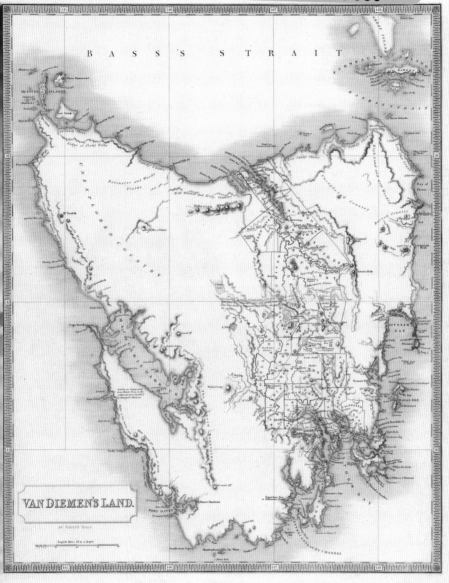

VAN DIEMEN'S LAND.

BY SIDNEY HALL.

Praise for
The Exiles

A *New York Times* bestseller
A *USA Today* bestseller
An Indie Next Pick
A *Real Simple* best of the year
A *Kirkus Reviews* best of the year

"Christina Baker Kline can tell a tale like nobody else. *The Exiles* is a riveting story, brilliantly told, full of characters the reader cannot help but care for desperately. Impeccable research infuses the story with rich and fascinating detail, but never gets in the way of the irresistible force of the narrative. From the first page to the last, you know you're in the hands of a master storyteller. This is historical fiction at its very best."   —Alex George, author of *The Paris Hours*

"Kline's tale gives powerful voice to the exiled and oppressed."
                —*People* "Pick of the Week"

"Intelligent and satisfyingly dramatic."   —*Newsday* (New York)

"Gorgeous. Brilliantly re-creates the beginnings of a new society."   —Kristin Hannah

"A tour de force of original thought, imagination and promise. . . . Kline takes full advantage of fiction—its freedom to create compelling characters who fully illuminate monumental events to make history accessible and forever etched in our minds."
                —*Houston Chronicle*

"Extraordinary. . . . Christina's level of research into characters, place and time to tell a powerful story of suffering and survival in an historical fiction is masterful. The beauty and brutality of Australian history narrated through the lives of these girls is wonderfully told."
                —Heather Morris, author of *The Tattooist of Auschwitz*

"Monumental. . . . This episode in history gets a top-notch treatment by Kline, one of our foremost historical novelists. This fascinating nineteenth-century take on *Orange Is the New Black* is subtle, intelligent, and thrillingly melodramatic."

—*Kirkus Reviews* (starred review)

"Christina Baker Kline's new novel *The Exiles* is . . . in some ways a quiet book, focusing on the innermost thoughts and feelings of its main characters—but it's also epic in scope, addressing matters of life and death, choices and consequences, and the founding of a new nation. These disparate elements combine to make it her best work yet."

—Greer Macallister, Chicago Review of Books

"Well-researched and boldly imagined."

—*Sydney Morning Herald*

"Master storyteller Christina Baker Kline is at her best in this epic tale of Australia's complex history—a vivid and rewarding feat of both empathy and imagination. I loved this book."

—Paula McLain, *New York Times* bestselling author of *The Paris Wife*

"A moving story set in Australia. Readers adored *Orphan Train*, Christina Baker Kline's 2013 novel. Now she's back with another winner." —AARP

"Both uplifting and heartbreaking, this beautifully written novel doesn't flinch from the ugliness of the penal system but celebrates the courage and resilience of both the first peoples and the settlers who came after, voluntarily or not, to create a new home for themselves and their children."

—*Library Journal* (starred review)

"*The Exiles* is that rarest of novels, a true page-turner. The action moves along; the reader feels himself to be in the hands of a professional." —Alabama Public Radio

THE EXILES

Novels by Christina Baker Kline

THE EXILES

A NOVEL

Christina Baker Kline

CUSTOM
HOUSE

A hardcover edition of this book was published in 2020 by Custom House, an imprint of William Morrow.

FIRST CUSTOM HOUSE PAPERBACK EDITION PUBLISHED 2021.

Designed by Bonni Leon-Berman

Library of Congress Cataloging-in-Publication Data has been applied for.

ISBN 978-0-06-235633-8

21 22 23 24 25 LSC 10 9 8 7 6 5 4 3 2 1

For Hayden, Will, and Eli—
adventurous wayfarers all

Let no one say the past is dead.

The past is all about us and within.

—*Oodgeroo Noonuccal, Aboriginal poet*

PROLOGUE

Flinders Island, Australia, 1840

BY THE TIME THE RAINS came, Mathinna had been hiding in the bush for nearly two days. She was eight years old, and the most important thing she'd ever learned was how to disappear. Since she was old enough to walk, she'd explored every nook and crevice of Wybalenna, the remote point on Flinders Island where her people had been exiled since before she was born. She'd run along the granite ridge that extended across the tops of the hills, dug tunnels in the sugary dunes on the beach, played seek-and-find among the scrub and shrubs. She knew all the animals: the possums and wallabies and kangaroos, the pademelons that lived in the forest and only came out at night, the seals that lolled on rocks and rolled into the surf to cool off.

Three days earlier, Governor John Franklin and his wife, Lady Jane, had arrived at Wybalenna by boat, more than 250 miles from their residence on the island of Lutruwita—or Van Diemen's Land, as the white people called it. Mathinna stood with the other children on the ridge as the governor and his wife made their way up from the beach, accompanied by half a dozen servants. Lady Franklin had a hard time walking in her shiny satin shoes; she kept slipping on the stones. She clung to her husband's arm as she wobbled toward them, the expression on her face as sour as if she'd bitten an artichoke thistle. The wrinkles on her neck reminded Mathinna of the exposed pink flesh of a wattlebird.

The night before, the Palawa elders had sat around the campfire, discussing the impending visit. The Christian missionaries had been preparing for days. The children had been instructed to learn a dance. Mathinna sat in the darkness on the edge of the circle, as she often did, listening to the elders talk as they plucked feathers from muttonbirds and roasted mussels in the glowing embers. The Franklins, it was widely agreed, were impulsive, foolish people; stories abounded of their strange and eccentric schemes. Lady Franklin was deathly afraid of snakes. She'd once devised a plan to pay a shilling for every dead snake turned in, which naturally spawned a robust market of breeders and cost her and Sir John a small fortune. When the two of them had visited Flinders the previous year, it was to collect Aboriginal skulls for their collection—skulls that were obtained by decapitating corpses and boiling the heads to remove the flesh.

The horse-faced Englishman in charge of the settlement on Flinders, George Robinson, lived with his wife in a brick house in a semicircle of eight brick houses that included rooms for his men, a sanatorium, and a dispensary. Behind this were twenty cottages for the Palawa. The night the Franklins arrived, they slept in the Robinsons' house. Early the next morning, they inspected the settlement while their servants distributed beads and marbles and handkerchiefs. After the noontime meal, the natives were summoned. The Franklins sat in two mahogany chairs in the sandy clearing in front of the brick houses, and for the next hour or so the few healthy Palawa males were made to perform a mock battle and engage in a spear-throwing contest. Then the children were paraded out.

As Mathinna danced in a circle with the others on the white sand, Lady Franklin kept looking at her with a curious smile.

The daughter of the chief of the Lowreenne tribe, Mathinna had long been accustomed to special attention. Several years ago, her father, Towterer—like so many of the Palawa deported to Flinders—had died of tuberculosis. Mathinna was proud to be the chieftain's daughter, but in truth she hadn't known him well. When she was three, she'd been sent from her parents' cottage to live in a brick house with the white schoolteacher, who made her wear bonnets and dresses with buttons and taught her to read and write in English and hold a knife and spoon. Even so, she spent as many hours a day as she could with her mother, Wanganip, and other members of the tribe, most of whom did not speak English or adhere to British customs.

It had only been a few months since Mathinna's mother had died. Wanganip had always hated Flinders. She'd often climb the spiny hill near the settlement and gaze across the turquoise sea toward her homeland, sixty miles away. This terrible place, she told Mathinna—this barren island where the wind was so strong it spun vegetables out of the ground and fanned small fires into raging infernos, where the trees shed bark like snakes shed their skin—was nothing like her ancestral land. It was a curse on her soul. On all of their souls. Their people were sickly; most of the babies born on Flinders died before their first birthdays. The Palawa had been promised a land of peace and plenty; if they did as they were told, the British said, they'd be allowed to keep their way of life. "But all of that was a lie. Like so many lies we were foolish to believe," Wanganip said bitterly. "What choice did we have? The British had already taken everything."

Looking into her mother's face, Mathinna saw the fury in her eyes. Mathinna didn't hate the island, though. It was the only home she'd ever known.

"Come here, child," the governor's wife said when the dance was over, beckoning with a finger. When Mathinna obeyed, Lady Franklin peered at her closely before turning to her husband. "Such expressive eyes! And a sweet face, don't you think? Unusually attractive for a native."

Sir John shrugged. "Hard to tell them apart, quite frankly."

"I wonder if it might be possible to educate her."

"She lives with the schoolteacher, who is teaching her English," Robinson said, stepping forward. "She's quite conversant already."

"Interesting. Where are her parents?"

"The girl is an orphan."

"I see." Lady Franklin turned back to Mathinna. "Say something."

Mathinna half curtsied. The arrogant rudeness of the British no longer surprised her. "What shall I say, ma'am?"

Lady Franklin's eyes widened. "Goodness! I am impressed, Mr. Robinson. You are turning savages into respectable citizens."

"In London, I hear, they're dressing orangutans like lords and ladies and teaching them to read," Sir John mused.

Mathinna didn't know what an orangutan was, but she'd heard talk of savages around the elders' campfire—British whalers and sealers who lived like animals and sneered at rules of common decency. Lady Franklin must be confused.

Robinson gave a short laugh. "This is a bit different. The Aborigines are human, after all. Our theory is that by changing externals you can change personalities. We are teaching them to eat our food and learn our language. We feed their souls with Christianity. They've surrendered to clothes, as you can see. We've cut the hair of the men and impressed modesty on the women. We've given them Christian names to aid the process."

"The mortality rate is quite high, I understand," said Sir John. "Delicate constitutions."

"An unfortunate inevitability," Robinson said. "We brought them out of the bush where they knew not God, nor even who made the trees." He gave a small sigh. "The fact is, we all must die, and we ought to pray to God first to save our souls."

"Quite right. You're doing them a great service."

"What is this one's name?" Lady Franklin asked, returning her attention to Mathinna.

"Mary."

"And what was it originally?"

"Originally? Mathinna was her Aboriginal name. She was christened Leda by missionaries. We decided on something less . . . fanciful," Robinson said.

Mathinna didn't remember being called Leda, but her mother had hated the name Mary, so the Palawa refused to use it. Only the British called her Mary.

"Well, I think she's charming," Lady Franklin said. "I'd like to keep her."

Keep her? Mathinna tried to catch Robinson's eye, but he didn't return her gaze.

Sir John looked amused. "You want to take her home with us? After what happened with the last one?"

"This will be different. Timeo was . . ." Lady Franklin shook her head. "The girl is an orphan, you said?" she asked, turning to Robinson.

"Yes. Her father was a chieftain. Her mother remarried, but recently died."

"Does that make her a princess?"

He smiled slightly. "Of a sort, perhaps."

"Hmm. What do you think, Sir John?"

Sir John smiled beneficently. "If you wish to amuse yourself in such a fashion, my dear, I suppose there's no harm in it."

"I think it will be entertaining."

"And if it isn't, we can always send her back."

Mathinna did not want to leave the island with these foolish people. She did not want to say goodbye to her stepfather and the other elders. She did not want to go to a strange new place where nobody knew or cared about her. Tugging on Robinson's hand, she whispered, "Please, sir. I don't—"

Slipping his hand from her grasp, he turned to the Franklins. "We will make the necessary arrangements."

"Very well." Lady Franklin cocked her head, appraising her. "*Mathinna*. I'd prefer to call her that. It will be more of a surprise if she achieves the manners of a lady."

Later, when the governor's party was distracted, Mathinna slipped behind the brick houses where everyone was gathered, still wearing the ceremonial wallaby-skin cape her father gave her before he died and a necklace of tiny green shells made by her mother. Wending her way through wallaby grass, silky against her shins, she listened to the barking dogs and the curra-wongs, plump black birds that warbled and flapped their wings when rain was on the way. She breathed in the familiar scent of eucalyptus. As she slid into the bush at the edge of the clearing, she looked up to see a geyser of muttonbirds erupt into the sky.

EVANGELINE

I never know an instance of any female convict coming out that
I would consider a fair character. Their open and shameless vice
must be told. Their fierce and untamable audacity would not be
believed. They are the pest and gangrene of the colonial society—
a reproach to human nature—and lower than the brutes, a disgrace to all animal existence.

—JAMES MUDIE, *The Felonry of New South Wales:*
Being a Faithful Picture of the Real Romance of Life
in Botany Bay, 1837

FROM WITHIN THE DEPTHS OF a restless dream, Evangeline heard a knocking. She opened her eyes. Silence. Then, more insistent: *rapraprap*.

Thin light from the small window high above her bed cut across the floor. She felt a surge of panic: she must have slept through the morning bell.

She never slept through the morning bell.

Sitting up, she felt woozy. She leaned back against her pillow. "Just a minute." Her mouth filled with saliva and she swallowed it.

"The children are waiting!" The scullery maid's voice rang with indignation.

"What time is it, Agnes?"

"Half nine!"

Sitting up again, Evangeline pushed back the covers. Bile rose in her throat, and this time she couldn't keep it down; she leaned over and vomited on the pine floor.

The knob turned and the door swung open. She looked up helplessly as Agnes twitched her nose and frowned at the viscous yellow splatter at her feet. "Give me a minute. Please." Evangeline wiped her mouth on her sleeve.

Agnes didn't move. "Did ye eat something strange?"

"I don't think so."

"Feverish?"

Evangeline pressed her hand against her forehead. Cool and clammy. She shook her head.

"Been feeling poorly?"

"Not until this morning."

"Hmm." Agnes pursed her lips.

"I'm all right, I'm just—" Evangeline felt a roiling in her gut. She swallowed hard.

"Clearly you're not. I'll inform Mrs. Whitstone there'll be no lessons today." With a curt nod, Agnes turned to leave, then paused, narrowing her eyes in the direction of the chest of drawers.

Evangeline followed her gaze. On the top, beside an oval mirror, a ruby gemstone ring glowed in the sunlight, staining the white handkerchief it lay on a deep red.

Her heart clenched. She'd been admiring the ring by the light of a candle the night before and had stupidly forgotten to put it away.

"Where'd ye get that?" Agnes asked.

"It was . . . a gift."

"Who from?"

"A family member."

"*Your* family?" Agnes knew full well that Evangeline had

no family. She'd only applied to be a governess because she had nowhere else to turn.

"It was . . . an heirloom."

"I've never seen ye wear it."

Evangeline put her feet on the floor. "For goodness' sake. I don't have much occasion, do I?" she said, attempting to sound brusque. "Now, will you leave me be? I'm perfectly fine. I'll meet the children in the library in a quarter of an hour."

Agnes gave her a steady look. Then she left the room, pulling the door shut behind her.

Later Evangeline would replay this moment in her head a dozen ways—what she might have said or done to throw Agnes off the trail. It probably wouldn't have mattered. Agnes had never liked her. Only a few years older than Evangeline, she'd been in service to the Whitstones for nearly a decade and lorded her institutional knowledge over Evangeline with supercilious condescension. She was always chiding her for not knowing the rules or grasping how things worked. When Evangeline confided in the assistant butler, her one ally in the household, that she didn't understand Agnes's palpable contempt, he shook his head. "Come now. Don't be naive. Until you arrived, she was the only eligible lass in the place. Now you're the one drawing all the attention—including from the young master himself. Who used to flirt with Agnes, or so she believed. And on top of that, your job is soft."

"It isn't!"

"It's not like hers, though, is it? Scrubbing linens with lye and emptying chamber pots from dawn till dusk. You're paid for your brains, not your back. No surprise she's tetchy."

Evangeline rose from her bed, and, carefully stepping around the puddle, went to the chest of drawers. Picking up the ruby ring, she held it to the window, noting with dismay how it caught and refracted the light. She glanced around the room. Where could she hide it? Under the mattress? Inside her pillowcase? Opening the bottom drawer, she slipped the ring into the pocket of an old dress tucked beneath some newer ones.

At least Agnes hadn't noticed the white handkerchief under the ring, with Cecil's cursive initials—*C. F. W.* for Cecil Frederic Whitstone—and the distinctive family crest embroidered onto a corner. Evangeline tucked the handkerchief in the waistband of her undergarments and went about cleaning up the mess.

MRS. WHITSTONE MATERIALIZED in the library while the children were taking turns reading aloud from a primer. They looked up in surprise. It wasn't like their mother to show up unannounced during their lessons.

"Miss Stokes," she said in an unusually high-handed tone, "please conclude the lesson as expediently as you can and meet me in the drawing room. Ned, Beatrice—Mrs. Grimsby has prepared a special pudding. As soon as you are done you may make your way to the kitchen."

The children exchanged curious glances.

"But Miss Stokes always takes us downstairs for tea," Ned said.

His mother gave him a thin smile. "I am quite sure you can find the way on your own."

"Are we being punished?" Ned asked.

"Certainly not."

"Is Miss Stokes?" Beatrice asked.

"What a ridiculous question."

Evangeline felt a tingle of dread.

"Did Mrs. Grimsby make a sponge cake?"

"You'll find out soon enough."

Mrs. Whitstone left the library. Evangeline took a deep breath. "Let's finish this section, shall we?" she said, but her heart wasn't in it, and anyway the children were distracted, thinking about the cake. When Ned reached the end of his sing-songy recitation of a paragraph about boating, she smiled and said, "All right, children, that's enough. You may run along to your tea."

THERE IT WAS: the ruby ring, sparkling in the glow of the whale-oil lamps in the gloomy drawing room. Mrs. Whitstone held it out in front of her like a treasure-hunt find. "Where did you get this?"

Evangeline twisted the corner of her apron, an old habit from childhood. "I didn't steal it, if that's your implication."

"I'm not implying anything. I'm asking a question."

Evangeline heard a noise behind her and turned, startled at the sight of a constable standing in the shadows behind a chair. His moustache drooped. He wore a black fitted waistcoat and a truncheon in a holster; in his hands were a notebook and pencil.

"Sir," she said, curtsying slightly. Her heart was beating so loudly she feared he could hear it.

He inclined his head, marking something in the notebook.

"This ring was found in your possession," Mrs. Whitstone said.

"You—you went into my room."

"You are in the employ of this household. It is not your room."

Evangeline had no answer to that.

"Agnes spied it on the dresser when she went to check on you. As you know. And then you hid it." Holding up the ring again, Mrs. Whitstone looked past Evangeline toward the constable. "This ring is my husband's property."

"It isn't. It belongs to Cecil," Evangeline blurted.

The constable looked back and forth between the two women. "Cecil?"

Mrs. Whitstone gave Evangeline a sharp look. "The younger Mr. Whitstone. My stepson."

"Would you agree that this is your stepson's ring?" His moustache twitched under his bulbous nose when he spoke.

With a pinched smile, Mrs. Whitstone said, "It belonged to my husband's mother. There is a question, perhaps, about whether the ring now belongs to my husband or to his son. It most certainly does not belong to Miss Stokes."

"He gave it to me," Evangeline said.

Only a few days earlier, Cecil had pulled a small blue velvet box from his pocket and rested it on her knee. "Open it."

She'd looked at him in surprise. A ring box. Could it be? Impossible, of course, and yet . . . She allowed herself a small surge of hope. Wasn't he always telling her that she was more beautiful, more charming, cleverer than any woman in his circle? Wasn't he always saying that he didn't give a fig about his family's expectations for him or society's silly moral judgments?

When she'd opened the lid, her breath caught in her throat: a band of gold, ornately filigreed, rose in four curved prongs to support a deep red stone.

"My grandmother's ruby," he told her. "She bequeathed it to me when she died."

"Oh, Cecil. It's stunning. But are you—"

"Oh, no, no! Let's not get ahead of ourselves," he'd said with a small laugh. "For now, just seeing it on your finger is enough."

When he extracted the ring from its slot in the cushion and slipped it onto her finger, the gesture had felt both thrillingly intimate and strangely constricting. She'd never worn one before; her father, a vicar, did not believe in adornments. Gently Cecil bent his head to her hand and kissed it. Then he snapped shut the velvet box, slipped it back into the pocket of his waistcoat, and withdrew a white handkerchief. "Tuck the ring into this and hide it away until I return from holiday. It will be our secret."

Now, in the drawing room with the constable, Mrs. Whitstone snorted. "That's ridiculous. Why in the world would Cecil ever give you . . ." Her voice trailed off. She stared at Evangeline.

Evangeline realized that she had said too much. *It will be our secret.* But Cecil wasn't here. She felt desperate, trapped.

And now, in defending herself, she had given away the real secret.

"Where is the younger Mr. Whitstone now?" the constable asked.

"Abroad," said Mrs. Whitstone, at the same time that Evangeline said, "Venice."

"An attempt could be made to contact him," the constable said. "Do you have an address?"

Mrs. Whitstone shook her head. "That will not be necessary." Crossing her arms, she said, "It's obvious the girl is lying."

The constable raised an eyebrow. "Is there a history of lying?"

"I have no idea. Miss Stokes has only been with us a few months."

"Five," Evangeline said. Summoning her strength, she turned to face the constable. "I've done my best to educate Mrs. Whitstone's children and help shape their moral character. I've never been accused of anything."

Mrs. Whitstone gave a dry little laugh. "So she says."

"Easy enough to find out," the constable said.

"I did not steal the ring," Evangeline said. "I swear it."

The constable tapped the notebook with his pencil. "Noted."

Mrs. Whitstone gave Evangeline a cold, appraising look. "The truth is, I've had my suspicions about this girl for some time. She comes and goes at odd hours of the day and night. She's secretive. The housemaids find her aloof. And now we know why. She stole a family heirloom and thought she would get away with it."

"Would you be willing to testify to that effect?"

"Certainly."

Evangeline's stomach dropped. "Please," she begged the constable, "could we wait for Cecil's return?"

Mrs. Whitstone turned on her with a scowl. "I will not tolerate this inappropriate familiarity. He is Mr. Whitstone to you."

The constable twitched his moustache. "I believe I have what I need, Miss Stokes. You may go. I've a few more questions for the lady of the house."

Evangeline looked from one to the other. Mrs. Whitstone raised her chin. "Wait in your room. I'll send someone for you presently."

IF THERE WAS any question in Evangeline's mind about the gravity of her predicament, the answer made itself clear soon enough.

On her way down the stairs to the servants' quarters, she encountered various members of the household staff, all of whom nodded soberly or looked away. The assistant butler gave her a wincing smile. As she was passing the room Agnes shared with another housemaid on the landing between two staircases, the door opened and Agnes stepped out. She blanched when she saw Evangeline and tried to duck past, but Evangeline grabbed her arm.

"What are ye doing?" Agnes hissed. "Let go of me."

Evangeline glanced around the hallway and, seeing no one, pushed Agnes back into the room and closed the door. "You took that ring from my room. You had no right."

"No right to retrieve stolen property? To the contrary, it was me duty."

"It wasn't stolen." She twisted Agnes's arm, making the maid wince. "You know that, Agnes."

"I don't know anything except what I saw."

"It was a gift."

"An heirloom, ye said. A lie."

"It *was* a gift."

Agnes shook her off. "'It *was* a gift,'" she mimicked. "Ye dimwit. That's only half the trouble. Yer *pregnant*." She laughed at Evangeline's befuddled expression. "Surprised, are ye? Too innocent to know it, but not too innocent to do the act."

Pregnant. The moment the word was out of Agnes's mouth, Evangeline knew she was right. The nausea, her recent inexplicable fatigue . . .

"I had a moral responsibility to inform the lady of the house," Agnes said, smugly self-righteous.

Cecil's velvet words. His insistent fingers and dazzling smile. Her own weakness, her gullibility. How pathetic, how foolish, she had been. How could she have allowed herself to be so compromised? Her good name was all she had. Now she had nothing.

"Ye think you're better than the rest of us, don't ye? Well, you're not. And now you've had your comeuppance," Agnes said, reaching for the doorknob and wrenching the door open. "Everyone knows. You're the laughingstock of the household." She pushed past Evangeline toward the stairs, knocking her back against the wall.

Desperation rose within Evangeline like a wave, filling her with such force and velocity that she was helpless against it. Without thinking, she followed Agnes out onto the landing and shoved her, hard. With a strange, high-pitched yelp, Agnes fell headlong down the stairs, crumpling in a heap at the bottom.

Peering down at Agnes as she staggered to her feet, Evangeline felt her fury crest and subside. In its wake was a faint tremor of regret.

The butler and head footman were on the scene within seconds.

"She—she tried to kill me!" Agnes cried, holding her head.

Standing at the top of the landing, Evangeline was eerily, strangely, calm. She smoothed her apron, tucked a wispy strand of hair behind an ear. As if watching a play, she noted the butler's contemptuous grimace and Agnes's theatrical sobs. Observed Mrs. Grimsby flutter over, squeaking and exclaiming.

This was the end of Blenheim Road, she knew, of primers and white chalk and slate tablets, of Ned and Beatrice babbling about sponge cake, of her small bedroom with its tiny window. Of Cecil's hot breath on her neck. There would be no explaining, no redeeming. Maybe it was better this way—to be an active participant in her demise rather than a passive victim. At least now she deserved her fate.

IN THE SERVANTS' hallway, lighted with oil lamps, two constables fastened Evangeline into handcuffs and leg chains while the constable with the droopy moustache made the rounds of the household staff with his notebook. "She were awful quiet," the chambermaid was saying, as if Evangeline were already gone. Each of them, it seemed to her, overplayed the roles expected of them: the staff a little too indignant, the constables self-important, Agnes understandably giddy at the attention and apparent sympathy of her superiors.

Evangeline was still wearing her blue worsted wool uniform and white apron. She was allowed to bring nothing else with her. Her hands shackled in front of her, her legs shuffling in irons, she required two constables to guide her up the narrow back stairs to the ground-floor servants' entrance. They had to practically lift her into the prison carriage.

It was a cold, rainy evening in March. The carriage was dank, and smelled, oddly, of wet sheep. The open windows had vertical iron bars but no glass. Evangeline sat on a rough wooden plank next to the constable with the droopy moustache and across from the other two, both of whom were staring at her. She wasn't sure if they were leering or simply curious.

As the coachman readied the horses, Evangeline leaned forward to look at the house one last time. Mrs. Whitstone was standing at the front window, holding the lace curtain back with her hand. When Evangeline caught her eye, she dropped the curtain and retreated into the depths of the parlor.

The horses lurched forward. Evangeline braced herself against the seat, trying futilely to keep the leg irons from cutting into her ankles as the carriage swayed and rattled along the cobblestones.

THE DAY SHE'D first arrived by hackney cab to St. John's Wood had also been cold and drizzling. Standing on the front step of the creamy white terrace house on Blenheim Road—its number, 22, in black metal, its front door a shiny vermilion—she'd taken a deep breath. The leather valise she clasped in one hand held all she possessed in the world: three muslin dresses, a nightcap and two sleeping shifts, an assortment of undergarments, a horsehair brush and washing cloth, and a small collection of books—her father's Bible with his handwritten notes; her Latin, Greek, and mathematics catechisms; and a dog-eared copy of *The Tempest*, the only play she'd ever seen performed, at an outdoor festival by a traveling troupe that passed through Tunbridge Wells one summer.

She adjusted her hat and rang the bell, listening to it trill inside the house.

No response.

She pushed the buzzer again. Just as she was wondering if she had the wrong day, the door opened and a young man appeared. His brown eyes were lively and curious. His brown hair, thick and slightly curly, draped over the collar of his untucked white shirt. He wore no cravat or tailcoat. Clearly this was not the butler.

"Yes?" he said with an air of impatience. "Can I help you?"

"Well, I—I'm . . ." Remembering herself, she curtsied. "Pardon, sir. Perhaps I should return later."

He observed her, as if from a distance. "Are you expected?"

"I thought so, yes."

"By whom?"

"The lady of the house. Sir. Mrs. Whitstone. I'm Evangeline Stokes, the new governess."

"Really. Are you quite sure?"

"P-pardon?" she stammered.

"I had no idea governesses came in this shape," he said, sweeping his hand toward her with a flourish. "Bloody unfair. Mine looked nothing like you."

Evangeline felt conspicuously dumb, as if she were performing in a play and had forgotten her lines. In her role as vicar's daughter, she used to stand a step behind her father, greeting parishioners before and after the service, accompanying him on visits to the sick and infirm. She met all sorts of people, from basket-makers to wheelwrights, carpenters to blacksmiths. But she'd had little contact with the wealthy, who tended to worship in their own chapels with their own kind. She had scant experience with the slippery humor of the upper classes and was unskilled at banter.

"I'm just having a bit of fun." The young man smiled, holding out his hand. Tentatively she took it. "Cecil Whitstone. Half brother to your charges. I daresay you'll have your hands full." He opened the door wide. "I'm standing in for Trevor, who is no doubt off fulfilling some caprice of my stepmother's. Come in, come in. I'm on the way out, but I'll announce you."

When she stepped into the black-and-white tiled foyer, clutching her valise, Cecil craned his neck out the door. "No more bags?"

"This is it."

"My word, you travel light."

At that moment, the door at the other end of the hall opened and a dark-haired woman who appeared to be in her midthirties emerged, tying on a green silk bonnet. "Ah, Cecil!" she said. "And this must be, I assume, Miss Stokes?" She gave Evangeline a distracted smile. "I'm Mrs. Whitstone. It's a little chaotic today, I'm afraid. Trevor is helping Matthew harness the horses so I can go into town."

"We all do double duty around here," Cecil told Evangeline conspiratorially, as if they were old friends. "In addition to teaching Latin you'll soon be plucking geese and polishing silver."

"Nonsense," Mrs. Whitstone said, straightening her bonnet in a large gilt mirror. "Cecil, will you inform Agnes that Miss Stokes has arrived?" Turning back to Evangeline, she said, "Agnes will show you to your quarters. Suppertime for the servants is at five o'clock. You'll take your meals with them if the children's lessons are finished in time. You look a little peaked, dear. Why don't you have a rest before supper."

It was a statement, not a question.

When Mrs. Whitstone left, Cecil gave Evangeline a sly smile.

"'Peaked' is not the word I would've used." He stood closer to her than felt quite proper.

Evangeline felt the unfamiliar sensation of her heart thumping in her chest. "Should you . . . um . . . let Agnes know I'm here?"

He tapped his chin, as if considering this. Then he said, "My errands can wait. I'll take you around myself. It will be my pleasure."

How might things have turned out differently if Evangeline had followed Mrs. Whitstone's instructions—or, for that matter, her own instincts? Had she not realized the ground beneath her feet was so unstable that it might crumble at the slightest misstep?

She had not. Smiling at Cecil, she tucked a stray piece of hair back into her bun. "That would be lovely," she said.

NOW, SITTING IN the drafty carriage, she moved her shackled wrists to the left side of her body and rubbed the place beneath her petticoat where she'd tucked the monogrammed handkerchief. With the fingers of one hand she traced its faint outline, imagining she could feel the thread of Cecil's initials intertwined with the family crest—a lion, serpent, and crown.

It was all she had, would ever have, of him. Except, apparently, for the child growing inside her.

The carriage made its way west, toward the river. No one spoke in the chilly compartment. Without realizing what she was doing, Evangeline inched closer to the solid warmth of the constable next to her. Glancing down, he curled his lip and shifted toward the window, widening the space between them.

Evangeline felt a prickle of shock. She had never in her life experienced a man's revulsion. She'd taken for granted the small gifts of kindness and solicitude that came her way: the butcher who gave her choice cuts of meat, the baker who saved her the last loaf.

Slowly it dawned on her: she was about to learn what it was like to be contemptible.

THIS PART OF LONDON WAS like no place Evangeline had ever seen. The air, dense with coal smoke, reeked of horse manure and rotting vegetables. Women in tattered shawls loitered under oil lamps, men huddled around barrel fires, children—even at this late hour—darted in and out of the road, picking through rubbish, shrieking at each other, comparing finds. Evangeline squinted, trying to make out what they had in their hands. Was it—? Yes. *Bones*. She'd heard about these children who earned pennies collecting animal bones that were turned to ash and mixed with clay to make the ceramics displayed in ladies' china cupboards. Even a few hours ago she might've felt pity; now she only felt numb.

"There she is," one of the constables said, gesturing out the window. "The Stone Jug."

"Stone Jug?" Evangeline leaned forward, craning her neck.

"Newgate." He smirked. "Your new home."

In tawdry penny circulars she'd read stories about the dangerous criminals locked up in Newgate. Now here it was, a block-long fortress squatting in the shadow of St. Paul's Cathedral. As they drew closer Evangeline saw that the windows facing the street were strangely blank. It wasn't until the coach-man shouted at the horses and pulled hard on the reins in front of the tall black gates that she realized the windows were false, painted over.

A small crowd, idling near the entrance, swarmed the car-riage. "Misery mongers," said the constable with the droopy moustache. "The show never gets old."

The three constables filed out of the carriage, barking at the crowd to stand back. Evangeline crouched in the cramped com-partment until one of them gestured impatiently. "Come on!" She hobbled to the lip of the door and he tugged at her shoulder. When she stumbled out of the carriage, he hoisted her like a sack of rice and dumped her on the ground. Her cheeks burned with shame.

Large-eyed children and sour-faced adults stared as she found her footing. "What a disgrace," a woman spat. "God have mercy on your soul."

A constable pushed Evangeline toward the iron gates, where their small group was met by two guards. As she shuffled through the entry, flanked by the guards, the constables behind, she gazed up at the words inscribed on a sundial above the arch. *Venio Sicut Fur*. Most of the prisoners passing through these gates probably didn't know their meaning, but Evangeline did. *I come as a thief*.

THE GATE CLANGED shut. She heard a muffled noise, like cats mewling in a bag, and cocked her head. "The rest of the har-lots," a guard told her. "You'll be with 'em soon enough."

Harlots! She cringed.

A slight man with a large ring attached to his belt, keys hanging from it like oversized charms, was hurrying toward them. "This way. Only the prisoner and two of ye."

Evangeline, the constable with the droopy moustache, and one of the guards followed him into a vestibule and up several flights of stairs. She moved slowly in the leg irons; the guard kept prodding her in the back with a baton. They made their way through a twisting maze of corridors, dimly lit by oil lanterns that hung from the thick stone walls.

The turnkey came to a stop in front of a wooden door with two locks. Riffling through the keys, he found the one he was looking for and inserted it in the top lock, then in the lock below. He pushed the door open into a small room with only an oak desk and chair, lighted by a lamp high on the wall, and crossed the room to knock on another, smaller door.

"Beg your pardon, Matron. A new prisoner."

Silence. Then, faintly, "Give me a moment."

They waited. The men leaned against a wall, talking among themselves. Evangeline stood uncertainly in her chains in the middle of the room. Her underarms were damp, and the irons chafed her ankles. Her stomach rumbled; she hadn't eaten since morning.

After some time, the door opened. The matron had clearly been woken up. Her angular face was heavily lined, her graying hair pulled back in a messy bun. She wore a faded black dress. "Let's get on with it," she said irritably. "Has the prisoner been searched?"

"No, ma'am," the guard said.

She waved toward him. "Go to."

Roughly he ran his hands over Evangeline's shoulders, down her sides, under her arms, even, quickly, between her legs. She pinked with embarrassment. When he gave the matron a nod, she made her way to the desk, lit a candle, and sank into the chair. Opening a large ledger filled with lines of tiny script, she said, "Name."

"Evangel—"

"Not you," the matron said, without looking up. "You have forfeited your right to speak."

Evangeline bit her lip.

The constable extracted a piece of paper from the inner pocket of his waistcoat and peered at it. "Name is . . . ah . . . Evangeline Stokes."

She dipped her quill into a pot of ink and scratched on the ledger. "Married?"

"No."

"Age."

"Ah . . . let's see. She'll be twenty-two."

"She will be, or she is?"

"Born in the month of August, it says here. So . . . twenty-one."

The matron looked up sharply, her pen poised over the paper. "Speak precisely, constable, or we'll be here all night. Her offense. In as few words as possible."

He cleared his throat. "Well, ma'am, there's more than one."

"Start with the most egregious."

He sighed. "First . . . she's an accused felon. Of the worst kind."

"The charge."

"Attempted murder."

The matron raised a brow at Evangeline.

"I didn't—" she started.

The matron held out the flat of her hand. Then she looked down, writing in the ledger. "Of whom, constable."

"A chambermaid employed by . . . aah"—he searched the paper—"a Ronald Whitstone, address 22 Blenheim Road, St. John's Wood."

"By what method."

"Miss Stokes pushed her down the stairs."

She looked up. "Is the victim . . . all right?"

"Seems to be. Shaken, but essentially . . . all right, I suppose."

Out of the corner of her eye, Evangeline saw a small movement where the floor met the wall: a thin rat squirming out of a crack in the baseboard.

"And what else?"

"An heirloom belonging to the owner of the house was found in Miss Stokes's room."

"What kind of heirloom?"

"A ring. Gold. With a valuable gemstone. A ruby."

"It was given to me," Evangeline blurted.

The matron put down her quill. "Miss Stokes. You have been reprimanded twice."

"I'm sorry. But—"

"You will not say one more word unless addressed directly. Is that clear?"

Evangeline nodded miserably. The panic and worry that kept her vigilant all day had given way to an enervating torpor. She wondered, almost abstractly, if she might faint. Maybe she would. Merciful darkness must be better than this.

"Assault and theft," the matron said to the constable, her hand on the page. "Those are the accusations?"

"Yes, ma'am. And she is also . . . with child."

"I see."

"Out of wedlock, ma'am."

"I understood your implication, constable." She looked up. "So the charges are attempted murder and larceny."

He nodded.

She sighed. "Very well. You may go. I'll escort the prisoner to the cells."

Once the men had filed out, the matron inclined her head toward Evangeline. "Long day for you, I suppose. I'm sorry to tell you it will not improve."

Evangeline felt a rush of gratitude. It was the closest thing to kindness she'd experienced all day. Tears gathered behind her eyes, and though she willed herself not to cry, they spilled down her cheeks. With her hands shackled, she couldn't wipe them away. For a few moments her strangled sobs were the only sound in the room.

"I need to take you down," the matron said finally.

"It wasn't like he said." Evangeline hiccuped. "I—I didn't—"

"You are wasting your breath. My opinion is irrelevant."

"But I hate for you to . . . to think ill of me."

The matron gave a dry laugh. "Oh, my girl. You are new to this."

"I am. Entirely."

Setting down the quill and closing the ledger, the matron asked, "Was it force?"

"Pardon?" Evangeline asked, uncomprehending.

"Did a man force himself on you?"

"Oh. No. No."

"It was love then, was it?" Sighing, the matron shook her head. "You're learning the hard way, Miss Stokes, that there's no man you can count on. No woman neither. The sooner you understand that, the better off you'll be."

She crossed the room and opened a cupboard, from which she pulled out two pieces of brown sackcloth, a wooden spoon, and a tin cup. After wrapping the spoon and cup in the cloth, she tied the bundle with twine, making a loop to hang from Evangeline's bound hands. Then she took the candlestick from the desk and a ring of keys from a drawer and motioned for her to follow. "Here," she said when they were in the hallway, "take this," and handed her the glowing candle, which Evangeline held awkwardly, spilling hot wax on her thumbs, while the matron fastened the locks. The candle smelled strongly of tallow. Mutton fat, meaty and greasy. She recognized it from visits to poor parishioners with her father.

They made their way down the corridor, past the hissing lights, and descended the stairs. At the main entrance the matron turned left into an open courtyard. Evangeline followed her across the damp cobbles in the dark, trying not to slip, listening to the moaning of the harlots. She wanted to lift her skirts, but the handcuffs made it impossible. Her wet skirts slapped against her bare ankles. The candle illuminated only a few feet in front of them, the path behind swallowed by darkness. As they approached the other side of the courtyard, the cries grew louder.

Evangeline must have made a noise herself, a self-pitying whimper, perhaps, because the matron glanced over her shoulder and said, "You'll get used to it."

Down another flight of stairs, through a short corridor. The matron stopped in front of a black iron door with a cross-hatched grate in the top half and handed Evangeline the candle again. Selecting a key from the ring, she inserted it into three separate locks before opening the door into a dark hallway.

Evangeline paused, gagging at the foul odor. It evoked a long-ago memory: the killing room of the butcher shop in Tunbridge Wells, which she'd only entered once and vowed never to set foot in again. She couldn't see the women in the cells, but she could hear them, muttering and groaning. The plaintive wail of an infant, coughing that sounded like a barking dog.

"Come along now," the matron said.

Only the feeble glow from the candle lit their way down a narrow passageway, lined with cells on one side. There was a *tap-tap-tapping* as they passed, sticks against the iron grating on cell doors. Fingers touched Evangeline's hair, grasped at her apron. She cried out and veered to the right, knocking her shoulder against the stone wall.

"You're a fine one, ain't ye?" one woman said in a mincing voice.

"That dress won't stay clean for long."

"What'd ye do, missy?"

"What'd ye do?"

The matron stopped abruptly in front of a cell door. Wordlessly she handed Evangeline the candle again and unlocked the door. Murmuring and rustling from the women inside. "Make room," the matron said.

"No room to make."

"Somebody fell over in 'ere, ma'am. She was awful sick. Now she's cold as a wagon tire."

"She's takin' up space."

The matron sighed. "Move her to a corner. I'll send someone in the morning."

"I'm hungry!"

"Slop jar's full."

"Take the girl someplace else!"

"She's coming in." The matron turned to Evangeline. "Lift your skirts and I'll remove your leg irons." Before she knelt, she touched Evangeline's trembling hand and said, in a quiet voice, "They're more bark than bite. Try to get some sleep."

As Evangeline entered the dark cell, she stumbled blindly over the stone lip and sprawled headlong into a huddle of women, hitting her shoulder on the floor.

Voices rose in a chorus of insult.

"What's wrong with ye?"

"Clumsy oaf."

"Get up, ye foozler."

She felt a kick in the ribs.

Struggling to her feet, rubbing her unshackled wrists, Evangeline stood at the cell door and watched the faint glow from the matron's candle retreat down the long hallway. When the door at the end clanged shut, she flinched. She was the only one who did.

One small window, high and grated, let in dull sooty moonlight. As her eyes adjusted, she surveyed the scene. Dozens of women filled the cell, which was about the size of the Whitstones' small front parlor. The stone floor was covered with matted straw.

She sank against the wall. The smell near the floor—the metallic scent of blood, the fermented tang of vomit, the foulness of human waste—turned her stomach, and when bile rose in her throat, she doubled over and retched onto the straw.

The women near her stepped back, grumbling and exclaiming.

"Nasty wench, she shite through 'er teeth!"

"Ugh, disgustin'."

Wiping her mouth with her sleeve, Evangeline mumbled, "I'm sor—" before heaving up what little remained in her stomach. At this, the women around her turned their backs. Evangeline shut her eyes and fell to her knees, dizzy and tired beyond sense, slicking her dress with her own bile.

After some time, she roused herself. She untied the bundle the matron had given her and tucked the tin cup and wooden spoon into the pocket of her apron. She spread one of the sackcloths above the muck-slick straw, wadded her petticoats beneath her knees, and sank to the floor, where she lay carefully on the too-small rectangle of cloth. Only this morning she had lain in her own bed, in her own room, dreaming about a future that seemed well within her grasp. Now all of that was gone. Listening to the women around her wheezing and snoring, grunting and sighing, she drifted into a peculiar half-sleeping, half-waking state—aware, even while dreaming, that few nightmares could compare to the misery she'd face when she opened her eyes.

THE DOOR AT THE END of the hallway clanged open, and Evangeline dredged herself from sleep. It took a moment to remember where she was. Soot-stained stones oozing damp, miserable clusters of women, a rusting iron grate . . . her mouth cottony, her petticoats stiff and sour-smelling . . .

How pleasant it had been to forget.

Daybreak wasn't much to speak of: hazy light filtered from the window above. Grasping a bar, she pulled herself up from the floor and stretched her sore back. A putrid piss bucket squatted in the corner. The *tap-tapping* had started again, and now she saw its source: women hitting the iron grate and walls with their wooden spoons.

Two guards appeared in front of their cell with a bucket. "Line up!" one shouted as the other unlocked the door. Evangeline watched him dip a ladle into the bucket and slosh the contents into a prisoner's outstretched cup. Digging into her apron pocket, she pulled out her own battered cup and flipped it upside down to remove the grit. Despite the dampness around her ankles, her full bladder, her aching limbs and nausea, she pushed her way to the front, hunger winning out.

When the guard filled her cup, she tried to catch his eye. Couldn't he tell she had nothing in common with these pathetic wretches with faces as dirty as those of coal miners?

He didn't give her a glance.

She stepped back and took a sip of watery oats, cold and bland and possibly rancid. Her stomach heaved slightly, but she willed herself not to vomit.

Women juggling cups and crying babies tripped over each other to reach the gruel, thrusting their cups toward the guards. A few hung back, too sick or defeated to fight their way to the door. One woman—probably the one they'd told the matron about the night before—wasn't moving at all. Evangeline looked at her uneasily.

Yes, she might very well be dead.

After the guards left, carrying the unconscious woman, the cell quieted. A group of prisoners huddled in a corner playing cards fashioned from what appeared to be the torn pages of a Bible. In another corner, a woman in a knitted cap read palms. A girl who appeared no more than fifteen cradled an infant against her neck, crooning a tune Evangeline recognized: *I left my baby lying here to go and gather blueberries . . .* She'd heard women in Tunbridge Wells sing this strange Scottish lullaby to their children. In it a desperate mother whose baby disappears retraces her steps: *I searched the moorland tarns and then wandered through each silent glen.* The mother discovers the tracks of an otter, the wake of a swan across a lake. *I found the trail of the mountain mist but ne'er a trace of baby, O!* Clearly an admonition to new mothers to keep an eye on their infants, the lullaby now seemed to her cruelly grim, the specter of loss almost impossible to bear.

EVANGELINE FELT A rough poke in her back. "So what'd ye do?"

She turned to face a ruddy-cheeked woman of substantial girth, half a dozen years older than her at least, with a frizzy blond bob and a snub nose.

Evangeline's first impulse was to tell her to mind her own business, but instinct hadn't served her particularly well lately. "What did *you* do?"

The woman grinned, revealing a row of teeth as small and yellow as corn kernels, with a wide gap in the front. "I took my due from a cad who didn't pay what he promised." She patted her stomach. "Soon to be a father, and now he'll never know."

With a sly wink, she added, "Hazard of my profession. Bound to happen sooner or later." She shrugged. Wagging her fingers at Evangeline's stomach, she said, "I'm not feelin' tewly anymore, at least. It doesn't last. So ye know."

"I know," Evangeline said, though she didn't.

"So what's your name?" When Evangeline hesitated, the woman said, "I'm Olive."

"Evangeline."

"Evange-a-*leen*," Olive repeated, as if saying the name for the first time. "Posh."

Was it? Her father had chosen the name, he told her, because it was a derivation of the Latin word *evangelium*, meaning "gospel." "I don't think so."

Olive shrugged. "We're all the same in here, anyway. I'm sentenced to transport. They gave me seven years, but it might as well be a life sentence, from what I heard. Ye?"

Evangeline recalled seeing small items in the newspaper over the years about the incorrigibles—men, she thought—transported on convict ships to Australia. Murderers and other deviants exiled to the far side of the earth, ridding the British Isles of the worst of its criminals. She'd shivered with horrified delight at the details, as strange and otherworldly as stories from Greek mythology: bleak gulags and workhouses carved into rock in the middle of nowhere, separated from civilization by miles of desert sand and deadly predators.

She'd never felt sorry for these men. They had it coming, after all, didn't they? They were predators themselves.

"I haven't been before the judge," she said.

"Well, who knows—maybe ye won't be sent away. Ye didn't murder someone, did ye?"

Evangeline wished Olive would keep her voice down. She hesitated, then shook her head.

"Theft?"

She sighed and chose the least incriminating charge. "I was accused—wrongly accused—of stealing a ring."

"Ah. Let me guess." Lacing her fingers together, Olive cracked her knuckles. "Some cad gave it to ye in exchange for favors. Then denied it."

"No! It wasn't in exchange for . . ." Was it? "He's . . . away. I was accused in his absence."

"Uh huh. He knows you're up the pole?"

Evangeline had never heard the expression, but its meaning was obvious. She shook her head.

Olive thumbed her chin, then looked Evangeline up and down. "Ye were the governess."

Was her tale of woe so utterly predictable? "How do you know that?"

Lifting her hand to her mouth, Olive made a starburst with her fingers. "The way ye talk. Book smart. But ye don't have the airs of a lady. Pity you're not so smart in the ways of the world, Evange-a-*leen*." She shook her head and turned away.

AS EVANGELINE WELL knew from her father's sermons, a woman's greatest possession was her chastity. While men were more advanced in nearly all ways—more intelligent and reasonable, stronger, more resourceful—they were also inclined to recklessness and impulsivity. It was the duty of women to slow them down, he always said, to bring forth their better natures.

She thought she'd absorbed this lesson, but in the small village where she was raised, forty miles and a world away from London, it had never been put to the test. Most people in Tunbridge Wells stayed close to their parents and married their neighbors, sustaining and fortifying a web of relationships that became more tightly woven as each generation succeeded the last. But Evangeline had not been part of such a web. Her mother died in childbirth, and her widowed father lived a life of the mind, with little interest in quotidian earthly details. He'd preferred that Evangeline keep him company in the library, reading side by side, rather than performing the usual female duties—and anyway, the vicarage came with a housekeeper.

Detecting a sharp curiosity in his only child, he hired a tutor to teach her Greek and Latin, Shakespeare and philosophy. These hours in the library of the vicarage shaped her destiny in a number of ways. She emerged far better educated than the average villager, but because she'd been raised without peers, she was woefully guileless. She had no confidantes with whom to gossip, and thus to learn. Her father wanted to insulate her, to shelter her from harm, and in doing so he denied her the inoculation required to survive. She could name the seven continents and identify the constellations, but she knew little, in a practical sense, about the world beyond her door.

When Evangeline was twenty, her father died after a short illness. Two days after the funeral an emissary of the bishop appeared at the door, politely inquiring as to her plans. A young curate with a wife and small children had been appointed to take over the vicarage. How soon could she vacate the premises?

With dismay, Evangeline realized that her father had given little—that is, no—thought to a future without him. And neither had she. Both of them had blithely assumed they'd go on reading together in the library, drinking tea in front of the fire. With only a small inheritance, no living relatives, and negligible practical skills, she had few options. She could marry, but whom? Despite her beauty, the eligible men in her village weren't exactly clamoring for her hand. She was, by temperament, much like her father: diffident, with a shyness often mistaken for aloofness, a bookishness perceived as snobbery.

Evangeline was in a quandary, the bishop's emissary acknowledged—educated quite beyond her station but without the means or social status to attract a gentleman of superior rank. Which left her, he counseled, with one viable option: she must become a governess, teaching young children and living with a family. Prompting her to enumerate her skills, he listened carefully, scratching notes on parchment with his quill pen: English literature, grammar, arithmetic, religion, Greek and Latin and French, some drawing. A little piano. Then he submitted an advertisement to newspapers and circulars in and around London:

GOVERNESS.—A clergyman is desirous of RECOM-MENDING A YOUNG LADY, the orphan of a vicar, to the situation of GOVERNESS in a family where she will have charge of their young children. She has been expressly educated for the purpose. Apply by letter, postpaid, to the Rev. P.R. at 14 Dorchester Street, Tunbridge Wells.

Envelopes began appearing in the vicarage post box. One letter in particular stood out. A Mary Whitstone, writing from a quiet street in northwest London, described a comfortable life with her barrister husband and two well-behaved children, Beatrice and Ned. The children had been brought up by a nanny, but it was time for them to begin a proper education. The new governess would have her own accommodations. She'd be with the children six hours a day, six days a week, and might be expected to accompany them on holiday. Other than that, her time would be her own. A well-rounded education, Mrs. Whitstone wrote, should, in her view, include occasional excursions to museums and musical concerts and even perhaps the theater. Evangeline, who'd never done any of these things, was intrigued. She answered Mrs. Whitstone's many questions dutifully and at length, sent off her letter, and waited for the reply.

Despite her provincial ingenuousness, or perhaps because of it, she impressed the lady of the house sufficiently to receive an offer of employment: twenty pounds a year, plus lodging and meals. It seemed to Evangeline an extravagant sum. To the bishop, and the young curate poised to begin his new life in the vicarage, it was a godsend.

OVER THE NEXT few days at Newgate, Evangeline thought desperately about reaching out to someone, anyone, who might come to her aid, but could think of no one who might testify with great conviction to her good name. Though as the vicar's daughter she'd been accorded a modicum of deference, her father's decision to keep her close to home meant she'd made no real friends in the village. She wondered about contacting the housekeeper at the vicarage, or maybe the butcher or the baker or one of the shop clerks she'd been friendly with, but she suspected the word of an ordinary villager wouldn't carry much weight. She didn't know anyone in London other than the Whitstones.

She hadn't heard from Cecil.

By now he would have returned from Venice. By now he should've gotten the news. A small part of her clung to the hope that he'd act honorably and step forward. Perhaps he'd send a letter: *You were wronged. I've told them everything.* Maybe he'd even come and find her.

She needed to look presentable if he arrived. When the guards brought a clean bucket of water, she scrubbed her face and neck and swiped under her arms with a rag. She blotted her bodice and parted her hair with her fingernail and smoothed it down, tying it back with a strip of rag.

"Who're ye cleaning up for?" Olive wanted to know.

"No one."

"Ye think he'll come for ye."

"No."

"You're hoping."

"He's a good man, deep down."

Olive laughed. "He isn't."

"You don't know him."

"Oh, poor girl," she said. "Poor Leenie. I probably do."

HE WAS A good man, though. Wasn't he? After all, he'd rescued her from loneliness in that house on Blenheim Road. She hadn't known, when she accepted the position, how isolated she would feel. Evangeline was usually with the children until close to their suppertime; by the time she was free, the servants had finished their own meal and were busy serving the family dinner. Mrs. Grimsby, the cook, saved a plate for her, which she ate by herself. By seven o'clock she was holed up in her small bedroom for the night.

Many evenings, down the hall from her room, she could hear the servants playing blackjack or hearts around the long table in the kitchen, their voices rising in a showy camaraderie that only made her loneliness more acute. On the few occasions when she ventured out, she'd stand awkwardly in the corner while they cheerfully avoided her. They considered her an odd duck, both an object of gossip for her eccentric habits (such as reading while eating), and a mystery they had little interest in solving. She spoke a vernacular that no doubt reminded them of their employers, and they were clearly relieved when she went back to her room and shut the door.

Into this void came Cecil, three years older and infinitely more worldly. The brush of his fingertips against hers, a private wink over the heads of the children, the flat of his hand on the small of her back when no one was looking: in these small ways he telegraphed his intentions.

Over the weeks and months of their acquaintance, his ardor became more persuasive, his entreaties more endearing. "Dear Evangeline!" he whispered. "Even your name is picturesque." He'd studied Chaucer at Cambridge for the sole purpose, he told her, of memorizing lines to whisper in her ear:

She was fair as is the rose in May.

And:

What is better than wisdom? Woman. And what is better than a good woman? Nothing.

Everything about him awed her. This man had sat in cafés in Paris at midnight, traversed Venetian canals by gondola, swum in the ice-blue waters of the Mediterranean. And then there was the matter of that brown tendril of hair that feathered against his neck, those rangy shoulders under a crisp linen shirt, the aquiline nose and lush red lips . . .

"You captivate me," he said, tugging at the strings of her bodice.

"You are the only woman for me," he breathed into her hair.

"But what about—what about . . ."

"I adore you. I want to spend every hour of every day with you."

"It is . . . immoral."

"It is moral to us. Why should we concern ourselves with the chiding of provincial bores?"

In the same way that it's nearly impossible to imagine the brutal cold of winter on a hot summer day, Evangeline basked in the heat of Cecil's affection with little thought of its ending. He promised just enough to persuade her that he shared the emotions she felt so deeply.

It was surprisingly easy to keep their rendezvous secret. Evangeline's small room was set apart from the other servants' bedrooms, down a narrow hallway past the kitchen. Because she was on a different schedule than most of the staff, nobody paid much attention to her comings and goings. The proximity to London was its own alibi. Coming back to her room between lessons, she'd find notes slipped under her door—*Half six, corner of Cavendish and Circus . . . Gloucester Gate, 7 p.m. . . .*

Dorset Square at noon—and hide them under her mattress. She told the cook she was going for a stroll, to see the lights on the Thames at dusk, to explore Regent's Park on a Sunday, and she wasn't even lying.

Cecil's best friend from Harrow was an amiable lad named Charles Pepperton. Unlike Cecil, who was studying to be a barrister like his father, Charles wasn't expected to pursue a vocation. He would inherit both the family estate and his father's seat in the House of Lords; all he needed to do for the next few decades was cultivate the proper friends, marry an age-appropriate woman from a comparable family (a minor royal, if possible), and improve his fox-hunting skills at the family's country estate in Dorset. He spent a lot of time in Dorset. His home in Mayfair was spacious, well-appointed, and almost always uninhabited.

The first time Cecil brought Evangeline to the house in Mayfair—early on a Saturday evening, when lessons were over and the Whitstones senior were at a party—she was shy and self-conscious in front of the servants. But soon enough she learned about the mechanisms in place designed to keep secrets, cover up indiscretions, and protect the upper classes from scandal. Cecil, well known to the staff, was treated with casual deference: a discreet lowering of the eyes, a careful coding of language. ("Will the lady be joining you for tea?") As time went on, Evangeline became more comfortable, more brazenly open. When Cecil pulled her onto his lap in front of the butler, she no longer felt compelled to protest.

It was in the shadowy parlor of Charles's town house that

Cecil gave her the ring. "To remember me while I'm on holiday. And when I'm back . . ." He nuzzled her neck.

She pulled away, smiling uncertainly, trying to parse the meaning behind his words. "When you're back?"

He put a finger to her lips. "You'll wear it for me again."

This was not, of course, the answer to the question she was asking. But it was the only answer he was prepared to give.

It wasn't until much later that she realized she had built gossamer connections between his words, sticky as spider silk, filling in the phrases she wanted to hear.

THERE WERE SOME THINGS SHE would never get used to: the screams that spread like a contagion from one cell to the next. The vicious fistfights that broke out abruptly and ended with an inmate spitting blood or teeth. The lukewarm midday broth that floated with bony pig knuckles, snouts, bits of hooves and hair. Moldy bread laced with maggots. Once the initial shock subsided, though, Evangeline found it surprisingly easy to endure most of the degradations and indignities of her new life: the brutish guards, the cockroaches and other parasites, the unavoidable filth, rats scurrying across the straw. The constant contact with other women, cheek to cheek, their sour breath on her face as she tried to sleep, their snoring in her ears. She learned to dim the noise: the clanging door at the end of the hall, the tapping spoons and wailing babies. The stink of the chamber pot, which had so sickened her when she'd first arrived, receded; she willed herself to ignore it.

Her relationship with Cecil had been so consuming that while she was at the Whitstones' she'd barely had a moment to miss the life she'd led before. But now her life in Tunbridge Wells was what came to mind most often. She missed her father:

his mild temperament and small kindnesses, how they'd chat for hours in the evening, watching the fire settle as rain pattered the roof tiles. She'd adjust the blanket on his legs and he'd read to her from Wordsworth or Shakespeare, lines she now mouthed to herself as she lay in the small space she'd carved out on the cell floor:

There was a time when meadow, grove, and stream, / The earth, and every common sight, / To me did seem / Apparelled in celestial light . . .

We are such stuff / As dreams are made on, and our little life / Is rounded with a sleep.

When she closed her eyes, Evangeline found comfort in recalling even the small routines she used to complain about: heating a kettle to wash dishes in the sink, scooping coal from the bin to keep the fire going in the stove, heading to the bakery with her shopping basket on a cold February morning. Ordinary pleasures now seemed unimaginable: black tea sweetened with sugar in the afternoon, with apricot cake and custard; her mattress at the rectory, stuffed with goose feathers and cotton; the soft muslin gown and cap she wore to sleep; calfskin gloves, dark brown, with mother-of-pearl buttons, molded to the shape of her hands through years of wear; her wool cape with its rabbit-fur collar. Watching her father at his writing desk as he worked on his weekly sermons, his tapered fingers holding a quill. The smell of the streets of Tunbridge Wells when it rained in the spring: wet roses and lavender, horse manure and hay. Standing in a meadow at dawn, watching a lemony sun rise in a wide-open sky.

She remembered something her father had told her as he knelt at the hearth one evening, building a fire. Holding up the cut end of a log, he showed her the rings inside, explaining that each one marked a year. Some were wider than others, depending on the weather, he said; they were lighter in winter and darker in summer. All of them fused together to give the tree its solid core.

Maybe humans are like that, she thought. Maybe the moments that meant something to you and the people you've loved over the years are the rings. Maybe what you thought you'd lost is still there, inside of you, giving you strength.

THE PRISONERS HAD nothing to lose, which meant they had no shame. They blew their noses into their sleeves, picked lice from each other's hair, crushed fleas between their fingers, kicked slithering rats out of the way without a second thought. They swore at the slightest provocation, sang bawdy songs about randy butchers and barmaids with swollen bellies, and openly inspected their monthly rags, stained dark with blood, to assess whether they could use them again. They had strange scabbed rashes and phlegmy coughs and sores oozing with neglect. Their hair was matted with dirt and vermin, their eyes bloodshot and runny with infection. Many spent their days hacking and spitting, a telltale sign, according to Olive, of gaol fever.

Accompanying her father on visits to the ailing and infirm, Evangeline had learned to tuck a blanket around a feeble form or spoon broth into a slack mouth, to murmur psalms to the dying: *Praise the Lord, my soul, and forget not all his benefits—who forgives all your sins and heals all your diseases, who redeems your life from the pit and crowns you with love and compassion.* But she had not actually empathized. Not really. Even after leaving the home of a sickly parishioner, she would turn with thinly veiled distaste from a beggar in the street.

How young she'd been, she realized now, how easily shocked, how quick to judge.

Here she couldn't pull the door behind her or turn away. She was no better than the sorriest wretch in the cell: no better than Olive, with her coarse laugh and rough manners, who sold her body on the street; no better than the unfortunate girl singing the lullaby, who held her infant for days until someone noticed it was dead. The most private, shameful parts of being human— the bodily fluids people spent their lives trying to contain and conceal—were what most deeply connected them: blood and bile and urine and shit and saliva and pus. She felt horrified to have been brought so low. But she also felt, for the first time, a twinge of true compassion for even the most despicable. She was one of them, after all.

The cell quieted as two guards came in to take the lifeless infant from its mother. They had to pry it from her arms as she stood humming a tuneless song, tears streaming down her cheeks.

Yes, Evangeline loathed this place, but she loathed more the vanity and naivete and willful ignorance that had landed her here.

ONE MORNING, ABOUT a fortnight after she'd been brought in, the iron door at the end of the hallway clanged open and a guard shouted: "Evangeline Stokes!"

"Here!" Struggling to be heard above the din, she pulled herself toward the cell door. She glanced down at her stained bodice, her hem weighted with filth. She smelled her own rank breath and sweat and swallowed the fear in her mouth. Still, whatever awaited her out there had to be better than what was in here.

The matron and two guards carrying truncheons appeared at the cell door. "Move aside, let 'er through," one of the guards said, thwacking the grate with his stick as the women surged forward. When she reached the door, Evangeline was hauled out, shackled, and escorted across the street to another gray building, the Sessions House. The guards led her down a narrow set of stairs to a windowless room filled with holding cells stacked on top of each other like chicken pens, each barely large enough for one hunched adult, with slatted iron bars on either side. Once she was locked inside, and after her eyes adjusted, she could see the shapes of prisoners in other cells and hear their groans and coughs.

When a hunk of bread thumped on the floor, Evangeline jumped, banging her head on the top of her cell. An old woman in the cage beside her reached through the slats and snatched it, chortling at her alarm. "Goes to the street," she said, pointing to the ceiling. Evangeline peered up: above the narrow aisle separating the cells into two sides was a hole. "Some people take pity."

"Strangers throw bread down here?"

"Mostly relatives, come for a trial. Anybody here for ye?"

"No."

Evangeline could hear her chewing. "I'd give ye some," the woman said after a moment, "but I'm starvin'."

"Oh—it's all right. Thank you."

"Your first time, I'm guessin'."

"My only time," Evangeline said.

The woman chortled again. "I said that once meself."

THE JUDGE LICKED his lips with obvious distaste. His wig was yellowed and slightly off-kilter. A fine sprinkling of powder dusted the shoulders of his robe. The guard assigned to Evangeline had told her on the way to the courtroom that the judge had already presided over a dozen cases so far today, probably a hundred this week. Sitting on a bench in the hallway, awaiting her trial, she'd watched the accused and convicted come and go: pickpockets and laudanum addicts, prostitutes and forgers, murderers and the insane.

She stood in the dock alone. Legal counsel was for the rich. An all-male jury sat to her right, gazing at her with varying levels of indifference.

"How will you be tried?" the judge asked wearily.

"By God and by my country," she said as instructed.

"Have you any witnesses who will vouch for your character?"

She shook her head.

"Speak, prisoner."

"No. No witnesses."

A barrister stood and recited the charges against her: Attempted Murder. Grand Larceny. He read from a letter that he said he had received from a Mrs. Whitstone at 22 Blenheim Road, St. John's Wood, detailing Miss Stokes's scandalous crimes.

The judge peered at her. "Have you anything to say for yourself, prisoner?"

Evangeline curtsied. "Well, sir. I didn't mean to . . ." Her voice faltered. She had meant to, after all. "The ring was a gift; I didn't steal it. My—the man who—"

Before she could continue the judge was waving his hand in the air. "I've heard enough."

The jury took all of ten minutes to announce a verdict: guilty on both counts.

The judge lifted his gavel. "Sentenced," he said, bringing it down with a bang. "Fourteen years transportation to the land beyond the seas."

Evangeline clutched the wooden bar in front of her so she wouldn't sink to her knees. Had she heard him right? Fourteen years? No one returned her gaze. The judge shuffled papers on his desk. "Summon the next prisoner," he told his page.

"That's it?" she asked the guard.

"That's it. Australia. Ye'll be a pioneer."

She remembered Olive saying transport was a life sentence. "But . . . I can come back when my time is served?"

His laugh was devoid of pity, but not exactly unkind. "It's

the other side of the world, miss. Ye might as well be sailin' to the sun."

As she made her way, flanked by the guards, back to Newgate and down the dark corridor to the cells, Evangeline forced herself to square her shoulders (as best she could, chained hand and foot) and took a breath. Years ago, she'd climbed to the top of the church spire in Tunbridge Wells, where the bells were rung. As she ascended the circular stone staircase in the windowless tower, the walls narrowed and the steps became steeper; she could see a shaft of light above her head but had no idea how much farther it was to the top. Trudging upward in smaller and smaller circles, she'd feared that she might end up penned in on all sides, unable to move.

That was how this felt.

Passing the cells filled with prisoners, she noticed the ragged, dark-rimmed nails of a woman clutching an iron grate, the large eyes of a baby too weak or too hungry to cry. She heard the thudding flap of the guards' boots, the dull clang of her leg irons. Under the pungent odor of human waste and sickness was the sour salty smell of vinegar, used every other week or so by the lowliest guards to scrub the walls and floors. A stream of liquid snaked toward a grate beneath her feet. She felt as if she were watching a play that she herself was in—*The Tempest*, perhaps, with its topsy-turvy world, its chaotic and menacing landscape. A line floated into her head: *Hell is empty, and all the devils are here.*

"Including you," the guard said, shoving her along.

She'd said the words aloud, she realized, as if reciting them to her father during a lesson.

EVERY FEW DAYS, regardless of weather, a group of prisoners was led out of the cell, shackled, and marched to a desolate exercise pen, separated from other pens by high iron-spike-tipped walls, to plod in a circle for the better part of an hour.

"How long do you think until we leave?" Evangeline asked Olive as they tramped around the pen one gray afternoon.

"Dunno. I heard they fill a ship twice or three times a year. One left just before I was nabbed. Midsummer, if I had to guess."

It was the beginning of April.

"I don't understand why they're sending us halfway around the world," Evangeline said. "It'd be a lot less money and bother if we served our sentences here."

"You're missing the point," Olive said. "It's a government scheme. A racket."

"What do you mean?"

"England used to send its dregs to America, but after the rebellion they had to find a new rubbish dump. Australia it was. Before they knew it there was nine men for every woman. *Nine!* Ye can't found a settlement with only men, can ye? Nobody thought that through. So they came up with arse-backward excuses to send us over there."

"Surely you don't mean . . . ," Evangeline said.

"Surely I do. By their reckoning we're already sinners."

Slapping her belly, Olive said, "Look at us, Leenie! No question we're fertile, is there? Plus we're bringing new citizens inside us. Bonus if they happen to be female. And it doesn't cost 'em much. Fix up a few slaving ships and they're good to go."

"*Slaving* ships?"

Olive laughed. Evangeline's naivete was one of her greatest amusements. "Makes perfect sense, if ye think about it. Dozens of seaworthy vessels just sitting there, rotting in the harbor, and all because a few do-gooders in Parliament got cold feet about owning human beings. Mind ye, nobody has any such qualms about breeding convicts."

A guard came over and grabbed Olive's arm. "Stop spreading gossip, you."

She yanked away from his grasp. "It's the truth, though, in'it?"

He spit on the ground at her feet.

"How do you know all this?" Evangeline asked after a few more turns around the pen.

"Hang around the pubs in this town after midnight. No telling what a fella will reveal when he's had a few drinks."

"They must be lying. Or exaggerating, at least."

Olive gave her a pitying smile. "Your problem, Leenie, is ye don't want to believe what's in front of your nose. That's what got ye here in the first place, in'it?"

ON SUNDAY MORNINGS the female inmates were herded into the prison chapel, where they were seated in the back, in a section of pews behind tall, slanted boards that allowed them to see the preacher but not the male inmates. A coal stove glowed below the pulpit, but its heat did not reach them. For more than an hour the women huddled in their flimsy dresses and heavy chains as the preacher rebuked, admonished, and berated them for their vices.

The gist of the sermon was always the same: they were wretched sinners paying an earthly penance; the Devil was waiting to see how much lower they could descend before they became irredeemable. Their only chance was to throw themselves on the stern mercy of God the Father and pay the price for their wickedness.

Sometimes Evangeline looked down at her hands and thought: these same fingers plucked flowers and arranged them in a vase. Drew Latin letters in chalk on a piece of slate. Traced Cecil's face from his forehead to his Adam's apple. Hovered over her father's still features and closed his eyes for the last time. And now look at them—dirty, grasping, defiled.

Never again would she describe something as unbearable. Almost anything, she now knew, could be borne. Small white vermin infested her hair, lingering sores developed from small scrapes, a cough burrowed into her chest. She was exhausted and sick to her stomach much of the time, but she wasn't dying. In this place that meant she was doing all right.

IN THE ETERNAL GLOOM OF the cell it was hard to tell how much time had passed, or even what time of day it was. Outside the small grated window, though, and in the shadow of the spiked wall of the exercise yard, the light from the sun grew warmer and lingered longer. Evangeline's morning sickness subsided and her belly began to swell. Her breasts, too, grew larger and more tender to the touch. She tried not to think too much about the child she carried inside her—visual proof of her degradation, a mark of sin as unambiguous as the Devil's red claw tracks on flesh.

Some time after breakfast one temperate morning, the gate at the end of the hall clanged open and a guard shouted, "Quakers here. Make yourselves presentable."

Evangeline looked around for Olive and, seeing her a few feet away, caught her eye. Olive pointed toward the cell door: *Get there.*

Three women in long gray cloaks and white bonnets materialized in front of the cell, each carrying a large sack. The one in the middle, wearing a plain black dress with a white shawl under her cloak, stood taller and straighter than the other two.

Her eyes were a milky blue, her skin unrouged, her gray hair parted neatly under her bonnet. She smiled at the women inside with an air of benign self-possession. "Hello, friends," she said in a quiet voice.

Remarkably, except for a fussing baby, the cell had gone silent.

"I am Mrs. Fry. The ladies accompanying me today are Mrs. Warren"—she nodded to her left—"and Mrs. Fitzpatrick. We are here on behalf of the Society for the Reformation of Female Prisoners."

Evangeline leaned forward, straining to hear.

"Each of you is worthy of redemption. You need not always be stained by your sins. You may choose to live your lives from this day forward with dignity and honor." Reaching through the iron grate with two fingers, Mrs. Fry touched the arm of a young girl staring at her wide-eyed. "What doest thou need?"

The girl shrank back, unaccustomed to being spoken to directly.

"Would you like a new dress?"

The girl nodded.

"Is there any poor soul here this day," asked Mrs. Fry, tilting her chin toward the larger group, "who wants to be saved from sin, so that you may be saved from woe, saved from misery? Friends, hold fast your hope. Remember the words of Christ: 'Open the door of thy heart, and I will overcome that by which thou hast been overcome.' If thou dost trust in the Lord, all will be forgiven."

When she finished speaking, a guard unlocked the door and the prisoners jostled to make room. Entering the cell, the

Quakers handed out oat biscuits from a cotton sack. Evangeline took one and bit into it. Though hard and dry, it tasted better than anything she'd eaten in weeks.

With the help of the guards, Mrs. Fry identified the new prisoners and gave each one a parcel tied with twine. Pressing a bundle into Evangeline's arms, she asked, "How long have you been here?"

Evangeline half curtsied. "Nearly three months, ma'am."

Mrs. Fry cocked her head. "You are—educated. And from . . . the South?"

"Tunbridge Wells. My father was a vicar there."

"I see. So . . . have you been sentenced to transport?"

"Yes."

"Seven years?"

Evangeline winced. "Fourteen."

Mrs. Fry nodded, seemingly unsurprised. "Well. You appear healthy. The journey is about four months—it's not easy, but most survive. You'll arrive at the end of the summer, which is the end of their winter. Much preferable to the reverse." She pursed her lips. "In all honesty, I am not convinced that transport is the answer. There are too many opportunities for abuse—too many ways, I believe, for the system to corrupt. But it is the system we have, and as such . . ." She looked at Evangeline intently. "Let me ask you something. Would your father have approved of"— she gestured vaguely toward Evangeline's belly—"this?"

Evangeline flushed.

"Perhaps it reveals a certain lack of . . . judgment. You allowed yourself to be taken advantage of. I urge you to be careful. And alert. Men don't have to live with the consequences of their actions. You do."

"Yes, ma'am."

When Mrs. Fry and her helpers turned their backs to hand out more parcels, Evangeline rifled through hers, pulling out and inspecting the items: a plain white cap, a green cotton dress, a burlap apron to wear over the dress. After the parcels were distributed, the Quakers came around to help the prisoners into their new clothes.

Mrs. Warren unbuttoned the back of Evangeline's soiled dress and helped her extract each arm from its sleeve. Evangeline was acutely aware of the stink under her arms, the sour tang in her mouth, her sludgy hem. Mrs. Warren smelled like . . . nothing; like skin. But if she was repulsed, she gave no hint of it.

Once the prisoners were clothed, Mrs. Fry asked if any of them were interested in needlework or quilting or knitting stockings. Evangeline raised her hand. Though she had little interest in stitchery, a break from the cell would be nice, and she missed being productive. Three dozen prisoners were divided into groups and led across the open courtyard to a large, drafty room filled with tables and rough benches, with tiny open windows cut high in the wall facing the courtyard. Evangeline's group was assigned knitting, which she'd never learned to do. Mrs. Warren settled on the bench beside her, gently guiding the long wooden needles in her hand through the coarse wool. Feeling this woman's soft, warm hands on hers, the touch of a person who was neither scornful nor contemptuous . . . Evangeline blinked back tears.

"Oh, my dear. Let me find a handkerchief," Mrs. Warren said, rising from the bench.

As Evangeline watched her cross the room, she ran her fingers down the slight bump of her midsection and over to her hipbone, tracing the faint outline of Cecil's handkerchief under her new green dress. After a moment she felt a flutter, like a tiny fish swimming at the bottom of her stomach.

It must be the baby. She felt suddenly protective of it and absentmindedly cradled her lower belly, as if holding the child itself.

This child would be birthed in captivity, in disgrace and uncertainty; it faced a future of strife and toil. But what had at first seemed like a cruel joke now felt like a reason to live. She was responsible not only for herself, but for another human being. How fiercely she hoped it would have a chance to overcome its unhappy beginnings.

THE RATTLE AND click of locks at the end of the long, dark hallway. The glow of lanterns splashing across stone. The clanking cart filled with chains and irons. The harsh voices of jailors: "Let's go now! Make it quick!"

"It's time," Olive said, poking Evangeline's shoulder. "They've come for us."

In front of the cell door stood three guards. One held a piece of parchment; another raised a lantern above it. The third ran his stick back and forth across the iron grate. "You lot listen up," he said. "If I call your name, step forward." He squinted at the paper. "Ann Darter!"

A rustle, a murmuring, and then the girl whose baby died crept to the front. It was the first time Evangeline had heard her name. "It'll be a miracle if that one makes it," Olive muttered.

"Maura Frindle!"

A woman Evangeline didn't know crept out of the shadows.

"Olive Rivers."

"I'm 'ere, hold your horses," she said, her hands on the grate.

The guard with the stick ran it across the grate again, *rat-tat-tat-tat*, forcing Olive to let go. "Last one. Evangeline Stokes."

Evangeline smoothed a strand of hair behind her ear. She ran a hand under her belly and stepped up.

The guard with the lantern held it up to get a better look. "This one's a jammy bit o' jam."

"She don't like fellas," Olive said. "Too bad fer ye."

"She liked some kind of fella," the lantern holder said, to general laughter.

"And look where it got her," Olive said.

With one guard in front and two behind, the prisoners trooped across the courtyard, up another set of stairs, and down the wide corridor with its hissing oil lamps to the matron's quarters. The matron, sitting behind her oak desk, appeared in no better mood than she'd been on the night Evangeline arrived. When she saw Evangeline she frowned. "You're too thin," she said accusingly, as if Evangeline had capriciously decided to lose weight. "Would be a pity to lose the child."

"Prolly be better off," a guard said.

"She probably would be." The matron sighed. Peering at the ledger, she ran a line through Evangeline's name.

When the prisoners were discharged, the guards led the shuffling procession down the stairs, moving slowly so they wouldn't tumble like dominoes. As she stood outside the tall black gates, Evangeline felt like a bear emerging from a cave, blinking into the early morning light.

The sky overhead was the warm white of fresh muslin, the leaves of the elms lining the street lily-pad green. A spray of birds rose, confetti-like, from a tree. It was an ordinary day in the city: a flower monger setting up his stall, horses and buggies clattering down Bailey Street, men in black waistcoats and top hats striding along the sidewalk, a boy calling in a high, thin voice, "Pork pies! Hot cross buns!"

Two ladies were strolling arm in arm, one in walnut brocaded satin, the other in a watery blue silk, both tightly corseted, with puffed upper sleeves that tapered fashionably to the wrist. Their parasols were ornamental, their bonnets tied with velvet bows. The one in blue caught sight of the manacled female prisoners and stopped in her tracks. Lifting a gloved hand to her mouth, she whispered in the other lady's ear. The two of them turned abruptly in the opposite direction.

Evangeline looked down at her heavy chains and burlap apron. She must seem a specter to them, she realized—barely human.

As she stood with the guards and the other prisoners near the street, a carriage with boarded-up windows, drawn by two black horses, clip-clopped to a stop in front of them. Half shoving, half lifting each woman, one of the guards managed to load them inside, where they sat across from each other, two by two, on rough wooden planks. When the guard closed the door and locked it, the interior was pitch dark. Springs wheezed as he took his place beside the driver. Evangeline strained to hear their voices but couldn't make out what they were saying.

The crack of a whip, the whinny of a horse. The carriage jolted forward.

It was stuffy inside the carriage. As the wheels creaked along the cobblestones, Olive bumping against her at every turn, Evangeline felt a bead of perspiration slide from her forehead to the tip of her nose. In an absentminded gesture that had become a habit, she found the edge of Cecil's handkerchief under her dress with her fingertips. Sitting on the hard plank in the dark, she listened for clues. Finally, the *caw-caw*s of seagulls, men yelling in the distance, the air sharp with brine: they must be near the water. The slaving ship. Her heart began to thump.

MATHINNA

We make no pompous display of Philanthropy. The Government must remove the natives—if not, they will be hunted down like wild beasts and destroyed!

—*THE COLONIAL TIMES* (Tasmania), December 1, 1826

THE EARLY MORNING AIR WAS cool, with a steady rain. Under a weeping pine, Mathinna pulled the wallaby skin around her shoulders and gazed out at the hairy brown ferns and the cloud gardens of moss hanging above, listening to the shirring rain and the chirping crickets. Fingering the delicate shells on the necklace looped twice around her neck, she thought about her predicament. She wasn't frightened of being alone in the forest, despite the tiger snakes that hid under logs and the venomous black spiders in their invisible webs. She feared more what awaited her back at the settlement.

Before Mathinna was born, Wanganip had told her, Mathinna's sister, Teanic, had been yanked out of her father's arms by British settlers attempting to capture him. Teanic was sent to the Queen's Orphan School near Hobart Town and they never saw her again. It was rumored that she died of influenza at the age of eight, but the Palawa had never been told that directly.

Mathinna did not want to be kidnapped like her sister.

After Wanganip died, Mathinna's stepfather, Palle, had done his best to comfort her. With one arm around her as they sat near the crackling campfire, he told her stories about the Palawa gods, so different from the one they were now forced to worship. The two main deities were brothers descended from the sun and the moon. Moinee made the land and rivers. Droemerdene lived in the sky, having taken the form of a star. He crafted the first human from a kangaroo, fashioning knee joints so the man could rest and removing the cumbersome tail.

Since the first Palawa was created, Palle told her, they had walked many miles a day. Lean and fit and small of stature, they roamed from the bush to the sea and to the top of the mountains, carrying their food and tools and eating utensils in bags woven from grass. Smeared with a layer of seal grease to protect them from the wind and cold, they hunted kangaroo and wallaby and other beasts with spears honed with stone knives and with wooden clubs called waddies. From campsite to campsite they carried water in kelp vessels and smoldering coals in baskets made of bark. They ate abalone and oysters and used the sharp edges of leftover shells to cut meat.

Long ago, their country had extended across what were now the waters of the Bass Strait, but one day the rising sea sliced the island from the continent. Ever since, the Palawa had lived on Lutruwita in splendid isolation. There was usually enough to eat; the water was fresh and wildlife plentiful. They built domed huts out of tree bark and twisted wide strands of bark into canoes. They crafted long necklaces, like those Mathinna's mother made, from vivid green Mariner shells the size of baby teeth and wore ceremonial red ochre in their hair. Many tribesmen wore raised scars shaped like suns and moons on their shoulders and arms and torsos, carved into their skin and filled with powdered charcoal. Their stories, spoken and sung, were passed from one generation to the next.

Unlike the British, Palle said, spitting on the ground with contempt, the Palawa did not need brick structures or constricting costumes or muskets to feel content. They coveted nothing and stole nothing. There were twelve nations, each containing half a dozen clans, each with a different language, and there was no word for property in any of them. The land was simply part of who they were.

Or perhaps more accurately, he said, they were part of the land.

It had been two hundred years since the first white men came to their shores—strange-looking creatures with freakishly pale skin, like white worms or ghosts out of legends. They appeared as soft as oysters, but the spears they carried roared with fire. For many years the only white people hardy enough to remain through the winter were the whalers and sealers, many of whom were so crude and vicious they seemed to the Palawa half man, half beast. Even so, over time, a bartering system developed. The Palawa traded crawfish and muttonbirds and kangaroo skins for white sugar, tea, tobacco, and rum—vile substances that took root in their brains and stomachs, Palle told Mathinna, fueling cravings and dependence.

Since the day the invaders arrived on—and named—Van Diemen's Land, they were as relentless as a rising tide. They seized the land and pushed the Palawa farther and farther into the mountains. The grasslands and open bush, their kangaroo and wallaby hunting grounds, became grazing pastures for sheep, penned in by fences. The Palawa loathed these stupid bleating animals that clogged their routes and pathways. They refused to eat their stinking meat and burned the fences that impeded their movements. Fearing the shepherds who had no qualms about killing them when they came near, they fought back the only way they could, with ambush and subterfuge.

A decade before Mathinna was born, the so-called Black War decimated the tribes. The white men, the Palawa realized too late, were devoid of morality. They lied while smiling at you and thought nothing of luring you into traps. The Palawa fought in vain with rocks and spears and waddies against roving parties of convicts and settlers who had been officially authorized by the British government to capture or kill any natives on sight. These men roamed the island with kangaroo dogs, hunting the Palawa for sport. As the Palawa continued to elude them, their tactics became more cunning. They camouflaged steel traps with eucalyptus leaves. They bound the men to trees and used them for target practice. They raped and enslaved Palawa women, infecting them with diseases that left them barren. They burned them with brands and dashed the brains of their children on the rocks.

When most of the Palawa had been killed off, the remaining few were rounded up and brought to Flinders. Here, they were forced into stiff British clothes with needless buttons and shoes that cramped their feet. The red ochre was scrubbed from their hair, which was clipped short, in the British style. They were made to sit in the dark chapel and listen to sermons about a hell they'd never imagined and moral instruction they didn't need, singing hymns that promised salvation in exchange for suffering.

The Palawa had been told that their time on Flinders would be temporary, that soon they'd be granted land of their own—or rather, given some of their own land back.

It had been ten years. They were still waiting.

THE RAIN FELL in sheets. It trickled down Mathinna's neck, finding the gaps in her cape, soaking through her cotton dress to the skin. Deep in her chest she could feel a thickening, the beginnings of a cold. Her eyes were itchy with exhaustion and her stomach was empty. She could hunt for swans' eggs, but that would mean heading into the open grasses. If she went to the beach in search of mussels, she'd be easy to spot from the ridge. Though she had never caught a muttonbird, she'd watched Palle do it: he dipped his hand inside a hole in the ground as wide as a large oyster shell, and if the air was cold, he pulled his hand out quickly; it might be a snake den—but if it was warm, it was probably a muttonbird nest. He'd reach in, grab the bird, and yank it out, twisting its neck to snap it.

The problem was, Mathinna didn't have fire. Even the hardiest elders, the ones who tore into the muttonbirds as soon as most of the sticky feathers were burned off, didn't eat them raw.

She gazed at the gum trees in the distance with bark as smooth and gray as wallaby bellies, and her eyes clouded with tears. She missed her pet, Waluka, an albino ringtail possum with pink ears she'd found abandoned and raised from birth. She missed the warmth of Palle's arms.

Her mouth watered at the thought of steaming oysters plucked from the coals.

By the time she made her way back to the settlement, the rain had stopped. Some of the Palawa and a few missionaries were milling about, but there was no sign of the Franklins. Mathinna's heart surged with hope. She slipped into the schoolroom, where a few children were learning their lessons. The schoolteacher looked up from his primer. He appeared to take no notice of her wet dress, the soiled wallaby skin, the frightened look in her eyes. He seemed unsurprised that she'd returned.

"Mary," he said, rising. "Come with me. They've been looking for you."

WHEN THE CAPTAIN LIFTED HER into the sloop, Mathinna looked back and saw her stepfather standing on the ridge, silhouetted against the sky, shading his eyes with his hand.

"Palle!" she cried, waving.

He raised his arm, his fingers outstretched.

"Palle . . ." His figure blurred through her tears.

"That's enough, now," the captain said.

She sobbed quietly as he pulled anchor and readied the sail. Deep in her bones, she felt certain that she would never see her stepfather again. She watched his figure recede into the distance as the boat left its mooring and headed into the open ocean.

Spitting on the deck, the captain said, "I was told to treat ye like a little lady. I'll do what they say, but ye don't look like any lady I ever saw."

Mathinna didn't answer. She wiped her eyes with her hands.

She'd never been out on the water before. Only the seafarers among the Palawa went out in canoes. She had not known to expect the gliding rises and sudden drops, the salty fizz in her nose, the hard brightness of the sun, the stomach-churning smell of fish innards rotting in a bucket.

Her mouth filled with saliva. Her eyes watered. Before they even lost sight of Flinders, she was vomiting into a pail.

"It's in your head." The captain tapped his temple. "Calm yourself."

When Mathinna had returned to the settlement, three days earlier, she was told that the Franklins were on their way back to Van Diemen's Land. They'd left behind *The Cormorant* and its captain from their small fleet for the express purpose of ferrying her to Hobart Town. George Robinson's wife, Maria, had helped her pack her meager belongings into an old steamer trunk for the trip: two plain, English-style cotton dresses, two sets of pantaloons, a bonnet, a pair of leather shoes. Mathinna made a nest of the wallaby-skin cape for Waluka in a rush basket Palle had woven for her, tucking three shell necklaces her mother had made beneath it.

"Bringing a rodent to the governor's residence hardly seems advisable," Robinson said when he saw Waluka.

"It's a marsupial, George." His wife pantomimed paws like a kangaroo. "It has a pouch. She raised it from birth; it's quite tame."

"It looks like a rat."

Maria put her hand on his arm. "This child is leaving behind everything she has ever known. What harm is there in letting her keep it?"

Now, crouching down, Mathinna opened the basket. She pulled out one of the shell necklaces and draped it around her neck, then lifted Waluka onto her lap. With his milky skin, pink nose, and long talons he did look a bit like a rat, she supposed. In her lap he was limp, motionless, but she could feel his tiny heart skittering as she stroked his chest with the back of a finger.

"I'm surprised they let ye bring that mangy thing," the captain said.

She ran a protective hand down Waluka's back. "Mr. Robinson said I could."

"Ever eaten possum?"

She shook her head.

"Not bad," the captain said. "Tastes like eucalyptus."

She couldn't tell if he was joking.

The sky was as gray as the flat stones in the cove. Waves glinted like shale. Spreading out his tattered map, the captain beckoned Mathinna over. He traced the coastline of a large landmass with his forefinger until he reached a narrow passage near the bottom. Tapping it, he said, "This is where we're headed. Ten days' journey."

It looked like nothing to her: jagged lines on a piece of paper. But as she examined the map, sounding out the names of towns and regions, she moved her own finger up the coastline, the reverse of their journey. Past Port Arthur, around tiny Maria Island, through Four Mile Creek and around Cape Barren Island, and finally back to Flinders, a speck in the ocean above the bulk of Van Diemen's Land.

Running a finger along the shells of her necklace, Mathinna remembered her mother placing it in her hands. "Every person you've ever cared about, and every place you've ever loved, is one of these shells. You're the thread that ties them together," she'd said, touching Mathinna's cheek. "You carry the people and places you cherish with you. Remember that and you will never be lonely, child."

Mathinna wanted to believe it. She wasn't sure it was true.

THE CAPTAIN SLEPT in fits and starts; at the slightest dip or flap of the sail he'd startle awake. She pretended not to notice when he moved behind a barrel to use the chamber pot or wash his armpits in a bucket. He was probably only in his midthirties, but to Mathinna he seemed ancient. He was coarse, but not unkind. His only task, he told her, was to deliver her safely to the governor, and by hook or by crook he would do that. Mainly he left her alone. When he wasn't tending the mainsail or charting their course, he sat on one side of the boat, whittling naked women out of wood with a small curved knife, and she sat on the other, fingering the tiny green shells around her neck and playing with Waluka.

Each morning the captain performed a checklist of tasks: recording barometer readings in a notebook, checking the sail for rips and tears, nailing down loose boards, splicing rope. He trailed a lure behind the boat and pulled in red-striped perch and jack mackerel and the occasional salmon. He'd stun the flopping fish before gutting it quickly with his carving knife, then make a fire in the cook box, a metal contraption with three sides on four sturdy legs, with a tray in the bottom for the fire and a grate on top.

Mathinna had never eaten scale fish; the Palawa ate only shellfish. They laughed at the missionaries when they saw them picking tiny bones out of their teeth. But now her mouth watered at the smell of crackling skin and the sight of white flesh melting from the bone. "Try it," the captain said one evening, catching her eye. He sliced off some chunks, dumped them on a pewter plate, and handed it to her. When she tried to pick up the chunks with her fingers, the fish separated into flat fleshy disks. She slipped them into her mouth one by one, marveling at the buttery flavor. He grinned. "Better'n hardtack, ain't it?"

The captain told her stories about his life—how he'd stolen rare coins to pay for medicine for his sick mother (or so he said), ending up on a convict ship to Van Diemen's Land, where he did six years of hard labor at Port Arthur. When he mentioned he'd been a sealer, Mathinna's heart thumped. But she hadn't seen any sign of savagery.

"Do you like . . . killing seals?" she asked.

He shrugged. "It's rough work. Dirty and cold. But I didn't have much choice, din' I? At least I knew I'd be paid for me labor. Anyway, I seen worse in prison. What people do to each other, ye wouldn't believe."

Why wouldn't she believe? Here she was, torn from her family and everyone she knew at the whim of a lady in satin slippers who boiled the skulls of her relatives and displayed them as curiosities. (What people do to each other, indeed.)

"That's all in the past," the captain said. "I'm on the straight and narrow now. When the governor pays your wages, ye jump when he tells ye. And as high."

Out on the open ocean, the water was white-tipped and choppy. It sprayed in their faces and sudsed over the sides as the small sloop plunged and turned. The captain began putting her to work, untangling the rigging, steadying the tiller while he adjusted the sails. He showed her how to clean the metal grill and nurse the coals to keep the fire going in the cook box. He told her he was assigning her the job of watch stander—when he needed a nap, or a break, she was to keep her eyes open for trouble. She grew to enjoy the work, an antidote to boredom. Her favorite moments were when the captain was asleep. Her senses sharp, she scanned the horizon and stoked the fire.

She began doing these tasks without being asked and he began to assume she would do them. "They say your people can't be taught, but look at ye," he said.

When the sky darkened, she pulled the fur cape around her shoulders and gazed up in search of Droemerdene, the bright southern star, allowing herself to close her eyes only when she'd found him.

IT WAS LATE afternoon when *The Cormorant* entered Storm Bay and made its way up the River Derwent toward Hobart Town. As they approached the harbor, surrounded by shrieking gulls, Mathinna tied down the bow dock line and the stern line. The captain let out the main sheet, slowing the sloop, and guided it gently toward a mooring. While he did this, she gathered her things, tucked Waluka into the basket, and covered him with the wallaby skin. She changed into a plain white dress with small pleats around the bodice, the one she'd been told to save for their arrival. She'd been barefoot for the entire journey, and the skin on the soles of her feet was as tough as horsehide. Now she slipped on the soft leather shoes. They felt strange, like bonnets on her feet.

Standing on the cobblestones at the wharf, holding her basket, she took tentative steps, trying to regain her balance after so many days at sea. She'd never seen such a swarm of activity. Men shouting at each other, women peddling wares, dogs barking, gulls squawking, horses whinnying and tossing their manes. Bleating goats and grunting pigs. The briny smell of seaweed, a whiff of horse manure, the earthy sweetness of roasting chestnuts. Against the side of a building, a cluster of men in garish yellow-and-black costumes stood toeing the dirt. When she looked closer, she saw that they were chained together.

Hearing the captain's distinctive laugh, Mathinna turned. He was several feet away, talking with two men wearing red uniforms, muskets slung over their shoulders. He raised his chin toward her. "That's the one."

"Ye hardly need to point 'er out."

"Where're her parents?"

"No parents," the captain said.

The first soldier nodded. "Just as well."

The captain crouched in front of her. "It's time to hand ye off. These two will take ye where ye need to go." He lingered for a moment as if he wanted to say more. Then he nodded at her basket. "Glad we didn't have to eat your possum."

The seats of the open carriage—horsehair, dyed royal

blue—were slippery. Mathinna had to grip the armrest to keep from sliding onto the floor. The horses' hooves made a slurping noise as they clip-clopped along cobblestones slick with mud. Looking back at the wharf receding into the distance as they jolted away, Mathinna felt more alone than she had ever been in her life. No one in this strange place looked like her. No one.

THE HORSES TURNED DOWN A short drive and lurched to a stop in front of a long, two-story, cream-colored building with blue trim and a wide front porch. One of the soldiers jumped down and lifted Mathinna out of the carriage. Instead of setting her on the stone apron of the driveway, he carried her to the entry stairs. "You're a proper lady, I'm told," he said in an exaggerated show of deference. "Wouldn't do to muddy your hem."

Mathinna craned her neck to look around. Though she'd never seen such a large and stately building, she felt oddly at ease, as if she were stepping into an etching in a book she'd read with the schoolteacher.

A stout middle-aged woman wearing a gray dress and a white apron and cap appeared on the porch. "Hello, Mathinna," she said, inclining her head. "We've been expecting you. I am Mrs. Crain, the housekeeper. This is Government House. Your new . . . home."

The schoolteacher on Flinders had a housekeeper, an old missionary woman who made his bed and prepared his breakfast. Mathinna had always ignored her. But she didn't know the customs of this place. Was she expected to curtsy? She curtsied.

"Don't waste your fine manners on me," Mrs. Crain scoffed. "I'm the one should be bowing to you, I suppose. A princess, I hear!" She raised her eyebrows at the soldiers. "Lady Franklin and her fancies!"

Hoisting the steamer trunk on his shoulder, one of them said, "Where d'ye want the lady's dowry?"

"Drop it at the servants' entrance. I doubt there's much to salvage." Turning back to Mathinna, Mrs. Crain frowned, assessing her. "Come with me. I'll find a maid to draw a bath. We'll need to make you presentable before Lady Franklin takes one look and changes her mind."

THE OLD WOODEN tub had been a horse's trough, the housemaid, Sarah, told Mathinna. Rubbing Mathinna's back and arms with a rough brick of lye soap, she said, "I was instructed to wash ye tip to toe. Mrs. Crain said be quick about it, so there was no time to heat the water."

Hunched in the tub, her teeth chattering, Mathinna nodded.

"Next is supper, and then you're to see Lady Franklin," Sarah said, lifting Mathinna's arm and swiping the soap underneath. "Mrs. Wilson is the cook. She's a good sort. Most of us housemaids are here because of her. She was at the Cascades for more'n a decade."

Mathinna flinched as Sarah squeezed a cold cloth over her shoulders. "What's the Cascades?"

"Stay still, I have to rinse ye. It's a prison. They call it the female factory. Horrible place. Though not as bad as Flinders, from what I hear. Now raise your chin."

Mathinna looked up as Sarah scrubbed her neck. She remembered what the captain had said about the convicts at Port Arthur—that they were ruthless; they'd cut your throat as soon as they'd look at you. She thought of the men she'd seen at the wharf, shuffling along in their shackles. "I didn't know there were lady convicts."

Sarah made a face. "We're hardly ladies."

Mathinna gazed at Sarah, with her curly brown hair and bright blue eyes, her neat gray dress. She seemed harmless enough, but who knew? "Did you murder somebody?"

Sarah laughed. "Only in me heart." Wringing out the cloth, she said, "Murderers aren't allowed out on day release. They pick tar out of rope in their cells all day long. Ruins your fingers. Best reason I can think of not to kill somebody."

After the bath, Sarah dressed Mathinna in a white petticoat, a pink gabardine dress, and white stockings, and smoothed her hair with oil. When she handed her a pair of stiff black shoes, Mathinna balked. "Ye have to put 'em on. I'll be in trouble if ye don't," Sarah said.

Though she'd dressed in the British style on Flinders, Mathinna had never worn lace-up shoes. She put them on, but Sarah had to tie them.

Before they left the room, Sarah inspected her, pulling up a stocking and adjusting her petticoat. "Miss Eleanor got a lot of wear out of this dress," she mused, fingering a frayed hem.

"Miss Eleanor?"

"Sir John's daughter. This is her hand-me-down. She's seventeen. You'll meet her soon enough. She's a plain girl, god bless her, but at least now her dresses come from London."

IN THE KITCHEN outbuilding Mathinna gazed at the enormous stone hearth, the sheaves of herbs hanging from the soot-blackened ceiling, the bins and pots and pans stacked on shelves.

Mrs. Wilson, her hands on her ample hips, gave Sarah a hard look. "Did you find lice? Any sign of scurvy?"

Sarah shook her head. "Fit as a butcher's dog."

Mrs. Wilson gestured for Mathinna to sit at the table, then slid a plate of food in front of her. Mathinna stared at it. Purplish fish, wobbly in its gelatin, and cold white potatoes.

"Eat up," Mrs. Wilson said, tying a napkin around Mathinna's neck. "I don't abide finicky appetites in my kitchen."

Sarah squeezed Mathinna's shoulder. "Do as she says and be quick about it. I barely have time to take ye to your room before you're to see Lady Franklin."

Mathinna choked down a few bites of the bland, slippery food, swallowing quickly to avoid the taste and texture. Then she followed Sarah down a long corridor in the main house, past half a dozen rooms that appeared both overstuffed and strangely empty. Tall silver candleholders rose from pedestals like writhing tiger snakes, blue-and-white china vases bloomed with lilacs, brocaded draperies puddled on carpets. Powder-white faces peered down from gilded frames. The gold and green tendrils of the wallpaper in the corridor reminded Mathinna of the scrolls of smoke the Palawa elders blew from their mouths as they sat around the fire.

At the end of the hallway, Sarah opened a door that led to a back staircase, and up they went. The walls were bare and white. "The schoolroom," she said as they passed a room with a chalkboard on an easel, a table and chairs, and a small bookcase. The next two doors were closed. At the second one, Sarah stopped and turned the white porcelain knob.

In the light from the hall Mathinna could make out a narrow bed covered with a faded red blanket, a tall armoire, and a small pine desk and wooden stool. The room was dark. Following Sarah inside, she went to the window, expecting to find a drawn shade or closed curtain. When a light bloomed behind her, she saw that four wide planks were nailed across the window frame.

She turned to Sarah in surprise.

Sarah blew out the match she'd used to light an oil lamp on the wall. "It was Lady Franklin's orders to shield ye from the view. She read somewhere that natives feel a painful longing for the wilderness from whence they came. That without sight of it, you'll be less . . . homesick."

Mathinna stared at her. "I must live here in the dark?"

"It seems strange, I know. But perhaps you'll come to find this room quite . . . restful."

Mathinna couldn't help it; her eyes welled with tears.

Sarah bit her lip. "Look . . . I'll leave some candles for ye, but ye must be careful. The last one wasn't, and he nearly burnt the house down."

"Do you mean Timeo?"

She nodded. "He left only a few months ago."

"Why did he leave?"

"Why?" Sarah shrugged. "Lady Franklin tired of him, that's why."

Mathinna considered this. "Where is he now?"

"Oh goodness, ye are full of questions. I don't know. Now, come—we need to go downstairs. Lady Franklin is waiting."

"BEFORE I TAKE ye in here, I should mention that the Franklins like to collect things," Sarah told Mathinna as she knocked.

Mrs. Crain opened the door with a scowl. "You've kept the lady waiting."

Stepping into the room holding her rush basket, Mathinna gazed around her. There was almost too much to take in. In a curio chest between two long windows, human skulls were lined up by size. On the wide mantel of the fireplace, under glass domes, a snake appeared coiled and ready to strike, spiders clung to branches, a colorful bird swooped in midflight. A wombat, wallaby, gray kangaroo, and pademelon peered out from a glass display case, so lifelike that they seemed merely captive.

A collection of waddies and spears lined one wall. Mathinna walked closer to get a better look. One of the spears, decorated with a distinctive pattern of ochre and red, was familiar.

"I was told it belonged to Towterer."

Mathinna turned. Lady Franklin was seated in a brown velvet chair, her back erect and her hands in her lap. Her gray hair was parted in the middle and pulled back in a bun, and she wore a burgundy shawl around her shoulders. "Your father, yes?"

Mathinna nodded.

"Eventually I'll donate it to a museum, along with most of these artifacts. No doubt they will help further our study of native life." Lady Franklin beckoned her with a finger. "I'm pleased to see you, Mathinna. What have you got in that basket?"

Dutifully Mathinna stepped forward and set the basket in front of Lady Franklin. She peered into it. "My word," she exclaimed. "What a strange-looking creature! What on earth is it?"

"A possum, ma'am."

"Wouldn't it be better off in the wild?"

"He has never lived in the wild. I've had him since he was born."

"I see. Well . . . I suppose it can stay, as long as it's healthy. Best keep it away from Montagu's dog. What else is in there?"

Mathinna reached into the basket, under Waluka's nest, and pulled out the now-tangled clump of tiny green shells, easing them into three separate strands. She handed one to Lady Franklin.

"Ah," Lady Franklin murmured, holding up the necklace and turning it in the light. "I've seen these from a distance. Remarkable handiwork."

"It is, madam."

"Did you know, Mrs. Crain, that natives spend weeks, months even, finding and stringing the minuscule shells? These necklaces will be a worthy addition to my collection."

Mathinna felt short of breath. She wanted to grab the necklace out of Lady Franklin's hand. "They're mine," she blurted. "My mother made them."

Mrs. Crain shook her head, clucking her tongue.

Lady Franklin leaned down, close enough that Mathinna could see a few dark hairs sprouting from her chin. "I'm sure your mother would be honored if she knew that the governor's wife appreciates her trinkets." She held out her palm.

Reluctantly, Mathinna handed over the other two necklaces.

Lady Franklin turned to Mrs. Crain. "I am keen to observe the influence of civilization on this child. Timeo was unable to overcome the unfortunate traits of his race—the lack of self-control, of course, and the innate stubbornness of will and temper that we are witnessing here." She looked back at Mathinna, evaluating her. "This girl is lighter in color, and her features are more pleasing to the eye. More . . . European. It gives one hope that she might be more acquiescent. That she'll be able to let go of the past and embrace a new way of life. It is possible, I believe. She's younger than Timeo. Perhaps more malleable. Do you agree, Mrs. Crain?"

"If you say so, madam."

Lady Franklin sighed. "Time will tell. Take her to her room. I imagine this will be the first night she's slept in a proper bed."

Mathinna had been sleeping in a proper bed since she was

three years old—though she would've preferred the soft kangaroo skins the Palawa slept on in their cottages. There was little point, she knew, in saying this to Lady Franklin.

WHEN SARAH OPENED the armoire in Mathinna's bedroom, Mathinna was surprised to discover an entire wardrobe of clothing in her size: six dresses in fabrics ranging from cotton ticking to linen; six pairs of stockings, linen caps to cover her hair; three pairs of shoes. Most of the dresses were practical, meant for everyday wear: white and blue checks, small sensible sprigs of flowers, modest stripes. But one was fit for a princess: a high-waisted scarlet satin frock with a pleated bodice and full skirt, two layers of petticoats, pearl-white buttons on the short sleeves, and a black velvet waistband.

"For special occasions," Sarah told her. "Not every day."

Mathinna stroked the fabric. The satin slid between her fingers.

"No harm in trying it on, I suppose." Sarah lifted it over her head. As she fastened the buttons in the back, Mathinna lifted the skirt and watched it billow down, puffing below the waist and rustling against her legs. Sarah opened the door to the armoire wide, and Mathinna's breath caught in her throat. Staring back at her was a slim girl with large brown eyes and short black hair in a shimmering red dress. She touched the glass and then touched her own face. The girl inside the glass was her.

LYING ON THE hard mattress after blowing out the candle, Mathinna gazed up into the blackness and thought of the green shell necklace around Lady Franklin's neck. She remembered watching her mother prick holes in tiny iridescent shells, hundreds of them, thousands, to string into necklaces. Wanganip liked to sit under the shade of a blue gum tree, singing as she worked: *Niggur luggarato pawé, punna munnakanna, luggarato pawé tutta watta, warrena pallunubranah, punna munnakanna, rialangana, luggarato pawé, rialanganna, luggarato . . .*

As the tune came back to her, Mathinna hummed it aloud: *It's wattle blossom time, it's springtime, the birds are whistling, spring has come. The clouds are all sunny, the fuchsia is out at the top, the birds are whistling. Everything is dancing because it's springtime . . .* Reaching into the basket on the floor, she pulled Waluka onto the bed. She stroked the ridge of his back, rested her palm between his tiny witchy hands, cupped his rounded belly. He nudged her neck with his wet nose, and she felt tears slide from her eyes, dampening her neck and pillow.

She missed her mother. She missed Palle. She missed the smell of the smoke that rose from the elders' pipes as they sat around the fire pit. She had spent her whole life in a place where she'd been free to roam barefoot as far as she pleased, where she could sit for hours on a rock on the hillside watching seals waffle in the surf, moon birds dip and soar in a choreographed whoosh, the sun slide into a glittery sea. Where everyone knew her. And now she was alone in this strange land, far from anything familiar.

Closing her eyes, she was back on Flinders, threading through wallaby grass on a windy day as it heaved and ebbed around her like waves on the sea, digging her toes into the white sand, running across the top of the hills. Watching embers glow and settle in the campfire on a cool evening, listening to Palle's languorous voice as he sang her to sleep.

EVANGELINE

Among other suggestions relative to the classification of prisoners we find one recommending the wearing of a ticket by each woman. Each ticket was inscribed with a number, which number should agree with the corresponding number on the class list. . . . In the case of convicts on board convict-ships proceeding to the penal settlements, Mrs. Fry recommended that not only should the women wear these tickets, but that every article of clothing, every book, and every piece of bedding should be similarly numbered. . . . She considered the most thorough, vigilant, and unremitting inspection essential to a correct system of prison discipline; by this means she anticipated that an effectual, if slow, change of habits might be produced.

—MRS. E. R. PITMAN, *Elizabeth Fry*, 1884

AS THE CARRIAGE GROUND TO a halt, Evangeline heard the groan of springs under the driver's seat and felt the tilt of the chassis. When the door creaked open, she winced. The darkness inside framed a too-bright world: a dirt road with a small crowd of people on the other side, and beyond that, anchored in the harbor between water and sky, a black wooden ship with three sails.

"Out," the guard barked. "Step quick."

Stepping quick was impossible, but one by one the women hobbled to the opening, where he grasped them by the upper arms and yanked them onto the dirt.

The crowd surged toward them: a few rough-looking boys, a frail old man with a cane, a ringleted girl hanging onto her mother's skirt. A woman holding a baby cried, "Slatterns!"

Ahead of them, tied to a dock, was a skiff with two sailors. One of them whistled. "Ay! Over here."

As the guard pressed the prisoners forward, the crowd tried to block their way, throwing a rotten cabbage, a spray of pebbles. An egg bounced off Evangeline's skirt and cracked at her feet.

"Dirty puzzles, ye should be ashamed," the old man said.

"God help your souls," a woman called, hands clasped in prayer.

Evangeline felt a sharp pain in her arm and looked down. A rock skittered in the dirt. Blood trickled from her elbow.

"Nasty buggers!" Olive turned to face the crowd, jangling her handcuffed fists. "I'll fight the whole boodle of ye."

"Settle down or I'll pound ye meself," the guard said, poking her hip with his truncheon.

Evangeline could feel the earth beneath the thin soles of her shoes. She had an impulse to lean down and rake her fingers through it, to clutch a handful of it. This would almost certainly be the last time her feet would touch English soil.

Far out in the harbor, on the three-masted ship, a line of men leaned over the railing, hooting and clapping. From this distance their catcalls sounded as innocent as birdsong.

THE TWO SAILORS at the skiff wore wide trousers and tunics tied with rope. Their forearms were covered in ink. One was swarthy and one pale, with a mop of sandy hair. The sandy-haired sailor leapt out and stood on the dock, grinning as the women approached. "Greetings, ladies!"

"We're glad to be rid of 'em," the guard told him.

"They'll have a warm welcome here."

He laughed. "No doubt."

"That one should clean up all right." The sailor jerked his chin toward Evangeline.

The guard made a face. "She's up the duff. Look at 'er." He motioned toward her belly. "That one, too," he said, scowling at Olive, "and she's a feisty munter. She'll claw your eyes out."

"Won't be so feisty when we're done with 'er."

"All talk," Olive said. "I know your type."

"Enough outta ye," the sailor said.

In the skiff the women were seated side by side, front and back, while the crewmen rowed in the middle. Evangeline sat perfectly still, listening to the splashing of the oars in and out of the water, a bell clanging in the distance. The hem of her skirt was soaked with seawater. As they got closer, she saw the name painted on the hull: *Medea*.

From this angle the ship loomed over them, terrifyingly large.

The sandy-haired sailor appraised Evangeline frankly as he rowed. His small eyes were dishwater gray and he sported a red-and-black tattoo of a topless mermaid on his biceps that writhed as he pulled on the oar. He blew a kiss into the air when he caught her eye.

As they reached the ship, bumping lightly against the side, the whooping of the men at the railing above them grew louder. The sandy-haired sailor jumped onto a small platform attached to a ramp and began tugging the prisoners out of the skiff.

The women were clumsy in their shackles. "Bloody chains," Olive grumbled as she clambered onto the dock. "Where the hell d'ye think we'll escape to?"

"Watch your mouth or we won't take 'em off at all," the sailor said.

She snorted. "Don't go actin' all superior. You're an ex-con yourself, no doubt."

"Mind your own—"

"As I thought."

He yanked the chain between her hands and she stumbled forward. When she caught her footing, he pulled her close to him, like a dog on a lead. "Listen, tart. Ye'll do well to remember who's in charge." With a sudden movement he jerked the chain down and she fell to her knees. He twisted it so the upper half of her body hovered over the water alongside the platform. "These irons are heavy. All I have to do is let go. Ye'll sink like a stone."

Olive made a small noise. A whimper. "Please."

"Please, *sir*."

She opened her hands helplessly. "Please, sir."

"*Kind* sir."

She was silent.

Evangeline, behind her in the skiff, leaned forward. "Olive. Just say it."

The sandy-haired sailor looked at the other sailor and winked. Then he nudged Olive's legs with his knee, pushing her closer to the water.

The men above them quieted. The only sound was the screeching of seagulls.

"Kind sir," Olive whispered.

The sailor pulled the chain up, and with it, Olive's body, so that she hung suspended over the water. He seemed poised to let go. Without thinking, Evangeline cried out and stood up.

The skiff rocked wildly side to side. "Fer Chrissake, wench, will ye go overboard too?" the sailor behind her said, pushing her roughly on the shoulder so that she fell hard on the wooden bench.

The sandy-haired sailor yanked the chain back toward him, and Olive collapsed on the platform in a heap. For a few moments she lay at the base of the ramp. Her wrists were scored with blood. Her back heaved oddly up and down, and at first Evangeline thought she was laughing. Then she saw that Olive's eyes were squeezed shut. Her body was shaking, but she didn't make a sound.

AFTER THE FOUR prisoners had been transferred to the ship, they stood on the main deck, waiting to be unshackled. A shirt-less sailor with a scaly green-and-black dragon inked across his torso held up a ring of keys. Except for Cecil, in the shadowy light of a bedroom with the drapes closed, Evangeline had never seen a man without his shirt, not even her father in his dying days. "You." The sailor gestured to Evangeline, motioning for her to sit on an overturned bucket.

A small crowd of sailors had formed. She'd never seen men like this, with faces leathery and as creased as walnut shells, hawklike eyes, sinewy arms covered in elaborate tattoos. The guards at Newgate had been contemptuous, but they didn't lick their lips in lascivious revelry, making obscene noises with their tongues.

The locksmith instructed another sailor to hold the chain

between Evangeline's manacles, then he knelt down and opened the irons around her ankles before unfastening the ones around her wrists. When her shackles fell to the ground, the men around her yelled and clapped. Evangeline shook out her sore hands.

The locksmith jerked his head toward the others. "They'll settle down. It's always like this with a new group."

Evangeline looked around. "Where are the other prisoners?"

"Most of 'em are down there." He raised his chin toward a dark, square opening from which a handrail jutted out. "In the bowels. The orlop deck."

The bowels. Evangeline shuddered. "Are they—caged?"

"No shackles on board. Unless ye do something to deserve it."

It surprised her that prisoners were allowed to move freely, but then she realized, of course. Unless they chose to leap into the water, there was nowhere to go.

She couldn't swim. But for a brief, wild moment, she considered leaping.

"NAME IS MICKEY," a midshipman told the women after the last of them was released from her chains. "I won't remember yours, so don't bother telling me. The ship'll be docked in the harbor another week or two, until they reach the quota. Quarters are tight and getting tighter. You'll take sponge baths—clothes on, mind ye—on the main deck once a week, to keep it bearable on the orlop deck."

He doled out coarse yellow sponges, bricks of lye soap,

wooden spoons and bowls, tin cups, and gray burlap shifts, and showed the women how to roll everything into horsehair blankets.

Pointing at a pile of bedticks, he said, "Each of ye, grab one of those."

The bedticks were heavy. Evangeline smelled hers: it was mildewed, filled with wet straw. But at least it would be better than the hard stone floor at Newgate.

Gesturing at the women's feet, Mickey said, "When it's not freezin' ye should go barefoot on the main deck. It can be rough at sea. Ye wouldn't want to pitch over."

"Does that happen?" one of the women asked.

He shrugged. "It happens."

Motioning for them to follow, he disappeared down the rope ladder. "Ye'll get the hang of it," he called from below as they crept down the ladder with their unwieldy bundles and bedticks. Pointing out the officers' quarters, he led them down the narrow hall to the lip of another opening. He dug a candle stub out of his pocket and lit it. "Hades, this way."

Struggling to balance their bulky loads, the women followed him down an even flimsier ladder into a low, cave-like space, weakly lit by swinging candle lamps. As soon as Evangeline reached the bottom rung, she dropped her bedtick on the floor and covered her nose with her hand. Human waste and—what could it be? A rotting animal? How quickly she'd recovered from the stench of Newgate and acclimated to fresh air.

Mickey gave her a lopsided grin. "Orlop's just above the bilge. A stew of filthy water. Fragrant, in'it? Add to that the

chamber pots and stinky candles and god knows what else."
Pointing at her bedtick he added, "I wouldn't set that on the
floor if I was ye."

She snatched it up.

Gesturing toward the narrow sleeping bunks, he said,
"There'll be close to two hundred women and children down
here at night. Cozy quarters. I advise ye to keep your soap and
bowl under your mattress. And hide anything ye care about."

Olive claimed an empty top berth. "Need me privacy." She
heaved herself up, grunting.

Evangeline dumped her bedtick onto the berth below Olive's and unrolled her blanket. The space was half a yard high
and half a yard wide. No room to sit up and not long enough to
stretch out. But it was hers. After unpacking her things, she took
Cecil's handkerchief, smoothed it out on the blanket, refolded
it with the crest and initials hidden, and pushed it deep under
the mattress behind her tin cup and wooden spoon.

"THE CAPTAIN STEERS the ship, but the surgeon runs it."
Mickey pointed toward the rafters. "He's your next stop. Can
any of ye read?"

"I can," Evangeline said.

"Ye first, then. Dr. Dunne. On the tween deck. Name on
the door."

She made her way to the ladder and clung to it tightly as it
swayed from side to side. In the narrow hallway she knocked on

the door with the brass plate. From behind the door she heard a curt: "Yes?"

"I was told to . . . I'm a-a convict." She blanched. It was the first time she'd identified herself that way.

"Come in."

Cautiously she turned the knob and entered a small oak-paneled room. A man with short dark hair sat at a mahogany desk facing the door, flanked by bookcases, with another door behind him. He looked up with an air of distraction. He was younger than she expected—perhaps in his late twenties—and was dressed formally in a double-breasted navy uniform braided in gold and lined with brass buttons.

Beckoning with his hand, he said, "Close the door behind you. Name?"

"Evangeline Stokes."

He ran his finger down the page of the ledger in front of him and tapped it. "Fourteen years."

She nodded.

"Attempted murder, larceny. . . . These are serious charges, Miss Stokes."

"I know." She looked at the surgeon's crisp white collar and gray-green eyes. The silver monogrammed cup and round glass paperweight on the desk. The Shakespeare volumes lined up neatly on a shelf in the bookcase behind him. This was a man she might've been acquainted with in her previous life.

He pursed his lips. Shutting the ledger, he said, "Let's get started, shall we?"

Opening the door behind his desk, he ushered her into a smaller room with a raised bed in the middle. She stood against the wall while he measured her height and around her waist with a cloth tape, checked her eyes, and asked her to stick out her tongue while he peered into her mouth. "Reach toward the ceiling. Now arms straight ahead. Good. Try to touch your toes." Feeling around her midsection, over her apron, he molded his hand around the bump as if palming a grapefruit. "Six months, give or take. This child will almost certainly be born in my care."

"Does it seem healthy?"

"If the mother is healthy, the child should be too." Looking her over, he said, "You're underweight and your skin is sallow, but your eyes are clear." Placing the wider end of a hollow wooden tube against her chest, he inclined his ear toward the other end.

When he removed it, Evangeline asked, "What is that for?"

"It's a way to check for tuberculosis, or what we used to call consumption. The scourge of any ship. You show no signs of it."

"And if I did?"

"Back to Newgate, into quarantine."

"No transport?"

"Certainly not."

"Perhaps I'd be better off."

He set the tube on a shelf behind him. "The voyage is a long one. And convict life is, no doubt, a . . . trial. But transport can, for some, be an opportunity."

"It will be a long time until I'm free."

"It will. But you're young. And with good behavior you

may earn your ticket of leave sooner. The most important thing is not to succumb to despondency. 'Though much is taken, much abides.'"

"'Made weak by time and fate, but strong in will,'" she said, almost without thinking.

He raised an eyebrow. "You've read Tennyson?"

She blushed. "I was a governess."

"How . . . unexpected." He gave her a funny smile, as if he couldn't quite absorb this bit of information. Then he stepped back. "Well. I suppose I must inspect your fellow travelers."

"Of course." She straightened her apron. She felt a little lightheaded, as if emerging from a trance.

Ascending the rope ladder to the main deck, she thought of those children's tales in which humans are transformed into frogs and foxes and swans, and only when someone recognizes them for who they truly are is the spell finally broken.

That was what this felt like: a faint glimmer of recognition.

WITHIN A FEW DAYS THE convicts' routine was established. They were roused at six in the morning by a series of bells and the unbolting of the hatch, a shaft of light piercing the darkness. Evangeline would lie in her berth for a few minutes listening to the slap of water against the hull, feeling the tug of the ship against the anchor that moored it, beams creaking as it rolled. Women waking, chattering, groaning. Squalling babies. Olive slept heavily, snoring above her, seldom woken by the bell, so Evangeline got in the habit of rapping on the bottom of her bunk until Olive groused, "All right, all right, I hear ye." They dressed quickly, tucking tin cups and bowls and spoons into apron pockets. Unless it was raining, the prisoners were expected to bring their blankets up the ladders to the main deck, where they'd hang them on netting to air.

After breakfast they queued for the surgeon to inspect their eyes, look inside their mouths, pour a thimbleful of lime juice mixed with a little sugar and wine into their cups, and watch them drink it. "For scurvy," he said. "It's sour, but better than losing your teeth."

THOUGH IT WAS a new experience for her, Evangeline had adjusted fairly easily to working for the Whitstones in St. John's Wood, deferring to them and submitting to their whims. She, and they, existed within a clearly defined social order. But she had little familiarity with people who were gratuitously cruel, driven by anger or boredom or revenge. People who got away with bad behavior because they could.

The sandy-haired sailor, she learned, was named Danny Buck. The sailors called him Buck. It was rumored he'd slit a woman's throat. He'd been sentenced to transport himself, as Olive had guessed, and became enamored of the sea on his own crossing. As soon as he'd served his time, he signed on to a crew that sailed back and forth between London and Hobart Town, the port city in Van Diemen's Land, Australia, ferrying female convicts.

One foggy morning, scrubbing the deck on her hands and knees, Evangeline heard voices from across the water. She stood and went to the railing. It had rained through the night; the water was the same dull hue as the sky and the air smelled of rotting fish. Shielding her eyes with her hand, she could barely make out the skiff leaving the dock. As it got closer, she could see Buck and another sailor in the middle seats, flanked by four women huddled like pigeons against the damp.

The skiff bumped against the ship and the women were unloaded. One by one they plodded up the ramp, their chains clinking. The first, plump and disheveled, appeared to be in her thirties. The next two were close to Evangeline's age. The final girl was much younger. She was ghostly pale, with unruly copper hair gathered in a loose bun against her neck—the only spot of color in the drab scene. Looking neither at Buck nor at the small crowd lining the railing above, she stared resolutely ahead, stepping carefully in her chains like a dancer to avoid the thick treads. She wore boys' breeches, tied with a cloth belt, and was as fine-boned as a sparrow.

Buck, walking close behind her, thwacked the girl's backside with his palm. She stumbled forward, barely catching her footing. "No dallyin'," he said, kissing his fingers and winking at the men above, who whistled and clapped.

The girl stopped. He came up short, bumping into her.

She turned slowly to face him, her chin thrust forward. Evangeline couldn't see her face or hear her words, but she watched Buck's smug leer vanish.

As the girl turned back around and continued up the ramp, Buck's expression changed again, from blank consternation to anger. Gripping the railing, Evangeline called, "Watch out!" but her voice was swallowed in the tumult.

When the girl reached the deck, Buck shoved her hard, and, tripping on her chains, she sprawled forward. She couldn't raise her arms to protect her face, but at the last second she twisted to the side, closing her eyes as she fell with a sickening thud.

Someone gasped. The hooting stopped. The girl lay still. Evangeline watched Olive push through the sailors and prisoners gathered around the prone body, and, kneeling, lift the girl to a sitting position, one arm around her shoulders. One side of her head was matted with blood, deep red, staining her curls and running down her neck.

Buck jumped lightly onto the deck. "Such a clumsy one," he said, nudging the girl's leg irons with his foot.

A few sailors laughed.

The girl's eyelids fluttered. With an arm around her back, Olive helped her to her feet. Evangeline could see the knobs of her backbone beneath her thin blouse and a small crescent moon tattooed in blue and black on her neck. She was quivering like an aspen. Olive's dress was smeared with blood.

"What happened here?" the surgeon asked, coming toward them.

Wordlessly the sailors dispersed, avoiding his eyes.

"Mr. Buck?"

"Seems the prisoner lost 'er balance, officer."

Dr. Dunne glared at Buck, as if wanting to reprimand him but not finding enough cause. He exhaled through his nose. "Get the locksmith."

"Will do, officer."

"Do it now, seaman." Dr. Dunne motioned for Olive to step away. Crouching down in front of the girl, he said, "What is your name?"

"Don't matter."

"I'm the ship surgeon. Dr. Dunne. I need to know."

She stared at him for a long moment. "Hazel."

"Hazel what?"

"Ferguson."

"Where are you from?"

She paused again. "Glasgow."

"May I?" He held his hands up, as if surrendering, then reached toward her, fingers spread. She let him cup her face. He turned her head this way and that, inspecting it. "Does that hurt?"

"No."

"The wound needs cleaning. As soon as you get these irons off, I'll take a closer look."

"I can take care of meself."

Stepping forward, Olive blurted, "That sailor shoved her. Buck. We all seen it."

"Is that what happened?" the surgeon asked the girl.

"Dunno."

"You don't know, or don't want to say?"

She lifted a bony shoulder in a shrug.

"Did the same to me," Olive said. "Savage as a meat axe, that one. Ye should throw him off the ship."

Dr. Dunne gave her a sharp look. "That's enough, Miss Rivers."

"What d'ye know." Olive grinned, nodding to the crowd. "He knows who I am."

The surgeon stood and faced her, hands on his hips. "Do not mistake my solicitude for affinity, prisoner," he said. "I am paid to know who you are. And to keep you alive. Though perhaps not enough to accomplish that feat."

EVANGELINE DIDN'T SEE the girl again until after chores were done for the day and the convicts were herded down to the orlop deck to be bolted in for the night. As she approached her berth with a nub of candle she saw that the bottom bunk across the aisle was occupied. The girl's narrow back was visible under the blanket, her curls spilling across it.

Evangeline motioned to Olive, just behind her: *Look there.*

Olive climbed up to her bunk and leaned across the aisle. "Ay, Hazel."

Silence.

"I been to Glasgow once."

The form shifted slightly.

"That cathedral. Big, in'it? Huge." Olive whistled through her teeth.

Hazel twisted around to look at them. "Ye seen it?"

"I have. You're a long way from home." When the girl didn't answer, she said, "I'm Olive. This here's Evange-a-leen. I call 'er Leenie. She floats along with her head in the clouds, but she's all right."

"Olive." Evangeline sighed.

"What? It's true."

"I've never been to Glasgow, but I read about it," Evangeline told Hazel. "*Rob Roy*. I loved that book."

"See what I mean?" Olive said. "She tries, god love 'er, but all she knows is books."

Hazel made a grunt. A laugh, maybe.

"You're pitiful young," Olive said. "Ye must miss your mum."

She snorted. "Hardly."

"Ah, it's like that, then. How old are ye?"

"Twenty."

"Pah. If you're twenty, I'm seventy-five."

"Quiet!" a woman shouted. "And kill that candle, or I'll do it for ye."

"Mind your business," Olive yelled back. "You're not a day over twelve," she said to Hazel.

In the glow of the candle Evangeline could see Hazel scowling at Olive. "I'm sixteen. Now leave me alone." She leaned across the narrow aisle, looked Evangeline in the face, and blew the candle out.

THE SHIP WAS at capacity. The day before they were to set sail, Evangeline heard voices from the water and saw the skiff coming toward the ship with three women, Buck, and another sailor in the middle, as usual, pulling on the oars. But this group was different. They were sitting bolt upright, for one thing, whereas convicts stooped; it wasn't easy to stay erect in chains. And their clothing looked clean. Each wore a neat dark cloak and a white bonnet.

As the skiff pulled alongside the ramp, Evangeline realized it was the Quakers. She recognized the figure in front: the wisps of gray hair, the light blue eyes. Mrs. Fry.

In an uncharacteristic display of gallantry, Buck stepped out of the skiff and held it steady for the women to disembark. He took each woman's arm as he helped her out of the boat: Mrs. Fry, then Mrs. Warren and Mrs. Fitzpatrick. The captain, who generally made himself scarce, had materialized at the railing in a formal uniform—a peaked cap with gold trim, a black tailcoat with gold buttons, braid, and epaulettes. The surgeon, in his navy blue uniform, was at his side. As the Quakers made their way up the ramp, the sailors below them hauled two large trunks out of the skiff. The sailors at the railing were quiet.

Evangeline had almost forgotten it was possible for women to be treated with such deference.

At the top of the ramp, Mrs. Fry spoke quietly to the captain and surgeon before turning to the small group of convicts nearby. "We'll begin with those present." Despite the creaks and clanks and the lapping of water against the hull, her voice was clear. Spying Evangeline, she beckoned her forward. "We have met previously, I believe?"

"Yes, ma'am."

"At Newgate." When Evangeline nodded, she said, "Ah, yes. You're literate. Your father was a vicar."

"You've a good memory, ma'am."

"I make it a point to remember." Mrs. Fry motioned to Mrs. Warren, who opened a trunk and brought out a small burlap sack, a book, and a bundle tied with twine. Mrs. Fry pressed the book into Evangeline's hands. A Bible. "May this bring you solace."

Evangeline rubbed the reptilian skin of the maroon cover with her thumbs. The sensation brought her back to the parish church in Tunbridge Wells, in the front pew, listening to her father's sermons. All of his talk about sin and redemption that had seemed so theoretical at the time came back to her, painfully, now.

"Most of these women are illiterate. It is my hope that you will share the gift of reading," Mrs. Fry said.

"Yes, ma'am."

"I have some things to ease your journey." Mrs. Fry picked up the bundle. "A knit cap for the cold—you won't need it now, but you'll be happy to have it later—an apron, and a shawl. Made for you by Quakers who believe in the possibility of salvation." She set the bundle down and gave Evangeline the sack. "In here you'll find all you need to make a quilt. For your child, perhaps."

Evangeline peered inside: a thimble, spools of thread, a red cushion pricked with pins and needles, a pile of patchwork pieces tied with string.

"Remember, my dear: we are but vessels," Mrs. Fry said. "You must labor to keep yourself humble, meek, and in a self-denying frame, that you may be fit to follow the Lord Jesus, who invites such to come to Him. Only through sorrow do we learn to appreciate kindness."

"Yes, ma'am," Evangeline said, though she hardly needed to labor, these days, to keep herself humble and self-denying.

"One last thing." Reaching into the trunk, Mrs. Fry pulled out a flat disk on a red cord and held it on her palm.

The disk appeared to be made of tin and was as wide as her thumb. A number was stamped into the metal: 171.

"From now on, you will be known by this number," Mrs. Fry said. "It will be printed on, or sewn into, every item you possess, and kept in a ledger that will be passed from the ship surgeon to the warden of the prison. You will wear this ticket for the duration of the journey. With God's blessing."

Evangeline frowned, feeling a flash of defiance. After all she'd been through, all she'd had to accept.

"What is wrong, my dear?"

"To be known by a number. It's . . . degrading."

Touching Evangeline's hand with her fingertips, Mrs. Fry said, "It's to be sure that you are accounted for. That you are not lost to the winds." Holding up the necklace, she said, "Bend your neck, please."

Evangeline felt like a horse resisting a bridle. Resistance, she knew, was pointless; the horse always ends up in the bridle. And so would she.

EARLY IN THE MORNING OF June 16, the *Medea* shifted off her anchor and lurched forward, towed down the Thames by a steamer. Seagulls circled above the ship, cawing and squeaking; a Union Jack fluttered from the stern. Sailors shouted to one another above the lapping river, the heaving deck, the flap and slither of the canvas sails, the creaking masts. They scrambled hand over hand up the ropes to the wooden platforms four stories in the air and to the top of the yardarm, swinging like squirrels.

Standing at the railing with the other convicts as the *Medea* reached the Thames estuary, Evangeline rubbed the tin disk between her fingers, running her hand along the cord, worrying the metal hook in the back. She watched the brick buildings, carriages, and mud-roofed huts recede, the people on shore turn to specks. All of them going about their daily lives without so much as a glance at the departing ship. She'd been on the ship for nearly ten days. In Newgate for three and a half months. In service to the Whitstones for almost half a year. She'd never ventured farther than forty miles from the village of her birth. She reached a hand into the mist: England was literally slipping through her fingers. A few lines from Wordsworth drifted into her head: *Turn wheresoe'er I may, by night or day. The things which I have seen I now can see no more.* As a young woman she'd been stirred by the poet's lament that when he became an adult he was no longer attuned to the beauty of nature; he saw the world through different eyes. But it struck her now that metaphysical melancholy was nothing compared with physical displacement. The world she knew and loved was lost to her. In all likelihood she would never see it again.

EVANGELINE FOUND OLIVE near the bow, sitting in a circle of women who were ripping apart their Bibles, folding the pages into rectangles to make playing cards and twisting them into curling paper for their hair. Olive looked up, holding her tin disk between her fingers. "From now on ye can call me one twenty-seven. My new friend Liza says it's a lucky prime, whatever that means."

A lanky woman with jet-black hair beside her grinned. "Number seventy-nine. Also a lucky prime."

"Liza's good with numbers. Managed the ledgers for a boarding house. Though how good are ye if ye get caught cooking the books?"

The women in the circle laughed.

Evangeline spotted Hazel sitting alone on a wide wooden crate, leafing through the Bible on her lap, and went over to her. "This cord around your neck feels strange, doesn't it?"

Hazel squinted up at Evangeline. "I've got used to worse."

WITHIN THE HOUR Evangeline's skin was clammy, her mouth full of saliva. Bile rose in her throat.

"Keep your eye on that line."

She turned.

Beside her was the surgeon. He pointed toward the horizon.

She followed his finger but could barely focus. "Please—stand away—" she said, before heaving the contents of her breakfast over the side. Glancing down the railing, she saw other prisoners leaning over, retching streams of liquid down the side of the ship and into the choppy water.

"Motion sickness," he said. "You'll get used to it."

"How?"

"Shut your eyes. Put your fingers in your ears. And try to move with the ship—don't fight it."

She nodded, shutting her eyes and putting her fingers in her ears. But his advice didn't do much good. The rest of the day was miserable, and nightfall brought little relief. All around her in the darkness of the orlop deck, women moaned and retched. Olive, above her, muttered curses. Across the aisle Hazel was silent, curled like a shrimp toward the wall.

Evangeline had thrown up so many times she felt faint with exhaustion, yet could not sleep. Once again, she sensed the roiling in her gut, her mouth filling with spittle, the sudsy wave rising in her throat. She'd been aiming into her wooden bowl, but now it was full and sloshing. She didn't care anymore. Leaning over the side of her narrow bed, she emptied what little remained in her stomach in a thin stream onto the floor.

Hazel turned over. "Can ye not control yourself?"

Evangeline lay there dully, without will to speak.

"She can't help it, can she?" Olive said.

Hazel leaned across the aisle, and for a moment Evangeline thought she might slap her. "Put out your hand." When Evangeline complied, Hazel put a small knobby bulb in her palm. "Ginger root. Scrape the skin off with your teeth and spit it out. Then take a bite."

Evangeline held it to her nose and sniffed. The scent reminded her of desserts at Christmastime: glazed cakes and hard candies, gingersnaps and puddings. She did as she was told, breaking the skin with her teeth and spitting it on the floor. The chunk of root was fibrous and tasted sharply sour. Like vanilla concentrate, she thought: seduced by the smell, betrayed by the flavor.

"Chew slowly 'til nothing's left," Hazel said. "Hug the wall. And give it back. It's all I got."

Evangeline handed her the root. Closing her eyes, she put her fingers in her ears and turned to the wall, concentrating only on the nub of ginger in her mouth, which softened and mellowed as she gnawed it. In this way, finally, she drifted to sleep.

BY THE TIME Evangeline emerged from below decks the next morning, a few hours after breakfast, the *Medea* had left the Thames and was heading into the North Sea. The water was choppy and white-capped, the sky above the sails a dull white. A thin finger of land was visible in the distance. Evangeline gazed out at the vast, glistening ocean. Then she sat carefully on a barrel and closed her eyes, listening to a cacophony of sounds: a woman laughing, a baby fussing, sailors calling from mast to mast, the squawk of gulls, a bleating goat, the slap of water against the hull. The air was cold. She wished she'd brought her blanket upstairs with her, stained and reeking as it was.

"How was your night?"

She blinked into the brightness.

The surgeon was staring at her with his gray-green eyes. "Feel any better?"

She nodded. "I did what you said. Fingers in my ears and all. But I think it was ginger that made the difference."

He gave her a quizzical smile. "Ginger?"

"The root. I chewed it."

"Where'd you get it?"

"That redheaded girl. Hazel. But she took it back. Do you know where I might get some more?"

"I don't. In the cook's galley, I suppose." His mouth twitched. "I've always considered it an old wives' tale. But if it seems to help, by all means continue with it. I tend to be skeptical of miracle cures."

"Well, I don't know if it's a miracle cure, but I do feel better," she said. "Maybe those old wives knew what they were talking about."

AT TIMES THROUGH strong headwinds, at others carving smoothly through the waves, the *Medea* journeyed the rough waters. The convicts gathered on the deck as the *Medea* passed the chalky Cliffs of Dover, as cleanly sliced as almond nougat, before heading into the lower Channel.

The cell at Newgate had been so crowded that all Evangeline had wanted was distance from other people. But now, to her surprise, she realized she was lonely. Every morning she rose with the clanging of the bell and lined up with the other women, who joked and complained and cursed as they stood with their dented cups and chipped spoons. She gulped her tea and gnawed hardtack, scrubbed the deck on her hands and knees. On temperate evenings, after her chores were finished and before the women were herded down to the orlop deck, she often stood alone at the railing and watched the sun drop in the sky and the stars appear, faintly at first, as if bubbling to the surface of a vast lake.

One morning, after chores, Evangeline found Hazel sitting alone, her curly hair half covering her face, whispering to herself and tapping at words in the Bible open in her lap. When she looked up and saw Evangeline, she shut it quickly.

"Do you mind if I sit?" Without waiting for an answer, Evangeline perched on a corner of the crate.

The girl gazed at her. "I have chores."

"Just for a minute." Evangeline cast about for something to talk about. "I keep thinking about Psalm 104: 'There is the sea, vast and spacious, teeming with creatures beyond number— living things both large and small.' You know the one I mean?"

Hazel shrugged.

Evangeline noticed the smattering of freckles across the girl's nose, her eyes, as blue gray as wood pigeon feathers, the russet fringe of her lashes. "Do you have a favorite?"

"No."

"You're a Presbyterian, aren't you?" When Hazel frowned, Evangeline added, "Scotland. I assumed."

"Hah. Well. Never been much of a churchgoer."

"Your parents didn't take you?"

She almost looked amused. "Me parents . . ."

They sat in awkward silence for a moment. Evangeline tried a different tack. "I noticed your tattoo." She touched her own neck. "A moon. It's a fertility symbol, isn't it?"

Hazel made a face. "I saw this play once. The characters were drunk, talking nonsense. 'I was the man i' the moon when time was.' I thought it was funny."

"Oh!" Finally, common ground. "*The Tempest.*"

"Ye seen it?"

"It's one of my favorites. 'O brave new world, / That has such people in't!'"

Hazel shook her head. "I don't remember much, to be honest. It was confusing. But it made me laugh."

"You know . . . the surgeon has a whole shelf of Shakespeare in his office. Maybe I could ask to borrow one."

"Eh. Don't have much use for reading."

Ah, Evangeline thought. Of course. "You know . . . I could teach you to read, if you want."

Hazel gave her a hard look. "I don't need help."

"I know you don't. But . . . it's a long journey, isn't it? Might as well have something to do."

Hazel bit her lip. Her fingers strayed absently over the cover of the Bible. But she didn't say no.

They started with the alphabet, twenty-six letters on a piece of slate. Vowels and consonants, sound and sense. Over the next few days, as they sat together, knitting words, Hazel shared small bits and pieces of her past. Her mother had built a thriving practice as a midwife, but something happened—someone had died, a mother or child or both. She lost her reputation, and with it, her paying clients. She started drinking. Leaving Hazel alone at night. She pushed her out the door to beg and pick pockets on the streets when Hazel was eight years old. Hazel was no good at thievery; she was nervous and indecisive, and kept getting nabbed by the police. The third time she was hauled into court—when she was fifteen, for stealing a silver spoon—the judge had had enough. He sentenced her to transport. Seven years.

She hadn't eaten in two days. Her mother didn't even come to the hearing.

Evangeline looked at her for a long moment. If she expressed any pity, she knew, Hazel would slip away. *E-A-T,* she wrote on the slate. *D-A-Y.*

Even after she'd lost everything, Hazel's mother still practiced in secret. There were plenty of desperate women who needed help. She treated wounds and infections, cough and fever. If a woman didn't want a baby, she made her problem disappear. If a woman did, she showed her how to nurture and protect the life growing inside her. She turned babies around in wombs and taught new mothers how to feed them after they were born. Many women were afraid to go to the lying-in hospital to deliver their babies because of the stories about child-bed fever, an illness that began with sweating and shaking and almost always ended in death, in an agony of vomit and blood. Hazel shook her head at the memory. "Only in hospital. Not in the tenements with the midwives. They say it's because the poor are hardy, like farm animals."

P-O-O-R. F-A-R-M.

"But that's not the reason," Hazel said. "The doctors touch the dead and don't wash their hands. Midwives know it, but no one listens."

Evangeline palmed her stomach. Prodded it to feel the lumpy limbs just beneath the skin. "Did you learn from your mother?"

Hazel gave her an appraising look. "You're afraid of birthing."

"Of course."

Hazel's lips twisted into a smile. It was peculiar on her, like a grin on a fox. "She was no good at being a mother. But she was a good midwife. Still is, for all I know." She tilted her chin at Evangeline. "Yes, I learned."

IN A GREAT WHOOSH OF flapping sails, the *Medea* cleared the English Channel and made her way into open ocean, heading south toward Spain. Nothing but water and sky visible for miles. Standing at the railing, gazing out at the expanse, Evangeline thought of a line from Coleridge: *Alone, alone, all, all alone, / Alone on a wide wide sea!*

In early morning, fog clung to the water like cotton batting. The air was cool and fresh after the stench of the orlop deck, and smelled of pine tar. Women jostled and bartered for places in line; if you were sick, unlucky, or lazy enough to come last, you got the gruel that was burned and congealed at the bottom of the pot. The water they drank, stored in a wine cask, was muddy and tasted as if it had been drawn from a ditch. Evangeline learned to wait a few minutes after it was poured in her cup for the sediment to sink to the bottom.

The gruel was supposed to hold them until midafternoon, when the women lined up once more, for their final meal of the day: a watery broth of cabbage and turnip and, if they were lucky, tough, salty beef or dried cod, with a hardtack biscuit and another cup of muddy water.

Evangeline was assigned to a work crew of six women. On

a revolving schedule they emptied chamber pots, boiled dirty laundry, cleaned the sheep and goat pens, collected eggs from the hens stacked in cages on the main deck. They coiled sodden rope that had been dumped in a tangle and scrubbed the orlop deck with stones and sand and a straw-bristle brush. They washed the main deck and privies with a mix of lime and calcium chloride that made their noses burn and eyes water.

As the days passed Evangeline adjusted to the swaying and creaking, the ebb and flow of the waves. Mimicking the sailors, she began walking flat-footed, rocking her hips and bending her knees with the movement of the ship, anticipating the pitch of the deck as it rolled from side to side. The motion of dancing, she thought. Of courtship. She discovered hidden handholds all over the ship, tucked under banisters and ledges and built into ladders, to grab when the sea was rough. Soon enough, despite her growing bulk, she could climb from orlop to tween, from tween to the main deck, as fast as any crewman. She learned where to sit or stand to avoid the spray, how to dodge puddles, how to navigate around rum barrels and tangles of rope without tripping, where to find sunlight at different times of the day. She skirted the grasping hands of sailors as she passed and avoided their sleeping rooms on the tween deck. She got used to the taste of salt on her lips, which she had to rub with lard and whale oil to keep from cracking. Her hands became tough and red and strong. She got used to the chaos: the toll of the bell every half hour, the constant bleating of goats and honking of geese, the reek of the privies and bilge.

On temperate afternoons the captain brought his orange pet

canary in a rusty cage onto the main deck, where it chirped shrilly for hours, perched on its tiny swing.

She got used to the chirping.

As if memorizing subject-verb agreements in Latin, she taught herself the language of sailing. Facing the ship's front—the bow—port was on the left, starboard on the right. The back of the ship was aft. Windward, naturally, meant the direction the wind was blowing; leeward, the opposite. The horizontal pole at the bottom of the mast, the boom, controlled the wind power of the sails.

The sailors were busy from dawn until dusk, raising and lowering the sails, climbing up and down masts like the acrobats in Covent Garden, patching huge sections of canvas, greasing cables, splicing rope. Evangeline had never seen a man with a needle and thread, and was surprised to learn how adept the sailors were at stitching. Two or three of them would sit amidships on the deck with legs outstretched, mending a sail with long needles and coarse thread, thimbles on the balls of their thumbs attached to their wrists by leather straps.

They spoke in a barely comprehensible shorthand that Evangeline only understood through context and pantomime. They called porridge burgoo. They called the stew they ate lobscouse. She didn't know why. That was just how it was. The sailors received far more daily provisions than the convicts: a pound of biscuits, a gallon of rum or wine, a cup of oatmeal, half a pound of beef, a half cup of peas, a slab of butter, and two ounces of cheese. Sometimes—rarely—the women would get a taste of their rations.

Some of the women learned to fish. When their morning chores were finished, they cast lines overboard baited with chum, using twine and thread, with padlocks and bolts for weights and hooks. In the afternoons they cured the mackerel and sea robins they caught in the sun. Before long a barter system developed between the convicts and the crew. Dried fish could be exchanged for biscuits or buttons, stockings the women knitted by hand traded for brandy, an even more desirable commodity.

If a convict did something wrong, punishment was swift. If she got into a fistfight or was caught gambling, she'd be locked in a small, dark room on the orlop deck called the hold. One woman, accused of stealing a crewman's tortoiseshell comb, was forced to wear a placard around her neck that said *THIEF* for a month. A narrow box chained to the main deck was used for particularly grave offenses, such as disrespecting the captain or surgeon. The unfortunate convict was buckled into a waistcoat that wrapped around her limbs, then locked inside the box. If she screamed or cried, a cistern of water was poured on her head through the breathing hole. The solitary box, sailors called it. Convicts called it the grave.

For repeated offenses, a convict's head was roughly shaved, like that of an inmate in an insane asylum.

Some prisoners complained to anyone who'd listen. Others bore their burdens with stoic good cheer. It was hard work to keep boredom at bay, and a number of them simply gave up. They ate with their hands and were unashamedly naked in front of one another, spitting and belching and farting at will. Some, out of sheer boredom, began making trouble. Two got into a brawl and took turns in the hold, subsisting on bread and water. Another who swore at the captain was locked inside the solitary box for an entire day. Her muffled yelling and swearing got her an additional half day, plus an unwelcome shower through the breathing hole.

Evangeline clung to her dignity like a life preserver. She kept her head down, minded her own business, attended divine service, worked on her quilt, and did her chores without complaint, even as her stomach swelled, and along with it her feet and hands. After breakfast, kneeling beside other convicts, she dipped a rag into a tub of seawater, wrung it out, and washed her face, the back of her neck, between her fingers, under her arms. Daily she aired her bedding; once a week, on washing day, she scrubbed her clothing, hanging it to stiffen and dry in the salty air. She still turned her back when she changed out of her dress.

At night, when the hatch was closed on the orlop deck, Evangeline felt entombed. But she came to welcome the time in her coffin-like berth; it was her only privacy. She'd tuck in her knees and pull the rough blanket up around her ears and shut her eyes. Resting her hand on the bulge of her stomach, she'd feel for a flutter of movement beneath the taut skin.

On mild afternoons in Tunbridge Wells she used to grab her bonnet from a peg in the foyer and wander down the rutted path to the stone bridge over a stream, passing tangled nettles, butterflies hovering above foxgloves, a field sprinkled with orange-red poppies, listening to the willows rustle in the wind. She made her way to a hill near her house, an easy ascent along a well-trod trail through spiky purple thistles, sheep so intent on grazing on clover that she had to push them off the path to continue on her way. When she reached the top, she'd gaze down at the terracotta roofs of the houses in the village, conjuring lines from the poets she read with her father—Wordsworth, say, or Longfellow, whose words enhanced her own observations: *As lapped in thought I used to lie, / And gaze into the summer sky, / Where the sailing clouds went by, / Like ships upon the sea . . .*

In the darkness of the orlop deck, she retreated to that mountain trail. Sidestepping small rocks and avoiding mud puddles, she breathed in the damp earth and the sour-sweet grass, felt the prickle of brambles on her legs and the sun on her face as she made her way toward the summit. She drifted to sleep to the distant bleating of sheep and the sound of her own beating heart.

MOST OF THE women on the ship were familiar with the accommodations of desperation, the compromises and calculations that went into staying alive day to day. Stealing, haggling, deceiving gullible children, trading a place to sleep or a bottle of rum for sexual favors; many had long since overcome any squeamishness about what they considered necessary transactions. Their bodies were just another tool at their disposal. Some simply wanted to make the best of a bad situation, finding protection wherever they could. Others were determined to carve a good time out of the rough timber of the trip. They laughed raucously, drank with the sailors, and made bawdy jokes, toeing the line of insub-ordination.

A few convicts, Evangeline noticed, had disappeared from the orlop deck.

"The sailors call it taking a wife," Olive explained.

"Taking a . . . wife?" She didn't understand.

"For the duration of the trip."

"Isn't that immoral?"

"Immoral," Olive chortled. "Oh, Leenie."

Though the surgeon did all he could to discourage it, there were clear advantages to taking up with a sailor, so long as he wasn't sadistic or downright repulsive. You were spared the hell of the orlop; you could sleep in his relatively comfortable berth, or even, depending on his rank, a private room. You might get extra rations, blankets, special attention. Your alliance protected you from other brutish crewmen, and even, to an extent, the threat of punishment from above. But it was a dangerous gam-bit. There were few repercussions for sailors who were cruel or sadistic. Women crept back to the orlop deck with welts on their legs, scratches on their backs, gonorrhea and syphilis and all manner of other diseases.

Despite her own sizable stomach, within a few weeks Olive had taken up with a barrel-chested, much-inked sailor with a snaggletoothed smile and a ruddy neck called Grunwald. She rarely slept in her own berth.

"I hope that sailor is nice to her," Evangeline said to Hazel one afternoon as they sat in the stern behind a wall of chicken crates, an out-of-the-way place they'd discovered to meet after their chores were done. Evangeline was working on her quilt, Hazel copying words from the Bible onto the slate with a nub of chalk.

UNTO. DAY. GOD. LORD.

"Let's just hope he leaves her alone for a spell to mend after the baby is born."

Evangeline arranged a section of fabric squares and started pinning them together. "Surely he will."

Hazel grunted. "Men do as they please."

"Come, now," Evangeline said. "Not all men."

"Yours did, didn't he?"

The observation stung. Evangeline concentrated on her stitches, inserting the needle in the front of the fabric, grabbing a bit of the back, running the thread through the layers. "Is anybody giving you trouble?"

"Not really."

"What about Buck?"

Hazel shrugged. "Nothing I can't handle."

Evangeline turned the fabric over, inspecting the line of stitches. "Be careful."

"Careful," Hazel scoffed. Reaching into her apron pocket, she pulled out a silver folding knife with a mother-of-pearl handle and held it on the flat of her palm.

Evangeline gaped. "Where'd you get that?"

"I'm a pickpocket, remember?"

"A failed one. For goodness' sake, put that away." Both of them knew that if Hazel were found guilty of theft from a sailor, she'd wear a placard and shackles in the hold until her feet touched land.

"No one but you will ever know," Hazel said, slipping the knife back into her pocket. "Unless I need to use it."

ONE AFTERNOON A sailor lost his footing and fell from the yardarm to the deck, a distance of about twenty feet, near where Hazel and Evangeline sat together prying apart wet rope. They looked up. No one was coming to his aid. Hazel dropped the rope and went to his side, leaning close and whispering in his ear. The sailor howled and groaned, clutching his leg.

Just then the surgeon emerged from the tween deck. Seeing Hazel bent over the sailor, he called, "Move aside, prisoner."

At first Hazel ignored him, running a hand down the crewman's leg to his shin, probing it with her fingers. A small crowd had gathered. Looking up at the surgeon, she said, "His leg is broken and needs to be reset."

Evangeline was struck by the girl's expression: an air of practiced attentiveness that gave her an unexpected authority.

"I'll determine that," the surgeon said.

The sailor groaned.

"He'll require a splint. And some rum," Hazel said.

"What experience have you?"

"My mother is an herbalist. A midwife."

The surgeon flicked his hand at her. "Stand over there." Crouching over the sailor, he repeated Hazel's movements: he felt down the man's leg, grasped it between his fingers, put a flat hand to his forehead. Sitting back on his heels, he said, "Some-one find a board to transport him to my quarters."

"As I said," Hazel murmured behind him.

Several days later, Evangeline awoke to find Hazel on the floor between their berths, hunched over sprigs of dried herbs, crushing leaves with two fingers.

"What are you doing?"

"Mixing herbs for a poultice. That sailor could die if infection sets in."

Hazel had been right: his leg was badly broken. A convict who brought his meals to the infirmary reported that he was delirious with pain, thrashing and cursing. They'd had to tie him to the bed.

"The surgeon knows what to do, doesn't he?" Evangeline said.

Hazel gazed at her with those implacable gray eyes. Then she gathered the herbs into a heap on a rag and tied them into a parcel.

Early in the afternoon, Evangeline sat on the main deck with a small group of convicts, mending a sail. She watched Dr. Dunne come up from the tween deck, a grim expression on his face, and vanish around a corner. Putting down her needle and thimble, she told the woman beside her she was going to the privy. She caught up with him at a spot blocked from view by a stack of crates. He stood at the railing, resting his chin on crossed arms.

"How is the sailor?"

He looked up. "Not well."

She, too, crossed her arms on the rail. "Hazel, the girl—"

"I know who she is."

"I saw her crushing herbs. For a poultice, she said."

"She's not a doctor."

"Of course not. But if there's nothing to lose . . ."

"Only a man's life," he said in a clipped voice.

"He's doing poorly, I hear. What harm is there in trying?"

Shaking his head slightly, Dr. Dunne gazed out at the shimmering line between sky and sea.

Back in the sewing circle, Evangeline watched as he called Hazel over, leaning toward her as she pulled a small packet from her apron pocket and opened it for him to inspect. He crumbled the herbs with his fingers, held them to his nose, tasted them with his tongue. Then he took the packet and disappeared down the ladder.

Perhaps the result was circumstantial. Perhaps the sailor would have recovered regardless. But three days later he sat lounging on the main deck in a wooden chair, his splinted leg propped on a barrel, pestering a blond-ringleted convict and bellowing with laughter at her retort.

THE SURGEON HAD HIS HANDS full. All the beds in the infirmary were occupied. Heatstroke, seasickness, diarrhea. Delirium, ulcerated tongues, dislocated limbs. He treated constipation with calomel, made of one part chloride and six parts mercury. For dysentery he prescribed flour porridge with a few drops of laudanum and a tincture of opium. To reduce fever he shaved women's heads, a treatment they feared more than delirium. For pneumonia and tuberculosis, bloodletting.

Word of Hazel's miracle cure had spread. Convicts who didn't want to see the surgeon or who were sent away untreated began lining up to see her. She scrounged herbs from the cook and planted some of the seeds she'd smuggled on board with her in a box of manure: arnica for pains and bruises, mandrake for sleeplessness, and pennyroyal, a flowering mint, for unwanted pregnancy. For dysentery, egg whites and boiled milk. For fainting spells, a tablespoon of vinegar. She created a paste from lard, honey, oats, and eggs as a salve for chapped hands and feet.

"That girl, Hazel, with her witchy powders and potions . . . ," the surgeon said irritably to Evangeline as she stood at the railing late one afternoon. "I'm afraid she'll only make things worse."

"You have plenty to do. Why should you mind?"

"It gives the women false hope."

She gazed out at the water. It was clear and green, as smooth as a mirror. "Surely hope isn't a bad thing."

"It is if they forgo proper medical treatment."

"The sailor who fell from the yardarm is much improved. I saw him shimmying up a mast."

"Correlation, causation. Who's to know?" His mouth tightened. "There's something about that girl. An insolence. I find it . . . off-putting."

"Have pity," Evangeline said. "Imagine being her age, condemned to this."

Giving her a sidelong look, he said, "The same could be said about you."

"She's much younger than I am."

"How old are you, then?"

"Twenty-one. For another month, at least." She hesitated, not sure whether it was appropriate to ask. "And you?"

"Twenty-six. Don't tell anyone."

He smiled, and she smiled back.

"Hazel's life has always been hard. She's never seen . . ." She struggled to find the words. "The . . . good in the world."

"And you have?"

"Of a sort."

"It seems to me you've had a rather rough go of it."

"Well, yes. But the truth is . . ." She took a breath. "The truth is, I was rash and impulsive. I have no one to blame for my misfortune but myself."

The wind was picking up. Sunlight splintered brightly in

shards across the waves. For a few moments they stood silently at the railing.

"I have a question," she said. "Why on earth would anyone choose to be on this ship if they don't have to?"

"I've wondered that many times myself," he said with a laugh. "The easy answer, I suppose, is that I'm restless by nature. I thought it would be an interesting challenge. But if I'm honest . . ."

He'd been a shy only child, he told her, raised in Warwick, a small village in the Midlands. His father was a doctor; it was expected that his son would join the practice and take over when he retired. He'd been sent to boarding school, which he loathed, and then to Oxford and the Royal College of Surgeons in London, where he discovered to his surprise that he actually did have a passion for medicine. On returning to the village he purchased a charming cottage with a housekeeper and set about expanding and updating the practice. As an eligible bachelor, he became a frequent guest at banquets, balls, and shooting parties.

Then disaster struck. A young lady from a prominent landholding family was brought in complaining of stomach pains and shaking with chills, and had a high fever. His father, having never seen a case of appendicitis, diagnosed typhoid, prescribed morphine for the pain and fasting for the fever, and sent her home. The heiress died in great agony, vomiting blood in the middle of the night, to the disbelieving horror of her family. Their heartbreak required a villain. The doctor and his partner-son were shunned, the practice ruined.

Some months later, an envelope arrived in the post from

his roommate at the Royal College. The British government sought qualified surgeons for transport ships and would pay handsomely. It was a particular challenge to find surgeons for the female convict ships because, "to be frank," his roommate wrote, "the ships are rumored to be floating brothels."

"A gross exaggeration, as I now know," Dr. Dunne hastened to add. "Or at least . . . an exaggeration."

"But you signed on anyway."

"There was nothing left for me at home. I would've had to start somewhere new."

"Do you regret it?"

The corners of his mouth turned up in bitter comedy. "Every day."

This was his third voyage, he said. He spent little time with the rough sailors, the boorish captain, or the alcoholic first mate, whose excesses he'd already treated several times. There was no one he could really talk to.

"What would you do, then, if you could do whatever you chose?" she asked.

He turned to face her, one arm on the railing. "What would I do? I would open my own practice. Maybe in Van Diemen's Land. Hobart Town is a small place. I could start again."

"Starting again," she said with a catch in her throat. "That sounds nice."

"YE SHOULD CHARGE for your services," Olive told Hazel on a rare afternoon away from her sailor. "People take advantage."

"How're they gonna pay?" Hazel asked.

"Not your worry. Everybody's got something to barter."

Olive was right. Soon enough Hazel was in possession of two quilts, a small store of silver pilfered from sailors' trunks, dried cod and oat cakes, even a down pillow made by an enterprising convict who plucked geese for the officers' meals.

"Look at all this," Evangeline marveled when Hazel lit a taper in a small brass candlestick with a finger loop—another bartered item—and pulled out a sack she'd stuffed under her berth.

"Want something? Help yourselves."

Evangeline sifted through the sack, with Olive peering over her shoulder. Two eggs, a fork and spoon, a pair of stockings, a white handkerchief . . . wait—

She snatched the handkerchief out of the sack and ran her thumb along the embroidery. "Who gave you this?"

Hazel shrugged. "Dunno. Why?"

"It's mine."

"Are ye sure?"

"Of course I'm sure. It was given to me."

"Ah, sorry, then. Nothing's safe, is it?"

Evangeline pressed the handkerchief on her bedtick, smoothing it, and folded it into a small square.

"What's so special about it?" Olive reached for the handkerchief and Evangeline let her take it. Holding it up to the candle, she peered at it closely. "Is this a family crest?"

"Yes."

"This must be from the cad who . . ." Olive gestured toward

Evangeline's stomach. "C. F. W. Lemme guess. Chester Francis Wentworth," she said, affecting a snooty accent.

Evangeline laughed. "Close. Cecil Frederic Whitstone."

"Cecil. Even better."

"Does he know you're here?" Hazel asked.

"I don't know."

"Does he know you're carrying his child?"

Evangeline shrugged. It was a question she'd asked herself many times.

Hazel set the candle on the ledge of the berth. "So, Leenie . . . why would ye keep this?"

Evangeline thought of the look on Cecil's face when he gave her the ring. His boyish eagerness to see it on her finger. "He gave me a ruby ring that had been his grandmother's. He wrapped it in this handkerchief. Then he went away on holiday and the ruby was found in my room, and I was accused of stealing it. They didn't notice the handkerchief, so I kept it."

"Did he return from his trip?"

"I assume he did."

"Why didn't he come to your defense, then?"

"I don't—I don't know what he knows."

Olive crumpled the handkerchief in her fist. "I can't see why you'd want this lousy piece of cloth, after he left ye high and dry."

Evangeline took it from her. "He didn't . . ."

But he did, didn't he?

She fingered the handkerchief's scalloped edges. Why *did* she want this lousy piece of cloth?

"It's—it's all I have left." The moment she said it, she knew that this was true. This handkerchief was the only remaining shred from the fabric of her previous life. The only tangible reminder that she'd once been somebody else.

Olive nodded slowly. "Then ye should put it in a place no one'll find it."

"There's a loose floorboard under my berth where I stash some bits and pieces," Hazel said, smoothing out the handkerchief and folding it. "I can hide it for ye, if ye want."

"Would you?"

"Later, when no one's looking." She tucked the cloth into her pocket. "So what happened to the ruby ring?"

"No doubt on someone else's finger," Olive said.

OVER THE NEXT SEVERAL WEEKS, the *Medea* passed the mouth of the Mediterranean, Madeira, and Cape Verde, crossing the Tropic of Cancer and heading toward the equator. By late morning, these days, the sun was hot overhead, the air thick and humid. There was no wind to speak of. What little progress the *Medea* made was gained by tacking, a job that required great effort by the sailors. The temperature in the lower decks soared above 120 degrees, the humidity so acute it felt like living inside a steaming kettle.

"They're boiling us alive," Olive said.

A cloud of malaise hung over the ship. More fell ill. Some women's feet were covered with oozing black sores, and swollen to double their size. The ones who could read carried their Bibles around with them, mouthing verses from Revelation: *And the sea gave up the dead which were in it; and death and hell delivered up the dead which were in them.* And Psalm 93: *The waves of the sea are mighty, and rage horribly; but yet the Lord, who dwelleth on high, is mightier.*

The choice for the convicts was to stay on the main deck and endure the unforgiving sun or suffer in the unventilated hold. The heat made the stink even worse. They aired their bedding, burned sulfur, dusted the surfaces with bleaching powder. Sailors fired pistols below decks in the belief that gunpowder dispelled infectious vapors. But the best the prisoners could hope for in the bowels of the ship was merciful sleep. Mostly, they lay around on the main deck, wrapped in perspiration like gauze, their eyes half closed against the unremitting glare. They made bonnets out of burlap and flour sacks to shade their faces. Some women, not particularly stable to begin with, took to banging their heads against the posts of their berths or the ship railings on the upper deck until they were doused with buckets of water. But most were quiet. It took too much energy to speak. Even the farm animals lolled about, their tongues drooping from their mouths.

Two and a half months after leaving London, the *Medea* rounded the jagged cliffs and pristine sands of the Cape of Good Hope near the southernmost tip of Africa and headed due east into the Indian Ocean. Ann Darter, the sickly girl whose baby died in Newgate, took a turn for the worse. When she died, Evangeline felt compelled to attend the makeshift service. Ann's body, in a weighted burlap sack, lay on a plank draped with a Union Jack. As two sailors held the plank on the railing, the surgeon said a few words—"We commit this prisoner to the deep, looking for the resurrection of the body when the sea shall give up her dead"—and tilted his chin at the sailors, who tipped the plank. The body slid from under the flag and splashed into the sea, floating on the surface for a moment before sinking beneath the waves.

Evangeline looked down into the water, as blackly iridescent as a raven's wing. A life extinguished. No one who loved this girl, or even knew her, to witness it. How many convicts had died on these ships, far from home and family, with none to mourn their loss?

She watched a shark, its fin dipping in and out of the water, following in the wake of the ship. "It smells death," Olive said.

WASHING DAY.

Evangeline was still amidships when the sun sank below the horizon. With all the seasickness and dysentery, the task of scrubbing and rinsing clothes and bedding was taking longer than usual, and she finished her task—wringing out the wet cotton, stretching it over the line, clipping it with wooden pegs—in the gray twilight, the pale moon hovering overhead. Her back ached; her feet were sore. In her third trimester now, she was large and slow.

All at once she was aware of a strange noise. A cry. She stood, alert, straining to hear. The mainsail flapped loudly above her head. Water lapped at the bow.

And then a woman's voice: *Stop! Get off me!*

Hazel. She was sure of it.

Evangeline slung the laundry over the line, wiped her hands on her skirt, and looked around. No one was near. There it was again: that cry. She hurried as fast as she could toward the starboard bow, from where the sound seemed to emanate, only to be blocked by a stack of crates. Turning back, she rounded the port bow, hugging the railing, and saw two figures ahead in the grainy darkness.

As she came closer, Evangeline realized with horror what she was seeing: Hazel, bent awkwardly over a barrel, her dress open to the waist and bunched around her thighs, her head twisted to the side—and a man behind her. It took a moment to realize that the man's fist grasped the red cord around Hazel's neck and was pulling it tight.

Glancing around her, Evangeline spied a wooden pole with a brass hook at the end, used for attaching sails. She grabbed it. "Get off!"

The man turned toward her. It was Buck. "Don't be stupid," he snarled. "You're in no shape."

Evangeline hoisted the pole above her head.

Buck let go of Hazel, who slid to the ground, gasping. As he advanced toward Evangeline, she saw the flash of a knife blade, the iridescent handle. Hazel's knife. He must've wrested it from her.

Evangeline moved toward him blindly, swinging the pole. With his free hand, Buck reached for it, missing several times before grabbing the end and yanking it toward him, knocking her off her feet. As he came toward her she was aware of Hazel, behind him, pushing the barrel onto its side and rolling it forward with both hands. It hit him behind his knees. He lost his balance, the knife flying from his hand, skittering across the deck. Without thinking, Evangeline lunged for it, wrapping her fingers around the handle.

Buck scrambled to his feet.

Holding the knife out in front of her, Evangeline turned to face him.

"Gimme that." He rushed toward her and she stabbed blindly in his direction, slashing his wrist and forearm as he reached for the knife. "*Whore!*" he spit, hunched over his bleeding arm. Blood gushed from the wound. Buck stumbled around like a wounded animal, cursing and whining, trying to stanch the flow.

"Go!" Evangeline yelled to Hazel, behind her. "Get help."

Hazel tugged her dress down and disappeared around the bow.

Buck sank to his knees. His white shirt was soaked with blood. As Evangeline stood over him, holding the knife, it took every ounce of self-restraint she possessed to keep from attacking him again. She trembled with adrenaline-fueled rage. She wasn't just furious at Buck; she was livid at all of the sailors and guards who treated the convicts worse than chattel. The crude catcalls and vulgar groping, the casual brutality, the arrogant assumptions of privilege—she was sick of it. And she was also, she realized, enraged at Cecil. He had merely been toying with her, using her for his own selfish ends. His delight in seeing his grandmother's ruby on her finger had been nothing more than egotistical self-gratification, an occasion to admire his two shiny ornaments—her and the ring.

Buck was moaning now, pressing his good hand against the wound. She watched with disinterest as he nursed his arm like a little boy. Presently she heard the clatter of footsteps; the surgeon came around the corner, followed by two crewmen with muskets. They stopped, mouths agape, at the sight of this heavily pregnant woman holding a knife, standing over a blood-soaked sailor on a bloody deck.

"I'll take that, Miss Stokes," Dr. Dunne said, holding out his hand.

Evangeline gave him the knife, and he passed it to one of the sailors. "Take your shirt off and tear it into strips," he ordered the other, who quickly complied. They watched in silence as he knelt in front of Buck and made a tourniquet to bind the wound. When he was finished, he sat back on his heels and turned to a crewman. "Is anyone in the hold?"

"Not at the moment."

"Shackle him and take him down."

Holding out his bandaged arm, Buck protested, "She stabbed *me*."

"Thwarting an attack, I understand."

Buck shrugged. "C'mon, officer. Just a bit o' harmless fun."

"Hardly harmless. Look at you," said Dr. Dunne.

"I'M SURPRISED YOU'RE not dead," Olive said, helping Hazel onto her berth an hour later.

"I would be, but for her." Hazel nodded at Evangeline, propped on an elbow in her bunk.

Olive tucked the blanket around her. "Not so long ago this kind of thing was just the way it was, and nobody batted an eye."

"Yes, it's so civilized now," Evangeline said.

"He's in the hold, at least," Olive said. "He won't be botherin' ye anytime soon."

Even days later, it was hard to deny the evidence of Buck's assault: the slight girl hobbling through her chores with the deep purple line of a bruise on her neck, one eye red and swollen, her split lip blown up like a sausage.

A sailor stepped forward to claim the pearl-handled knife, which, he said, had gone missing weeks earlier. Buck had threatened her with it, Hazel told Dr. Dunne. She'd only picked it up.

The captain sentenced Buck to twenty lashes and twenty-one days in the hold.

Some of the convicts stood on the deck with the sailors to watch the flogging. When he was brought up from the hold, Buck caught Evangeline's eye and stared at her until she looked away.

After he was tied to the mast, she slipped from the crowd and went to the other side of the ship, trying to ignore the whistle of the whip and Buck's anguished grunts. One day soon she would give birth to this baby, and the ship would land, and she'd serve her time, and then perhaps she could put all of this behind her. She wouldn't be too old. She had some skills: she knew how to sew and how to read. She possessed within herself a cache of poetry, a vault of her father's sermons. She could translate Latin and recall, at a moment's notice, the Greek myths she'd studied as a girl. That must count for something.

She thought of those two fine ladies she'd seen strolling down Bailey Street in front of Newgate Prison, encased in corsets and silks, tethered to convention, alarmed by everything beyond the bounds of their own narrow sphere. She knew more about life than they ever would. She'd learned that she could withstand contempt and humiliation—and that she could find moments of grace in the midst of bedlam. She'd learned that she was strong. And now here she was, halfway around the world. The sheltered, unworldly governess who'd entered the gates of Newgate was gone, and in her place was someone new. She barely recognized herself.

She felt as flinty as an arrowhead. As strong as stone.

DEEP IN THE INDIAN OCEAN, far from land, Evangeline saw creatures she'd only read about in legends: dolphins and porpoises leaping around the prow, bottlenose whales plunging in and out of the spray in the distance. One afternoon she noticed that the water was undulating with dozens of strange, translucent beings, some resembling cut lemons, others parasols that became luminous as light faded from the sky. It was as if the ship were gliding through molten fire.

"They're known as jellyfish."

Evangeline turned her head. Dr. Dunne was standing beside her, wearing dark trousers and a white shirt open at the collar. "Jellyfish?" She laughed. "It's a surprise to see you out of uniform."

He glanced down at himself. "I've been in surgery. A gangrenous leg."

"Oh dear. Did you have to amputate?"

"I'm afraid so. He waited too long, as these sailors tend to do. Think they're invincible."

Watching the horizon line quiver in the heat, she asked, "How is Mr. Buck?"

"Rather . . . unhappy, as you might imagine. It was brave what you did, Miss Stokes."

"Or foolhardy."

"Bravery often is."

She looked up into his greenish eyes, fringed with dark lashes.

A voice from behind them said, "Excuse me, sir."

Dr. Dunne turned quickly. "Yes, sailor?"

"A convict is in labor and appears to be having a hard time of it. Can ye come?"

IT WAS OLIVE. Hours later, long after the women had been bolted in for the night, Evangeline could hear her cries.

The next morning, after breakfast, she and Hazel paced the deck.

"It's taking too long," Hazel said.

"Do you think you could help?"

"I don't know."

Olive's snaggletoothed sailor passed them, swigging from a bottle of rum.

A cry pierced the air.

"Maybe I could," Hazel said.

"Let me ask." Evangeline hurried to the ladder and descended into the gloom of the tween deck. A sailor standing outside the surgeon's room moved to block the door.

"I need to see Dr. Dunne," she said.

"You're a convict."

"Evangeline Stokes. Number one seventy-one. Will you let him know I'm here?"

The sailor shook his head. "No convicts allowed."

"It's urgent."

The sailor looked her up and down. "You're about to . . ." He motioned at her belly.

"No, no," she said impatiently. "Just—please. Tell him it's me."

He shook his head. "He's busy, can't ye tell?"

"Of course I can tell. I have someone who can help."

"I'm sure the good doctor has things under control."

"But—"

"Stop wasting me time." He waggled his fingers to ward her off. "You'll be seeing him soon enough."

The day became interminably hot. Steam rose from the newly washed deck as if from a griddle. Hazel opened the Bible, mouthed some lines, closed it. Evangeline worked on her baby quilt, trying to concentrate on the stitches.

Olive's cries lessened, then stopped.

Evangeline looked at Hazel. She wore a grim expression and was knitting and unknitting her fingers.

They didn't speak. There was nothing to say.

The sun slid down the sky, its reflection puddling on the water before seeping underneath, like liquid on a porous surface. When the convicts were herded below decks, Hazel and Evangeline hunkered down in the stern, behind the wall of chicken crates.

A passing sailor, seeing them in the shadows, did a double take. "Hey, you two. They're locking up."

"We're waiting for the surgeon." Evangeline clutched her stomach. "I'm—I'm due."

"Does he know you're here?"

"Could you inform him?"

The sailor stared at them for a moment, clearly unsure of what to do. He swiped his hand at Hazel. "She don't need to stay."

"She's a"—would it help or hurt to say it?—"a midwife."

"Huh. Me auntie's a midwife."

"Is she, now?" Evangeline winced theatrically. "Oof. Will you please . . ."

As they watched him cross the deck and disappear down the ladder, Hazel whispered, "Well done."

"Wish I'd thought of it earlier."

A few minutes later, the sailor reemerged, followed by Dr. Dunne, grimly pale.

Evangeline stepped forward. "Is Olive—"

"She's resting."

"And the baby?" Hazel asked, behind her.

"Stillborn. I did what I could."

"The cord around its neck," Hazel said.

He nodded. Running his hands along the buttons of his jacket, he found the top one undone and buttoned it. "I was told a prisoner is in labor. Is that a lie?"

Evangeline swallowed. "I think it was . . . a false alarm."

He gave her a sharp look. Turning to the sailor, he said, "To the orlop deck with both of them."

OLIVE APPEARED ON the main deck the next afternoon, her face as pale as dough, with deep hollows under her eyes. Evangeline brought her tea with purloined sugar. Hazel crushed dried chamomile blossoms and stirred them into the tea. "To soothe your nerves," she said.

Olive had given birth to a boy, with a shock of dark hair and pearly fingernails. She glimpsed him for only a moment before he was covered with a towel and taken away.

They didn't ask what became of him. They knew.

Clutching her bosom, Olive said, "Christ, they hurt."

"Just your body doing what it's meant to do. I can give ye something," Hazel said.

She shook her head. "No. I want to feel it."

"Why, Olive?" Evangeline asked.

She sighed. "I didn't want the child. Many times I wished I was rid of it. But then . . . he was perfect. A perfect baby boy." Tears glinted in her eyes. "God's punishment."

"Not God. Just the way it is sometimes," Hazel said.

Evangeline nodded. For a moment all of them were quiet. Then she said, "Well, I don't know if this will help, but . . ." She took a breath. "When you cut down a tree, you can tell how old it is by the rings inside. The more rings, the sturdier the tree. So . . . I imagine I'm a tree. And every moment that mattered to me, or person I loved, is a ring." She put the flat of her hand on her chest. "All of them here. Keeping me strong."

Olive and Hazel exchanged dubious glances.

"I know it sounds silly. But what I'm trying to say, Olive, is that I think your child is still with you. And he always will be."

"Maybe so." Shaking her head, Olive managed a small smile. "I never thought of meself as a tree, Leenie, but it doesn't surprise me that ye do."

"At least she made ye smile," Hazel said.

THE CONVICTS HAD LEARNED TO watch the sky as closely as the sailors. So three days later, when the sky turned a sickly yellow, they knew that a big storm must be on the way. In early afternoon they were sent below decks. Wind lashed the sea into huge waves, sending the ship plunging into a deep crevasse, only to be borne to the crest and dropped again. Lightning tore through the sky, forking over the ship. The rain fell in torrents as sailors skidded along the deck, wrangling ropes and pulleys. Climbing the shroud of the foremast, they swayed like flies in a spiderweb.

As the ship lurched and tilted, the orlop deck was thrown into chaos. Women were dumped from their berths, groaning with seasickness, screaming and crying in terror. Water seeped through cracks above, streaming onto their heads. Bibles flew through the air; children wailed. Evangeline tied a corner of her blanket to her bedpost and tucked the rest around her, a makeshift hammock. She huddled close to the wall, fingers in her ears, and somehow, improbably, drifted to sleep.

Some hours later she was woken by a searing pain in her abdomen. She lay still for a moment, listening to the thrumming rain, trying to decide what to do. It was so dark she couldn't even see the ribs of the bunk above.

"Hazel." Leaning out of her berth, she reached across the aisle and poked the place she knew the girl would be. "*Hazel*. I think it might be time."

She heard a rustling. "What does it feel like?" Hazel's voice was groggy.

"Like what I did to Buck."

Hazel laughed.

"I'm not joking."

"I know you're not joking."

Over the next few hours, as waves pounded the hull and the ship pitched in the sea, Hazel talked Evangeline through the clenching and unclenching. Breathe, she told her; *breathe*. The pain in Evangeline's gut spiked and ebbed. When the hatch of the orlop deck was finally unlocked, Hazel helped get Evangeline up the stairs. "The air will do ye good," she said.

The women around them were mostly silent. Everyone knew what had happened to Olive.

The sky was the colors of a bruise, yellow and purple, the dark sea strafed by wind and sudsed with white. The air was thick with brine. Sailors shouted from pulpit to jib, tightening the sails as the ship heaved and slashed through the waves.

Hazel and Evangeline paced the deck, pausing when the pain surged or a cloud emptied rain. Sips of tea, a bite of hardtack. Trips to the privy. A distracted game of whist. In midafternoon a commotion lured them toward the stern: Buck—filthy, wiry, with matted hair and sunken eyes—had been released from the hold. Twenty-one days it had been.

He narrowed his eyes at them. Spit on the deck.

"Mr. Buck."

Evangeline turned.

Dr. Dunne stood several feet away, hands clasped behind his back. "Consider this a warning. Stay away from these prisoners or you'll be back in the hold."

Buck held up his hands. "I ain't done nothin'." Twisting his lips into a smile, he slunk away.

Hazel looked at Evangeline. "Put him out of your mind."

She tried. But it was hard to dismiss the menace of that smile.

Time passed slowly. The pain became more intense: a searing clamp. Evangeline could barely stand.

"I think she's ready," Hazel told the surgeon.

He nodded. "Bring her down."

Hazel guided Evangeline down the ladder to the tween deck. Behind a screen in the surgeon's office, she helped her into a cotton shift. When she was finished, Hazel stood in a corner of the room, making no move to leave. The surgeon didn't say a word.

EVANGELINE WAS DELIRIOUS, bathed in sweat.

Dr. Dunne began asking Hazel to help in small ways. *Hand me a wet cloth. Mop her brow.* She brought him a basin filled with water and a bar of lye soap, and after he washed his hands, she gave him a towel to dry them. When she noticed Evangeline tugging at the red cord around her neck, Hazel unfastened the necklace and placed it on a shelf.

After two hours it became clear that the birthing process

was stalled. Evangeline wiped her tears with the back of her hand. "What's happening?"

"Breech." Dr. Dunne sat back on his stool and rubbed his forehead with his arm.

"Breech?"

Hazel stepped forward. "Your baby is special," she told her. "Feet first." To the surgeon, she said, "May I help? I know how to do it. The turning."

He sighed, then lifted his arms from the elbows as if to say, *Come on, then.*

Hazel spread her fingers out on Evangeline's stomach, feeling all the way around it.

Evangeline gazed at her with alarm. "Is the baby in trouble?"

She felt Hazel's cool hand over hers. "You'll both be grand. Just listen to my voice. Breathe in."

She breathed in.

"Now out."

She breathed out.

Hazel stroked her hair. "Move toward the pain. Think of it as . . . a lantern guidin' your way."

The surgeon sat back on his stool, observing.

Surrendering to Hazel's demands, Evangeline breathed when she told her to, pushed when she told her to, followed the pain as if it were a lantern along a winding path. She began to sense the contractions before they happened, as they gathered force within her, and rode each wave of pain to its crest, the agony so intense that at a certain point it became a kind of euphoria. Rain drummed on the deck above their heads, muting her cries. She felt Hazel's small hands inside her, shifting, turning, coaxing the baby down. She no longer knew whether she was screaming or silent, writhing or still. And then . . . and then . . . a release. An emptying.

A baby's piercing cry.

She lifted her head.

Time flattened. Widened. Her senses returned. She smelled the fishy odor of the whale oil in the lamps, the muttony candle wax, the iron sweetness of her own blood. She gazed up at the wide beams in the ceiling, nailed in place by long iron spikes. Heard the soft patter of rain on the deck, the last remnants of the storm.

At her feet, Hazel was smiling her foxy smile. Auburn curls were plastered damply to her forehead, blood splattered on her apron. A naked infant in a blanket in her arms. "A girl."

"A girl." Evangeline struggled up on her elbows to see.

Dr. Dunne placed another pillow behind her head and Hazel handed her the featherweight bundle and all at once she was looking into the dark eyes of a baby. Her daughter. Staring at her intensely. Had anyone ever stared at her so intensely?

"Do you have a name?" Hazel asked.

"I didn't dare to think that far ahead." Holding the child in the crook of her arm, Evangeline inhaled the yeasty smell of her hair, stroked the tiny mollusk-shell ears and sea anemone fingers. Was that her father's nose, perhaps?

Hazel motioned to her to open her shift. She guided the baby toward Evangeline's breast and tapped her bottom lip, prompting her to open her tiny mouth. When the baby latched on,

Evangeline felt as if a string had been yanked from her nipple to her gut. "The more she suckles, the faster you'll heal," Hazel said.

As Evangeline cupped the infant's small head, her forefinger found a soft spot in the middle. She looked at the surgeon with surprise.

He smiled. "So the brain can grow. Don't worry. It will close."

"So the brain can grow. How could I not have known?" she marveled.

And thought of all the things she had not known.

IT WAS EARLY in the evening in the surgeon's quarters. The baby was swaddled in a blanket, tucked into the curve of Evangeline's arm. The surgeon was in the infirmary, attending a sailor with influenza. Hazel sat in a chair with his volume of *The Tempest*, mouthing words to herself.

Evangeline pointed at the book. "Where are you?"

"'This rough magic I here ab-abjure, and, when I have . . .'" Her voice trailed off.

"'Required.' Q-U is like K-W."

Hazel nodded. "Re-KW-ired. 'Required some heav-en-ly mu-sic, which even now I do, to work mine end upon their senses . . .'"

"'That this airy charm is for.'"

"It's bloody hard," Hazel said. "'Ye taught me language; and my profit on't is, I know how to curse.'"

Evangeline smiled. "Well done."

Hazel closed the book. "How d'ye feel?"

"Sore. And it's so hot. This room is stifling."

"It's always hot these days. Even after the rain."

Evangeline lay back against her pillow. Tossed her head from side to side. "I must get some air." She glanced down at the sleeping infant. "Before she wakes."

"You want to go up the ladder *now*?" Hazel frowned. "The deck will be slippery. And it's dark."

"Just for a minute."

Hazel put down the book. "I'll come with ye, then."

"No, stay with her. Please."

"But ye've just—"

"I'll be careful, I promise. I don't want her to be alone." Evangeline swung her legs over the side of the bed, and Hazel helped her to stand. Suddenly lightheaded, she swayed back against the bed.

Hazel eyed her. "This is not a good idea."

"Hazel, please. 'Gentle breath of yours my sails must fill, or else my project fails.'"

Hazel rolled her eyes. "'You cram these words into mine ears against the stomach of my sense.'"

"Oh!" Evangeline said, clasping her hand. "You're my best student."

"Well, you're my best teacher. My only teacher, truth be told." She smiled that vulpine smile.

Evangeline smiled back. "Look after my daughter while I'm gone, will you?"

"She's sleeping. She'll be fine. Hurry back."

EVANGELINE'S BELLY WAS loose under her gown, her bare feet unsteady. She climbed the ladder slowly, stopping to catch her breath with each rung. At the top she paused, her heart beating in her ears, gazing up into the velvet darkness at a thin disk of moon. Though the sky was clear, the air still smelled of rain. Taking a breath, she crossed the sea-slick deck to the railing. Inky water roiled beneath the ship, glittering in the moonlight. She looked out at the whole beautiful expanse of the sea.

Hearing a noise behind her, she turned.

A figure was sprinting toward her. A man. In the dim light she could see his sandy hair and bare arms, the sharp angle of his jaw. And then he was on her, his hands on her shoulders.

Buck.

"No," she gasped. "What are you—"

He pushed her against the railing. "You'll pay."

She smelled him, alcohol and perspiration. Felt his breath on her neck. He slammed her against the railing again with such force that the brass nails jutted into her back and she felt her legs buckle, her feet slip out from under her. And then he was lifting her up, up, to the top of the rail, the ropy muscles of his arms taut around her back. "No—no! What are you—"

"Stop!" a woman shrieked. It was Hazel. "Stop!"

For a moment Evangeline hovered on the hard wood of the railing. Then Buck let go, and the world tilted. She screamed as she fell backward through the darkness. Her baby lay swaddled in the surgeon's room, and here she was, falling, falling through the air. Her mind refused to believe it. This couldn't be happening. It made no sense.

The water hit her shoulder first, a hard slap, a shock of pain. She moved her legs instinctively, though they were tangled in her gown and she didn't know what she was doing. I don't know how to swim, she thought; I don't know how to stay afloat.

Her daughter on the birthing bed, alone.

I left my baby lying here to go and gather blueberries . . .

She was sinking. Sinking. Slowly at first, and then her chin was underwater. Her lips. Her nose, her eyes. She strained to see in the grainy darkness, eyes stinging from the salt. Frantically she moved her arms, struggling in her gown, eyes wide open as she tried to fight her way toward the surface, toward the light. But she was falling, still, suspended in space. *Alone, alone, all, all alone, / Alone on a wide wide sea!* Her gown rose up, filmy as a handkerchief . . . Cecil's white handkerchief; lion, serpent, crown . . . *And she was fair as is the rose in May.* . . . All lost, lost. The ruby ring. The handkerchief. The tin ticket on the red cord.

In the dim recesses of her mind she remembered something she'd once read about the act of drowning—that the terror was in resisting, in refusing to accept. Once you let go, it wasn't so hard; you just sank into the water, cool and obliterating.

By night or day, / The things which I have seen I now can see no more.

She closed her eyes. Pushing away the terror, she withdrew deeper into herself. Here she was now in the foyer of the vicarage in Tunbridge Wells, grabbing her bonnet from the peg, opening the heavy front door and stepping out onto the stone stoop, pulling the door closed behind her. Setting off on the footpath, a straw basket over her arm. *There was a time when meadow, grove, and stream, / The earth, and every common sight, / To me did seem / Apparelled in celestial light* . . . She meandered past the privet hedge tangled with roses, that old willow shushing in the wind. Heard the chimes of a church bell, a woodpecker knocking on a tree, a barking dog. Before long, she'd cross the stone bridge over the stream that led to the mountain trail, with its craggy rocks and sour-sweet grass, its grazing sheep and purple thistles. Her favorite place on earth, just around the bend.

MATHINNA

The last Aborigines were caught about a fortnight ago, and sent to Flinders Island, so that our little native girl is the only one remaining here. She is improving I think, though it will be a long time before she becomes quite civilised.

—DIARY OF ELEANOR FRANKLIN, 1840; daughter of
Sir John Franklin, Lieutenant-Governor of
Van Diemen's Land, 1837–1843

TALL, SLOPE-SHOULDERED, WITH A BROAD forehead, translucent eyelashes, and yellow hair, Eleanor Franklin was, indeed, rather plain. She was also the first person Mathinna had met on Van Diemen's Land who seemed utterly nonchalant about her presence. "Oh. Hullo. They're hard boiled," she said by way of introduction, waving her hand wearily toward a bowl of eggs when Sarah introduced Mathinna to her in the nursery the morning after she arrived. "I *despise* hard boiled."

As they ate, they could hear the housekeeper, Mrs. Crain, speaking in a low whisper with an elderly woman—Miss Williamson, a governess who'd come with the family from England. "It was quite enough to try this experiment once, with that incorrigible boy," the governess huffed. "To expect me to attempt to educate another savage is too much to ask."

"It is Lady Franklin's request, not mine," Mrs. Crain said. "You may take it up with her, if you wish."

Eleanor looked up. "I could tutor the girl. Might as well put my French to good use, since I'm not doing anything else with it. This place is so *dull*."

And so it was that for three hours a day, three days a week,

Mathinna and Eleanor met in the schoolroom after breakfast. Eleanor treated Mathinna the same way she treated her dog, Sandy: with a mild, lukewarm affection. What she lacked in smarts, Eleanor made up in effort; she dutifully taught Mathinna to add and subtract and spell. One week she devised a lesson on architecture. She showed her pictures of Gothic design, with its thrilling gargoyles and grotesques, and classical, with its emphasis on proportion and harmony. The fashion in Hobart Town was for boring Georgian, she said, all tiled roofs and sandstone exteriors. Like Government House, the building they were in.

Eleanor explained how the calendar worked, days turning into weeks into months into years, and though Mathinna paid attention, she didn't much see the point. The schoolteacher on Flinders had kept a date book open on his desk in which he jotted precise notes about the seasons, particularities of the weather, and his perambulations around the island, but the Palawa elders scoffed at such recordkeeping. Didn't these colonists know that time doesn't move in a line from past to present but instead is continuous? That spirits and humans, animals and plants, are connected by the land, which binds ancestors to descendants in an eternal moment? Mathinna started to explain this, as best she could remember, but Eleanor's eyes got a faraway, glazed look and she picked at her fingernails until Mathinna stopped talking.

More successful was the study of French. They practiced with Eleanor's collection of marionettes. After several weeks, their puppets—a blond princess in a powder-blue ball gown and a tiara, and a mountain maid wearing a dirndl—were conversing:

> *Bonjour, comment vous appelez-vous?*
> *Bonjour, madame, je m'appelle Mathinna.*
> *Enchanté de fair votre connaissance.*
> *Merci, madame. Je suis enchanté également.*

Mathinna grew to love the melody of the language. It seemed to her logical and beautiful—much nicer than English, pocked as it was with maddening contradictions and inelegant phrasings. Though she did like a play that started on a Scottish heath with witches around a cauldron and featured a royal couple who reminded her ever so slightly of Lady Franklin and Sir John. And another about a shipwreck on a remote island that Eleanor decided they should read aloud.

"'But thy vile race,'" Eleanor intoned, in character as Miranda, "'Though thou didst learn, had that in't which good natures / Could not abide to be with. Therefore wast thou / *Deservedly* confined into this rock, / Who hadst deserved more than a prison.'" And Mathinna-as-Caliban responded, "'As I told thee before, I am subject to a tyrant, a sorcerer that by his cunning hath cheated me of the island.'"

Spinning a wooden sphere, Eleanor identified the seven continents and five oceans. "Here," she said, putting her finger on a kangaroo-like shape in the northern hemisphere on the other side of the globe from Van Diemen's Land. "This is where I was born." She tapped London, and Paris, and Rome—all the important cities, she said—and ran her finger down the spiky coastline to the bottom of Africa, and across a wide blue expanse. "And this is the route we took to get to this godforsaken place. We spent four months at sea!"

Mathinna touched the heart-shaped mass of Van Diemen's Land. She traced her own reverse journey with her finger, as she'd done on the captain's map, up the right side of the island to the tiny speck where she was born. On the captain's map, Van Diemen's Land had been huge and Flinders Island small. On this globe, it was merely a rock in the ocean, too slight and insignificant to have a name. It was as if the place she loved, and the people on it, had been erased. No one even knew they existed.

IN THIS STRANGE new place Waluka clung to Mathinna. His own fear raised in her a protectiveness that calmed her. He spent most of the day sleeping in a wide pocket of her pinafore, but climbed out now and then to make his way up to her neck, where he nestled against her, nuzzling her with his wet nose. In the evenings she was expected to put him in a cage that was brought to her room for that purpose, but after shutting the door and blowing out the candle, she unlatched the cage and let Waluka run across the floor to the bed.

She spent as little time as possible in her bedroom, with its boarded-up window and looming candle-made shadows. On mild days, when she wasn't with Eleanor in the schoolroom, she rambled around the cobbled courtyard with Waluka in her pocket, watching the stablemen brush and feed the horses, scratching the backs of the hogs in the piggery and listening to the gossip between the convict maids as they scrubbed laundry and hung it on the clothesline behind the house.

It was generally agreed that Lady Franklin possessed the brains and the ambition to rule this unruly colony, while Sir John, with his knighthood, provided the status. The maids spoke of him with a kind of benevolent contempt. In their eyes, Sir John was a foolish man, constantly getting himself into trouble and barely getting himself out. They recounted endless stories about his haplessness, such as the time he'd charged out of the house shouting for the carriage with his face half shaved and half lathered. They scoffed at how he combed his few remaining strands of hair across the top of his head. They tittered at how comical he appeared on horseback, with his stomach bulging over his trousers, the buttons on his waistcoat straining at the seams.

Sir John had achieved fame as an explorer, but each voyage he'd led was more calamitous than the last. There was one expedition to northern Canada that ended in survivors eating their own boots and possibly each other, and another to the Arctic Circle that grew increasingly dire before the remaining few gave up and fled back to England. Only after a vigorous marketing campaign by Lady Franklin was he rewarded with a knighthood for these failed attempts.

Lady Franklin's treatment of Eleanor was another source of amusement. Eleanor was the product of Sir John's first marriage to a woman who'd died tragically young; Lady Franklin, who had no children of her own, tolerated her with barely concealed impatience. When she couldn't avoid Eleanor, she poked at her with criticism masquerading as concern. "Are you quite well? You're frightfully pale." "Dear girl, that dress is so unflattering! I must have a word with the seamstress."

Mathinna saw this for herself one day when she and Eleanor passed Lady Franklin in the corridor. "Posture, Eleanor," Lady Franklin said, barely breaking stride. "You don't want to be mistaken for a scullery maid."

Eleanor looked as if she'd been splashed in the face with water. "Yes, ma'am," she said. But when Lady Franklin disappeared around the corner, she slumped comically, tucking her arms into wings and crouching into a penguin's waddle, making Mathinna giggle.

LADY FRANKLIN HAD little time for Mathinna, preoccupied as she was with entertaining dignitaries, writing in her journal, taking picnics up Mount Wellington on daylong expeditions, and departing on overnight trips with Sir John. But a few times a month she invited a group of ladies, wives of merchants and government officials, to drink tea and eat cake in the red-paneled drawing room, and on these occasions she summoned Mathinna to show off her newly acquired French and good manners.

"What would you like to say to these ladies, Mathinna?"

She curtsied dutifully. *"Je suis extrêmement heureux de vous rencontrer tous."*

"As you can see, the girl has made remarkable progress," Lady Franklin said.

"Or is a clever mimic, at least," one of the ladies said behind her fan.

The ladies asked lots of questions. They wanted to know if Mathinna had ever worn proper clothing before coming to Hobart Town. If she ate snakes and spiders. If her father had many wives, if she'd grown up in a hut, if she believed in the occult. They marveled at her brown skin, turning her hands over to inspect her palms. They patted her spongy dark hair and peered inside her mouth to confirm the pinkness of her gums.

Mathinna grew to dread these afternoons in the drawing room. She disliked being pawed over and whispered about. Sometimes she wished she were white, or invisible, just to avoid the stares and whispers, the rude, patronizing questions.

When they tired of her, Mathinna sat in a corner playing patience, a game of solitaire that Eleanor had taught her. As she squared and fanned her cards, she listened to the ladies commiserate about the inconvenience of living so far from civilization. They complained about how they couldn't get the supplies they wanted—Leghorn bonnets from Tuscany and opera-length kid gloves, mahogany bed frames and glass chandeliers, champagne and foie gras. They bemoaned the lack of skilled artisans. The impossibility of finding good help. The dearth of amusements, like opera and theater. "Good theater," Lady Franklin clarified.

"You can attend an atrocious production in Hobart Town every day of the week." They fretted about their skin: how it burned and dried out, blistered and freckled, how vulnerable it was to rashes and insect bites.

So many odd customs these ladies had! They stuffed themselves into elaborate costumes: corsets with whalebone stays, hats with bows and ribbons, impractical shoes with pointy heels that disintegrated in the mud and dirt. They ate extravagant meals that upset their stomachs and made them fat. They appeared to exist in a perpetual state of discontent, constantly comparing their lives to those of their contemporaries in London and Paris and Milan. Why did they stay here, Mathinna wondered, if they disliked it so much?

ON MONDAY MORNINGS, like clockwork, a black carriage arrived at Government House carrying John Montagu, the Colonial Secretary, and his dog. A balding man with a perpetually smug expression, Montagu wore a double-breasted jacket over a tight-fitting waistcoat, a high-collared shirt, and a floppy black tie. His dog, a muscular beast with an attenuated snout and short, floppy ears, was unfriendly to everyone except its master, who seemed to delight in its twitchy aggression. "Jip can overpower a kangaroo in four paces," Montagu would brag to anyone who'd listen. It was rumored that he brought the dog with him to Government House to impress, or possibly intimidate, Sir John, with whom he had a simmering rivalry.

During the hour that the two men met each week, the dog

roamed the courtyard. One Monday a convict maid, hanging laundry in the yard, was attacked by the dog. It grabbed her skirt and yanked her to the ground, breaking her arm. "It's a pity," Montagu said when he learned of it. "But I did warn those prison wenches to stay out of Jip's way."

ON FLINDERS, MATHINNA had often gone to bed hungry. The Palawa had been accustomed to hunting and foraging from the coast to the highlands on Van Diemen's Land, but the smaller island was largely barren, and the missionaries did not share their food. Here there was plenty to eat, though much of it tasted strange in her mouth. Mutton chops and mushy peas, cold toast that stood upright in a silver server, small white kernels of rice she first mistook for grubs. The Franklins drank bitter herbs steeped in boiling water at every meal, redeemed only by the sugar that Mathinna soon discovered made everything taste better.

One Sunday afternoon Mathinna was invited to join the Franklins at a luncheon in the dining room for a visiting English bishop and his wife and young daughter. Over cold pheasant pie and calves' brains in aspic, the bishop asked Mathinna what natives liked to eat. She told him about hunting muttonbirds, how they'd pull the bird out of a hole, snap its neck, and toss it into a fire. She demonstrated how they'd pluck most of the feathers and spit out the rest as they bit into the skin.

"Mathinna!" Eleanor gasped.

Sir John chuckled. "She's quite right, you know. Why consume some birds and not others? Many an explorer has perished from unnecessary scruples about what he's willing to put in his mouth."

The rest of the table was silent. The bishop wore an expression of disgust. Lady Franklin looked aghast. Mathinna was annoyed at herself. For a brief moment she'd forgotten how peculiar these people were. She wished she hadn't said anything.

"It's not true," she said quickly. "I made it up."

After a moment, the bishop laughed. "What a peculiar creature!" he exclaimed, turning to Sir John. "I might believe anything she tells me about her people, so remote is their experience from ours."

"Perhaps it's time for the girls to leave the table," Lady Franklin said. "Sarah, will you take them outside for some fresh air?"

Mathinna sighed. Lady Franklin had invited her friends' children to play with her before, and it rarely went well. They did not seem to know whether to treat Mathinna as an equal, or as a servant, or with a wary, forced politeness, as if she were the pet of an acquaintance you might not trust not to jump or nip.

When they were in the garden, Mathinna scampered up a blue gum tree, hand over foot, shimmying across its elephant limbs while the bishop's daughter, Emily, shivered in the cool air below. Peering down at her through the ragged leaves, Mathinna called, "Climb up here with me!"

"My mama won't allow it. It's dangerous," Emily said, gaping up at Mathinna in her formal clothes.

Mathinna climbed down. "What do you want to do, then?"

"I don't know."

"Do you want to see my pet possum?"

"I suppose."

"Mama has one of those," Emily said when Mathinna brought out Waluka. "It's dead, though. She wears it as a fur around her neck. It still has its tiny black eyes."

Mathinna tucked Waluka back in her skirt pocket. It was becoming clear that the things that had made her happy on Flinders were considered childish, impetuous, and strange here. A young lady wasn't supposed to run around barefoot and half dressed, or shout into the air, or climb to the tops of the trees, or have a possum as a pet. From now on, she would keep Waluka out of sight when strangers were around. She wouldn't talk about hunting muttonbirds. She would stay quiet about her past.

That night, in the darkness of her bedroom, she danced with Waluka on her shoulders as she had on the white sand on Flinders, one hand on his small back to keep him steady. Perhaps, as Lady Franklin said, it would be easier if she could let go of Flinders in her mind—forget her people and their way of life. Perhaps it would make living in this strange place easier. Perhaps she would feel less painfully alone.

THE FRANKLINS HOSTED A BOATING party for Eleanor when she turned eighteen. On the occasion of Lady Franklin's forty-ninth, Sir John surprised her with a signed edition of *Oliver Twist* and a trip to Melbourne. Lady Franklin threw a large formal banquet in honor of Sir John's fifty-fifth. Mrs. Wilson, with a great show of fanfare, was granted her birthday off, with pay.

The Franklins didn't know Mathinna's birth date, and neither did she, so they picked a random date on the calendar: May 18, three months to the day after she'd arrived in Hobart Town. "Mrs. Wilson could make a cake for her, at least," she overheard Eleanor say to Lady Franklin a few days before. "She's turning nine. Old enough to notice."

"Don't be silly," Lady Franklin replied. "Her people don't notice such things. It would be like commemorating the birth date of the family pet."

But Mathinna did notice. To have been assigned a birth date and then denied the customary acknowledgment felt particularly callous. She woke up and practiced French with Eleanor (who seemed to have forgotten that the day had any significance), ate an ordinary midday meal in the kitchen with Mrs. Wilson, and spent the afternoon roaming the property with Waluka. She kept hoping that she might be surprised with a cake after all, but the hours passed with nothing. Only Sarah, putting away laundry in Mathinna's room after her solitary supper, mentioned anything about it. "So it's your birthday, I heard. Nobody says a word about mine neither. Just another year closer to me ticket of leave."

UNLIKE LADY FRANKLIN, Sir John seemed to genuinely enjoy Mathinna's company. He taught her cribbage—which she called the kangaroo game because of how the stick markers jumped up and down the crib board—and often summoned her to play it with him in the late afternoons. He invited her to join him and Eleanor in the garden before breakfast, under the shade of the gum trees and sycamores that dotted the property, for his daily morning constitutional, as he called it. On these strolls he taught her to identify the flowers they'd imported from England: pink-and-white tea roses, daffodils, purple lilacs with tiny, tubular flowers.

One morning when Mathinna arrived in the garden, Sir John was standing next to a box draped in a sheet. With a magician-like flourish he removed the sheet to reveal a wire cage containing a formidable black bird with patches of yellow on its cheeks and tail. "Montagu gave me this blasted cockatoo and I don't know what to do with it," he said, shaking his head. "No one wants to go near it. Now and then it makes a dreadful sound, a sort of . . . caterwaul."

As if on cue, the bird opened its beak and emitted a piercing *kee-ow, kee-ow*.

Sir John winced. "See what I mean? I've done a bit of research, and it turns out that a British naturalist named George Shaw discovered this species. Named it *Psittacus funereus* because, well, as you can see, it appears dressed for a funeral. Though there is some question about the Latin name of the eastern versus southern yellow-tailed cockatoo . . . well, never mind. At any rate, it appears that I am stuck with it."

"Why don't you let it go?" Mathinna asked.

"I'm tempted, believe me." He sighed. "But apparently creatures like this, raised in captivity, lose the ability to survive in the wild. And I can ill afford to insult Montagu while he's overseeing the question of convict discipline. You seem to have tamed that . . ." He gestured toward Mathinna's pocket, at the lump of Waluka's body. "The truth is, your people are more naturally attuned to wildlife than we Europeans. Closer to the earth, and so on. I hereby grant this bird to your care."

"To me?" Mathinna asked. "What do you want me to do with it?" She peered through the bars at the sullen-looking cockatoo as it hopped from one foot to the other. She watched it lift a green cone with its foot and root around with its beak for the seeds. Its crest, short and ink black, gave it an intimidating air. *Kee-ow*.

"Just . . . I don't know. We'll find a maid to feed it and clean its cage. You can . . . talk to it, I suppose."

"You can't talk to it?"

Sir John shook his head. "I tried, Mathinna, I really did. The two of us don't speak the same language."

MATHINNA WAS IN the schoolroom with Eleanor, practicing her handwriting, when Mrs. Crain popped her head in the door. "Lady Franklin requests the girl's presence in her curio room. Wearing the red dress. Sarah has ironed it and is waiting in her room."

Mathinna felt a familiar dread in the pit of her stomach. "What does she want with me?" she asked.

Mrs. Crain gave Mathinna a curt smile. "It is not your place to ask."

When she left the room, Eleanor rolled her eyes. "You know how Jane likes to show you off. To take credit for civilizing you."

Sarah helped Mathinna dress and escorted her downstairs.

"Ah! Here she is." Lady Franklin turned to a thin, stooped man in a black wool coat standing beside her. "What do you think?"

He cocked his head at Mathinna. "Extraordinary eyes, you're quite right," he said. "And the dress is splendid against that dark skin."

"Did I mention she's the daughter of a chieftain?"

"You did indeed."

"Mathinna," Lady Franklin said, "this is Mr. Bock. I have commissioned him to create your portrait. For the purposes of science as well as art. Scientific research, as you may know, is a keen interest of mine," she told Mr. Bock.

"One gathers as much," he said, looking around at the taxidermied menagerie.

"I think people will be much interested in seeing this remnant of a native population that is about to disappear from the face of the earth," she said. "Don't you?"

"Ah, well . . ." The tips of Mr. Bock's ears reddened slightly, and he slid his eyes toward Mathinna. She looked behind her to see if he meant to communicate with someone else, but no one was there.

Oh. He was embarrassed on her behalf.

She thought she had become inured to the way Lady Franklin spoke about her in her presence as if she had no feelings or didn't comprehend what she was saying. But Mr. Bock's acknowledgment of it made her realize how insulting it was.

Every afternoon for a week, Mathinna sat for hours in front of Mr. Bock's easel in the least-used drawing room. He was quiet for long periods of time, speaking only to admonish her not to fidget or look away, to sit up straight, lay hands in her lap. Sarah told her it was rumored that Mr. Bock was a famous painter in England before he was sentenced to transport for stealing drugs. The fact that he might be an ex-convict made him somehow less intimidating.

Each day, when Mr. Bock dismissed her, Mathinna left the room without looking at the painting in progress. She'd seen the framed pictures on the walls in Lady Franklin's quarters—natives with exaggerated features, bulbous noses, and saucer eyes. She was afraid of how she might appear on Mr. Bock's easel.

Late on Friday afternoon, he announced that he was finished. He called for Lady Franklin to take a look. Scrutinizing the portrait, she cocked her head. Nodding slowly, she said, "Well done, Mr. Bock. You've managed to convey her mischievousness. And that woolly hair. What do you think, Mathinna? Doesn't it look like you?"

Mathinna slid off her chair and walked slowly to the easel. The girl in the portrait did resemble her. She gazed directly at the viewer with large, blackish brown eyes, her hands folded in her lap, bare feet crossed, lips turned slightly upward. But she didn't look mischievous. She seemed melancholy. She had an air of preoccupation, as if she were waiting for something, or someone, beyond the canvas.

Mathinna's heart quavered.

The painter had captured something about her that she knew to be true but had not consciously understood. Wearing the scarlet dress had felt like a game to her, an elaborate charade. It was not a dress her mother would've worn, or any other woman on Flinders. It had nothing to do with the traditions she'd grown up with or the way of life of the people she loved. The dress was an impersonation.

But the truth was, her past was slipping away. It had been a year since she'd arrived in Hobart Town. She could no longer see her mother's face. She couldn't summon the smell of the rain in the Flinders cove, or the grainy feel of the sand beneath her feet, or the expressions of the elders around the fire. In bed at night she mouthed words in her language, but her language was disappearing. *Mina kipli, nina kanaplila, waranta liyini. I eat, you dance, we sing.* It was an eight-year-old's vocabulary; she had no words to add. Even the songs she once knew seemed to her now like nursery rhymes filled with nonsense words.

Seeing herself on the canvas showed her how much her life had changed. How far she was from the place she'd once called home.

MRS. WILSON WAS IN A foul mood, grousing about the day's delivery, a random collection of ingredients that even a seasoned cook like herself was hard pressed to turn into dinner. "Turnips and gristle!" She bustled around the small space like a hedgehog in its burrow. "What the good Lord am I expected to do with that?" Rooting around in baskets, she found celery root and a few limp carrots. "Suppose I'll make a turnip pudding," she muttered, "and some crackling from this sorry excuse for a roast."

Mathinna sat in a corner of the kitchen, as she often did, working on a floral needlepoint of dark green leaves and pink trumpet-shaped flowers. Waluka lay curled around her shoulders, his hot-water-bottle belly against her neck. She watched as Mrs. Wilson gathered ingredients, slapping lard into a cast-iron skillet, shaving bits of fatty meat off the hunk in front of her and tossing them into the pan. A maid came in with Lady Franklin's tray from lunch, which only exasperated the cook further. "Don't stand there gawping. Give that here! Move along!" She cleared a space on the crowded table, plunked down the messy tray, and shooed the maid out the door.

Neither she nor Mathinna noticed that spatters of lard, sloppily thrown toward the skillet, had landed on the coals and ignited a fire. The room filled with smoke.

Mrs. Wilson let out a cry and flapped her arms. "Don't just sit there, child. Help me!"

Mathinna leapt to her feet. A spear of flame had jumped from the hearth to the wall and now lapped at a hand towel hanging to dry. She started to ladle water out of the barrel, then, realizing it was taking too long, grabbed a pile of dishtowels and dumped them into the water. She handed the dripping towels one by one to Mrs. Wilson, who used them to bat at the flames. When the towels ran out, Mathinna scooped water from the barrel with a small bowl and flung it toward the hearth. It was several minutes before the two of them, working feverishly, were able to extinguish the fire.

When it was finally out, they stood in the middle of the kitchen floor, surrounded by clumps of soggy towels, surveying the now-even-blacker wall above the fireplace. Mrs. Wilson sighed, patting her bosom. "Good thinking, you. It's lucky I have a kitchen left to cook in."

Mathinna helped her clean up the mess. They dumped the wet towels in the sink, mopped the floor in front of the hearth, and cleared the table. When they were finished, Mrs. Wilson said, "Now where did that creature of yours get off to?"

Instinctively Mathinna reached up to her neck, but of course Waluka wasn't there. He must've slid away when she sprang to her feet, but she had no memory of it. She looked in the rush basket, under the old wooden cupboard, behind the breakfront where the bowls were kept.

"Hiding in a corner, no doubt," Mrs. Wilson assured her.

But he wasn't.

Mathinna felt a sudden coldness—a sickening alarm. Waluka didn't stray. He was afraid of everything. But the fire . . . the tumult . . . Her gaze drifted toward the doorway, which Mrs. Wilson had thrown wide when the room filled with smoke. She could make out something . . . something in the courtyard.

She moved as if in a trance through the doorway and out into the cold air. As she got closer, stumbling over the cobblestones, her eyes fixed on the small white lump.

Matted fur, a trickle of red.

No . . .

When she reached it, she collapsed on her knees. She touched the soft body, slick with something viscous. It was broken and bloody, its eyes dull, half open.

She heard a low growl, and then a shout: "Move away!" She looked up, her vision murky with tears. Montagu's dog was charging toward her, nose down, trailing a chain that clanged along the cobbles, Montagu waving madly behind it. "Bloody hell, get away from that thing or Jip will eat you too!"

Mathinna lifted the small possum, cradling him in both hands. He was still warm. "Waluka, Waluka," she keened, rocking back and forth. When the dog bounded up, snarling, she staggered to her feet and lunged at it, baring her own teeth. A guttural howl traveled up through her body until she vibrated with it.

She howled until the dog backed away and the convict maids dropped their baskets; until Mrs. Crain burst through the servants' door of the main house and Mrs. Wilson came running across the courtyard; until even Lady Franklin emerged on the balcony above the green drawing room, with a look of mild annoyance, to see what all the fuss was about.

FOR MONTHS, MATHINNA felt the ghost of Waluka's presence. The weight of his body on her shoulders, his soft, warm belly and shallow breath against her neck. The tap of his paws on her skin when he ran up the length of one arm and down the other. The bony ridge of his spine as he lay next to her in bed. The possum had been her only remaining link to Flinders—his beating heart linking her to her mother, her father, Palle, the elders around the fire. And now that heart was still.

So many losses piled up, one on top of the other, each tamping down the last. Her chest heavy with the weight of them.

"Maybe it was for the best," Lady Franklin told her. "A wild animal like that isn't meant to be domesticated."

Well, maybe Lady Jane was right. Maybe it was for the best. Without him, perhaps she could finally leave Flinders behind, tuck away her few remaining memories and embrace her role as the girl in the portrait in the red satin dress. It would be a relief, she thought, to let it go. She'd become accustomed to stiff shoes; she ate aspic without complaint. She conversed in French and kept track of dates on a calendar. She was tired of feeling as if she lived between worlds. This was the world she lived in now.

HAZEL

As to the females, it is a melancholy fact, but not the less true, that far the greater proportion are utterly irreclaimable, being the most worthless and abandoned of human beings! No kindness can conciliate them, nor any indulgence render them grateful; and it is admitted by everyone, that they are, taken as a body, infinitely worse than males!

—LIEUTENANT BRETON, *Excursions in New South Wales, Western Australia and Van Diemen's Land During the Years 1830, 1831, 1832, and 1833*

WHAT HAZEL REMEMBERED MOST VIVIDLY—WHAT she would always remember—was the hem of Evangeline's gown as she hovered on the railing, her arms flailing in the air. Her disbelieving shriek as she tumbled overboard. The cold rage on Buck's face when he turned, startled by Hazel's scream. The quickening in her chest, the disorienting horror.

After that, all was chaos. The surgeon yelling behind her, two crewmen rushing to apprehend Buck, two others peering over the side. Dunne stripping off his jacket, preparing to jump, and the captain's shouted reprimand: "Dr. Dunne! Stand down, sir."

"One of the crew, then," Dunne said. "An experienced swimmer—"

"I will require no man to risk his life for a convict."

Hazel and Dunne stayed on the deck for what felt like hours after everyone else had left, standing wordless, helpless, at the railing, scanning the glittery water. Was that a floating cloth, just under the surface? A glimpse of hair?

The sea, blackly silent, gave up nothing. No sign of her. Evangeline was gone.

FOR MONTHS, YEARS, afterward, Hazel would dream of Evangeline underwater. The fathomless silence. The absence of sound.

A TINNY WAIL rose from the tween deck.

Hazel and Dunne looked at each other. The baby. They'd forgotten about the baby.

In the surgeon's quarters, Hazel held the swaddled infant close to her chest, trying to soothe her. "She needs to be fed."

"Goats' milk will do. We can mix it with water and a little sugar."

"Mothers' milk is better."

"Of course it is, but . . ."

Wet nurses were common in Glasgow, where the infant mortality rate was high and mothers of dead children learned that they could at least earn money from their misery. But there were no wet nurses on the ship.

Hazel looked at Dunne wordlessly. Olive had given birth less than a week earlier. He nodded: he'd had the same thought. Yes, it was worth a try.

Dunne found a crewman to unbolt the orlop deck. Carrying a candle, Hazel made her way down the narrow corridor to Olive's berth. Since Olive had lost her baby, she'd been glum and withdrawn. She'd abandoned her sailor's bed and crept back to her own like an animal licking its wounds. Now she lay hunched under the covers and facing the wall, lightly snoring.

Hazel tapped her back. When there was no response, she tugged her shoulder.

Olive turned toward her. "Fer Chrissakes, what."

"You're needed."

Olive turned. The flickering candlelight cast ghoulish shadows on her face. She peered closer at Hazel. "Are ye . . . crying?"

"It's—it's Evangeline."

Olive didn't ask any questions. She hoisted herself off the bunk, dragging her blanket with her and pulling it around her shoulders like a cape, and followed Hazel past the rows of sleeping women, up the swaying ladder and into the surgeon's quarters.

At the sight of Dunne cradling the infant, Olive stopped in her tracks.

"It's hers," Hazel said.

"I didn't know she was ready to—"

"You've been a bit preoccupied."

Olive looked back and forth between them. "Where is she, then?"

There was no easy way to say it. "She's gone, Olive," Hazel said.

"Gone?"

It was still so unfathomable to Hazel that she hardly believed it herself. "Buck pushed her over the side."

Olive looked at Dunne, as if asking him to dispute it.

"I'm afraid it's true," he said.

"No." Olive placed a hand to her forehead.

"She went under and never came up." He swallowed. "I wanted to go after her, but . . ."

Tears glinted in Olive's eyes. "No need to explain."

For a moment all of them were quiet, trying to absorb the enormity of it. Evangeline had been here, and now she was gone. Her life had such little value that the ship wouldn't even attempt a rescue.

Olive sniffed. Wiping a tear with the back of her hand, she said, "To hell with all of 'em."

The baby, in the surgeon's arms, gave a lamblike bleat.

Dunne glanced at Hazel, then back at Olive. "The child is hungry. She needs a wet nurse."

She squinted at him.

"I thought—well, Hazel and I wondered—"

"It's a girl," Olive said.

"Yes."

"Ye want me to feed it. Her."

"Yes."

With a hard look at Dunne, Olive said, "Ye couldn't save my baby but now ye want me to save Evangeline's?"

He pressed his lips together. There was no answer to that.

"It's all terrible, Olive," Hazel said.

Slowly she shook her head. "I don't think I can."

"But—"

"Ye shouldn't ask me to. Babies survive without mothers' milk, don't they?"

"Some do," Dunne said. "Many don't."

Hazel knew that Olive genuinely cared for Evangeline. And

yet, like Hazel's mother, her top priority was her own survival. "I know it won't be easy. But . . . you'd get extra perks," Hazel said, glancing at Dunne.

He nodded. "Better rations."

"Me sailor gets me those."

"You'd never scrub the deck again."

Olive gave a short laugh. "I weasel out of chores as it is." She cleared her throat. "Look. I would help. I would. But me sailor wants me back. And he would not take kindly to an infant in his bed."

"Ye don't need to keep the baby," Hazel said. "Just feed her now and then."

"Where will she sleep?"

It was a good question. The baby would need to be fed at night. If Hazel slept with her on the orlop deck, they'd be locked in until morning.

Dunne pursed his lips. Then he said, "Miss Ferguson can stay with the infant in a room on this floor and bring her to Mr. Grunwald's quarters when she needs feeding."

Silence stretched across the space between them.

"Her baby will probably die, Olive," Hazel blurted. "Both of 'em dead, and for no reason. You'd be giving her a chance."

"I don't even know if I still have milk."

Dunne handed her the small bundle.

Sighing heavily, Olive sat on the bed. After a few moments she pulled open her nightshirt and Hazel coaxed her forward, helping her to position the infant at a slight angle. The child fretted and squirmed.

"It's no good," Olive said.

"Shh," Hazel said. "Give it time." Reaching over, she swiped a droplet of milk and wiped it onto her finger. When she rubbed it on the infant's lips, the baby rooted in the air, craning her neck, and Hazel gently guided her mouth to Olive's breast. "Feels strange at first, I know. But she'll get the hang of it, and so will ye."

Olive gazed down at the child as she suckled. "Poor Leenie," she said. "She was never meant for this kind of life, was she?"

IT SURPRISED HAZEL that she felt so bereft. She'd never been a crier, but here she was, sobbing into her apron, wiping away tears before anyone could see. She was *fine*, she told herself. She hardly knew Evangeline, after all. It was her own fault she'd allowed herself to feel for her.

Even so, her true heart whispered: you are not fine. Evangeline was the only person in her life who had been wholly kind. She was gutted.

Before meeting Evangeline, Hazel had wondered if she'd ever feel a real connection to another human being. Because she never had, not really. As a child, she'd yearned to feel the warmth of her mother's love. She searched her eyes, desperate to see herself reflected back, but all she saw was her mother's own need, her unquenchable desire. When Hazel sought affection, her mother pulled away. When she cried, her mother was annoyed. Her mother ignored Hazel until she needed something, and even then, it was rare that her gaze settled on Hazel's face.

In time Hazel had come to feel insubstantial—not invisible, exactly, but not quite seen.

Her mother bought rum instead of food. She went out for hours, leaving Hazel alone in the cold, dark room they lived in on that narrow Glasgow street as the fire died out. Hazel learned to fend for herself, combing Kelvingrove Park for branches to feed the woodstove, stealing clothes from backyard lines and food from neighbors' tables. On the way home she'd pass the glow of candlelight through thick windowpanes and imagine the happy lives within, so remote from her own.

Over time, she grew deeply angry. It was the only emotion she allowed herself to feel. Her anger was a carapace; it protected her soft insides like the shell of a snail. From a bitter distance she watched her mother place gentle hands on the girls and women who came to see her, carrying their shame in front of them, those telltale swollen bellies. Eyes wide with terror or weary with grief, they were afraid of dying, of the child dying, of the child living. Their burdens the result of misplaced love, or drunken fumbling, or the predatory advances of men they didn't know—or, worse, men they did. Hazel's mother calmed their fears and soothed their pain. She treated them with a kindness and compassion she was never able to show her own daughter, watching from the shadows.

Now, faced with Evangeline's helpless infant, Hazel wanted to turn away, to retreat into her shell. It wasn't her responsibility; she didn't owe the child a thing. No one would blame her if she stepped aside. She knew—didn't she?—that it was a mistake to allow herself to have feelings. Here she was, abandoned again.

But this was Evangeline's baby. And she was all alone. They both were.

THE CONVICT WAS not in her right mind, Buck told the captain. She was loony. Vindictive. She'd lunged toward him and he pushed her away in self-defense. It wasn't his fault she pitched overboard.

Hazel was the only witness. She told the captain what she saw.

"The word of a convict against the word of a sailor," the captain mused.

"I can corroborate," Dunne said. "I was there just after it happened."

"You didn't actually witness the crime."

Dunne gave him a thin smile. "As you are aware, Captain, Buck is a convicted criminal. With a history of violence and a motive for revenge. Miss Stokes had just given birth. She was hardly in any state, physical or emotional, to attack him. And why would she? He'd been punished for his crime. Justice was served."

Buck was given thirty lashes, and this time Hazel and Olive stood with the surgeon at the front of the crowd, watching him writhe and whine. Most of the throng melted away as soon as the whipping ended. But the three of them watched as Buck was untied from the mast, the stripes on his back already puffing and oozing blood.

Hazel looked him in the eye. He stared at her dully. "What

will happen to him?" she asked Dunne when they dragged him off.

"He'll be kept in the hold until we land, and then a court of law will decide his fate. Port Arthur, probably, for a long time."

It felt good to stand like a sentinel, to witness Buck's humiliation and pain. But it didn't lessen the heartache of losing Evangeline.

HAZEL'S ONLY TASK now, Dunne told her, was to care for the infant. He moved her into a small room off the infirmary, where she slept with the baby at night. She made a crib out of a drawer from a dresser and set it beside the bed. She'd almost forgotten what it was like to sleep on a real mattress with clean cotton sheets and a blanket that didn't chafe her skin. To light an oil lamp when she pleased. To relieve herself in private.

As the days passed, Olive, too, settled into her role. When the two women sat together in the afternoons, Dunne brought them stewed plums and mincemeat pies and fresh mutton, delicacies forbidden the prisoners and most of the sailors, available only to the top brass.

"Does the captain know you're feeding the animals?" Olive asked as they sipped tea with milk and sugar and ate toast with blackberry jam.

Dunne gave a small laugh. "He has no say in the matter."

Olive slathered butter on her toast. "I suppose it'll be different when we land."

"No doubt. Enjoy it while you can."

AT FIRST HAZEL and Dunne were wary around each other, carefully formal. She still found him high-handed and arrogant, and reluctant to take her seriously. But as the days passed he began talking with her about his patients' cases, and even asked her opinion on their treatment. She didn't know whether it was that she'd earned his respect during the breech birth or simply that he liked having someone to talk to, but she enjoyed sharing what she knew. Many convicts had vague symptoms of anxiety—hysteria, Dunne called it—for which he had no cure. Hazel suggested a tea of motherwort. For menstruation cramps, powdered red raspberry leaves. For fainting, a tumbler of vinegar down the throat. For cuts and sores, a sticky bandage of cobwebs.

Dunne began inviting her to sit with him in front of the small fire in the grate in his quarters before turning in for the night.

"The child needs a name," he said one evening. "Shall we call her Evangeline?"

The infant in Hazel's arms was gazing up at her. She lifted her up and kissed her nose. She saw the slope of Evangeline's nose, her large expressive eyes. The father, she thought, must've been handsome too. She shook her head. "No. There's only one of her."

Early the next morning, she took Evangeline's tin ticket on

its red cord from the shelf in the surgeon's quarters and made her way down to the orlop deck. Confronted by the now-unfamiliar stench, the sounds of women hacking and moaning, the over-whelming malaise and disquiet, Hazel nearly turned around. While living in it, she'd acclimated to it. But now, from the dis-tance of only a rope ladder, she felt so far removed from it that even a brief exposure made her heart palpitate.

The women in the bunks stared at her as she passed.

"Look at 'er, so fancy now, in the surgeon's quarters and all," one singsonged.

"Ye have to wonder if she shoved the poor girl over the side herself," said another.

When she reached her berth, Hazel felt for the loose floor-board and pried it open with her fingertips. Finding the sack, she sifted through the items: a few spoons, a dented cup, a pair of stockings . . . Ah—here it was. Evangeline's hand-kerchief. Tucking it in her pocket, she made her way back up the ladder.

In her room on the tween deck, she spread the small white square on the bed and ran a finger along the scalloped border, the initials embroidered in the corner, *C. F. W.* Cecil Frederic Whitstone. This flimsy cloth had been the locus of Evange-line's hopes and dreams, unrealistic as they may have been. Now it was all her daughter would ever have of her. Hazel placed the ticket on the handkerchief, thinking of the ruby ring that Evangeline had hidden in it—the ring that became the cat-alyst for her journey. She'd once told Hazel that her vicar fa-ther considered jewelry a vice; the only ornaments she'd ever worn were the ruby ring and this ticket on a red cord around her neck.

The first a marker of seduction, Hazel thought. The second its result.

Folding the ticket in the handkerchief and tucking it in her pocket, she thought about what Evangeline had said about the rings of a tree, how the people we love live on inside us, even after they're gone.

Ruby.

It wasn't a name Evangeline would've chosen. But to Hazel it was a way to mend a broken heart. To erase a false accusation. To reclaim a treasure.

Ruby. Precious girl.

A SHOUT CAME FROM HIGH in the rigging: "Van Diemen's Land!"

On the main deck, there was an excited rustling. The *Medea* had spent nearly four months at sea, through storms and suffocating heat and icy rain. The women were sick of each other and even sicker of the ship. They ran to the railing, but there was little to see. A distant smudge on the horizon.

Hazel made her way down the ladder to gather her things. She'd become adept at navigating the crowded deck and going up and down the swaying ladders with Ruby tied to her front. Thanks, in part, to the better food and clean bedding, Hazel was stronger, her eyes were brighter, her skin a little rosy. Even getting up twice in the night to carry Ruby to Olive's bed, she slept better than she ever had on the orlop deck.

Dunne was at his desk in the anteroom, writing in a ledger, when she knocked on the door and went in. "I'm glad you're here," he said, rising. "There's something we need to discuss. I have not yet filled out the birth certificate. If I state officially that you are Ruby's mother, you'll be permitted to visit her in the nursery at the prison. Would you want that?"

Hazel cupped Ruby's warm head in her hand. "Yes."

He nodded. "I'll note on the chart that you had an infection and cannot feed her, and she'll be given a wet nurse. Olive, if she agrees. You'll be allowed to spend your days with her, at least for a few months. Eventually they'll send her to an orphanage."

"An orphanage?" She held Ruby a little closer.

"It's protocol," he said. "But as her mother, you can claim her when you're released, if you wish."

Hazel thought of the women in the bunks, envious of her privileges. "What if someone tells the authorities I'm not the mother?"

"Why would anyone do that?"

"Have ye never felt jealousy, Dr. Dunne?"

"You saved this child's life, Miss Ferguson. I believe you've earned the right to call yourself her mother."

She couldn't help smiling. She had earned the right, hadn't she?

"At any rate," he said, "it would be a convict's word against mine."

Back on the deck a little while later, Hazel stood at the railing with Olive and her sailor, holding Ruby in her sling as the ship turned toward the harbor.

They sailed past whalers and a cargo ship and a litter of small boats. Dolphins dipped in and out of the water; white gulls with gray wings cawed overhead. A narrow strip of shoreline sloped into hills of multihued green, with glassy sheets—lakes, Hazel supposed—in the distance. Seals lounging on outcroppings of rock reminded her of the prostitutes who picnicked in Kelvingrove Park in Glasgow in the summer, hiking their dresses above their knees and fanning themselves with newspapers.

Above them, a square flag, half red and half white, fluttered on a mast in the breeze. "To warn the whole island that this vessel is filled with female incorrigibles." Olive's sailor grinned.

"Will ye miss him?" Hazel asked her.

Olive swatted him on the behind. "Parts of him, at least," she said.

FROM THE COVE where the *Medea* was anchored, Hazel could see the busy wharf, and behind it, a tall mountain covered thickly in trees. She watched from the railing as Dunne and two sailors boarded a small boat. Under Dunne's arm he carried the ledger in which she'd watched him write each day's account, along with a binder filled with the women's court records and other documents—including Ruby's newly filled-out birth certificate.

When the boat made its way back from the pier to the ship several hours later, it held two extra men who turned out to be the superintendent of convicts and a British soldier in a scarlet uniform.

Over the next two days, the convicts were called to a makeshift office on the upper deck where they were catalogued, examined for infection, and quizzed about their skills. They were told that many of them would be sent out daily from the prison on assignment to work in settlers' homes and shops as housemaids, cooks, flax spinners, straw plaiters, weavers, seamstresses, and laundresses. Others would work inside the prison. Insubordinates would be separately confined.

The superintendent began the assessments. When he called "Ferguson!" Hazel stepped forward.

He ran his finger down the ledger. "Height?"

"Five foot, one inch," the British soldier said, holding a measuring stick against her back.

"Build?"

"Slight," he said.

"Age?"

"Seventeen," Hazel said. Dunne had mentioned offhandedly a few weeks earlier that September had come and gone, and she'd realized that her birthday had, as well.

Freckled complexion. Oval head. Red hair. Wide forehead. Auburn eyebrows. Gray eyes.

"Literate?"

"Somewhat."

"Trade?"

Dunne stepped forward. "She has an infant, so it is my recommendation that she work in the nursery. She is quite . . . capable."

She raised her eyebrows at him, and he gave her a smile that vanished so quickly she was the only one to see it.

TWELVE HOURS LATER, as she stood on the main deck with the other convicts, Hazel gazed up at the moon, as yellow as a yolk in a cast-iron sky. By its light she could make out the phalanx of rowboats waiting to ferry the convicts to shore. The air was damp and cool. The women surged forward as the crew began loading them into boats. "Slow down, ye lot, or you're never getting off this ship!" the British soldier shouted. "No skin off my nose to keep ye here. A prison's a prison."

A light rain began to fall. After some time, Olive came to stand beside Hazel, and, without a word, reached for the baby. She'd learned to anticipate when Ruby was hungry, and often appeared at the door to Hazel's room just before she woke. Now Olive held Ruby in one arm and deftly unbuttoned her blouse with the other.

"I can't stop thinking about poor Leenie, tumbling over," Olive said, looking down at Ruby as she nursed. "I see her in this one's face and it breaks me heart."

After a few minutes, Dunne made his way over to them. He brought the Quakers' bundle, the needle and thread and Bible that Hazel had left in the surgeon's quarters. "I didn't know if you wanted these."

She shrugged. "I don't have much use for a Bible, to be honest."

"Maybe you'll find some use for this." He handed her his copy of *The Tempest*.

She looked at him with surprise. "It breaks up your set, Dr. Dunne."

"Perhaps I shall get it back one day."

"Ye do know where to find me," she said.

THE SKY LIGHTENED, washing everything in a grayish tinge. Rain fell steadily. From her seat in the rowboat, Hazel gazed back across the water at the ship. It looked small and ordinary from this distance—no longer the terrifying hulk that loomed over her when she'd seen it from the skiff in London. As she sat there, contemplating how far she'd come, she saw a wiry man in shackles being led down the ramp to the boats. Buck, she realized. Following them ashore.

She nudged Olive, sitting beside her. "Look who's out here."

"Should've murdered him when we had the chance," Olive said under her breath.

HAZEL'S LEGS WOBBLED WHEN SHE stepped out of the boat and onto the dock. She hadn't realized how accustomed she'd become to the rhythm of the waves until she was on solid ground, unable to find her footing. Afraid of losing her balance and dropping Ruby, she fell to her knees. All around her, women were doing the same.

By the time all 192 women and children had been ferried over and marched across the rickety causeway to the wharf, it was midmorning. Hazel looked at the gulls circling overhead, the fog wallowing on the sea behind them. Listened to the tide ramp against the shore, a low, rhythmic roar. A cool breeze came off the water, twisting up her skirt and winding between her legs. She tucked the blanket around Ruby and pulled her shawl tighter around her shoulders.

As they made their way across the slick cobblestones of the wharf, Hazel became aware of a strange whooping noise. A crowd of rough-looking men was moving toward them. Coming closer, they leered at the women, grabbing their skirts, waving hats in their faces, calling them names Hazel had never heard before, even on the streets of Glasgow.

"Look a' that flash bit o' mutton! . . . nasty bunters . . . stinkin' fish drabs . . . moon-eyed hens . . . dirty cracks . . ."

"Droolin' animals," Olive muttered, behind Hazel. "Can't abide that we're heading to prison instead of warming their beds."

The women shuffled along, looking down, trying to avoid the muddy puddles in the dirt road, pushing the men back with their elbows. Behind them, soldiers in scarlet uniforms carrying muskets on their shoulders stood watching. "Let's go, pick it up!" they yelled. The soldiers pushed the women roughly if they got out of line and pulled them to their feet if they tripped and fell, their hands lingering too long on waists and backsides.

Macquarie Street, the sign read just ahead. They trudged up a hill past brown government buildings and a brick church with a black dome and a three-faced clock, women moaning, children pleading, "How much longer? Where are we going?" Ruby, too, was fussing, hungry; Hazel tried to bobble her in the sling. Her own stomach rumbled. They hadn't been offered anything but hardtack in the darkness before they left. Spoiled by the real food she'd been eating lately, she'd turned up her nose. She regretted it now.

They passed two-story sandstone houses, small neat cottages, lean-to shacks that appeared to have been nailed together in a day. Roses twined up trellises and cherry trees bloomed in shades of pink. The morning air smelled peaty and fresh. Hazel gazed ahead at the high rocky bluffs of the mountain she'd seen from the harbor, the top of it clouding into sky. On either side of the road were trees with pinkish gray bark that reminded her of shorn sheepskin. She was startled to see birdlike creatures in a fenced-in garden that were taller than humans, with skinny legs and oblong bodies, strutting and pecking the dirt.

After some time, the long parade of women descended into a valley. A weak sun slipped from behind the clouds as they made their way past wooden shanties, a sawmill, a brewery. A group of green birds, massed as thickly as mosquitoes, whizzed through the air above their heads. The mud was deeper here, tamped down by the women at the front of the line but squishy nonetheless. It seeped through the seams of Hazel's shoes. All of this walking felt strange and unnatural after so many months at sea. Her legs ached and her feet were sore. She was thirsty and needed to pee.

Olive tapped Hazel's arm. "Look at that."

In a field about a hundred yards away, a cluster of large brown animals with deerlike faces and rabbity ears stood on their hind legs, staring at them. One turned and hopped off and the others followed, bounding after it like balls tipped from a basket.

"What in the world," Hazel breathed. This place was stranger than she'd dared to imagine.

As they marched forward, she became aware of a murmuring from the front of the line, and then, a few moments later, a terrible smell. She looked down: they were crossing a small bridge over a rivulet filled with sewage. Gray rats scurried in and out of the water.

Olive nudged her from behind. "Look up."

Straight ahead, in the shadow of the mountain, a windowless fortress rose from the earth. At the front of the line a soldier rapped on the huge wooden gate. When it opened, he barked at the convicts and children to form two lines. Slowly, they began to file inside.

A THIN, WHISKERED man in a blue uniform and a woman in a black dress buttoned to the neck stood near the far end of a desolate courtyard. Behind them, three women in shapeless prison garb swept the gravel. One, a woman with braided white hair, stopped her work and watched the new prisoners file in. When Hazel caught her eye, she put a finger to her lips.

Except for a clanging pot and the sound of someone chopping wood in the distance, the place was eerily quiet.

After the last woman entered, and the gate was closed and locked, the whiskered man stepped forward. "I am Mr. Hutchinson, superintendent of the Cascades Female Factory," he said in a high, reedy voice, "and this is Mrs. Hutchinson, the matron. As long as you are imprisoned here, you will be under our command." He shifted from foot to foot, speaking so quietly that the women had to lean forward, straining to hear. "Your personal effects will be taken from you and returned when you are released, unless they are deemed too foul, in which case they will be incinerated. Utmost cleanliness and submission are expected at all times. You will attend daily chapel at eight in the morning, after breakfast, and at eight at night, after supper. Lateness and absences will be severely punished. Profanity and smoking tobacco are even graver offenses. It is our belief that silence prevents disruptions and bad influences. Talking, laughing, whistling, and singing are strictly forbidden. If you break this rule, you will be punished."

Hazel glanced furtively around. The courtyard was damp and shadowed, pocked with puddles. It smelled of mold. The walls rose twenty feet around them. Ruby was whimpering. Her diaper sagged, sodden, and she needed to be fed.

"You'll be assigned to one of three classes, depending upon your sentence, reports of your conduct filled out by the ship's surgeon, and our assessment of your character. Assignables—those of you who are well behaved and presentable, and who possess a useful skill or ability—will be accorded the privilege of leaving the premises to work in free settlers' homes and businesses."

Olive poked Hazel in the back. "'Privilege,'" she scoffed. "To be worked like horses and treated like dogs."

"If you fail to perform your work, show signs of insolence, become intoxicated, or attempt to run away, this privilege will be revoked." The superintendent spoke in a monotone, his voice droning on. "Crime-class prisoners are employed at the prison, making and repairing clothing and working at the tubs in the washing yard. If you are found guilty of disobedience, profanity, obscenity, insubordination, sloth, or disorderly conduct, your hair will be sheared and you will be placed in a dark cell in solitary confinement, picking oakum until your sentence is served.

"If you become pregnant you may care for your infant for six months in the nursery before serving six months in the crime yard for the offense of unwed pregnancy. Older children will be sent to an orphanage. Mothers on good behavior may be permitted to visit on Sundays."

Though Hazel knew that mothers and children would be separated, most of the women did not. Their cries and exclamations filled the courtyard.

"Quiet!" the superintendent barked.

Ruby's whimpering turned into a wail. Olive whispered, "Should I feed her?"

Hazel pulled Ruby out of the sling and handed her over. "You'll be Ruby's nurse, then?"

Olive shook her head. "If I do, they'll make me a wet nurse. I can't be stuck to babies all day long."

When at last the superintendent finished speaking, the convicts queued for the midday meal, a hunk of bread and a pint of watery soup. Mutton, they were told, though Hazel tasted only fat and gristle. It was sharply sour, rancid. Despite her hunger, she spat it back in the bowl. For the rest of the afternoon, she stood with the other women in the drafty courtyard, jiggling Ruby on her hip, waiting to see the doctor. She watched as, one by one, they disappeared into a small brick house and emerged in gray uniforms.

"Show me your hands," the dour-faced doctor said when it was finally her turn. Hazel set Ruby on a wooden chair and held out her palms. Hands up, hands down. "Open your mouth." Looking at her papers, he raised a bushy eyebrow. "It says here your child needs a wet nurse."

She nodded.

"It's because you're too thin," he said irritably. "You convicts don't take care of yourselves, and others are forced to carry your burden. Who fed her on the ship?"

Hazel knew better than to implicate Olive. "A woman who sadly died."

"That's unfortunate." He made a note in her chart. "It is recommended that you work in the nursery. What are your skills?"

She hesitated. "I was a midwife."

"You delivered babies?"

"Yes. And I have some experience treating infants' maladies."

"I see. Well . . ." He sighed. "The ship surgeon's report is quite positive. And we are understaffed." Looking up from her chart, he said, "In the morning, you may walk with the new mothers and wet nurses. I'll make a note for you to assist in the birthing room as needed."

"Thank you." She picked Ruby up and held her against her shoulder.

"What are you doing?" he said sharply.

"I'm—I'm taking my baby."

"No you are not. We will transport this child to the nursery. You may see her tomorrow."

She felt her heart thudding in her chest. "She has always slept with me."

"Not anymore. You relinquished that right—indeed, any rights—when you committed your crime."

"But—"

"That will be all, convict." Stiffly, he held out his arms.

She hesitated. But what else could she do? She gave him the baby.

He took her as if he were handling a fireplace log.

With one last lingering look at Ruby, who was starting to fuss, Hazel was escorted from the room.

Across the hall, the matron, wearing a pair of long gloves, lifted the hair from the nape of her neck. "No apparent lice," she reported to a convict scratching notes. "Luckily for you, you may keep your hair," she said to Hazel.

After being sent to bathe in cold dirty water in a metal tub, Hazel put on her uniform—a coarse gray dress, dark stockings, and sturdy black shoes—and surreptitiously tucked Evangeline's handkerchief in her wide front pocket. The matron handed her a parcel containing another dress, a shawl, an apron, several shifts, another pair of stockings, a rough straw bonnet, and two folded rags. "For your monthlies. If you're of age," she said, adding, "Are you?"

"I have a baby."

"I would not have guessed." The matron shook her head. "Pity. A young girl like you."

AT SEVEN THIRTY, when the supper bell clanged, Hazel was so ravenous that the foul-smelling oxtail soup was almost appealing. She gulped it down and hurried to the chapel for the eight o'clock service, where she huddled on a crowded pew with the other convicts in the near darkness, listening to the chaplain harangue them as he banged his fist on the lectern. "Servants, you must obey in all things your masters; not with *eye service*, as *men pleasers*; but in singleness of heart, fearing God!" he shouted, spittle flying from his lips. "You of depraved and vicious habits, given up to debauchery and idleness, must be brought into habits of decency and industry!"

As the words washed over her, Hazel was reminded of the few times she'd dipped into St. Andrews Cathedral in Glasgow to get warm during Sunday morning services. Even at a young age, she'd bridled against all the talk of sin and depravity. It seemed there were different rules for rich and poor, and the poor were always blamed. They were told that only by confessing their sins would they triumph over illnesses, like typhoid, but the streets and water were filthy. And girls and women had it worst, she'd always thought. Mired in the mud, no way to get out.

When the sermon finally ended, the convicts were divided into groups of twelve and herded into cells filled with four rows of three hammocks. There was barely room to move. "You'll notice two buckets," the guard said. "One's drinking water and one's a chamber pot. You'll be smart to remember which is which."

The bare canvas hammocks crawled with fleas. The floor was sticky. The room smelled sharply of urine and blood and feces. When the door clanked shut, the women were in total darkness. Sitting on a moldy hammock, listening to the moans and coughs and sobs around her, Hazel thought only of Ruby, alone in the nursery. Was she wet? Was she crying? Hungry? It was the first night they'd spent apart. She felt bereft without the warm weight of her in the crook of her arm.

After changing into her nightshirt in the dark, Hazel pulled the white handkerchief from the pocket of her apron and unfolded it. She tied the red cord around her neck and tucked the tin ticket under her nightshirt, tracing the number with her finger: 171. If she couldn't be with Ruby at night, she would at least wear Evangeline's ticket. How strange that this visual marker of their incarceration had come to feel like something else: a memento. A talisman.

ROUSED FROM SLEEP BY THE clanging of a bell, the women dressed hurriedly in the dark and lined up in the chilly kitchen yard for gruel before sitting through another interminable sermon. By the time they emerged from the chapel, a queue of free settlers was filing in to the first yard to choose convicts for assignment. Hazel joined the group of new mothers and wet nurses waiting by the gate to walk to the nursery. It was on Liverpool Street, they were told, near the wharf.

Accompanied by a guard, the women reversed their trip of the day before, passing the high stone wall of the Cascades before turning left across the bridge over the stinking tributary and up the incline of Macquarie Street. Fog hung thickly over the top of the mountain above them, a false ceiling for an enclosed world.

Green lizards darted across the road in quick bursts. Royal blue birds swooped among the trees. As they tramped along in silence, Hazel marveled at the beauty of this new world: the flowering purple shrubs, the golden grass by the side of the road shiny with dew, the feathery gray scrub. She thought of her neighborhood in Glasgow, where she'd had to tread carefully along streets coated with a paste of coal particles and manure and stay alert to avoid rubbish thrown from windows. The cramped room she lived in with her mother, with its single clouded window that let in no air and little light, the dirt floor that turned to mud when it rained. The water in the River Clyde that was so lethal that most people, young and old, drank beer instead. How children as young as six worked in factories and mines and were sent out to steal for their parents, as Hazel had done.

Even so, her life in Glasgow wasn't all anguish and despair. There was plenty she missed. She'd loved navigating the wynds, the winding cobblestone streets that led to the shops in the West End filled with colorful scarves, leather gloves, bolts of shiny fabric. She'd loved picking at the flaky crust of a Scotch pie and feeling it melt on her tongue. Tatties and neeps and haggis, the rare treat of a trifle. The buttery sweetness of shortbread. Drinking chamomile tea laced with honey at the kitchen table on winter evenings, blowing into the steam to cool it. Her mother, she remembered, would put apples in an earthen jar with a sprinkle of cloves, a bit of sugar, some lemon peel, and a splash of red wine. After an hour in the fireplace it became a delicious mash that they ate straight from the jar with spoons.

Hazel felt a surprising surge of longing for her mother—and then, just as quickly, a spike of anger. She was here, in this terrible place, because of her. Hazel didn't think she could ever forgive her mother for that.

THE BUILDING THAT housed the nursery was dilapidated. Inside, the air reeked of vomit and diarrhea. Hazel made her way through a warren of tiny rooms, searching for Ruby. Infants lay three or four to a crib on soiled, flea-ridden bedding. Those old enough to crawl and walk peered out at her silently, like puppies in cages.

"Why are they so quiet?" she asked a guard.

He shrugged. "A lot are sickly. Some of them older ones were never taught to talk."

When Hazel found Ruby, in an upstairs crib, she, too, was unusually quiet. Hazel scooped her up and took her to the changing room. Her waste was a brackish green.

There were no doctors on the premises. No medicines or other supplies. Not even enough linens for bedding and cloths. All Hazel could do was hold the baby, so she did. Every now and then, Ruby whimpered. Hazel knew she was hungry, but no wet nurse was available. She would have to wait.

After about an hour, an exhausted-looking woman appeared in front of Hazel and took Ruby from her. Without a word, she swung her expertly under her arm and latched her on.

"Ye know what you're doing," Hazel said.

"I've had practice."

"How many babies do you feed?"

"Four, at the moment. Used to be five, but . . ." An expression flitted across her face. "They don't all make it."

Hazel nodded, her breath catching in her throat. "It must be . . . hard, sometimes."

The woman shrugged. "Ye get used to it. When my own wee bairn died, they gave me a choice. I could go to the crime yard for six months and wring laundry. Or I could do this."

After a few minutes, she pulled away and started buttoning her dress. Ruby twisted her head from side to side, opening and closing her mouth.

"She's still hungry," Hazel said.

"Sorry. This cow is dry."

At the end of the day, Hazel loitered by Ruby's crib, her throat closing up, her eyes brimming with tears.

"Please—let me stay with her. And help the others too," she begged the guard.

"You'll be reported missing and add years to your sentence, is that what ye want?"

All night, on her hammock, Hazel tossed and turned. The next morning, she was the first one up the hill, the first in the door at the nursery. Ruby was all right, but another infant in her crib, a boy, had died in the night.

"Where's his mother?" Hazel asked the guard when the body was taken away.

"A lot of 'em never show up," he said. "They prefer to serve their time in the crime yard and move on. Can't say I blame 'em."

Even many of the ones who did show up, Hazel noticed, were listless, blank-eyed and gray-faced, turned in on themselves. Some barely looked at their babies.

The boy who died would be buried in a children's cemetery at the corner of Harrington and Davey Streets, the guard told

Hazel, in a gumwood crate. They'd wait until the end of the day, in case there were more.

THAT EVENING HAZEL found Olive in the main courtyard with Liza, the crooked accountant, and some newfound friends. "Can we talk?"

"What d'ye need?"

Hazel got straight to the point. "Ye have to feed her, Olive."

"I told ye, I don't want to nurse six piglets."

"Ye can tell the doctor ye only have enough milk for one."

She shook her head. "I heard it's disgusting over there."

"Ruby'll die if ye don't."

"You're a regular Chicken Little, aren't ye, Hazel?" Olive shook her arms in the air in mock panic.

The women around her laughed.

"I'm begging ye," Hazel said, ignoring them. She took a breath. "Think of Evangeline." It was shameless to evoke their dead friend's name, she knew. But Hazel had no shame. "Babies die every day in that place, and they're dumped in a mass grave to rot. They're not even given a proper funeral."

Olive gave a loud, exasperated sigh. "Jesus, Mary, and Joseph," she said, rolling her eyes.

But the next morning, and each morning after that, when Hazel showed up in the courtyard, there Olive was, waiting with the other wet nurses and new mothers to walk to the nursery.

ONE DAY, WALKING beside Olive up Macquarie Street, Hazel spied a clump of sage by the side of the road and hurried over from her place in the line to pluck some leaves. As she was twining the leaves together and tucking them into her apron pocket, the convict behind her asked, "What're ye doing with that?"

Hazel turned around. It was the woman with the white braid she'd seen in the courtyard when they arrived. "I'll make a poultice," she said. "For rash."

"Ye know your milk is good for that," the woman said.

Hazel glanced at Olive, who snorted. "I suppose I'm a walking miracle cure."

This old woman was not a new mother or a wet nurse. "Are ye a midwife?" Hazel asked.

"I am. You?"

Hazel nodded.

"Working in the nursery isn't much of a prize for anyone, but I thought I could be of use. Most convicts in the birthing rooms and the nursery have no experience. I do."

Her name was Maeve, she said. Maeve Logan. She hailed from a landlocked part of Ireland called Roscommon. She'd always been outspoken, mouthy with complaint; some even accused her of being a witch, and maybe she was. Her landlord had died a day after she cursed him for starving his tenants. Though there was no evidence she had anything to do with it, she was charged with insurrection. Seven years. She'd been on Van Diemen's Land for four.

Over the next few weeks, while Olive was with Ruby, Hazel

began working with Maeve to improve conditions at the nursery. They boiled water to wash the linens and took them outside to scrub. They mopped the floors. To reduce fever, they bathed babies in water with lemon; for hives, they made a tea out of catnip. Maeve taught Hazel to identify local plants and showed her how to use them: Bark from the black peppermint tree could be brewed into tea for fevers and headaches. Sap from the white gum was good for burns. Juice from the hop bush plant soothed toothaches. Nectar from leatherwood flowers treated infections and other wounds.

Some of the native plants were dangerous—and dangerously tempting. In small quantities they produced a pleasant sensation, but if misused they caused hallucinations, or even death: yellow oil from the sassafras tree, the combination of ingredients that made up absinthe—wormwood, hyssop, anise seed, and fennel, marinated in brandy. Maeve pointed out a bush along the side of the road with fluted pale pink flowers hanging upside down. "Angel's trumpet. Beautiful, in'it? Eating these flowers makes your troubles go away. Problem is, too much will kill ye." She laughed. "It got its name because it's the last thing you'll see before ascending into heaven."

LIFE AT THE Cascades, Hazel learned, was all about waiting in line. The women queued for their daily pound of bread and pint of gruel for breakfast, their pint of mutton soup at midday, and their oxtail soup thickened with old vegetables for supper. They queued for chapel and queued for assignment. At Sunday muster, they queued in the second yard, facing the wall, to be roughly searched for contraband.

The prison had been built for 250 women and now held more than 450. There were only eight staff members, which meant both that the convicts got away with a lot and that they were punished severely if caught. Convicts smuggled in rum and wine traded for favors while on assignment. They buried tobacco and pipes, tea and biscuits beside the washtubs and behind bricks in the yard. The weaker prisoners—those who were small or sick, or had lost a child, or were depressed, or not right in the head—were overpowered by the strong, who stole their rations and anything else they could get their hands on. On the ship, as unpleasant as it was, convicts had only been punished if they caused a fight or disruption. Here, you could be thrown into the crime yard for the flimsiest of reasons: for picking up a heel of bread that had been tossed over the fence, for singing or bartering, for getting caught with rum.

A few of them escaped—or at least there were rumors. Two women supposedly used sharpened spoons to tunnel out of solitary. Another, it was said, tore her blanket into strips and knotted them to make a rope to scale the stone wall. But most women didn't risk it. They served their time quietly, hoping to gain their freedom before they were too old or sick to enjoy it.

One Sunday at muster the superintendent announced that an expansion was going to be built, a second crime yard with more than a hundred new cells, in two rows of double-tiered cellblocks. Two days later a work crew arrived, made up of male convicts from prisons all over the island. With men regularly in the factory now, the women had access to gin, rum, tea, and sugar, which they exchanged for favors and fresh bread baked in the cookhouse.

Olive took up with an unruly group of convicts who called themselves the Flash Mob. These women smuggled in grog, tobacco, tea, and sugar in coal bins or tied to brooms tossed over the walls. They paraded about in contraband silk scarves and pantaloons; they swore openly and drank until they were senseless. Defying the superintendent's orders, they sang bawdy songs in the full-throated voices of men and called to each other across the courtyard. They ridiculed the chaplain, jeering and gesturing as he passed: "Hey, Holy Willie, want some of this?" They got away with more than they were nabbed for, but even so, many of them drifted in and out of the crime yard, shrugging it off as a small price to pay for their revelry.

Olive and Liza, the crooked accountant from the ship, had become inseparable. They emboldened each other. Olive altered her uniform, trimming and tying and hemming it to show more cleavage and leg. Liza painted her lips with berry juice and rimmed her eyes with charcoal. They nuzzled each other's necks in the courtyard and pinched each other's backsides when the guards' backs were turned. By bribing a susceptible guard, they even managed to sleep together in the same bed.

One afternoon, when several dozen members of the Flash Mob were singing and dancing loudly in yard one, the matron arrived, flush-faced, to see what the commotion was about.

"Who is the ringleader?" she demanded.

Usually the Flash Mob fell silent when the matron showed

up, but this time they did not. They squatted on the floor, hooting and stamping their feet, chanting, "We are all alike, we are all alike, we are all alike."

"This is your chance to declare that you are not a member of a mob," Mrs. Hutchinson shouted. "Every one of you risks severe punishment!"

The women yelled and clapped and clacked their tongues.

In the chaos of the moment, Olive managed to slip out of sight. But nine convicts were sentenced to the crime yard for six months, with a month in solitary after that, and two of the instigators had years added to their time.

Hazel watched from a distance. She wasn't interested in getting away with anything. Her only goal was to earn her ticket of leave as early as she could for good behavior, like some women did, and make a new life for herself and Ruby, somewhere safe and free.

AT THE HEIGHT of summer, the sun was so hot that it burned the tips of the leaves on the trees and baked the dirt on Macquarie Street until it cracked. But deep in the valley, inside the high stone walls of the prison, it was gloomy and damp. The stone floors were often soupy and slick. When the rivulet overflowed, the entire place was ankle-deep in foul water. It was a relief to leave the premises each day, to walk to the nursery past picturesque cottages with neat picket fences and hills wheaten in the distance, dotted with sheep.

Over the weeks and months, the faces of the women walking to the nursery changed, but the numbers stayed roughly the same. New mothers joined the line; those whose babies were six months old were sent to serve their time in the crime yard. When Ruby turned six months old she was forcibly weaned, and Olive was discharged. Hazel was only allowed to stay in the nursery because of her skills in the delivery room and treating sickly infants. Knowing that the eyes of the overseer were always on her, she was careful to make the rounds, to hold and change the other children, but her heart kept tugging her back to Ruby as if tied to the baby by a string.

"What makes ye so special?" a loud, coarse woman in the hammock beside her said one night, back at the Cascades. "We're working our fingers to the bone, and ye get to sing to babies."

Hazel didn't answer. She'd never cared what people thought of her—it was one of the few benefits of having been underestimated for her entire life. Ever since she was old enough to know anything, she'd been preoccupied with survival. That was all. Just trying to stay alive. And now keeping Ruby alive. Nothing else mattered.

ONE MORNING, WHEN HAZEL ARRIVED at the nursery, Ruby was gone. She'd been taken to the Queen's Orphan School in New Town, the guard said, four miles away.

"But I received no notice," Hazel sputtered. "She's only nine months old!"

He shrugged. "The nursery's overcrowded, and another ship is arriving in a few days. Ye can visit 'er at the end of the week."

Every minute Hazel spent at the nursery reminded her that Ruby was alone. Worry lived inside her like a parasite, gnawing at her as she went about her days and causing her to wake, gasping, in her hammock at night. *Ruby, Ruby* . . . four miles away, in the hands of strangers. Her big brown eyes. Her high hairline and curly brown hair. Old enough to smile when she saw Hazel and pat her cheeks with her hands, but not old enough to know why she was alone, and what she'd done to deserve her exile.

Hazel could hardly hold another baby without crying. Before the week was out, she had requested a new assignment.

That Sunday Hazel stood with nearly two dozen convicts at the front gate of the Cascades to make the slow trek on foot to the orphanage. Some brought small gifts, toys and trinkets they'd bartered for or fashioned out of scraps, or clothing they'd sewn, but Hazel brought nothing. She hadn't known that she could.

The soft light of late morning washed over Mount Wellington. The air was cool and mild. Making their slow way to New Town, the women passed apple orchards, yellow marigolds, fields of wheat. Though it was a beautiful day, Hazel barely noticed. Her stomach was twisted in knots. All she could think about was Ruby.

They tramped up an incline. The large parish church flanked by two low buildings looked welcoming, with its pretty sandstone turrets and arches. But inside the rectory it was dark and austere.

One by one, the children were brought to their waiting mothers.

"Ma-ma," Ruby said, choking on the word. Her nose was crusted, and she had dark bruises on her arms and scabs on her knees.

"Ruby, Ruby, Ruby," Hazel whispered over and over.

The walk home was an agony.

The next morning, Hazel watched a new group of convicts stream in through the wooden gates of the Cascades, bedraggled and wide-eyed. She felt nothing but resentment toward them: more women fighting for food and hammocks and space. More babies crowding the nursery. More misery all around.

HAZEL WAS ACCUSTOMED to Glasgow's harsh winters. The apartment she'd shared with her mother was damp and drafty;

wind slithered under the front door and through cracks around the window frame. But the generally temperate weather in Van Diemen's Land had lulled her into thinking winter would be mild. The brutal cold, when it came, was a shock.

It was bleak and windy when Hazel joined the assignables in the courtyard for the first time one July morning. The cobblestones were slick with ice; the sky was white, mottled with gray, the color of dirty snow. The convicts stood like horses in two lines, stamping their feet. Their breath smoked the air. When the gate was opened, about a dozen free settlers entered, their thick coats and wool hats in marked contrast to the convicts' thin dresses and wraps.

Hazel's hair was neatly pulled back and her face washed. She wore a clean white apron over her gray dress, and a shawl over that. Maeve had told her that the more respectable-looking and polite a convict was, the nicer her placement. A fancy house didn't necessarily mean kinder employers, but it did mean better conditions. Sometimes there were even perks: extra rations, clothes, shoes. Perhaps a discarded toy or book she could give to Ruby.

The settlers strolled up and down the lines, asking questions: *What are your skills? Can you cook? Can you sew?*

Yes, sir. I was employed as a plain cook and housemaid.

I'm a farm servant, ma'am. I can wash and iron. Milk cows and make butter.

A plump older woman in a navy-blue dress, heavy overcoat, and fur cap paused in front of Hazel and moved on, making her way down the line. A few moments later she circled back. "What is your name, prisoner?"

"Hazel Ferguson, ma'am."

"I haven't seen you before. What was your past assignment?"

The woman had a haughty air. She'd probably never been a convict, Hazel thought.

"I worked at the nursery."

"You have a child?"

"A daughter. She's at the Queen's Orphan School now."

"You hardly look—"

Hazel told the truth. "I'm seventeen."

The woman nodded. "What are your skills?"

Hazel chewed her lip. No one wanted a nurse or a midwife, Maeve said; they didn't trust convicts for that. "I'm qualified to be a housemaid, ma'am. And a ladies' maid."

"You're experienced with laundry?"

"Yes."

"Ever worked in a kitchen?"

"Yes, ma'am," Hazel said, though she hadn't.

The woman patted her lips with two fingers. "I am Mrs. Crain, housekeeper to the governor of Hobart Town. The standards of my household are exacting. I tolerate no slackness or misbehavior. Do I make myself clear?"

"Yes, ma'am."

"I am only here today because I had to let the last convict maid go. Quite frankly, I would prefer not to use prison labor, but it can't be helped. There are simply not enough free settlers." Mrs. Crain lifted her arm, and the matron hurried over.

"This one should do all right, Mrs. Crain," she said. "We've had no complaints."

Hazel followed the housekeeper out onto the street, toward a horse-drawn open carriage with bright blue seats. Mount Wellington, looming above, was blanketed with snow.

"You'll sit across from me today," Mrs. Crain said brusquely. "Starting tomorrow, you will travel in a cart with the other convict maids before sunrise."

Hazel hadn't been in a proper carriage since she was six years old, visiting the seaside village of Troon, on the only holiday she'd ever taken with her mother. There'd been another person, a man, in the carriage. His breath had smelled of alcohol and he kept putting his hand on her mother's knee. Her mother had promised that she and Hazel would share crumpets and cream cakes at a tea shop and take long walks along the scenic shore, but as it turned out, Hazel spent a lot of time shivering on the windy beach alone while her mother and her new friend were "exploring the shops," as her mother put it.

One more disappointment. But the carriage was nice, as Hazel remembered.

Now she sat beside Mrs. Crain, trying not to shiver in her shawl.

The horses trotted briskly along Macquarie Street before turning down a long driveway lined with gum trees. They came to a stop in front of a stately sandstone building with two curving staircases that led to the front door. Hazel followed Mrs. Crain to the servants' quarters, where, she was told, she would change clothes before and after her shifts. Blue cotton dresses for the convict maids to wear hung on a pole; aprons, caps, clean undergarments, and stockings were folded on shelves. Mrs. Crain showed Hazel where to wash her face and hands before beginning work each day, and gave her a comb—which the convicts weren't allowed at the prison—to part her hair in the middle before tying it back and securing her cap on her head.

A convict maid must always be busy, Mrs. Crain said. She must not gossip or laugh loudly or sit down, unless she is mending clothing or polishing silver. "You are expressly forbidden from opening the front door; that is the butler's job," she said as she took Hazel through the house. "You may not talk directly to any member of the Franklin family or their visitors. You will use the back staircases and hallways. As much as possible, you must stay out of sight."

Two of the maids Hazel spoke with later in the morning offered a different sort of advice. Sometimes Sir John grabbed you when and where you least expected it, so you had to stay alert. Lady Franklin blamed anything that went wrong on the staff. Miss Eleanor was not very bright and could be demanding: once she insisted that a convict maid stay awake all night to hem a dress she might wear to a party. (And ended up wearing a different one.) They also told Hazel that the Franklins had taken in a native girl as a strange kind of experiment. She lived in the nursery. One of Lady Franklin's whims.

"What is the girl like?" Hazel asked.

"Seems lonely, poor thing. She had a pet weasel, but Montagu's dog ate it."

"A possum, I think it was," the other one said. "I'd heard that the natives speak only gibberish, but this one knows French as well as English."

"Maybe the clever ones can be trained," said the first. "Like dogs."

Hazel was curious about this child. She'd never seen a native; were they really that different? But she said nothing. She was not going to gossip, or ask questions, or otherwise jeopardize her new position. All she wanted to do was to hold on to her place in this household with both fists, to serve her time and get out.

OVER THE NEXT few weeks at the governor's house, Hazel acclimated to the routine. Just after dawn, as soon as she arrived, she hurried to the shed behind the kitchen outbuilding to get wood for the hearth. After lighting the fire, she filled two big black kettles with water from the cistern in the kitchen and hung them on iron hooks above the flames. When the cook arrived, Hazel and another convict maid went through the main building, lighting fires in the breakfast room and the drawing rooms so that they'd be warm when Sir John and Lady Franklin emerged from their chambers. The maids swept the foyer and front steps and veranda and set the breakfast table for the family, then crossed the courtyard to the kitchen to make toast and scoop butter into tiny dishes. While Lady Franklin and Sir John were eating, the maids went into their bedrooms and knelt in front of the fireplaces, sifting cinders and cleaning the grates, then opened windows and aired feather beds, turning and plumping them. (How different these downy mattresses were from the hard canvas hammocks at the Cascades!) They dusted picture frames and chair upholstery and shelves filled with books. They carried the family's chamber pots to the outdoor privy behind the stables, where they emptied them and rinsed them with well water.

When the Franklins had finished breakfast, Hazel cleared the table and took the dirty dishes to the kitchen to wash in the stone sink, using care not to chip the delicate teacups. Now she could eat her own breakfast: slow-cooked oats, with tea and toast and honey.

Then she cleaned the candlesticks and trimmed the lamps.

She refilled kettles all day long. Twice a day, she knelt in front of the kitchen hearth, sifting the cinders and cleaning the grate.

Once the morning chores were done, Hazel's work varied by day. On Mondays she cleaned the kitchen, scouring the pantry and the drawers and scrubbing the stone floor on her hands and knees, trying her best to stay out of the way of the cook. Tuesdays and Wednesdays were washing days. She pulled linens off the beds and collected clothing from each room, removing buttons and ribbons before dunking them in large copper urns. Three convict maids fed the washing through the mangle before setting it out on the drying lawn or hanging it on the clothesline. Inevitably, they got soaking wet. They had to change into dry uniforms before hanging clothes in the frigid air.

Sir John's white dress shirts, half-frozen on the line, looked like an army of ghosts.

Bedrooms were cleaned on Thursdays, the dining room and drawing rooms on Fridays. Once a week, on Friday mornings, three maids filled the Franklins' bathtubs with warm water brought by the stable boys, adding oil scented with lavender.

For the first time in her life, Hazel had a steady job. The house was orderly and warm and redolent of lilacs. She liked the sounds of the courtyard: the horses clip-clopping up the drive, the crowing roosters and grunting pigs. She liked the smells of the kitchen: fruit pies cooling on the counter, lamb roasting slowly on the turnspit. She would have considered herself quite fortunate were it not for the fact that Ruby languished in the orphanage, captive behind its walls.

Every day, in the midafternoon, Hazel was permitted to take a quarter-hour break in the kitchen and wrap her hands around a cup of tea sweetened with jam. She'd begun collecting pieces of rags from old clothing and sheets too worn to be used by the Franklins, and in quiet moments she pulled out the scraps she'd cut into small, uniform pieces, and worked on a quilt to bring to Ruby.

ONE FRIDAY MORNING Hazel was cleaning the grate in the green drawing room when Lady Franklin came in with Mrs. Crain. Hazel gathered her brushes quickly and stood to leave, but Lady Franklin waved at her and said, "I'd rather you finish your work than leave ashes on the hearth."

The two women sat at a small round table, discussing plans for the day. A tinker was stopping by with his cart; Mrs. Crain would need to gather utensils that needed fixing. The display cases in Lady Franklin's quarters required dusting: could Mrs. Crain assign that task to a convict maid? Oh—and she should inform the cook that Sir John had invited another guest to the dinner this evening. "He'll need a place card. His name is ... let's see ..." Lady Franklin peered at the paper in her hand through a magnifying glass. "Caleb Dunne. *Doctor* Caleb Dunne."

Hazel, startled, dropped her brush. Mrs. Crain shot her a glance.

"Sir John met him at a luncheon a few days ago," Lady Franklin was saying. "He recently moved to Hobart Town and set up a private practice. Apparently, he is unmarried. It's a pity I can't think of a young lady with whom to pair him."

"Miss Eleanor?" Mrs. Crain suggested.

"Goodness no," Lady Franklin said with a small laugh. "Dr. Dunne is an intellectual. He was educated at the Royal College of Surgeons. Seat him next to me."

When, later that day, Hazel encountered Mrs. Crain in the courtyard, she offered to stay late to help with the dinner. Mrs. Crain shook her head. "We only employ free settlers at evening events. Lady Franklin doesn't want the convict maids on the property after dark."

The next morning, Hazel casually inquired about the party, but all she managed to glean was that the roast was overdone (according to the cook), and the guests polished off the last of the sherry (according to Mrs. Crain). Neither of them had a word to say about Dr. Dunne.

ON SUNDAYS, STANDING in front of the wooden prison doors with the other mothers, waiting to walk to the orphanage, Hazel marveled at their dogged calmness, and her own. They trudged the four miles in silence, in the cold, waiting for an hour or more to be let in, then spent two hours trying desperately to make up for a long week of absence.

We should be rending our clothes, she thought. We should be howling in the streets.

The warden at the orphanage watched the mothers carefully, afraid they might grab their children and try to escape. He wasn't wrong to be worried. Every fiber of Hazel's being longed to snatch Ruby and flee. She spent hours, days, thinking about it. It was thrilling to imagine doing so. To imagine doing anything.

Hazel recited rhymes from Mother Goose that she remembered from childhood—stories about a boy who tumbled down a hill and cracked his skull, and London Bridge going up in flames, and a man who went to bed and bumped his head and couldn't get up in the morning. One-year-old Ruby babbled along; the verses delighted her. But Hazel couldn't help thinking about the heartache and calamity lurking beneath the words. A bleeding child, a bridge on fire, a man dying in his bed. *When the bough breaks, the cradle will fall, / And down will come baby, / Cradle and all.*

The rhymes seemed ominous to her now. They felt like warnings.

Each week, Ruby was paler and more withdrawn. No longer did she cling to Hazel when she arrived or cry piteously when she left. She had become almost indifferent, examining Hazel coolly under her eyelashes. Within several months she was treating her like a benevolent stranger. She allowed Hazel to play pat-a-cake with her, but seemed to barely tolerate it, like a cat struggling against an embrace it didn't invite.

One Sunday, Ruby's upper arms were bruised; another week red strips were visible across the backs of her legs. "Did someone hurt you?" Hazel asked, searching her eyes. Ruby pulled away, discomfited by Hazel's intensity and too young to understand what she was asking. When Hazel complained to the warden, he tilted her chin and said, "No marks appear on children who don't deserve them."

Hazel's heart was a wound that wouldn't heal.

What was happening to Ruby that she didn't know about?

Everything.

OLIVE WAS STANDING just inside the main gate at the Cascades, waiting for her, when Hazel returned from the governor's house one evening. Hazel hadn't seen her in a while. She'd been sentenced to three weeks in the crime yard for profanity and insubordination—no surprise.

Lifting her chin toward a group of women across the courtyard, Olive said, "Ye need to be careful. Some think you're getting special treatment. First the surgeon's quarters on the ship, then the nursery. Now the governor's house."

Hazel nodded. She knew Olive was right. Other convicts had it much worse. Their employers drank, worked them to the bone, beat them. How many women were pregnant now with babies they didn't ask for? She'd seen women do almost anything to avoid their assignments, including sucking on copper pipe to turn their tongues blue and upset their stomachs so they'd be too sick to work.

"Just watch out for yourself," Olive said.

MATHINNA

It is increasingly apparent the Aboriginal natives of this colony are, and have ever been, a most treacherous race; and that the kindness and humanity which they have always experienced from the free settlers has not tended to civilize them to any degree.

—GEORGE ARTHUR, Governor of Van Diemen's Land,
in a letter to Sir George Murray, Secretary of State for War
and the Colonies, 1830

THE WINTER, IT SEEMED TO Mathinna, was lasting forever. The courtyard still wore a thin crust of frozen mud that
crackled when she walked across it. Her bedroom was un-
heated; the cold seeped deep into her bones. She crept around
the main house, searching for a place to get warm. Shooed out
of the public rooms by Mrs. Crain, she sought refuge in the
kitchen.

Slicing a pile of potatoes, nursing a tumbler of sugar-laced
gin, Mrs. Wilson talked about her long-ago life in Ireland—
how she'd once been a cook on a fine estate on the outskirts of
Dublin but was unjustly accused of stealing linens to sell on the
street. Her employer had recently returned from Paris with a
steamer trunk of linens, and Mrs. Wilson was under the admit-
tedly mistaken impression that she was doing the household a
favor by disposing of the old ones. No one would've caught on
if the napkins weren't monogrammed; it was her mistake not
to remove the stitching. She genuinely believed that her ladyship would've been pleased to know that her old cloths—rags,
really—were being put to good use.

"She'd be pleased to know the cook was pilfering her linens?" the newest convict maid said with a smirk, ironing a sheet in the back of the room.

Mrs. Wilson looked up from her potatoes. "Not *pilfering*. Disposing of."

"Ye pocketed the profits, yes?"

"It wasn't her ladyship turned me in," she huffed. "The butler had it in for me. My mistake, I suppose. Pushed off his advances one too many times."

The maid smiled at Mathinna. "What d'ye suppose Lady Franklin would do if I had a mind to lift a table runner or two?"

"Don't be getting high and mighty. You're one to talk. Silver spoons I hear it was," Mrs. Wilson said.

"Just one spoon."

"All the same."

"At least I'll admit to my crime."

Mathinna looked back and forth between them. She'd never heard a convict maid challenge the cook. The maid gave her a wink.

"I'm just teasin' ye, Mrs. Wilson. Something to do on a cold gray morning."

"You're lucky to be here, Hazel. Ye should know your place."

The maid held up the sheet and folded it by the corners. "There's none of us lucky to be here, Mrs. Wilson. But your point is taken."

"I should certainly hope it is," Mrs. Wilson said.

A FEW DAYS later, when the cook was doing her daily rounds at the abattoir and the dairy shed and the henhouse, the new maid came into the kitchen again with a basket of linens. She lifted a black iron from a row of irons on a shelf and set it flat on the glowing coals of the fire. Then she fell into a chair. "Ah, me feet." She sighed. "It's too long a walk from there to here."

Mathinna was standing close to the hearth, warming her hands. "I thought they brought you in a cart."

"They're making us walk now. Say it's good for us. Bloody torturers."

Mathinna looked over at her. Hazel was as slight as a sapling, with wavy red hair pulled back under a white cap. Like the other convict maids, she wore a blue dress and white apron. "Have you been at the Cascades for long?"

"Not really. This is my first outplacement." She rose from the chair and wrapped a rag around her hand, then went to the fireplace and lifted the iron out of the coals. "What's your story, then?"

Mathinna shrugged.

The maid licked her finger and touched the iron's flat surface before carrying it to the ironing board and setting it on a trivet. "Where're your real mum and dad?"

"Dead."

"Both of 'em?"

Mathinna nodded. "I have another father, though. He's alive, I think. On Flinders."

"Where's that?"

She drew a line upward in the air with her finger. "A smaller island. Up north."

"Ah. That's where you're from?"

"Yes. It's a long way from here. I came on a boat." Nobody had asked Mathinna these questions. Or any questions, really. Her answers felt strange in her mouth—they made her realize how little she'd told anyone about herself. How little most people wanted to know.

"You're alone then, aren't ye?" the maid said. "I mean, there are plenty of people here"—she gestured vaguely around them—"but no one's really looking out for ye."

"Well . . . Miss Eleanor."

"Really?"

No, not really. Mathinna shook her head. She thought for a moment. "Sarah used to, I guess. But one day she stopped coming."

"From the Cascades?"

Mathinna nodded.

"Hmm. Dark curly hair?"

She smiled. "Yes."

The maid sighed. "Sarah Stroup. She's in solitary. Caught drinking."

"Oh. Does she have to pick tar out of rope?"

"How d'ye know about that?"

"She said it's a horrid job. A good reason not to murder someone."

"Well, she didn't murder anybody. But they need that rope for the ships. They'll use any excuse to make ye do it." Plucking a napkin out of a basket at her feet, the maid said, "I could try to get a message to her, if ye want."

"That's all right. I don't really . . . know her."

The maid smoothed the napkin on the ironing board. "It's hard being here. I'm from far away too. Across the ocean."

"Like Miss Eleanor," Mathinna said, thinking of the globe in the schoolroom, that wide expanse of blue.

She gave a dry laugh. "Miss Eleanor was on a different kind of ship."

Mathinna liked this maid Hazel. She was the first person she'd met in this place who talked to her like a real person. Nodding at the jumbled linens in the basket, she said, "I could help you fold those."

"Nah. It's me job."

Mathinna sighed. "I've finished my schoolwork. There's nothing else to do."

"I'll get in trouble if I let ye." Hazel pulled a pile of napkins out of the basket. "But . . . maybe later I could teach ye something. Like how to make a poultice. For if ye skin your knee." She pointed at the bundled dried herbs hanging from the ceiling. "Ye start with mustard. Or rosemary. And grind it up with lard, maybe, or soft onions."

Mathinna gazed up at the hanging herbs. "How do you know how to do that?"

"My mother taught me. A long time ago."

"Is she still alive?"

Hazel's face clouded. She turned back to the linens. "I wouldn't know."

TO CELEBRATE THE advent of spring, it was decided that the Franklins would host a dinner dance in the garden. In a short visit to the schoolroom, Lady Franklin announced that Mathinna's studies would be suspended while Eleanor taught her to dance. "If she is to attend, she must learn to waltz, and do the Scotch reel, and the cotillion, and the quadrille," she told Eleanor.

"But we're memorizing times tables," Eleanor said. "She's right in the middle of them."

"Oh, for goodness' sake. Learning to dance will matter more to her social prospects than times tables, I assure you."

"You mean *your* social prospects," Eleanor said under her breath.

"I beg your pardon?"

"Nothing. What do you think, Mathinna? Would you like to learn to dance?"

"I know how to dance," Mathinna said.

Eleanor and Lady Franklin looked at each other.

"This is different," Eleanor said.

For the first few days, Eleanor sat with Mathinna at the table in the schoolroom, mapping steps on a chalkboard, with *X*s for each participant and arrows designating where they should go. Then the two of them began practicing together in the yard behind the henhouse. Eleanor was too self-absorbed, not to mention intellectually incurious, to be a particularly inspiring schoolteacher. She plodded from subject to subject as if checking items off a list. But these same traits, as it turned out, made her an excellent dance instructor. Color rose to her cheeks and her eyes sparkled as her every step was admired and emulated. She looked so pretty as she turned! And as soon as she tired of one dance, she could move to another. She was playful and persistent, happy to spend hours demonstrating the moves.

Out in the courtyard one sunny afternoon, Eleanor conscripted a stable boy, two convict maids, two idling buggy drivers, and the butcher to practice with them. Upon learning that the head butler, Mr. Grimm, had taken up the fiddle, she persuaded him to saw a jaunty tune. The air was mild and the atmosphere convivial, and it was thrilling to touch another person's hand in public without fear of rebuke.

To Mathinna, the dances, with their choreographed footwork, were as logical as mathematics: the careful fitting together of a sequence; a series of movements that, done in the correct order, produced the intended result. Once she mastered them, it was as if her body moved on its own. Soon enough she was helping Eleanor corral the other dancers into their proper places. She loved the pace of the songs that drove them forward: *one–two–three–four, one–two–three . . . step-step-step-step, stepstepstep . . .*

"She will be ready in time, won't she?" Lady Franklin asked Eleanor a week before the party.

"She will. She's learning."

"Her dancing must be a triumph, Eleanor. Otherwise, what's the point of including her?"

The big event was four days away, then three, then two. Mathinna watched as a crew of workers erected a large sailcloth tent in the side garden and laid the wooden dance floor. As soon as the tent was up, half a dozen convict maids were enlisted to decorate it, overseen by Lady Franklin, who did not so much as lift a teacup but could spy a misplaced chair or wobbly table leg at five hundred paces.

The music played in Mathinna's head on a continuous loop. In bed at night she moved her toes—*one–two–three–four, one–two–three*—and tapped her fingers to the rhythm. She danced instead of walked, held her head a little higher and fluttered her arms in the air as she went about her day. The household staff was friendlier to her than they'd ever been. They smiled when they saw her coming down the corridor, complimented her footwork, quizzed her about the differences between a waltz and quadrille.

Only Mrs. Crain, passing through the courtyard as Mathinna practiced her steps, offered a critique. "Remember that these are formal English dances, Mathinna," she said with a frown. "You must control your native flourishes."

THE SCARLET DRESS still fit Mathinna around the waist, but it was too short, and the sleeves were tight.

She stood on a stool in the center of the room while Hazel sat on the floor, pinning the skirt around her. "Bloody dark in here," she muttered. "I can barely see what I'm doing."

Mathinna looked down at the part of Hazel's russet hair, the smattering of freckles on her forearms. A round metal pendant around her neck glinted in the weak amber light. "What's that?" she asked, pointing.

"What?" Hazel touched her throat. "Oh. I forget I have it on. Turn around, I need to pin the back. It belonged to a friend."

Looking over her shoulder at her, Mathinna said, "Why doesn't your friend wear it?"

Hazel was silent for a moment. Then she said, "She's dead. This is all I've left of her. Well, except . . ."

"Except what?"

"Oh . . . this and that. A handkerchief." Pushing Mathinna gently off the stool, Hazel said, "We're done. Let's get it off ye and I'll hem it before I leave."

As Hazel stood behind her, undoing the buttons, Mathinna said, "I used to wear a necklace that my mother made out of green shells, but Lady Jane took it."

"Ach. I'm sorry. Shall I steal it back for ye?"

Mathinna shook her head. "You'll end up in solitary like Sarah Stroup, and I'll never see you again either."

THE DAY OF THE DANCE was unseasonably humid. By late morning the golden wattle on the tables under the tent were drooping in their vases. By noon a hazy scrim enveloped the trees. Sir John was the one who'd decided the party should be held outdoors, Lady Franklin complained to whoever would listen. Easy for him to insist, since he had nothing to do with the planning! In the late afternoon she sent two convict maids into town to find paper fans—"Three dozen. No, four"—and directed Hazel to prepare a lavender bath in her chambers.

At six o'clock, when the first guests arrived, the air was still thick with heat. Lady Franklin, consulting with the musicians and Mrs. Crain, decided to push back the time of the dancing until half eight, when surely it would be cooler.

Sir John, sleek as a wombat in a form-fitting tuxedo, met Mathinna and Eleanor—wearing a custard-colored, scoop-neck taffeta gown that matched her hair—on the stone apron of Government House. "Don't we all look smart! Lady Franklin insists that I dance with you, Mathinna. Are you ready to be the center of attention?"

She was. All day she'd felt a flutter of anticipatory pleasure.

Now her skin gleamed with rose balm and her hair was oiled and sleek, tied in velvet ribbons that matched the black ribbon around her waist. She wore new red stockings and spit-polished shoes. Her scarlet dress had been ironed with starch, and the full skirt swished around her legs.

"I can't imagine she'll embarrass you, Papa, as long as she remembers the steps," Eleanor said.

"My only worry is that I may embarrass *her*," Sir John replied with a gallant flourish. "Frankly, I'd thought my cotillion days were behind me."

Offering his elbows, he escorted them to the tent, where Eleanor joined a gaggle of young ladies in sherbet dresses and Mathinna and Sir John were quickly surrounded by a throng. Some of the partygoers were familiar to Mathinna, but many were strangers. She greeted the people she recognized with a smile and tried to ignore the ones staring at her, mouths ajar.

A dowager with cake-icing hair tottered over. "I heard you acquired a savage, Sir John, but I hardly believed it. And here it is—in a ball gown!"

A dozen heads pivoted toward Mathinna like a school of fish toward a heel of bread. Feeling herself flush, she took a deep breath and looked at Sir John. He gave her a wink, as if to say that the woman's rudeness was merely part of the game.

"It is a *she*, Mrs. Carlisle," he corrected the dowager, "and *she* is called Mathinna."

"Does it—*she*—understand us?"

"Indeed. In fact, I would say that she probably comprehends far more than she lets on. Isn't that so, Mathinna?"

She knew what Sir John was asking her to do. He wanted her to astonish them. With a regal nod, she said, "*Vous serez surpris de voir combien je sais.*"

Gasps and a smattering of claps.

"Extraordinary!"

"What did she say?" Not everyone spoke French, of course.

"I believe it was, 'You'd be surprised how much I know,'" said Sir John, looking around with a self-satisfied grin. "She's cheeky, this one."

"Charming," the dowager said. "Where did you find her, exactly?"

"Well, it's quite a story," Sir John said. "On a trip to Flinders Island we spotted her cavorting around a campfire, with no shoes and barely any clothes. A pure primitive."

"Fascinating. And here she is, in a satin dress!"

"I can't help showing her off. Say a few more words in French, Mathinna," Sir John said.

Say a few more words in French, Mathinna. All right, then, she would. "*Bientôt je te danserai sous la table.*"

Sir John wagged his finger. "No doubt you *will* dance me under the table, my dear. She has been practicing, and I have not!"

"She appears quite comfortable with you," a woman mused.

He inclined his head in agreement. "Natives are surprisingly capable of forming attachments."

"I must say, I am impressed," the dowager said. "To have rescued this savage from a life of primeval ignorance—and to have given her an appreciation of art and culture—is a tremendous accomplishment. Almost as great, perhaps, as conquering the Arctic."

"And nowhere near as dangerous," Sir John said.

The dowager arched an eyebrow. "That remains to be seen."

When Sir John was distracted by a pile of cakes, Mathinna slipped away and wandered through the crowd. Someone handed her a small goblet filled with a golden liquid, and she took it with her as she made her way toward the far corner of the tent, near the dance floor, where the musicians were setting up their instruments: a small piano, an accordion, a fiddle, a harp, a wide shallow drum. Watching them warm up, chatting among themselves with easy familiarity, she felt an aching loneliness.

As she took a sip from the glass, her throat filled with molten fire. After a moment the heat subsided, leaving a sweet, warm taste in her mouth. She took another sip. Then drained the glass.

"ARE YOU READY, *ma fille?*" Sir John said, bowing to the ground in a showy display of formality. Lightly he took Mathinna's hand in his white-gloved one for the Grand March. Partygoers began flocking to the dance floor two by two, falling in line behind Sir John and Mathinna like Noah's animals as they circled the large wooden dance floor, the ladies as colorful and fragrant as freesia, the men as sleekly tailored as pigeons.

Mathinna put her shoulders back and her chin up. Here she was, the girl in the portrait in her red satin dress.

The first dance was a quadrille, one of her favorites. Following Sir John's lead, she executed each move fluidly, her footwork light and precise as she glided around the floor. *One–two–three–four, one–two–three, step-step-step-step, stepstepstep.* But the joy she'd felt in mastering the dance was gone. At the round tables just beyond the perimeter, people chattered behind their fans, exclaiming and pointing, but she ignored them. (She was two-dimensional, after all. Impervious to stares and whispers.) Circling her, Sir John whispered, "You are making quite an impression, my dear. You know that, don't you? Twirl! Show them what a lady you've become."

Taking small steps in time to the music, the girl in the portrait turned, the scarlet skirt billowing around her. As she and the three other ladies in her group came together in the middle, it meant nothing to her that two of them only pretended to touch her hands.

Between dances—as was the custom—accompanied by a jaunty piano tune, Sir John and Mathinna made a show of visiting the other dancers, pantomiming conversation and laughter. She widened her eyes and stuck her chin even higher in the air, imitating Lady Franklin's obsequiousness when dignitaries from London came to stay. Sir John, who seemed to recognize the mimicry, observed her with bemused delight.

After a few dances, his face became alarmingly flushed. He kept blotting his forehead with a handkerchief, attempting to stanch the sweat that trickled down his neck, dampening his collar. Eleanor, dancing beside them, looked concerned. At the end of a quadrille, she took her father's hand. "Let's rest, shall we?"

"I'm fine, daughter dear!" he protested as she guided him to an empty table. "I don't want to foil your chances with that eligible bachelor."

"It's all right," she said. "Dr. Dunne may be handsome, but he's a bit of a bore. He keeps going on about convicts' rights."

"Then, by all means, use me as an excuse to evade him." Sir John sank into a chair. "Tell your mother you forced me off the dance floor."

"Stepmother. And she should thank me," Eleanor said tartly. "At least someone is looking out for you."

MATHINNA, PARTNERLESS NOW, stood beside a wooden tent pole watching Noah's animals line up for the Scotch reel. Spying another goblet of that golden liquid on a silver tray, she took a sip, then swallowed it quickly, feeling the heat slide down her throat all the way to her stomach.

The music began with a merry fiddle. The women turned, their skirts flouncing up as they circled their partners. As the tune grew louder and more insistent, the women clapped in time to the fiddle while the men hopped in the air, snapping white-gloved fingers. Watching the pale-skinned, pastel-hued party-goers from a distance, Mathinna saw something clearly for the first time, as if through a lifting fog. Yes, she could pose as the girl in the portrait, wearing a pretty satin dress and ribbons in her hair; she could master the steps to the quadrille and the co-tillion and the Scotch reel; she could speak English and French and curtsy like a princess. But none of it would be enough. She could never be one of them, even if she wanted to. She would never belong in this place.

Well, maybe she didn't want to belong.

Her head felt fuzzy, as if she'd been spinning in a circle and stopped to catch her breath.

Slowly, slowly, she began to sway from side to side. She felt the music seep through her soles, the percussive snap of the fiddle like the beat of a drum. Her feet moved lightly under her dress, her small steps mimicking the dancers' exaggerated ones. She felt the rhythm inside her gathering force, rising from her toes to her thighs to her gut to her shoulders and up through her arms to the tips of her fingers. Closing her eyes, she felt the warmth of a long-ago campfire on her legs, saw the orange glow of it through her lids. Heard Palle brush his hand across a drum skin and begin to shush out the rhythm as the Palawa elders chanted to the tempo and a spray of muttonbirds rose into the sky.

Moving faster now, Mathinna arched her back, responding to the music with her entire body. She remembered things she thought she had forgotten: Droemerdene leaping and turning through the night sky, Moinee dancing across the land, down toward the ground and up to the stars, rocking and swaying, hunching and whirling. An ecstasy of movement, an obliteration of sadness. A celebration of life, hers and all of theirs: her mother's, her father's, Palle's, Waluka's, those of the elders she didn't remember and the sister she'd never met . . .

The music dwindled, then stopped.

Mathinna opened her eyes.

The entire party, it seemed, was staring at her. As her senses sharpened, she heard the tinkle of silver on china. A shrill laugh. Ladies huddled in groups, whispering behind fans. Eleanor stood alone, her face a rictus of disbelief.

Mathinna smelled rose water, and under it the tang of vinegar. The strong perfume of the golden wattle. The raisiny whiff of liquor on her own breath.

Lady Franklin was marching toward her, a smile frozen on her face, spots of red high on her cheeks, like a painted doll. Coming to a halt, she leaned down and hissed, "What—on earth—was *that*?"

Mathinna looked into her eyes. "I was dancing."

"Are you trying to humiliate us?"

"No," she said.

"You are clearly intoxicated. And have . . . I don't know"— Lady Franklin was so close that Mathinna could feel her vibrating with rage—"reverted to your natural savage state."

"Perhaps, my dear," Sir John said, coming up behind his wife, "it's best to let the wretched girl be."

Mathinna looked at Lady Franklin, with her wattlebird neck and red-rimmed eyes, and Sir John, moist and disheveled in his too-tight tuxedo. The two of them seemed like strangers to her, both terrifying and grotesque. She blinked swiftly to keep from crying. "*Peut-être*," she said.

Lady Franklin sighed. She raised her fan, motioning for Mrs. Crain. "Tell the band to begin again, and take this girl to her room," she told the scowling housekeeper. "The sooner we forget this unfortunate incident, the better."

BUT NOBODY FORGOT.

Almost imperceptibly, at first, things were different. The next morning Sir John did not summon Mathinna for his morning constitutional. From the schoolroom window, she watched him stroll through the gardens, his hands behind his back and head down, Eleanor by his side.

The tea-drinking ladies came and went; Mathinna was not asked to join them in the parlor. Eleanor left for a six-week trip to Sydney without saying goodbye.

Mrs. Crain informed Mathinna that from now on, especially with Eleanor away, she would no longer be served breakfast in the nursery but would instead take all her meals in the kitchen outbuilding with the cook.

"I hear ye caused quite a scandal," Mrs. Wilson said to Mathinna as she ladled cooked oats into a bowl. "Dancing like a primitive, were ye?" She looked around to be sure no one else was listening, then whispered, "Well, I think it's grand. They thought they'd mold ye in their likeness, didn't they, with a few French lessons and some fancy petticoats. But ye are who ye are. They can build their fancy houses and import their china teacups and dress in silks from London, but they don't really belong here, and deep down they know it. They don't understand a damn thing about this place, or you. And they never will."

ONE DAY MATHINNA awoke to find that Sir John and Lady Franklin had departed for a holiday in the riverside town of Launceston, a two-day journey, and that she would be staying at Government House in the care of a houseguest, a Mr. Hogsmead, from Sussex.

Mr. Hogsmead was imposingly tall, reed-thin, wore a pince-nez, and appeared to have little interest in anybody other than one particularly buxom convict maid named Eliza, whom the entire household observed coming and going from his chambers at all hours of the day and night.

With the Franklins gone, there was little for the staff to do. When Mrs. Wilson discovered a group of convict maids lolling on barrels and gossiping in the courtyard, she directed them to remove every last pot and ladle from the shelves and scrub the kitchen with lye and vinegar. The stable boys washed out the horse stalls and scoured the carriages; the maids aired linens and polished candlesticks to a gleam.

Without a routine or schoolwork, Mathinna existed in a strange purgatory. She wandered the property, forlorn and forgotten. Nobody seemed to realize that she was alone—or if they did, they didn't give it much thought. She lingered in the kitchen with Mrs. Wilson, hung upside-down from a branch of the gum tree in the far corner of the garden, played with Eleanor's collection of marionettes. She ate when she felt like it, which wasn't often. She didn't bathe. Sometimes she visited the cockatoo, desolate in its cage, squawking its mournful refrain. *Kee-ow, kee-ow.*

At night in her bedroom, dark as a tomb, Mathinna listened to the rustling of the trees outside her boarded-up window and the creaky lament of the gray galah birds, and curled into a ball, trying to evade the loneliness that crept under the covers and nestled in beside her. After a few days she took to sleeping in Eleanor's room, with its tall windows overlooking the garden. Eleanor would be horrified if she knew, but she didn't, did she? Each morning Mathinna slept in longer; it became harder and harder to pull herself out of bed. When she did emerge, in late morning, she spent hours on the upholstered window seat, staring out at the weepy fronds of the blue gums, listening to the warble of the magpies.

Perhaps Lady Franklin had been right—a view of the outdoors did make her melancholy.

No. She was melancholy already.

One rainy afternoon, Mathinna slipped into Lady Franklin's curio room and gazed at her father's ochre-and-red patterned spear and the skulls gleaming white in the gloom. Her mother's shell necklaces pinned to a board behind glass. The portrait Mr. Bock had painted of her in the red satin dress. In the entire time she'd been with the Franklins she had never seen another brown-skinned person. She looked down at the backs of her hands and turned them over to look at her palms. She thought about the tea-drinking ladies and their prurient questions. The dance-party guests and their horrified stares. Why wasn't it obvious before? She was just another piece of the Franklins' eccentric collection, alongside the boiled skulls and taxidermied snakes and wombats.

A marionette in a pretty dress. A cockatoo in a gilded cage.

In the courtyard she unlatched the door to the wire cage and reached inside. Despite her aversion to it, she felt a strange kinship with the poor creature—separated from its own kind, at the mercy of people who didn't even try to understand it. When she lifted it out, it was as bulky and lightweight as a hen. Its ashy feathers were silky soft. The bird allowed her to carry it to the trees just beyond the garden and set it on a branch, where it stared at her with its head tilted, seemingly confused. *What are you doing with me? Kee-ow.*

She turned and went back to the house.

Several hours later, when she returned, the cockatoo was gone. She wondered whether it had flown into town or into the bush, and whether it would ever come back. She wondered what would happen if she tried to leave, herself. Would anyone even notice? Maybe not.

But where would she go?

EARLY MORNING. SHE winced into the light. Thick-headed, ears clogged and aching, throat so sore it was hard to swallow. She lay in bed all day, floating in and out of sleep, feeling like a muttonbird burrowed in a hole. Sunlight thinned and faded as she stared at the pink-flowered canopy above her head. Her throat was parched but she had no water. She felt hollowed out with hunger, but too weak to move. After a while she dozed off again, waking in a fever in the dark and tossing off her blankets before drifting back to sleep.

When she woke she was shivering, her teeth chattering. Daylight, gray this time. Rain pattering the mullioned windows. She thought of Flinders, of how the rain thrummed the roofs of the cottages. The smell of sweet grass through the open doorway, babies swaddled in wallaby skins, her mother singing, her father puffing on his pipe, blowing smoke into the gloom. Her memories drifted, changing shape. Now she was running, running through the wallaby grass on a brilliantly sunny day, up the hill to the spiny ridge, her face tilted to the sky, the sun warm on her eyelids . . .

A FAINT KNOCK at the door. A voice. "Mathinna? Are ye in there?"

She opened her eyes, closed them. Too bright. Lemony. Midmorning, perhaps. *Yes.* She cleared her throat. Croaked, "Yes."

The door opened. "Good lord," Hazel said. "I knew something was wrong."

HAZEL BROUGHT MATHINNA lamb broth, tea made from sassafras leaves, and a paste made of ground fenugreek seeds for her phlegmy cough. She made her gargle with salt water. She brought a pot filled with lukewarm water that she dipped towels into before wringing them out and placing them on Mathinna's forehead and chest to cool the fever.

Feeling a trickle of water down her cheek, Mathinna opened her eyes. She looked up into Hazel's face: the smattering of orange freckles, ginger lashes, her clear gray eyes.

"Mrs. Crain sent us back to the Cascades," Hazel told her. "She said we're not needed while the Franklins are away. But I knew I should come back. I had a feeling." Leaning closer, she tucked in the blanket. The disk she wore around her neck swayed against Mathinna's cheek.

Mathinna reached up and touched it.

"Is it bothering ye?"

"I don't mind. I was trying to see what's written on it."

Hazel held it out. "It's a number. One seventy-one. They made us wear these on the ship. So if any of us went missing, they'd know it."

Mathinna nodded. "Did your friend go missing?"

"Well, she went overboard. So I guess she did." Hazel removed the spongy cloth from Mathinna's forehead and put her hand where it had been. "Fever's down. Shut your eyes." Draping another cloth on her forehead, she gave Mathinna a long look. "I'll tell ye a secret. Just before she died, my friend had a baby. A girl. Ruby. She's mine now. They've taken her to the Queen's Orphan School, but I'll get her back when I earn my ticket of leave." She traced the blunted edge of the disk with her finger. "It's a bad place, that orphanage."

"I know," Mathinna said. "My sister died there."

"Did she?" Hazel gave a long sigh. "I'm sorry."

"It was before I was born."

Hazel shook her head slowly. "Ruby has to survive. I don't know what I'll do if she doesn't."

After Hazel left the room, Mathinna closed her eyes. She thought of all the people she'd lost. The sister she never knew and her long-dead parents. Her stepfather, Palle, standing on the ridge on Flinders as she sailed away. Did he think of her? Did he worry? She wished she could let him know that she was all right, but she had no way to reach him. And besides, she didn't know that she was.

MATHINNA WAS SITTING IN THE kitchen outbuilding one morning, a week after the Franklins returned from Launceston, practicing times tables on a slate, when Mrs. Crain appeared in the doorway. "Good morning, Mathinna. Lady Franklin requests your presence in the red drawing room."

She looked up, heart thumping in her chest. Lady Franklin had not requested her presence since the dinner dance. "What does she want with me?"

Mrs. Crain pursed her lips. "She did not say. And it is not for you to inquire." She would not meet Mathinna's eyes.

The brocaded draperies in the drawing room were closed. The oil lamps cast strange shadows. Mathinna had to squint to make out the figure of Sir John, standing at the bookcase with his back turned, hands clasped behind him, motionless as a gargoyle. Lady Franklin sat in a chair, a book of maps open in her lap.

"Come in, come in. Mrs. Crain, you may stay. This won't take long." She motioned Mathinna forward with an impatient flutter of her fingers. Closing the atlas, she said, "How are you, then? Well enough?"

The question allowed only one response. "Yes, Lady Franklin."

"How do you occupy yourself these days?"

"She was studying mathematics when I found her, madam," Mrs. Crain reported.

"Ah. Good for you, Mathinna. I wouldn't have expected that, in Eleanor's absence."

"I have nothing else to do," Mathinna said sulkily. She'd never spoken to Lady Jane in such a tone, but there seemed little point in niceties now.

Lady Franklin didn't seem to notice. She gave a light laugh. "Boredom is a great motivator, I always say. You know, Mathinna, there are those who believe that higher learning is beyond the grasp of your people. Perhaps you are proving them wrong. Of course, there are certain . . . limitations to what can be taught and the progress one might expect to make. No doubt it has been as frustrating for you as it has been for us. Certainly we have tried . . . twice." Addressing her husband's back, she said, "Would you like to participate in this conversation, Sir John?"

Without turning around, Sir John said, "I would like for you to get on with it."

Mathinna stared at his back. She thought of their early morning strolls. She thought of the cockatoo. *The two of us don't speak the same language.*

Lady Franklin clasped her hands together. "Mathinna, in a few months' time we—Sir John and I, with Eleanor, of course— will return to London. Sir John has been recalled. And . . . after much thought, and discussion with our family physician, we have reluctantly decided that it will be better for you to remain here. For your health."

So. It was happening. They were abandoning her. In a way, it was a relief to know for sure. Even so, Mathinna felt a spike of anger at the flimsiness of the excuse. Where had they been when she was lying in bed, sick and alone? The Franklins had taken her from the only home she'd ever known, and she had not complained; she'd done everything they'd asked of her. But she had mattered to them only as an experiment. Now that the experiment had failed, they were done with her. She wanted them to squirm a little, at least.

"My health?" she said. "I am much better, ma'am."

"Nonetheless, your bout of pneumonia is cause for concern. Dr. Fowler has concluded that you have a weak chest. Which is best treated in temperate climates like this one."

"Dr. Fowler has not examined me."

Abruptly Sir John pivoted to face them. He cleared his throat. "It is scientific fact that Aborigines are constitutionally disadvantaged in colder regions."

"I'm afraid it's true," Lady Franklin said. "England is no place for a native."

"It's cold here sometimes," Mathinna said.

Lady Franklin's neck was splotchy. "This is not up for debate. Our decision has been made."

Mathinna gave her a steady look. "You are getting rid of me because you think I am wild, like Timeo."

Lady Franklin slid her eyes toward Sir John.

He turned back to the bookcase.

Mathinna lifted her chin. "When will I go back to Flinders, then?"

Lady Franklin gave a heavy sigh. "We are making arrangements for your care and will let you know in due course what has been decided. Now, Mrs. Crain, you may return Mathinna to her mathematics. I must begin to plan our voyage."

"JUST LIKE THAT!" Mrs. Wilson exclaimed, snapping a finger. "Back to England! And now all of us is wondering will the new governor keep the staff or dismiss us all? I've half a mind to find employment elsewhere and let them feed themselves for the next two months."

Hazel was crushing herbs with a pestle. "Your mistake was imagining they ever gave ye the slightest thought." Turning to Mathinna, she asked, "What will become of ye, then?"

"I'll be sent to Flinders."

Mrs. Wilson grimaced and shook her head. "I don't think so. The Queen's Orphan School, I heard. Maybe it's a rumor."

ONE MORNING AFTER breakfast, several weeks later, Mathinna returned to her room to retrieve a book. When she opened the door, she stepped back in surprise. The room was filled with light. She went over to the window and looked out at the garden, and, beyond it, the grove of gum trees and sycamores. She rubbed the edge of the window frame, feeling the holes where the nails had been. Turning around, she surveyed the room. Everything else appeared normal. Her books were on the shelf. Her bed was as she'd left it, neatly made. She pulled open the top drawer of her dresser.

Empty.

Then the second drawer, and the third.

She opened the wardrobe. All of her clothes were gone except for the red dress, which hung forlornly on a hook.

"Yes, my dear, today is the day," Mrs. Crain said, her voice falsely cheerful, when Mathinna tracked her down in the main dining room. "We've packed a nice steamer trunk with all your shoes and dresses. The wallaby skin you came with is in there too. And you'll find a mince pie and an apple in that old rush basket. The driver will be here soon, so you might want to hurry along and say goodbye to . . . well, to whomever you wish."

"Where are Lady Franklin and Sir John?"

"Out, I'm afraid. A previous commitment. But they said to tell you that . . ." For the first time, Mrs. Crain seemed to fumble over her words. "Well, that they feel certain that this decision . . . this next step . . . is the right one. For you, and for them. For all of us, frankly. And that we must rise to meet the challenges ahead with . . . with fortitude."

When Mathinna left the dining room and went out onto the stone apron of the driveway, she encountered a wooden cart with open sides holding a small trunk and her rush basket. The driver, wearing a patched jacket, slouched against a wheel. Seeing her, he nodded. "There's certainly no mistaking ye. Ready?"

"You're here for me?" she said with surprise. She'd never ridden in a cart.

"You're the only black girl here, ain't ye? Going to the orphan school?"

Mrs. Wilson had been right. She felt a chill in her bones.

"There's a plank in the back," he said, sensing her trepidation. "Ye don't have to sit on the straw."

"Oh." It was difficult to swallow. "I—I was told I'd have time to say goodbye."

He shrugged. "Take your time. I'm in no hurry to get back to that place."

Hazel was in the far courtyard, hanging clothing on the line. When Mathinna told her she was leaving, she dropped the damp clothes into a basket. "Now?"

"There's a cart out front."

"A cart." Hazel shook her head.

"They're sending me to the orphanage." Mathinna felt her heart constrict as if it were being squeezed. "I'm . . . I'm scared."

"I know ye are," Hazel said with a sigh. "But you're a strong girl. It won't be so bad."

"You know it will," Mathinna said in a quiet voice.

Hazel's eyes met hers. She did. "I come on Sundays to see Ruby. I'll try to find ye."

"They won't allow it, though, will they?"

Hazel cocked her head. Then she nodded toward a barrel. "Sit there for a minute. I'll be right back."

Mathinna sat on the barrel, gazing up at the gum trees with their stocking-cap leaves and straggly white flowers, the clouds beyond like spun sugar. A parrot alighted on a bush near her and cocked its head, its eyes as dark as seed. Just as suddenly, it rose into the air, a flash of red against the sky.

"I have something for ye." Hazel was beside her now, on the barrel. "I'm going to slip it in your pocket." She sat closer, and Mathinna felt a tug on her apron. "Put your hand in."

It was . . . tiny shells. Strung together. A big clump of them. She looked at Hazel.

"All three necklaces. Yes, I nicked 'em. I doubt Lady Franklin will notice. Anyway, I don't care. They belong to ye." Reaching for Mathinna's hand, she said, "There's something I want to tell ye."

Mathinna looked down at her brown hand in Hazel's pale freckled one. They were almost the same size.

"My friend—the one who died—taught me a trick to play in your mind when you're troubled. Ye think of yourself as a tree, with all the rings inside. And every ring is someone ye care about, or a place you've been. Ye carry them with ye wherever ye go."

Mathinna remembered what her mother had said about thinking of yourself as the thread of a necklace, the people and places you treasure as the shells. Maybe Wanganip and Hazel were saying the same thing: that if you love something it stays with you, even after it's gone. Her mother and her father and Palle . . . the spiny mountain ridge and the white sand beach on Flinders . . . Waluka . . . the sister she never knew. Hazel, even. Each a separate shell. All embedded in the rings.

Maybe she would always be alone and apart. Always in

transition, on her way to someplace else, never quite belonging. She knew both too much and too little of the world. But what she knew, she carried in her bones. Her mother's love. The shelter of her stepfather's arms. The warmth of a campfire. The silky feel of wallaby grass against her shins. She'd seen a strip of land from the open ocean and learned to rig a sail. Felt the shapes of different languages in her mouth and worn a dress of scarlet satin. Posed for a portrait like the daughter of a chieftain that she was.

She felt her fear unspooling like a tight fist opening. It was as if she'd been standing on a precipice and suddenly tipped forward. There was no point in feeling afraid. She was already falling, falling through the air, and her future, whatever it held, was rushing up to meet her.

HAZEL

Beautiful as it was, it was sown in blood, as indeed we may say of the whole civilized structure of this island.

—OLINE KEESE, *The Broad Arrow: Being Passages from the History of Maida Gwynnham, a Lifer*, 1859

WITH THE FRANKLINS' DEPARTURE DATE approaching, Hazel's days were now spent packing linens into cedar chests, wrapping china in rags, cataloguing silverware and figurines, and filling wooden crates.

The convict maids were told that their employment would end when the Franklins embarked. The new governor might or might not use labor from the Cascades. It was often a surprise to newly arrived British gentry that convicts, not even ex-convicts, would be working in their homes, with convictions ranging from vagrancy to murder. But free-settler labor came with its own problems. You had to pay them, for one thing, and unlike a captive labor force, if they decided to walk off the job there wasn't much you could do to stop them.

"CONVICTS ARE ONLY permitted to visit their own children," the warden at the Queen's Orphan School told Hazel when she inquired about Mathinna. "Even that is a privilege."

"But I was her maid at Governor Franklin's residence," she said, stretching the truth only a little.

"That is irrelevant."

"I promised I'd visit. To make sure she's all right."

"If you continue to argue, you may be barred from seeing your own child as well."

She tried one last tack: "I told the Franklins I'd keep an eye on her."

"Unlikely. Besides, Lady Franklin was here only a few days ago," the warden said with a dismissive wave.

Hazel was stunned. "She was? For what reason?"

"She didn't say. Who knows, perhaps she'd . . . reconsidered. At any rate, the girl had so reverted to her natural savage state, in such a short amount of time, that Lady Franklin chose to leave without seeing her."

"What do ye mean, her 'savage state'?"

The warden shook his head, clucking his tongue. "It is a mistake to attempt to civilize the natives. The Franklins meant well, no doubt, but the result is a creature who possesses both the natural belligerence of her race and a rather unnatural precocity. Within the space of only a few days here she had become quite ungovernable. We had to separate her from the general population."

"But she is only eleven years old."

The warden shrugged. "It is a pity, but we had no alternative."

SEVERAL SUNDAYS LATER, when Hazel was waiting with a group of convict mothers at the front gate of the Cascades to begin their walk to the orphanage, the matron pulled her aside.

"The superintendent needs to see you at once."

"But I'm going to visit my daughter."

The matron didn't reply; she simply turned toward the superintendent's quarters. Hazel hesitated. But she knew she couldn't disobey.

Inside his office, Mr. Hutchinson stood behind his desk. "We received an anonymous letter, Miss Ferguson, informing us that you are not who you purport to be."

Her mind raced. Her head felt light. "Sir?"

"You are not the mother of the child you claim as your own."

Hazel stopped breathing. "But ye have—ye have the birth certificate." Her voice came out as a croak.

"Indeed we do. So we undertook an inquiry. The convicts and sailors we spoke with said that at no point during the crossing did you appear to be with child. A convict with whom you were frequently seen"—he moved his glasses down his nose as he consulted the sheet on the table in front of him—"a Miss Evangeline Stokes, was, in fact, due to give birth. And . . . where is . . ." He rifled around the desk. "Ah, yes. The death certificate. She was murdered, apparently. There was an investigation, and . . . yes, here it is. A crewman, Daniel Buck, was charged with the crime. He was confined on the ship and later sentenced to life in prison. You, Miss Ferguson, gave testimony as a witness." He thrust the report toward her across the desk. "Is this your name?"

It was her name. She nodded.

"Did you not testify to what you saw?"

"Yes." She bowed her head.

"Did you not report that you were present in the room when Miss Stokes gave birth to"—he consulted the sheet—"a 'healthy female'?"

Hazel couldn't speak. She stood before him, trembling.

"Well, prisoner?"

"I did," she said quietly.

He set the report on a stack of papers. "The evidence is undeniable. You claimed the child in order to receive preferential treatment, to be allowed to stay with the infant instead of being sent out on assignment."

Her heart was oozing now, dripping into a puddle. "I did it to save the baby's life."

"Did you nurse this child, prisoner?"

"No, sir, but—"

"Then you cannot claim that you saved her life. The woman—women, I suppose—who nursed her have more of a legitimate claim to her than you do."

"But sir—"

"Do you deny these charges?"

"Please, let me explain."

"Do you deny them, prisoner?"

"No, sir. But—"

The superintendent held up his hand. He looked at the matron, and then back at Hazel. "You are hereby sentenced to three months' imprisonment in crime class, a fortnight of which will be spent in solitary confinement."

"But . . . my daughter—"

"As we have established, the child is not your daughter. Your visiting rights are revoked."

Hazel looked tearfully from the superintendent to the matron. How could this be happening?

Two guards grabbed her roughly by the upper arms and dragged her past the group of women she'd been standing with only a few minutes earlier, now staring at her open-mouthed.

"Please," she blurted, "tell my daughter . . ." Her voice trailed off. Tell my daughter . . . what? That I'm not really her mother? That I might never see her again?

"Tell her that I love her," she wept.

IN THE CRIME yard, the matron handed Hazel a spool of yellow thread and a needle and instructed her to embroider the letter *C*, for "crime class," on her sleeve, the hem of her petticoat, and the back of her shift. Hazel sat on a barrel and bent her head over the task. It was hard pulling the thread through the coarse fabric, and she kept pricking her fingers. When she was finished, the yellow thread was smudged with blood. The matron motioned for her to stand. Two guards held Hazel's arms while a third pulled out a large pair of scissors.

"Use care with this one," the matron said. "Cut it cleanly."

"What does it matter?" the one with the scissors said. "It's only to be mixed with clay for bricks."

The matron fingered Hazel's thick, wavy hair. "I think it can be salvaged for a wig. Titian hair is in fashion these days, you know."

THE SOLITARY CELLS were at the back of the crime yard, separated from the rest of the yard by a stone wall. The guards gave Hazel one sour-smelling, flea-ridden blanket and let her into a narrow cell with a grated open window above the door that let in a weak filtered light. They dropped a heavy bucket on the floor filled with oakum, a caulking compound used to plug holes in ships. Oakum was made of hemp rope, one of the guards explained, fused with tar and wax and crusted with salt. Hazel's task was to separate the strands by loosening the coils, to unpick the fibers and toss them in a metal bucket. "Ye best get to work. If ye don't unravel five pounds of this a day, you'll be beaten with a rod," he said.

The other guard tossed a heel of moldy bread on the floor. "If you're standing when we open the door in the morning, you'll be let out in the yard for a few minutes," he told her as they left. "If you're lyin' down, you'll be left in here all day." They locked her inside with a skeleton key.

The cell was as cold and deathly quiet as a tomb. Shivering in her shawl against the stone wall in the darkness, Hazel pulled the greasy blanket around her shoulders. She heard the *thwack* of hammers and the echoey voices of male convicts in the next yard, working on the prison expansion. Smelled the residue of waste in the bucket in the corner, the mold creeping up the walls, her own monthly blood. She rubbed the oval disk around her neck, tracing the numbers with her finger: 1–7–1.

She thought of Ruby in the dormitory at the orphanage, waiting in vain for her to arrive. She thought of Mathinna, isolated in some dismal room. Evangeline as she fell to her death—a glimpse of gown, arms flailing in the air.

She'd been no good to any of them.

Hazel banged her head against the wall. She wailed and sobbed until a guard rapped on the door of her cell, telling her to quiet down or he'd make her quiet down.

IN THE MORNING, frost dusted her blanket. When she heard the clang of a bell and the clacking of locks being undone, she struggled to stand.

The cobblestones in the courtyard were treacherous with ice. Her vision was blurry, her limbs stiff and achy, her feet unsteady as she plodded back and forth.

For the rest of the day she sat in the darkness of her cell picking oakum. As her cold fingers worried the rope, she tried to view the task as a puzzle rather than a punishment, a way to endure the minutes. *This goes here, that goes there.* A way to escape the torture of her thoughts. But she could not escape them. Could not stop thinking of Ruby, alone in her bed, wondering why her mother hadn't come. Hazel seethed like a kettle on a low flame, picking at the oakum, picking at the question of who betrayed her. Which of her fellow inmates was so jealous, so vindictive, that she would ruin the life of a child?

Her hands cracked and bled. Salt seeped into the cuts; they felt as if they were on fire. She tried to manage the pain, as she'd taught women in labor to do: to think of it as a part of her, as much a part of her as her limbs. Without the pain, she could not complete the task. She needed to listen to it, breathe through it. Be alert to its ebbs and flows. Dwell inside it.

At the end of the day, a guard arrived to weigh her bucket. "Five pounds," he said. "Just."

SOMETIMES SHE MADE a sound just to hear a sound. Smacked the wall. Flicked her finger through the water bucket. Hummed to herself. Maybe she could drown out the noises in her head, the fear and loneliness and self-recrimination.

A person could go crazy. People did.

She remembered things she thought she had forgotten. She muttered lines from *The Tempest* she'd memorized on the ship.

I was the man i' the moon when time was.

You may deny me, but I'll be your servant / Whether you will or no.

Hell is empty / And all the devils . . .

I wish mine eyes / Would, with themselves, shut up my thoughts.

Even the nursery rhymes she'd sung to Ruby, the ones that made her shudder: *Ring a ring o' roses . . .*

Sometimes, on the way to assignment, or in their hammocks

at night, the convict women sang a dirge that Hazel had considered maudlin. But now, in her dark cell, she sang it loudly, wallowing in self-pity:

I toil each day in grief and pain
And sleepless through the night remain
My constant toils are unrepaid
And wretched is the Convict Maid.
Oh could I but once more be free
I'd ne'er again a captive be
But I would seek some honest trade
And ne'er become a Convict Maid.

She ran her ragged fingernails down her arms. She didn't even have the satisfaction of seeing the blood. She smelled it, though, and felt it slick on her skin. She thought, as she often did, about her mother pushing her out on the street to pick pockets. She thought of all the times her mother had sent her out to steal rum, or something she could trade for rum.

That final time she'd stolen for her mother: the silver spoon.

How could any mother do that to her child? Hazel's anger was a hot coal burning a hole in the center of her chest. In the dark, in the cold, she stoked it, feeling its glow.

When the guard opened the door the next morning, she saw him flinch at the sight of her arms through the threadbare shawl. She looked down at the red crusted streaks, then gazed at him and smiled. Good. See my pain.

"You're only hurtin' yourself, lassie," he said, shaking his head.

THE FIRST TIME her mother was too drunk to help a woman in labor, when Hazel was twelve, she knew what to do. She'd always been a quick learner. "Nothing gets past ye," her mother said—not necessarily a compliment. It was true; once something was in her head, she didn't forget. For years she'd accompanied her mother to the homes and hovels of women about to give birth, because if she didn't, she'd be left at home alone. She'd paid close attention when her mother concocted pastes and potions, noting which herbs to crush with which liquids, how to make a salve or a tonic or a cure. Her mother allowed her to stay in the room, to fetch the water and grind the herbs. She grew to tell the cries apart and to anticipate the most welcome cry: that of the newborn.

Alone with that frantic pregnant woman, Hazel boiled rags and made her comfortable, showing her how to breathe and calming her fears. She told her when to push and when to stop. She lifted the slippery newborn onto its mother's stomach and cut its umbilical cord, then taught the woman to nurse.

A boy, it was. Named Gavin, she remembered, after his no-good father.

That was the day Hazel knew she would be a midwife. She had the touch, like her mother.

Sitting in the darkness now, prying apart strands of rope, she thought about all the convicts in other cells, each stewing in her own heartache and misery. This place was filled with women who'd had wretched childhoods, who'd been used and deceived, who felt unloved. Who were bitter and spiteful and couldn't let

go of their wounded feelings, their outrage at having been betrayed. Who couldn't forgive. The truth was, Hazel could stoke
her own hot coal until the day she died, but what good would it
do? Its warmth was scant.

It was time to let go. She was no longer an angry child. She
didn't want to carry that burning coal around anymore; she was
ready to be rid of it. Yes, her mother had been selfish and irresponsible; yes, she sent her out onto the streets to steal and
turned her back when she was caught. She also taught her the
skills that would save her.

The guard, heartless bastard, was right: Hazel was only
hurting herself.

AT THE END of the fourteenth day, when the cell door opened,
Hazel was crouching in a corner. She rubbed her tar-gnarled
fingers and blinked into the light. "It's like the den of a fox in
here," the guard said, hauling her out by an arm.

WHILE PREFERABLE TO SOLITARY, LIFE in the crime yard was its own version of hell. Hazel joined a line of convicts hunched over stone washtubs along the walls in the gray winter light. The work was endless. Not only were they responsible for scrubbing the prisoners' clothing; they washed all the clothing and linens for the ships and the hospital and the orphanage. With broomsticks, they fished the sopping linens out of a tub of warm water and dunked them in a tub of rinsing water and then a tub of cold water—three heavy lifts. Standing ankle-deep in the water that overflowed from the tubs, they fed the linens through a mangle, two rollers and a hand-turned crank. Another group hung wet items on half a dozen clotheslines stretched across the center of the yard. Water pooling in the yard quickly turned to mud.

The women were drenched from morning until night. They shook with chills. Their oakum-ravaged fingers stiffened in the water and bled on the coarse linens. They were not allowed to speak; mainly they communicated through facial expression and gesture. Locked inside stone cells at night for more than twelve hours, they huddled together against the frost like mice in a drain. Twice a day they were berated by the chaplain in a small, dark chapel, separate from the other convicts:

Upon the wicked he shall rain snares, fire and brimstone, and an horrible tempest: this shall be the portion of their cup.

The earth shall quake before them; the heavens shall tremble: the sun and the moon shall be dark, and the stars shall withdraw their shining.

Some of the women gave in to despair. You could see it in their eyes: a smoky haze. They stopped thrusting their bowls forward or trying to secure a space at the tubs. Every few days one of them was discovered unconscious, collapsed in a heap. When the guards came with food, they'd drag the body to a corner of the courtyard by the heels, leaving it for hours, sometimes days, before carting it away.

The only way to get through this, Hazel saw, was to just . . . let go. She couldn't think; she only needed to react. If she thought too much she would be paralyzed with dread, and that wouldn't do her any good at all.

Hazel tried not to think of Ruby, alone at the orphanage. She focused her attention on the sopping laundry, the stains and spots, the bar of lye soap in her hand. Warm water, rinsing water, ice water, mangle. As soon as she finished one piece, she started another. She did not retort when provoked by the guards. When she needed to move, she did so stealthily, like a cat. At mealtimes she wended her way toward the gruel without drawing attention. She stayed as quiet as she could. This, she found, was the trick: you didn't have to react to each little thing. You could just exist. Let your mind simmer over a low fire.

ONE MORNING, A month after arriving in the crime yard, Hazel looked up from the washtub to see Olive coming toward her. She sat back on her heels in surprise.

Olive grinned. "Ahoy."

"What're ye doing here?" Hazel whispered.

The guard gave them a sharp look. Hazel put a finger to her lips.

Olive knelt at the tub. "I needed to see ye, so I whistled at muster. As I figured: three days at the tubs." She looked around. "Can't believe I'm back in this shithole."

She glanced at the guard. Hazel followed her gaze. A convict had slipped in the mud, and he was prodding her to her feet.

"I had to let ye know," Olive stage-whispered. "Buck's the reason ye lost Ruby. He got his mate from the ship to smuggle the ledgers to Hutchinson."

Hazel's mouth went dry. "How do ye know?"

"Buck was here. On a crew building the new cells. He was bragging about it. Thing is, he escaped. Climbed over the wall."

"That's enough, ye two," the guard called. "C'mon now, up!" he said gruffly, poking the woman in the mud with his shoe as she struggled to rise.

Olive stuck her hands in the water and sucked her teeth. "Forgot how bloody cold it is." Splashing loudly, she said, "He's out there talking revenge to anybody who'll listen. Says it's just a matter of when."

Hazel thought of the way Buck's eyes had bored into her as she stood before the captain on the ship, telling him what she'd seen.

"He wants Ruby. He's been asking around, trying to find someone to get her from the orphanage."

Hazel's heart seized. "No. They wouldn't allow it. I'm the . . ."

Olive tilted her head. "You're not, though. Are ye?"

Hazel looked at the stone walls rising all around her. The laundry dripping icicles. The woman still splayed on the cobbles. Buck was out there, trying to get to Ruby, and she was in here. Trapped.

All day long, muddling the laundry and slopping it into buckets and running each piece through the ringer and dragging it to the clothesline, she turned the situation over in her mind. Lying in the straw in the stone cell that night, she stared up into the dark. Would anyone be willing to intervene? Mrs. Crain? Mrs. Wilson? Maeve? One of the mothers with a child at the orphanage? She thought of how impossible it had been for her to see Mathinna and was overcome with despair.

The convict women were powerless. The people with power had no reason to help.

Except . . . maybe . . .

She sat up, gripped by an idea.

The next morning, Hazel took the tin ticket from around her neck. Pressing it into Olive's hand, she told her what to do.

SIX WEEKS LATER, when Hazel was released from the crime yard, Olive was waiting.

"It's done," she said.

THE ASSIGNABLES STOOD in the long, narrow main yard in two straight lines, facing each other. Shifting nervously from one foot to the other, Hazel scanned the faces of the free settlers as they filed in through the wooden gate. At the end of the line was a man in a long black coat, light gray trousers, and a black top hat. His dark hair curled over the collar of his shirt, and he wore a short-cropped beard.

Once inside the courtyard, he removed his hat and smoothed his hair. Hazel gulped.

It was Dunne.

When he looked over at the rows of women, Hazel caught his eye. He raised an eyebrow in acknowledgment.

A jowly man in shiny leather boots had stopped in front of her. "Ever worked as a cook?"

"No, sir," she mumbled.

"Can you sew?"

"No."

"How're you at laundry?"

"No good, sir."

"What's that, prisoner?" the man said loudly, looking around to see if anyone else had witnessed her impudence.

"I'm not any good at all at laundry. Sir."

"Ye never been a housemaid?"

She shook her head.

"Useless wench!"

"How are you at needlepoint?" asked the next person, a matronly housekeeper.

"Dreadful, ma'am," Hazel said.

The woman flared her nostrils and moved along.

Finally Dunne was standing in front of her. She did not dare look up. "Your hair is so short," he said quietly, moving a step closer. "I almost didn't recognize you."

Self-consciously, she touched the nape of her neck.

He cleared his throat and stepped back. "I have a child in my care and need someone to look after her," he said. "Have you any experience, prisoner?"

"I have." She looked up, searching his eyes, but remembered herself. Looking down, she added, "Sir."

"Of what sort?"

"I—I worked in the nursery. Here, at the Cascades."

"Do you know how to treat scrapes and runny noses?"

"Of course."

"Crankiness?"

She smiled. "I am an expert."

"I will need someone to teach her to read. Are you literate?"

"'You may deny me, but I'll be your servant / Whether you will or no,'" she said softly.

He paused. The corners of his mouth twitched. "I'll take that as a yes."

She couldn't help it; she smiled again.

He pulled a handkerchief out of his pocket and dropped it at her feet. She watched it fall, a crisp white pocket square. Bending down, she picked it up and waved it toward the superintendent.

Mr. Hutchinson strode over. "Good morning, Mr. . . . ," he said to Dunne.

"Frum," he said. "Doctor Frum. Good morning."

"I see you've selected Miss Ferguson. For what kind of employment, may I ask?"

"To take care of a child."

Hutchinson grimaced showily.

"Is that a problem, superintendent?"

"Well . . . I must warn you, Dr. Frum, that this particular convict may not be the most appropriate choice. She was recently sent to the crime yard for a related offense."

"What was it, may I ask?"

"She impersonated a mother in order to get preferential treatment. To work in the nursery."

Dunne gave Hazel an appraising look. "And what does the real mother say?"

"The real mother? I believe she is deceased."

"And the father?"

"I—nothing is known about the . . . father," Hutchinson stammered.

"So this girl—what is your name?" Dunne asked abruptly, turning to Hazel.

"Hazel Ferguson, sir."

"This girl, Hazel Ferguson, assumed the care of a parentless child."

"Well, yes. But—"

"Did she take adequate care of the child?"

"As far as I know."

"Were there complaints about her conduct?"

"Not to my knowledge."

"And as superintendent you would know, would you not?"

"I suppose I would."

Dunne stood back on his heels. "Well, Mr. Hutchinson, it is precisely her experience caring for a parentless child that qualifies her to work for me. Her ability to do the job is my only concern."

The superintendent shook his head and sighed. "If I were you, I might be concerned about the deceit, sir. The . . . impersonation. There are other suitable—"

"I think," Dunne said, "I'll take my chances with Miss Ferguson."

Hazel fought to keep her eyes down and her posture submissive as he made arrangements for the assignment. She felt as if they were conspiring to pull off an escape, or a heist. When he beckoned her forward, she followed him through the wooden gate with her head bowed, like any dutiful convict maid. She trailed him down the street to his dun-colored horse and four-wheeled open buggy, and when he sprang up onto the driver's seat, she climbed onto the bench behind. Without looking back, he handed her a small parcel, then took the reins. He swatted the horse with a leather whip and they jolted off down the road.

She opened the parcel. Inside was Evangeline's ticket.

It was a chilly day in early spring. A silver disk of sun washed the grasses on the side of the road in a pale white light. Broombristle branches reached toward a sky streaked with wisps of cloud. As they made their way up the hill to Macquarie Street, Hazel looked back at the convicts trudging along on foot and riding in rickety carts.

Dunne flicked the whip again and the horse trotted on, leaving them behind.

AFTER SOME TIME, THEY TURNED from the long stretch of Macquarie Street onto a narrower side street lined with small cottages. When they reached a sandstone cottage with a red tile roof and a blue front door, Dunne pulled down the dirt drive. A sign hung on a post in the yard: *Dr. Caleb Dunne, Physician and Apothecarie*. It felt quite secluded; the house next door was hidden behind a tall hedge.

Dunne jumped down from the driver's seat and unbuckled the harness, then freed the horse from its bridle and hitched it to a post.

"Where is she?" Hazel asked, the first words she had spoken since they left the Cascades.

He walked toward the front steps, motioning for her to follow.

Hazel held her breath as she stepped over the threshold into the cottage. Dunne, ahead of her, turned into a room. Her heart racing, she hurried after him.

And there she was: Ruby. Sitting on the floor, building a tower out of wooden blocks.

"Oh," Hazel breathed.

Ruby looked up, a block in her hand.

It had been more than four months since Hazel had seen

her. She was heartbreakingly older. Her face had thinned and lengthened. Brown curls spilled down her back. She gazed at Hazel for a long moment, as if she couldn't quite place her.

"Give 'er time." A woman's voice.

Hazel looked up. "Maeve!" The woman was sitting in the shadows in a rocking chair, holding two knitting needles, a pile of yarn heaped in front of her.

"Welcome. We've been waiting for ye."

"What are ye doing here?"

With a broad smile, Maeve reached up and touched her white braid. "Glad to see yours is growing back."

"A small price to pay, if it led to this," Hazel said, tucking a short strand behind her ear.

Ruby's attention had shifted back to the blocks. Hazel knelt on the floor and crept closer. When she handed Ruby a block, the girl balanced it carefully on top of her tower.

Hazel wanted to give her a hug, but she was afraid of startling her. "Clever girl."

"Clever . . . mama," Ruby said.

"Clever mama," Hazel said, laughing through tears.

DUNNE STOOD ASIDE as Hazel inspected his surgery, ran her fingers along his implements, lifted the lids from tinctures and powders and held them to her nose, tasted them on her tongue. After Evangeline's death, he told her, he'd had enough of convict ships. But it took three more voyages before he'd saved enough to set up a practice. Almost a year ago, he resigned from his post as surgeon on the *Medea* and bought this cottage on Campbell Street in Hobart Town, with three bedrooms, a shed with a cistern, and a long narrow garden in the back.

A few weeks earlier, an unsigned letter had been slipped under Dunne's door, explaining that Buck had exposed Hazel's lie and threatened to take Ruby. The letter mentioned that Maeve, a midwife, had recently gotten her ticket of leave; if Dunne took Ruby in, perhaps he could employ Maeve to take care of her until Hazel was released from the crime yard.

Dunne made an appointment with the warden at the Queen's Orphan School and presented himself as Ruby's father, Dr. Frum. The warden seemed relieved to release her to his care; she was sickly, he said, and needed medical attention the orphanage couldn't provide. One fewer death on the ledger was always a good thing. As soon as Dunne saw the child, it was clear to him that she had typhoid. He brought her back to the cottage and set up a nursery in a sunny room facing the garden, then hired Maeve, who lived in a boardinghouse on Macquarie Street. The two of them slowly nursed Ruby back to health. Before long, Maeve was helping out with the details of his practice: organizing surgical implements, stripping cloth into bandages, meeting with patients. She wasn't literate but could remember every detail of a patient's complaint.

"I can't believe how big Ruby has gotten," Dunne said to Hazel. "These years have flown."

"For you, perhaps," she said.

THE NEXT MORNING, Hazel stood at the entrance to the Cascades with the other assignables who had ongoing placements. When Dunne arrived, she climbed into his buggy without a word.

Ruby was waiting on the front stoop when they got to the cottage. "You're here!" she cried.

Hazel wanted to shout to the rooftops, to sweep Ruby into her arms. But she didn't. "Of course I am," she said nonchalantly, getting down from the buggy. "I promised I'd be back, and here I am."

All day long, the two of them played seek-and-find, built fairy houses in the back garden out of sticks and leaves, read stories and drank sweet tea in the kitchen.

Hazel could hardly believe her good fortune. She would get to spend entire days with Ruby. She would get to be her mother.

On the floor of Ruby's bedroom sat a large dollhouse. Dunne had seen it in a shop window, he said, and couldn't resist. It was three stories tall and had many rooms, with servants' quarters at the top.

"Let's play," Ruby said to Hazel. "I'll be the lady. You be the maid."

"May I come downstairs, please, madam?" Hazel asked in a high voice, her thumb and forefinger around the doll in the attic. "It's so dark up here."

"No," Ruby said as the lady of the house. "You must be punished."

"What did I do wrong?"

"You talked too much at supper. And ran down the hallway."

"How long must I stay up here?"

"For two days. And if you are very naughty, you will be beaten with a cane."

"Oh." A cane. Hazel's heart froze. "But I am all alone. How could I be naughty?"

"You might spill your porridge. Or wet the bed."

"Everyone spills their porridge sometimes. And wets the bed."

"Not everyone. Only very bad girls."

Hazel looked at her for a long moment. "Not only bad girls, Ruby. Good girls too, sometimes."

Ruby shrugged. "All right. Anyhow, it's time for you to serve my tea."

AS THE WEATHER warmed, Hazel and Ruby planted flowers in the front, beside the house, and seeds for herbs in a small patch between the house and barn. When the herbs sprouted, they hung them in the sandstone shed behind the house to dry. The front garden became a riot of color. A golden wattle tree grew beside the barn, white roses climbed a trellis, a leafy bush with pale pink, trumpet-shaped flowers sat by the front door.

Dunne's practice was flourishing as free settlers poured into the port city. It wasn't unusual for Hazel to show up in the morning from the Cascades with Dunne and find a huddle of people waiting patiently for his return. He'd been corresponding with a group of doctors in Melbourne who were forming an association of licensed physicians, and was learning all about the latest medical procedures. Word of his innovative techniques was spreading.

Curious about the herbs Hazel and Maeve were growing, he pinched a few stalks with his fingers and held them to his nose. "How do you use these?" he asked.

Motherwort, they told him, with its leaves like the palms of an old woman, quieted anxiety. A syrup made of water and the bark of the umbrella bush relieved coughing. The stewed bark of hickory wattle soothed inflamed skin. Crushed leaves of the spotted emu bush could be inhaled to clear nasal passages. Catnip tea fought croup; red alder eased hives.

Hazel could see him fighting to overcome his skepticism. All those years of training—of being told to disregard the natural world, to dismiss the unwritten remedies of women as folk superstition—weren't easy to overcome.

As time went on, she began assisting in the surgery, along with Maeve. Dunne asked them to monitor the women in labor, and then to help with the births. Hazel was required to return to the Cascades at sundown, but Maeve could stay all night. Soon enough Dunne was delegating most of the obstetric cases to them, and only consulting with them when they asked him to.

THE TICKET OF leave, when it came, was almost anticlimactic. Several months after Hazel began working for him, Dunne wrote a formal letter vouching for her and offering paid employment and lodging.

"Your ticket of leave is a privilege, not a right," the superintendent said before releasing her. "If you commit an infraction of any kind you will be incarcerated again. Is that understood?"

Yes, she understood.

Reading the letter upside down on his desk, she saw that Dunne had signed his real name. Hutchinson either didn't notice or didn't care.

The matron handed Hazel the small bundle of tattered clothing she'd come in with, as well as Dunne's copy of *The Tempest*. Hazel smiled. She would put it on his bookshelf where it belonged, with the rest of the Shakespeare.

Before she left, she went in search of Olive. She found her with Liza, playing a game of whist. Despite multiple stints in the crime yard, they would soon be eligible for tickets of leave as well, they told her. "Hutchinson is glad to be rid of us troublemakers," Liza said. "We was never any good at wringing laundry anyhow."

"Remember me sailor? Grunwald?" Olive asked.

Hazel nodded.

"He opened a grog shop in Breadalbane. Asked me to barkeep. I told him I'll only consider it if he hires Liza to do the ledgers. He's writing letters for us both."

"Does he know about . . ." Hazel pointed back and forth at the two of them.

Olive grinned her gap-toothed grin. "He won't mind. The more the merrier."

"I won't skim off the top this time unless I absolutely have to," Liza said with a cackle.

Olive hoisted herself to her feet and pulled Hazel into a

smothering hug. "Take care of yourself," she said. "You're a better woman than I am, toleratin' that stiff surgeon. But I s'pose we all take our ticket of leave where we can find it."

Later, in the buggy with Dunne, Hazel gazed at the long high wall of the prison on her left, felt the rumble under her feet as they went across the tributary bridge, caught a whiff of the sewage. Then it was gone. She was done with that place. She felt as if she were seeing this world anew: woolly sheep in a field of yellow flowers, gray-green hills in the distance, blue butter-flies darting in and out of flaxen grass. Black-and-white magpies laughing in the trees. She half worried that if she turned around she'd see someone coming after her, that she'd be hauled back to the Cascades for some infraction, real or imagined.

She did not look back.

THAT NIGHT, SHE and Dunne stood awkwardly in the hall-way after Ruby went to sleep. She had made up one of the twin beds in Ruby's room for herself. Dunne's bedroom was down the hall.

"Is there anything you need?" he asked, leaning against the doorframe.

"No thank you." All of a sudden she was aware of his mus-cular forearm under his crisp cotton shirt. The bristles of his short beard. His smell, a not-unpleasant blend of perspiration and lye soap. She heard her own heart pulsing in her chest.

Feeling herself blush, she stepped back. Did he notice? She couldn't tell.

In Ruby's room, Hazel took Evangeline's tin ticket on its red cord and wrapped it in the white handkerchief. (Those faint initials, that family crest.) She opened the top drawer of the dresser and tucked the small bundle under a pile of clothes, then slid the drawer closed.

Someday she would share it with Ruby. Not yet.

IT WAS STRANGE TO FEEL so free. Free to feel the air on her face as she sat on a bench at the wharf with Ruby, watching the ships come in. Free to sit under the shade of a yew and marvel at the wide expanse of sky. To peel an orange—or two, or three— with her fingers, and slip the sweetly sour slivers into her mouth. To watch dough puff into pastry in a cast-iron skillet. To go to bed when she pleased, sleep in if she didn't feel well, laugh out loud without restraint, put her belongings in a drawer without fearing they'd be stolen.

It was strange to feel like a person in the world.

Hazel sewed herself some blouses and several pairs of trousers, so wide-legged that unless you were paying close attention they looked like skirts. Her own mother had always worn trousers like this; they were more comfortable in the birthing room, she said.

"You'll be known as the odd lady who wears trousers," Maeve teased.

Hazel grinned. "Maybe I'll start a fashion."

One warm afternoon, Hazel brought Ruby with her to shop at the crowded open-air market near the waterfront and saw a group of women, fresh off a convict ship, plodding toward

Macquarie Street. Tugging Ruby's hand, she turned away. She couldn't bear to watch.

HAZEL WAS AT the market with Ruby several days later, shopping for fruits and vegetables, debating whether to buy cherries or plums, when she became aware of a small commotion ahead of them. A rustling that sounded like wind through the trees. A few people crossed to the other side of the street, shaking their heads and casting quick glances behind them.

"What is she doing here, in polite society?" one woman said to another as they passed. "I thought they'd sent her back to live with her own kind, where she belongs."

Taking Ruby's hand, Hazel threaded through the crowd.

It was Mathinna. She stood in the middle of a group of gawkers with her chin raised, her mouth half open. She was taller. Thinner. Her cheekbones jutted sharply and her lips were chapped. Her hair was matted. The hem of her dress was caked with dirt. She looked around her with disinterest, absently rubbing the necklaces of tiny green shells she wore around her neck.

"Fer shame," a man said, full of scorn. "She's on the sauce."

Now that he said it, Hazel realized it was true. "Mathinna," she called.

The girl turned with a frown. Then broke into a half smile as recognition dawned. "Hazel," she said in a lazy lilt. "It's you." She swayed a little. "I still have them," she said, patting the necklaces.

"I'm glad."

The onlookers were quiet, appraising the exchange.

Fixing her eyes on Ruby, Mathinna said, "Is this your girl?"

"Yes. Ruby."

"Ru-by," she said in a singsong. She smiled broadly. "Hello, Ru-by."

"This is Mathinna," Hazel told Ruby. "Can you say hello?"

"Hello," Ruby whispered, stepping shyly behind Hazel.

Mathinna tilted her head at Hazel. "They let you out."

A murmur rippled through the crowd. Hazel felt her cheeks go pink. Though ex-convicts were everywhere, it wasn't considered civil to mention this fact in public. Taking Ruby's hand, she pointed at a small green park across the street. "Shall we go over there?"

"All right." Mathinna pushed her arms out in front of her and then to the side, her fingers spread wide. "Step *back*," she said loudly. When the crowd parted, she led Hazel across the street. Gazing straight ahead, her gait overly deliberate, she ignored the people pointing and staring, whispering behind their hands.

When they reached the park, Hazel said, "I tried to see ye at the orphanage. They wouldn't allow it."

"I know."

"They told ye?"

"They didn't tell me anything. They locked me in a room. But you said you would, and I believed you."

Hazel felt an ache in her throat. "How long were ye there?"

Mathinna wagged her head slowly, as if trying to remember. "I don't know. I couldn't even tell how much time passed." She reached up and touched her head. "They beat me. Shaved my head. Dunked me in ice water. I don't know why. They said I was insolent, and maybe I was."

"Oh, Mathinna. Ye were a child."

"I was." Her voice trembled. She looked down.

Still are, Hazel thought. The crowd across the street had mostly dispersed, though some were still gaping at them. She motioned toward a bench under a gum tree, facing in the other direction. "Will you sit with us for a minute?"

Mathinna nodded.

On the bench, Hazel pulled Ruby onto her lap. Mathinna sank down beside them. Sun filtered through the drooping leaves and dandelion-like flowers of the tree above them, dappling their faces with light.

"When did ye leave the orphanage?" Hazel asked.

Mathinna lifted her shoulders in a shrug. "All I know is one day they pulled me out and put me on a boat back to Flinders. But it wasn't the same. My stepfather had died. Influenza, they said." She shook her head again. A tear slid down her face. "Most of the people I knew were dead. The rest were wasting away. And anyway I'd lost the language. I was too . . . different. So they sent me back."

"To the orphanage?"

"Yes, for a while. Then to a wretched place called Oyster Cove. An old convict station. Everyone was sick and dying there too."

Hazel looked into the girl's glistening eyes. Tears welled in her own. "So how did ye end up here?"

"I ran away. Found work with a seamstress who runs a grog shop outside of town. She lets me rent a room."

"And what do ye do for her?"

"Sew. Serve rum. Drink rum." She laughed a little. "Go to bed and get up and do it again. The nights are long, but I sleep all day, mostly. For one thing, to avoid . . ." She gestured toward the other side of the road.

"People are rude."

"I'm used to it."

Ruby pointed at Mathinna's necklaces. "Pretty."

Mathinna ran her fingers along the shells. She seemed happy to change the subject. "My mother made these," she told Ruby. "And your mother"—she raised her chin at Hazel—"stole them back from the lady who took them from me."

Hazel winced a little. "I didn't really *steal* them," she told Ruby. "They never belonged to . . . that person."

Mathinna bent toward Ruby. "Would you like one?"

Ruby beamed, reaching toward the necklaces.

"Oh, no. Ye really shouldn't." Hazel closed her hands over Ruby's grasping fingers. She looked at Mathinna over the top of Ruby's head. "They're yours, Mathinna."

"I don't need all of them. They're meant to be shared. It's just I've never had anyone to give one to." She jiggled them with her fingers. "The thing is, they're tangled together. Will you help?"

"I want one, Mama," Ruby said.

Mathinna lifted the clump of necklaces over her head and handed them to Hazel. "You were the only person who was truly kind to me in all the years I lived with the Franklins."

Hazel felt her heart twist. She hadn't done much, after all. It was terrible to realize that her paltry gestures were the only real affection Mathinna had been shown. She thought of how Mathinna had wandered around the property after the Franklins had gone on holiday without her.

Looking down at the necklaces in her hands, Hazel took a breath. "Well . . . I have become skilled at knots." Running her fingers over the shells, she worried the clusters until they loosened and the necklaces fell into three separate long strands. She looped them over the web of her thumb and forefinger and held them out.

Mathinna took two necklaces and draped them around her own neck. Then she slung the third around Ruby's and held it up, showing her the iridescent green shells. "I watched my mother make this. She used a wallaby tooth to prick these tiny holes, then rubbed the shells with muttonbird oil to make them shiny. See?"

Ruby touched the necklace daintily with the tip of her finger.

"Just imagine you're the thread," Mathinna told her. "And the people you love are these shells. And then they'll always be with you." When she leaned in close, Hazel caught a whiff of alcohol on her breath. "It's good to know you are loved. You know your mama loves you, don't you, Ruby?"

Ruby nodded, a smile spreading across her face.

Hazel thought of her own childhood—how little tenderness she'd been given. She and Mathinna both had had to take whatever scraps they could get. "Come with us," she said impulsively. "We live just a few streets away, in the home of a doctor. There's a room, a small room, but it would be your own. Ye could get back on your feet."

Mathinna laughed, a laugh that started deep in her gut and rose into her throat. "I am on my feet, Hazel."

"But drinking, and—and staying up all night . . . You're too young, Mathinna. You're not meant for this kind of life."

"Ah—I don't know. What kind of life am I meant for?"

For a moment both of them were silent. It was hard to know what to say. Hazel listened to the cawing of seagulls, the raised voices of vendors hawking their wares in the market across the street.

"If I'd stayed on Flinders, I'd probably be dead," Mathinna said finally. "If the Franklins had taken me to London, I'd still be trying to be somebody I will never be. Here I am. Living the only life I was given." Abruptly, she stood, swaying slightly. "Don't worry about me, Hazel. I'm a wanderer. I'll be all right." Spreading her open hand across her chest, she said, "*Tu es en moi. Un anneau dans un arbre*. You are in me, like a ring inside a tree. I won't forget it."

Sitting on the bench with Ruby, watching Mathinna make her way down the street, Hazel felt a strange and unquench-able sadness. They were, both of them, éxiles, torn from their homes and families. But Hazel had stolen a spoon to earn that status; Mathinna had done nothing to deserve her fate. Hazel was marked with the convict stain and would be for many years, but it erased itself as time went on. She could already feel it less-ening. She could stroll through the market with a basket over her arm, and Ruby's hand in hers, and no one would guess.

Mathinna had no such luxury. She would never be able to melt into the crowd, to go about her business without judgment and suspicion.

"Where's she going, Mama?" Ruby asked.

"I don't know."

"She's nice."

"Yes."

Ruby fingered the shells around her neck.

"Do ye like your necklace?" When Ruby nodded, Hazel said, more sharply than she intended, "It's special. Ye must take good care of it."

"I know. I will. Can we get cherries, Mama?"

"Yes." Hazel sighed, rising from the bench. "We can get cherries."

THE FIRST MEETING OF THE Association of Licensed Physicians in Melbourne was scheduled for mid-February, and Dunne had decided to attend. It was several days' journey by ship; he planned to remain on the mainland for a week to learn about some surgical innovations. Maeve would stay in a small spare room at the back of the house while he was away, and she and Hazel would mind the practice. If emergencies arose that they couldn't handle, they'd send patients to Hobart Hospital for treatment.

It was a temperate afternoon. Clouds drifted across a powder-blue sky. Gulls swooped overhead, yawping their plaintive lament. The ship to Melbourne was scheduled to depart from Hobart Town at three o'clock, and Hazel decided to accompany Dunne to the wharf, a ten-minute stroll. As they walked, they discussed a patient's ongoing treatment, a Dickens novel Hazel was reading that featured a character sentenced to transportation, a lesson plan for Ruby.

"Eleven days," Dunne said at the gangplank. "You'll be fine without me?"

"Of course we'll be fine."

"I know you will." He squeezed her hand. "Tell Ruby good-bye for me."

"I will." Ruby had been building fairy houses with Maeve in the back garden when they'd left.

Sitting on a bench at the Elizabeth Street Pier after Dunne had boarded, Hazel watched the crew of the large wooden ship scurry to raise its gangplank. The air smelled of burning wood, wildfires from just beyond the perimeter of town. She gazed out at the spinachy seaweed on the pebbled shore and the boats nodding in the harbor. Sunlight glittered on the waves, an inverse of stars.

She thought, as she often did when looking out at the water, about Evangeline, out there in the deep. She remembered a line from *The Tempest*: *Full fathom five thy father lies. / Of his bones are coral made*. Ariel tells Ferdinand that his father, who drowned, underwent a sea change: his bones transformed into coral, his eyes pearls.

A sea change. Perhaps that was true for all of them.

After Dunne's ship was released from its moorings, Hazel meandered up Campbell Street, making a mental list of all the things she needed to do. It was a Sunday; the practice was closed. When she got back to the house, she would read a chapter in a medical book Dunne had suggested and prepare some remedies with the herbs she'd hung to dry. Perhaps she and Maeve would take Ruby to Mount Wellington for a picnic supper: cured ham, boiled eggs, cheese, apples. They'd bring the currant cake Maeve had baked that morning and left on the table to cool.

As she approached the house, Hazel saw Maeve kneeling in the herb garden. It was a perfectly ordinary scene, Maeve gathering mint. But something seemed amiss.

Hazel felt a finger of fear run down her back. Why wasn't Ruby with her?

"Maeve," she called, trying to keep her voice steady.

Maeve turned with a smile. "There you are!"

"Where's Ruby?"

Maeve sat back on her heels and dusted off her hands. "In the back, with a friend of Dr. Dunne's. I told him the doctor was away, but he wanted to meet her—said he was on the ship when she was born. I told him I'd make tea. He asked for mint." Maeve held up a sprig.

Hazel's skin felt clammy. She couldn't quite catch her breath. "What is his name?"

"Tuck. I think."

"Buck," Hazel breathed. "No. No."

"Oh dear," Maeve said, seeing Hazel's stricken expression, "did—"

Hazel ran up the steps and flung open the front door. "Ruby?" she called. "Ruby!"

No one was in the parlor or the examining room or the kitchen. She threw open the door to Ruby's room. Empty. She looked in Dunne's bedroom, then in the small room Maeve was staying in. She could hear her own jagged breathing. Her thudding footsteps.

Maeve, behind her now, said, "I'm sorry, Hazel, I didn't—"

"Shh." Hazel held up a finger and stood very still, her head cocked like a hound's. She went to the back door and looked through the pane.

There he was, about fifty feet back in the long garden, standing beside Ruby as she bent over the fairy houses. Too close. His sandy hair was slicked back from his forehead, his beard roughly trimmed. His shirt and trousers looked clean. Respectable, even. But there was a strangeness to his look, something off-kilter. He was painfully thin. Gaunt. As if he hadn't eaten in weeks.

Hazel saw the glint of a knife in his hand. "Stay here," she told Maeve. Stepping outside, she called, "Hello!" Fighting to keep her voice calm.

Ruby flapped her hand. "Come see my new fairy house!"

Buck gave Hazel a long look across the grass.

Her heart tick-ticking in her chest, Hazel walked toward them. She felt like a deer in a clearing, aware of the hunter, every fiber of her alert. She saw the scene in front of her with heightened clarity: a cluster of insects above the lavender, two orange-breasted kingfishers swooping among the trees, the tiny green shells looped around Ruby's neck. Buck's grimy fingernails. The dirt that rimmed his collar.

"Your hair's still short," he sneered. "And them breeches. Ye look like a boy."

Steady, Hazel thought; don't react. "It's been a while."

"It has. I been biding my time."

"I heard ye escaped. Are they after ye?"

He made an odd stuttering sound, a kind of snigger. "Maybe so. But I know how to disappear."

"It's rough out there in the bush."

"Ye got no idea." He vibrated with a kind of maniacal energy. "Ever eat kangaroo?"

She shook her head. She'd heard stories about the ex-cons and fugitives who lived like savages among the snakes and wild dogs and wallabies in the bush. Bushrangers, they were called. Pirates who roamed the land instead of the sea. They raided farms and small businesses, stealing horses and rum and weapons.

"Ye smoke 'em over the fire. Bind 'em to sticks." He held his arms wide, demonstrating. "After they're dead, usually." When he laughed, she saw his small gray teeth. "Sometimes, if we're lucky, we get ahold of a lamb."

Buck ran the tip of his knife down the side of Ruby's small head. She didn't notice, didn't even see the blade as she crouched over her stick houses. He sliced off a curl and held it out toward Hazel. "See how easy that was? Ye can always use a sharp knife. As ye know yourself."

He dropped the curl in the grass.

Hazel breathed through her nose, feeling the air fill her lungs. She smelled the lavender in the garden, and even from here, blocks from the harbor, the briny scent of the sea. Glancing toward the house she smelled the currant cake fresh from the oven.

"Ye must be hungry," she said. "Maeve made a cake. We have fresh butter. She said ye wanted tea."

Buck gazed at her. "It's true I haven't eaten in a while. And I confess I'm thirsty. Ye got any sugar?"

"We do," she said.

She thought about the twice-a-day tirades in the chapel at the Cascades, enough sermons to last a lifetime. *Let the wicked forsake his way, and the unrighteous man his thoughts: and let him return unto the Lord, and he will have mercy upon him.* Buck had been an infant once. A child. Maybe he was cast out, or betrayed, or beaten. Maybe he never had a chance. She didn't know, would never know. All she knew was her own hard story. How easy it would've been to sow bitterness, the way he did. To nurture it until it bloomed like a noxious flower. "We believe in forgiveness here, Mr. Buck," she said.

"Vengeance tastes better to me," he said.

Ruby looked up, sensing a change in tone. "Mama?"

"That's what she told ye?" Buck reached out and grabbed Ruby's arm, yanking her to her feet. "She's not your mama, little girl."

Hazel couldn't help it; she gasped.

Ruby made a small sound, a whimper.

Hazel had to fight the urge to lunge at him. She knew it would be foolhardy; there was too much at stake. "It's all right, Ruby," she said, her voice wobbling only slightly.

With the knife, Buck motioned toward the house. "Lead the way."

Hazel raised her eyebrows at Maeve as they entered the gloamy kitchen. She saw Maeve taking it all in: Buck holding the knife, his other hand on Ruby's arm.

The kettle was on a tripod over the hearth. The knives were in a drawer. The cast-iron skillet and pots were hanging from hooks on the other side of the room.

Buck looked back and forth between them. Gazing directly at Hazel over Ruby's small head, he whispered, "Don't even think about tryin' anything. I'll slit her throat as quick as I'd kill a lamb."

Hazel was aware of each breath passing through her. Her eyes flitted over the knife in Buck's hand, Maeve standing at the table, the green sprigs of mint behind her. "Maeve," she sighed, "your eyesight has gotten so bad. Ye picked the wrong herb. The mint's in a different part of the garden, remember?" She turned to Buck. "Ye asked for mint, yes? Not sage?"

Nodding slowly at her, Maeve slid the mint into her pocket. "Oh, dear. What was I thinking? Would you be an angel, Hazel, and get a few sprigs? I'll put out the cake."

"Nope," Buck said. "She's not leaving."

Maeve set the currant cake and the slab of butter in front of him. He cut into the cake with the knife he still clutched in his hand, then roughly sliced a chunk of butter and smeared it on the cake. For a few moments the only sound was of him chewing. The click of his jaw.

"I don't mean to blow me own trumpet, Mr. Buck, but I make a lovely pot of mint tea," Maeve said.

"I'll take water."

"Cold water's in the cistern in the shed. I have hot here. Boiled for tea."

His mouth twitched. "Get the mint, then. You, not her." He pointed the knife at Maeve, then Hazel. "Don't even think about yellin' for help."

"She's right, though. Me eyes aren't what they used to be." Maeve ran a hand back and forth in front of her face. "It's all fuzzy. Mint looks like every other green herb to me, I'm afraid."

"Let me do it, Mr. Buck. I know right where it is," Hazel said. "You've got Ruby," she added quietly. "Why would I try anything?"

Ruby gazed at her with her big brown eyes. Hazel gave her a tremulous smile.

Looking straight at Hazel, Buck held the knife near Ruby's cheek, pointing the tip toward her temple. "Make it quick," he said.

Hazel took a small earthenware bowl from the counter and went outside and down the steps. Bending over the herb patch, she collected several sprigs of mint with quaking fingers. Then she stood and turned back toward the house, toward the green bush with floppy leaves and pale pink, trumpet-shaped flowers that sat by the front door.

MAEVE FILLED A cup from the teapot and handed it to Buck. "Sugar? Or honey?"

"Sugar."

She pushed the pot of sugar in front of him. He added two heaping spoonfuls and stirred it. Ruby, beside him, asked, "May I have some?"

"Ye already had your tea," Hazel said. "How about a piece of cake?"

Ruby nodded.

"Our mint is strong, Mr. Buck," Maeve said. "Better with lots of sugar. There's nothing nicer than sweet tea, is there?"

Buck added two more spoonfuls. He took a sip, then drank noisily. Sliced off another hunk of currant cake and ate it in gulps.

"Can I play with my dollhouse?" Ruby asked.

"She's not leavin'," Buck said.

"It's only in the next room," Hazel said.

"I want her where I can see her."

Ruby shifted restlessly. "I'm tired of sitting here."

"I know," Hazel said. "Our friend will be leaving soon."

Buck leaned back in his chair. "I'm not goin' anywhere." He lifted the knife in the air, ran a finger along the blade as if examining its sharpness.

Hazel looked at him, at his thin sandy hair and sunburnt lips, the tail of the red-and-black mermaid on his forearm disappearing into his sleeve.

Buck rubbed his eye with a finger and blinked a few times. "Ye got some meat? Long as it's not kangaroo." He grunted a laugh. "Too gamey for my taste."

Maeve took the cured ham from the larder and he carved off two large slabs and ate them with his fingers. That's right, Hazel thought, quench your thirst with salt.

He gulped a second cup of tea and asked for a third. When she handed it to him, he drained it and wiped his lips with the back of his hand. "I was thinking," he said to Hazel, "we might finish what we started on the ship."

She watched a bead of perspiration roll down his neck and into the collar of his shirt. "Ye were thinking that, were ye?"

He wagged his head toward the front of the house. Sweat dappled his upper lip. "One of them rooms would do fine."

She watched him closely. He took a deep breath, then another. He rubbed the hair back from his scalp, and then, with curiosity, glanced at his hand. It was shiny wet. He stared, opening his eyes wide as if to allow in more light.

"The thing is, it's too late for that, Mr. Buck."

"What?" He took a gulp of air. "What in the . . ." He stood up fast, knocking over his chair. His legs buckled and he sagged against the table. "Don't move," he barked, holding the knife out like a sword.

"Mama?" Ruby looked up. "What's wrong with the man?"

"He's feeling poorly."

Ruby nodded. It wasn't unusual to see people in the house who felt poorly.

Turning to Maeve, Hazel said, "Take her out."

"She's not going anywhere," Buck shouted, choking oddly on the words.

"I don't want to leave you alone with him," Maeve said to Hazel. "He still has the knife."

"Look at him. He can barely stand." Hazel stepped closer to Buck. When she reached over and touched his wrist, he swung the blade at her wildly. Then he grimaced and sank sloppily onto a chair. The knife slid from his hand and clattered on the floor.

Buck shook his head as if trying to wake from a nap. "What—what's happening?"

Hazel picked up the knife, watching him, and touched the blade. Sharp, indeed. She placed it on a shelf.

Maeve nodded. "All right." Turning to Ruby, she said, "Let's go to the harbor and see if we can spot some seals on the rocks." She grasped the girl's hand and led her out of the kitchen.

When they were alone, Hazel sat in the chair across from Buck. His pupils were huge and black, his shirt soaked through with perspiration. She reached for the earthenware bowl on the sideboard behind her. Inside it were some sprigs of mint and three long, pale pink flowers with pointed tips, elegant as bells. She set the bowl on the table.

"There's a saying among healers and midwives, Mr. Buck. 'Hot as a hare, blind as a bat, dry as a bone, red as a beet, mad as a hatter.' Have ye heard it?"

He shook his head uncertainly.

"Well, it describes a set of symptoms. Starting with 'hot as a hare.' You're feeling quite warm right now, aren't ye?"

"It's broilin' in here."

"No it isn't. Your body temperature is rising. Next is 'blind as a bat.'" She pointed at her own eyes. "Your pupils are dilated. Things are getting blurry, yes?"

He rubbed his eyes.

"Dry as a bone." She touched her own throat. "You're parched."

He swallowed.

"You're not quite as red as a beet, but your skin is awfully flushed. And 'mad as a hatter,' well . . ."

It seemed to require a great effort to dredge himself out of his stupor. "What're . . . ye . . . talking about?"

She tipped the bowl so he could see. "These pretty blossoms are called angel's trumpet—though some call them breath of the devil, and for good reason. We have a plant just outside the front door. I'm sure you've seen it before; it's fairly common. There's a bush in the neighbor's garden across the street. Even a few at the governor's house." She set the bowl back on the sideboard. "If you're lucky—and I think there's enough poison in your bloodstream that ye are—you'll become delirious before the convulsions start. You'll probably end up in a coma before ye die. So that's a mercy."

"Ye—ye nasty bunter!" he gasped.

"Don't worry. It's not as bad as drowning. From what I hear. Though maybe it is." She shrugged. "Do ye feel spoony? Short of breath?"

He nodded, his Adam's apple bobbing.

"It shouldn't take long. By morning . . ." Her voice trailed off. She held up her palms as if in apology. "There's really nothing anyone can do."

He lurched forward, struggling to pull himself to his feet. Sagging against the table, he knocked the empty teacup onto the floor, where it shattered. He collapsed in a heap beside it. "You'll pay," he groaned.

Looking down at him, she said, "I don't think so, Mr. Buck.

Ye came in to the practice complaining of stomach pains. Turned out you'd eaten a poisonous flower, probably to feel its effects. I didn't judge ye for it. Only God can do that. Sadly, there's no antidote. All we could do was try to make ye comfortable."

He lunged toward her, wrapping his hand around her ankle. Leaning down, she peeled his fingers off her leg one by one. "Ye are no longer strong enough to overpower me, Mr. Buck. That moment has come and gone."

BY THE TIME Maeve and Ruby returned, Buck was in the shed out back. Hazel had led him, panting, drooling, to the cistern for fresh cold water, and then she'd locked him in. Every now and then, over the next few hours, they heard an odd noise, a shriek or a cry, but it sounded very far away. The walls of the shed were made of sandstone and lined with wood that Dunne had cut and stacked to get them through the winter.

Later that evening, Hazel opened the back door of the house and walked out into the dewy grass. She gazed up at the moon, a smear of yellow in the purple bruise of the sky. Then she went to the door of the shed and stood quietly, listening. She heard the purring of insects in the undergrowth, the lazy chirping of birds singing themselves to sleep. There was no sound from inside.

When she and Maeve unlocked the door of the shed the following morning, Buck was dead.

The authorities were glad to put the matter to rest. Buck was an escaped criminal, after all. A convicted murderer and a hardened fugitive. He was known to be an alcoholic and an addict;

it was no surprise he'd overdosed on a readily available hallu-cinogen.

Two days later, a pair of convict laborers transported Buck's body in a cart to St. David's Park, a formal English garden with sandstone walls. At the far end of the park was the prisoners' cemetery, surrounded by shrubbery and foliage, including a commonplace but lovely bush with pendulous pink flowers. They buried Buck without ceremony in an unmarked grave.

FOR SO LONG, FEAR HAD cramped Hazel's heart. Now she felt only relief, as if she had killed a venomous snake that was lurking under the house. Even so, she was afraid to tell Dunne the truth about what had happened. She could live with it, but she didn't know if he could.

"I don't know how he'll react. He's so . . . moral," Hazel said to Maeve.

"And we're not?"

She thought about this for a moment. "I'd say we live by a different code."

Maeve shook her head. "I'd say ye can't know what code ye live by until it's tested. You're afraid he'll go to the authorities?"

"No, no." She hadn't even considered that. But—might he?

"He's no saint. He altered that birth certificate," Maeve pointed out.

"True. But that's hardly murder."

A week later, when Dunne's ship was scheduled to arrive from Melbourne, Hazel was standing at the bottom of the gangplank with Ruby, waiting for him.

He broke into a smile when he saw them. "What a pleasant

surprise!" Crouching down, he gave Ruby a hug. "How have you been?"

"I showed a man my fairy garden and then he got very sick," Ruby said.

Hazel cringed. It hadn't occurred to her that Ruby would blurt it out.

"Did he? And is he all better now?" Dunne asked.

"No, he isn't."

"Oh dear." He looked up at Hazel, seeking explanation.

"Yes. It's . . . a long story." Her heart quavered in her chest. "I've got the horse and buggy. I thought we might take a picnic to Mount Wellington. Would that be nice?"

"Very nice," he said.

"IN MELBOURNE THERE'S talk of ending transport altogether," Dunne said. "Lots of newspaper editorials. It doesn't look good in the eyes of the rest of the world." They were sitting on a large flat rock, the picnic spread out around them. The wind from the sea was warm on their faces and the trees were lush and green. Eagles dipped and soared; low-hanging clouds puffed in the sky. Below them, long swells frothed into sandstone rocks as white as bone.

"Do ye think it will happen?" Hazel asked.

"I do. It must."

Children and grandchildren of the early convicts were settled citizens now, he said. The place was becoming almost respectable. "It would be wise for Britain to remember the rebellion of the American colonies before they lose what goodwill they've got left," he said.

Hazel gave him a distracted smile. Go slow, she thought. Ease into it. But that wasn't her style. When Ruby slid off the rock in search of sticks to build a fairy house, Hazel turned to him. "I need to tell ye what happened."

"Oh—yes," he said, sitting back. "The man who got sick."

She took a breath. "Danny Buck was in the garden with Ruby when I returned from the wharf ten days ago. He had a knife. He said he would kill her, and he threatened to rape me."

His eyes widened. "My god. Hazel."

"Ye know that bush by the front step?" she said, forging ahead. "Angel's trumpet, it's called."

"The one with pink flowers."

"Yes. The sap is toxic. Too much of it is fatal."

"I didn't know that."

"It is. And—anyway—it was."

He looked in her eyes. "It was."

"Yes." When he didn't respond right away, she added, "We called the police, and they took him away. The plant is a narcotic; overdoses aren't unusual."

"I see." He exhaled through his nose. "My god," he said again.

For a few moments they sat in silence, watching Ruby in the distance as she snapped tiny sticks in half and arranged them in piles. Was he horrified? Appalled? She couldn't guess. "I don't . . ." Hazel paused, picking her words carefully. "I don't regret it."

Dunne nodded slowly.

"I'm relieved he's gone."

He sighed, running his hand through his hair. "Look. I actually think you were . . . that was . . . incredibly brave. You saw what you needed to do, and you did it. You saved your life, and Ruby's. I'm only sorry I wasn't there."

He reached for her hand, and she let him hold it. She looked down at Ruby in the grass, bending over a clump of flowers, and then back at Dunne, at his dark hair curling around his ears, his trim beard and dark lashes. She listened to the dull roar of seawater in the distance, gushing out of caves.

Tentatively she ran a hand along Dunne's forearm. He turned clumsily toward her, knocking over the plate of cheese and apple slices between them. Reaching up to his face with both hands, she pulled him close. She felt his skin warm beneath his beard and smelled his sweet, appley breath, and then his lips found hers, his hands through her still-cropped hair. Closing her eyes, she breathed him into her.

"Mama, let's make a bracelet!" Ruby shouted, running toward them, holding up a cluster of daisies.

When Hazel pulled away from Dunne, she felt as she had when her feet touched solid ground for the first time after four months at sea. Unsteady, disoriented, the world around her vibrating.

AFTER WEAVING A daisy chain, Hazel sat on the rock while Dunne helped Ruby construct her fairy village in the clearing below. As light faded over the mountain, Hazel gazed out at the jagged, green-tinged cliffs rooted in the sea. How far she had traveled to get here! From the wynds of Glasgow to the bowels of a slave ship to a prison halfway around the world. And now to a sandstone cottage in a frontier town where she was free to ply her trade. To mother a child who needed her. To live in peace with a man she might be beginning to love.

She thought of the moments that had saved her. Watching *The Tempest* in Kelvingrove Park. *I was the man i' the moon when time was.* Evangeline teaching her to read. Olive's unexpected generosity and Maeve's camaraderie. Dunne's compassion. Ruby, the good that had overcome the heartbreak, the promise that Evangeline never lived to see fulfilled. Maybe Hazel had saved Ruby's life, or maybe she would've survived regardless. But Hazel knew with certainty that Ruby had transformed hers.

She was starting to believe that she belonged in this terrible, beautiful place, with its convict-built mansions, its dense bush and strange animals. The eucalyptus with their half-shed bark and woolly foliage, orange lichen that spread like molten lava across the rocks. Here she was, rooted to the earth. Her branches reaching toward the sky, the rings inside as dense as bone. She felt ancient, as if she'd lived forever, but she was only nineteen years old. The rest of her life in front of her like a ribbon unfurling.

RUBY

If society will not admit of woman's free development, then society must be remodeled.

—DR. ELIZABETH BLACKWELL, 1869; British physician,
mentor to Dr. Elizabeth Garrett Anderson

IT WAS SURPRISINGLY EASY TO track down the address.
Armed with his full name—Cecil Frederic Whitstone—Ruby
charmed a receptive clerk at the Metropolitan Board of Works
near Trafalgar Square, who, within minutes, produced a ledger
of London taxpayers and located a Mr. C. F. Whitstone at 22
Blenheim Road.

"Barrister," the clerk told her. "Lives alone, apparently. No
marriage or birth certificates linked to the name. Are you staying in London for long, Miss Dunne?"

Ruby had come to England to apprentice with Dr. Elizabeth
Garrett, a physician who founded St. Mary's Dispensary in
Marylebone, a place for poor women to receive medical care. It
was the first of its kind, staffed entirely by women. Dr. Garrett,
only four years older than Ruby, was the first female in Britain
to qualify as a doctor and a surgeon. Shortly after opening the
dispensary, she placed a notice in London newspapers, seeking
college-educated women who wished to become doctors and
nurses. In Hobart Town, five months later, Ruby opened the
Saturday Review and spied it.

In her long letter to Dr. Garrett, Ruby explained that she'd grown up with a surgeon father and midwife mother in a frontier town on an island off the coast of mainland Australia. From a young age, she'd been put to work polishing instruments, cataloguing medication, and assisting in the operating room. As the town expanded, so had the family practice. Eventually her father founded Warwick Hospital, named after the town in the Midlands where he was raised. Ruby's dream was to help her father run the practice one day.

But she had learned all she could from her parents. Her mother's medical skills were based on folk remedies and trial and error, not scholarship. Her father had taught her anatomy and the rudiments of surgery, but now, at twenty-eight, she craved the kind of formal education he'd received at the Royal College of Surgeons in London. Women were not allowed to apply to medical school in Australia, so this opportunity would be life changing. She proposed studying with Dr. Garrett for three months so that she might return to Warwick Hospital with the latest information and techniques.

Dr. Garrett wrote back: "I will find you reasonable lodgings, and you will stay for a year and earn a degree."

A month after receiving this letter, Ruby was on a ship bound for London.

Ruby had never met a woman as frank, outspoken, and boldly revolutionary as Dr. Garrett. Determined to go to medical school, in 1862, at the age of twenty-six, she'd found a way in on a technicality. The Society of Apothecaries had not thought to forbid women from taking their exams until after Dr. Garrett passed them all. Later, as a member of the British Women's

Suffrage Committee, she presented petitions to Parliament demanding the vote for female heads of household.

"Penal transportation to Tasmania only ended fifteen years ago," she said with characteristic bluntness when Ruby arrived in Marylebone. "I must ask: Are you related to a convict?"

Ruby blanched slightly. This still wasn't spoken of freely where she was from. But she was determined to be as forthright as Dr. Garrett. "I am," she said. "My mother is from Glasgow and was sent to Australia at the age of sixteen. Many people in Tasmania have similar origins, though few talk about it."

"Ah—the 'hated stain' of transport. I read that they changed the name from Van Diemen's Land to lessen the unsavory association with criminality."

"Well, that wasn't the official reason given, but . . . yes."

"What was your mother's offense, if you don't mind my asking?"

"Stealing a silver spoon."

Dr. Garrett gave an exasperated sigh. "This is why we can't leave the making of laws to men. They result in travesties of injustice that unfairly burden the poor. And women. Those high and mighty aristocrats, in their black robes and powdered wigs—they have no idea."

Ruby had been to Melbourne once, on a summer holiday, but had never imagined a city as vast and sprawling as London, with its north and south banks bisected by a winding canal and linked by half a dozen bridges. (She was surprised to discover that London Bridge, familiar from the nursery rhyme, was quite intact.) She shared a room in a boarding house on Wimpole

Street with another of Dr. Garrett's protégés, a young woman from the Lake District whose family believed she was employed as a ladies' maid. In fact, as Dr. Garrett pointed out when she arrived, Ruby was the only one of her students whose parents encouraged her desire to become a doctor. "It is my sense that, despite its hardships and limitations, living in a new world accords one certain freedoms. Social hierarchies are not as rigidly enforced. Would you agree that this is true?"

"I don't know," Ruby said. "I've never lived in any other world."

"Well, now you will, and you can see for yourself," Dr. Garrett said.

In her free time Ruby explored the sights, from the British Museum to St. Paul's Cathedral, from verdant parks to bustling teahouses. She sampled strawberryade and fried fish and chips at an outdoor market in Covent Garden. She attended a performance of *The Tempest* at the Lyceum Theatre and a trapeze show at a pleasure garden in North Woolwich. On one such outing she found herself in front of the imposing stone fortress of Newgate Prison and remembered the stories that Olive, her mother's friend, had told about life inside its gates—how she'd met Evangeline there and found herself sentenced to transport on the same ship. How a Quaker reformer handed out Bibles and hung tin tickets around their necks—one of which Ruby had brought with her, wrapped in an old white handkerchief, to London.

During her last week with Dr. Garrett, Ruby visited an orphanage. Stepping inside the front gate, she felt lightheaded. She'd never been able to remember much about her early years at the Queen's Orphan School in New Town, but now she had such an overwhelming sense of panic that she thought she might faint.

Dr. Garrett gave her a curious look. "Are you all right?"

"I—I'm not sure."

"Let's sit for a moment."

On the settee in the reception room, at Dr. Garrett's insistence, Ruby tried to identify the feelings that had dredged up, seemingly out of nowhere: dread and anxiety and fear.

"It's only natural that you'd have such a response," Dr. Garrett said. "You were a child taken from her mother." She patted Ruby's hand. "Your understanding of what it's like to feel abandoned is yet another reason we need qualified doctors like you, Miss Dunne, working with vulnerable populations in far-flung places like Australia."

Now Ruby was scheduled to return to Tasmania two days hence. Before she departed, there was one thing left to do. Here she was, in front of the house of the man whose monogrammed handkerchief had made its way to Australia twenty-eight years earlier. She'd walked through the neighborhood half a dozen times in the past few months, trying to summon the courage to seek him out.

The creamy white paint of the residence was patchy in spots and peeling from the eaves. Its vermillion front door was chipped; the hedges on either side of the front gate were pocked with brown. Weeds sprung from between the bricks of the walkway.

Ruby pushed the bell and heard it warble inside the house.

After an uncomfortable delay, the door opened, and a man winced into the light. "Yes? Can I help you?"

It was too late to turn around. "Does a Mr. Whitstone reside here, by chance?"

"I am Mr. Whitstone."

The man appeared to be in his early fifties. His hair was graying around the temples. He was thin, with pronounced cheekbones and slightly sunken brown eyes. It struck Ruby that he had probably been handsome once, though now he was somewhat frail, the skin on his face like a peach past its prime.

And then, as if observing an object under a microscope come into focus, she noticed his resemblance to her. The same wavy brown hair and eyes and narrow build. The shape of the lips. Even an unconscious gesture, a certain tilt of the chin.

"I am"—she put a hand to her chest—"Ruby Dunne. You don't know me, but . . ." She reached into her purse and extracted the handkerchief. She held it out and he took it from her, examining it closely. "I believe you knew my . . ." She swallowed. She had imagined this moment many times in the past year. Contemplated every possible scenario: He might shut the door in her face or deny ever having known Evangeline. Or perhaps he'd died or moved away. "The woman who gave birth to me. Evangeline Stokes."

Ruby felt him inhale at the mention of the name. "Evangeline." He looked up. "I remember her, of course. She was briefly governess to my half siblings. I've long wondered what became of her." He paused, his hand on the knob. Then he held the door open. "Would you like to come in?"

THE HOUSE WAS gloomy after the afternoon brightness of the street. Mr. Whitstone hung Ruby's cloak in the foyer and led her into a parlor room with lace curtains in the windows. It smelled musty, as if the windows hadn't been opened in a long time.

"Shall we sit?" He gestured toward a set of well-worn uphol-stered chairs. "How is . . . your mother?"

She waited until they were settled, then said, "She died. Twenty-eight years ago."

"Oh, dear. I'm sorry to hear it," he said. "Though I sup-pose . . . I suppose it was quite a long time ago." He narrowed his eyes, as if calculating something in his head. "I thought she left here around then, but maybe I'm mistaken. My memory isn't what it used to be."

Ruby felt a prickle on the back of her neck. Was it possible that he didn't know?

"Your accent is unusual," he said. "I've never heard anything like it."

She smiled. All right, then, they would change the sub-ject. "I'm from an island off the coast of mainland Australia— Tasmania, it's called now. Settled by the British. My accent is a hotchpotch of dialects, I suppose, English and Irish and Scottish and Welsh. I didn't realize how strange that was until I came to London."

He laughed a little. "Yes, in this hemisphere we generally stick to our own kind. Do you live here now?"

"Only temporarily."

A plump, gray-haired housemaid in a blue dress and white apron materialized in the doorway. "Afternoon tea, Mr. Whitstone?"

"That would be lovely, Agnes," he said.

When the housemaid left, they talked about the weather for a few minutes—how it had been miserably wet until a week ago, but now it was all sunshine and daffodils, and wisteria, even. The summer would probably be hot, given what a long, cold winter they'd endured. Ruby had grown accustomed to this English style of throat-clearing, but still found it mystifying. In Tasmania, conversation tended to be more straightforward.

"When do you return to Australia?" he asked.

"The ship leaves Friday."

"Pity. You'll miss the roses. We're rather known for them."

"We have lovely roses too."

Agnes reappeared, bearing a silver tray with a teapot and two bone china cups, a platter with slices of currant cake, and a small bowl of jam.

"This household is quite diminished," Mr. Whitstone said as the housemaid poured the tea into the cups and went through the motions of parceling out cake. "It's only the two of us now, isn't it, Agnes?"

"We get on all right," Agnes said. "But don't forget Mrs. Grimsby. Ye don't want me messing around in the kitchen."

"No, we can't forget Mrs. Grimsby. Though I'm not sure how much longer she'll be with us. I found her putting the eggs in the post box the other morning."

"She has got a bit barmy."

"Well, I don't really care what I eat. And we certainly don't entertain like we used to. It's quiet around here these days. Wouldn't you agree, Agnes?"

She nodded. "Quiet as a fly on a feather duster."

The two of them sat in silence for a moment after Agnes left. Ruby looked around the room at the gilt-faced grandfather clock in the corner, the faded brocade sofa, the filigreed bookshelves. To the right of their chairs was a curio chest filled with figurines: porcelain ladies in pastoral settings stepping over turnstiles, leaning against trees, swooning over pastel-painted flowers. "My stepmother's collection," he said, following her gaze.

Twee tributes to a mythical past, Ruby thought but did not say.

His father and stepmother retired to the country a few years ago, he told her. Beatrice, his half sister, had gone off to New York City to become an actress but ended up in Schenectady. His half brother, Ned, married an older heiress and moved to Piccadilly, where he dabbled in . . . something. Real estate? "I regret to say that we've fallen lamentably out of touch," he said, pouring more tea through the strainer into Ruby's cup. "So. Perhaps you might tell me what happened to Evangeline."

She took a sip. Lukewarm. She put it down. "I'm not sure where to start. How much do you know?"

"Very little. She worked here only for a few months, as I recall. I went off to Venice on holiday, and when I returned, she was gone."

Ruby gave him a sidelong look. "She was accused of stealing the ring you gave her."

"Yes, I do know that."

She felt a pit of anger in her stomach. "You never . . ." She pressed her bottom lip with her teeth. "You never told the authorities that you gave it to her?"

Sighing, he rubbed the back of his neck. "My stepmother knew. Of course she knew. Before I left for Italy, she'd warned me to stay away from the governess. But then . . . apparently Evangeline flew into a rage and pushed Agnes down the stairs. So it wasn't even about the supposed theft, in fact; it was a charge of attempted murder."

"Agnes. Your housemaid?"

"Yes. Still here, after all these years."

Still here. Alive and well. Ruby shook her head. "Did you ever try to find Evangeline, to hear her side of the story?"

"I . . . didn't."

Ruby remembered how Olive had described Evangeline in prison, holding out hope that this man would come, and felt close to tears. "She was in Newgate for months. And then sentenced to transportation for fourteen years and locked inside a slave ship. She was murdered by a sailor on the voyage over, an ex-convict."

He breathed in quietly through his nose. "I did not know. That is truly . . . unfathomable."

"She was a woman alone, with no means and no one to speak for her. You might've at least vouched for her character."

He seemed a little startled at her nerve. She was surprised, herself. It occurred to her that Dr. Garrett's bluntness may have worn off on her.

He sighed. "Look," he said, "I was told in no uncertain terms to let it be. That it was not appropriate to get involved. That I had narrowly avoided bringing scandal to the family, and they had taken care of it, and I was not allowed to make a mess of it again. If it's any consolation, I felt wretched about it."

"Not wretched enough to defy your stepmother. You were an adult, were you not?"

He gave her a faint smile. "You are quite . . . direct, Miss Dunne."

All at once Ruby felt an almost physical aversion to this man sitting across from her. Opening the clasp of her purse, she pulled out a small disk on a faded red cord. Holding it up, she said, "The prisoners were required to wear these around their necks on the ship. This was Evangeline's. It is all that I have of her." She dropped it into his open palm. "Except your handkerchief, I suppose."

He rubbed it with his finger, and turned it over, squinting to see the number, 171, etched faintly on the back. Then he looked up. "What do you want from me?" His voice was almost a whisper.

Ruby listened to the *tock tock tock* of the grandfather clock in the corner. She felt the metronomic beating of her own heart. "You are my biological father. You must realize that by now."

He gazed at her in the honeyed lamplight, his hands on his knees, rubbing the fabric of his trousers.

"You knew she was pregnant," she said. "And you did nothing."

"I didn't really know. No one ever said it. But I suppose if I'm honest I must admit I . . . suspected." He took a deep breath. "There's a deep moral cowardice at the root of the Whitstone family character, I'm afraid. I hope you haven't inherited it."

"I have not."

Silence spiked the air between them.

"I was lucky enough to be taken in," she said finally. "I have parents who love me, who fought for me. I don't want anything from you."

He nodded slowly.

"Except one thing, perhaps. I would like to see the room where Evangeline lived when she was here."

"It's been closed up for years." He tapped his lips. "But I suppose there's no harm."

He handed her the ticket and she wrapped it in the threadbare handkerchief and tucked it back inside her purse. Then she followed him down a long hallway wallpapered in green-and-pink stripes and around the corner to a door that opened onto a set of narrow stairs. Down they went past a large kitchen and into a humble dining room, where a small, white-haired lady sat at a table snapping beans.

She squinted up at them behind thick round glasses. "Mr. Whitstone!" she cried. "Where did you find Miss Stokes? She is not allowed here, after what she's done!"

"Oh—no, no," he stammered, putting out his hand. "You are mistaken, Mrs. Grimsby. This is Miss Dunne."

"I think I've seen a ghost," she murmured, shaking her head.

Mr. Whitstone gave Ruby an embarrassed glance and they continued past the dining room and turned down a hallway. He opened the door on the right and she followed him into a small room.

The only window, high on the wall, was shuttered. In the weak light from the hall Ruby could make out a narrow bed stripped of bedding, a side table, and a chest of drawers, all coated with a film of dust. She went and sat on the mattress. The ticking was lumpy.

Evangeline had lain here, in this bed. Paced this floor. She'd been younger than Ruby when she came to this house, trying to find her way in the world, and she left it pregnant and scared, with no one to help her. Ruby thought of all the women who came into Warwick Hospital and St. Mary's Dispensary, seeking treatment. Heavy with child, or writhing in pain from venereal diseases, or carrying newborns and toddlers. All the burdens of being poor and female, as Dr. Garrett put it. No one to catch you if you fell.

Looking down at the worn pine floor, Ruby was struck by a realization: she'd been in this room before, when she was barely more than a whispered thought.

"Will you excuse me?" Mr. Whitstone said. "I'll just be a minute."

She nodded. It was late in the afternoon. She wanted to get back to her lodgings before dark. Though she wasn't looking forward to the long voyage back to Tasmania, she was eager to share what she'd learned during her year abroad.

This moment in Evangeline's room, she knew, had nothing to do with the rest of her life and everything to do with it. She would leave this house changed, but no one would ever know she'd been here.

WHEN MR. WHITSTONE returned, he was carrying a small blue velvet box. He gave it to her, and she opened it. There, couched on yellowed ivory satin, was a ruby ring in a baroque gold setting. "A bit tarnished, I'm afraid," he said. "It's been in a drawer all these years. My stepmother insisted that it would go to my wife someday, but as it turned out, I never married."

Ruby extracted the ring and studied it carefully. The stone was larger than she'd imagined. It shimmered wetly in its setting. The color of velvet drapes, a lady's dress at Christmastime.

"You should be the one to rescue it from ignominy," he said. "You are . . . my . . . daughter, after all. I would like for you to have it."

She turned the ring in her hand, observing how the gem caught and refracted the light. She imagined Evangeline holding it in this room nearly three decades ago. She thought of the lies told and promises broken. How desperate Evangeline must've felt—how miserable. Ruby put the ring back in its blue velvet box and snapped it shut. "I can't take this," she said, handing it back. "It is your burden to bear, not mine."

He nodded a little sadly and slipped the ring box into his pocket.

Standing in the doorway, a few minutes later, he pulled a collection of coins out of his pocket. "Let me pay for your cab."

"That's not necessary."

"It's the least I can do, after you've come all this way." He dropped several shillings into her hand.

"Well. All right."

He seemed to be stalling, trying to keep her there. "I want to tell you that . . . that she was a lovely girl, your mother. And very intelligent. Always with her nose in a book. She had a gentleness about her, a kind of . . . innocence, I suppose."

"You took that from her. But you know that, don't you?"

Ruby didn't wait for his reply. As she walked down the front steps, the air was cool and smelled of rain. Soft early evening light washed over the brick walkway, the ancient cobblestones, the purple wisteria climbing a trellis. When she reached the gate, she piled the coins on the flat top of a fence post.

She would leave London behind now and return to the place and the people she loved. She would live the rest of her life in Australia, and her days would be busy and full. She would help her father run his practice, as he had done, long ago, with his own father. She would meet a man and marry him, and they would have two daughters, Elizabeth and Evangeline, both of whom would attend the first medical school in Australia that opened its doors to women, in 1890. In the last year of the nineteenth century, with nine other female physicians, they would establish the Queen Victoria Hospital for Women in Melbourne.

Ruby was under no illusions about the place she was returning to—that fledgling colony on the other side of the world that had taken root in stolen soil, choking out the life that already existed and flourishing under the free labor of convicts. She thought of the native girl, Mathinna, wandering through Hobart Town like an apparition, trying in vain to find a place to call home. She thought of the convict women shamed into silence as they struggled to erase the stain of their experience—a stain woven into the very fabric of their society. But she also thought of Dr. Garrett's observation about social hierarchies. The truth was, Hazel had made a life for herself that would not have been possible in Great Britain, where the circumstances of her birth would've almost certainly determined the story of her future.

Ruby turned and looked back. It was the last time she would ever see this man, Cecil Whitstone, without whom she would not exist. This was how she would remember him: hovering on the threshold, one foot out and one foot in. He'd been given so much, and yet he'd done so little. If she came back in five years, or ten, or twenty, she would know where to find him.

She thought of all the women she knew who'd been given nothing, who'd been scorned and misjudged, who'd had to fight for every scrap. They were her many mothers: Evangeline, who gave her life, and Hazel, who saved it. Olive and Maeve, who fed and nurtured her. Even Dr. Garrett. Each of them lived inside her, and always would. They were the rings of the tree that Hazel was always going on about, the shells on her thread.

Ruby tilted her chin at Cecil. He went inside and shut the door.

And she was on her way.

ACKNOWLEDGMENTS

ATTEMPTING TO IDENTIFY the genesis of a novel can be a fool's errand. Inspiration is as often unconscious as conscious; our imagination is stirred by myriad events, beliefs, and philosophies, by art and music and film, by travel and family history. It wasn't until I'd finished writing *The Exiles* that I realized I'd twined together three disparate strands of my own life history to tell the story: a transformative six weeks in Australia in my mid-twenties; the months I spent interviewing mothers and daughters for a book about feminism; and my experience teaching women in prison.

When I learned, as a graduate student living in Virginia, that the local Rotary Club was sponsoring fellowships to Australia, I leaped at the opportunity. I'd been obsessed with the place since my father, a historian, gave me his marked-up copy of Robert Hughes's 1986 book *The Fatal Shore: The Epic of Australia's Founding*. (He spent a year teaching in Melbourne when I was in college.) Only one chapter in Hughes's six-hundred-page book, "Bunters, Mollies and Sable Brethren," specifically addressed the experiences of convict women and Aboriginal people. This was the chapter that interested me most. I wanted to learn more.

As one of four Rotary "ambassadors" to the state of Victoria, I toured farms and factories, met mayors and minor celebrities, and learned Australian folk tunes and slang. I fell in love with the wide-open vistas, the offhanded friendliness that seemed to be a hallmark of the culture, and the vividly colored birds and flowers. The Aussies I met were happy to talk about their national parks, their pioneering spirit, and their barbecued shrimp, but seemed reluctant to discuss some of the more complicated aspects of their history. When I did press them to talk about race and class, I was gently, subtly, rebuked.

Several years later, in the mid-1990s, my mother, Christina L. Baker, a women's studies professor, worked on an oral-history project at the University of Maine in which she interviewed so-called second-wave feminists who'd been active in the women's movement in the 1960s, '70s, and '80s. I'd recently moved to New York City and met a number of young women who identified themselves as third-wave feminists, literal and figurative daughters of my mother's subjects. My mother and I decided to write a book together: *The Conversation Begins: Mothers and Daughters Talk About Living Feminism*. The experience became a powerful lesson for me in the value of women telling the truth about their lives.

Some years later, after learning about the limited resources available to women in prison, I created a proposal to teach memoir writing at the Edna Mahan Correctional Facility for Women, an hour from my house in New Jersey. My class of twelve maximum-security inmates wrote poems, essays, songs, and stories; it was the first time many of them had shared the most painful and intimate aspects of their experience. They were terrified, relieved, and searingly honest. When I read aloud a Maya Angelou poem that contains the lines "You may trod me in the very dirt / But still, like dust, I'll rise," more than one inmate wept with recognition.

AS A NOVELIST I've learned to trust a particular tingle, a kind of spidey sense. Until I stumbled on the little-known historical fact of the orphan trains, I had little interest in writing about the past. But the minute I heard about the American social experiment to send two hundred and fifty thousand children on trains from the East Coast to the Midwest, I knew I'd found my subject. The research I did for the novel *Orphan Train* laid the groundwork for another novel about rural life in early-to-mid twentieth-century America: *A Piece of the World*, the real-life story of an ordinary woman on the coast of Maine who became the subject of Andrew Wyeth's painting *Christina's World*. These leaps of time and place inspired me to pursue an even more ambitious story, this time a century earlier and half a world away—one that would address those questions I'd had about Australia's complex past that were never answered to my satisfaction twenty-five years earlier.

As I began to delve into the topic, I found the website of Dr. Alison Alexander, a retired lecturer at the University of Tasmania who has written or edited thirty-three books, including *The Companion to Tasmanian History; Tasmania's Convicts: How Felons Built a Free Society; Repression, Reform & Resilience: A History of the Cascades Female Factory; Convict Lives at the Cascades Female Factory*; and *The Ambitions of Jane Franklin* (for which she won the Australian National Biography Award). These books became primary sources for this novel. Dr. Alexander, who is herself descended from convicts, became an invaluable resource and a dear friend. She gave me a massive reading list and I devoured it all, from information about the prison system in England in the 1800s to essays about the daily tasks of convict maids to contemporaneous novels and nonfiction accounts. On my research trips to Tasmania, she introduced me to experts, took me to historic sites, and answered question after question, providing vital clarification and insights. She and her lovely husband, James, hosted me for dinner in their Hobart home on numerous occasions. Most of all, she read my manuscript with a keen and expert eye. I am grateful for her rigor, her encyclopedic knowledge, and her kindness.

Notable among the contemporary books I read on the subject of convict women are *Abandoned Women: Scottish Convicts Exiled Beyond the Seas*, by Lucy Frost; *Depraved and Disorderly: Female Convicts, Sexuality and Gender in Colonial Australia*, by Joy Damousi; *A Cargo of Women: Susannah Watson and the Convicts of the Princess Royal*, by Babette Smith; *Footsteps and Voices: A Historical Look into the Cascades Female Factory*, by Lucy Frost and Christopher Downes; *Notorious Strumpets and Dangerous Girls*, by Phillip Tardif; *The Floating Brothel: The Extraordinary True Story of Female Convicts Bound for Botany Bay*, by Sian Rees; *The Tin Ticket: The Heroic Journey of Australia's Convict Women*, by Deborah Swiss; *Convict Places: A Guide to Tasmanian Sites*, by Michael Nash; *To Hell or to Hobart: The Story of an Irish Convict Couple Transported to Tasmania in the 1840s*, by Patrick Howard; and *Bridget Crack*, by Rachel Leary. Books I read about Australian history and culture include, among others, *In Tasmania: Adventures at the End of the World*, by Nicholas Shakespeare; *30 Days in Sydney: A Wildly Distorted Account* and *True History of the*

Kelly Gang, by Peter Carey; *The Songlines*, by Bruce Chatwin; and *The Men that God Forgot*, by Richard Butler.

A number of articles and essays were useful, especially "Disrupting the Boundaries: Resistance and Convict Women," by Joy Damousi; "Women Transported: Myth and Reality," by Gay Hendriksen; "Whores, Damned Whores, and Female Convicts: Why Our History Does Early Australian Colonial Women a Grave Injustice," by Riaz Hassan; "British Humanitarians and Female Convict Transportation: The Voyage Out," by Lucy Frost; and "Convicts, Thieves, Domestics, and Wives in Colonial Australia: The Rebellious Lives of Ellen Murphy and Jane New," by Caroline Forell. I found a wealth of information online at sites such as Project Gutenberg, Academia.edu, the Female Convicts Research Centre (femaleconvicts.org.au), the Cascades Female Factory (femalefactory.org.au), and the Tasmanian Aboriginal Centre (tacinc.com.au).

Nineteenth-century novels and nonfiction accounts I read include *Life of Elizabeth Fry: Compiled from Her Journal* (1855), by Susanna Corder; *Elizabeth Fry* (1884), by Mrs. E. R. Pitman; *The Broad Arrow: Being Passages from the History of Maida Gwynnham, a Lifer* (1859), by Oline Keese (a pseudonym for Caroline Leakey); *For the Term of his Natural Life* (1874), by Marcus Andrew Hislop Clarke; *Christine: Or, Woman's Trials and Triumphs* (1856), by Laura Curtis Bullard; and *The Journals of George Augustus Robinson, Chief Protector, Port Phillip Aboriginal Protectorate, Volume 2* (1840–1841).

As I researched Mathinna's story, I found the following resources especially valuable: *The Last of the Tasmanians: Or, The*

Black War of Van Diemen's Land (1870), by James Bonwick; Dr. Alexander's biography of Jane Franklin (mentioned above); *Wanting*, a novel by Richard Flanagan; *Tunnerminnerwait and Maulboyheenner: The Involvement of Aboriginal People from Tasmania in Key Events of Early Melbourne*, by Clare Land; "Tasmanian Gothic: The Art of Tasmania's Forgotten War," by Gregory Lehman; "Extermination, Extinction, Genocide: British Colonialism and Tasmanian Aborigines," by Shayne Breen; "In Black and White," by Jared Diamond; and "From Terror to Genocide: Britain's Tasmanian Penal Colony and Australia's History Wars," by Benjamin Madley. I was inspired by excerpts from the Bangarra Dance Theatre's performance of "Mathinna," choreographed by Stephen Page.

I am grateful to Dr. Gregory Lehman, Pro Vice-Chancellor of Aboriginal Leadership at the University of Tasmania and a descendant of the Trawlwulwuy people of northeast Tasmania, for critiquing the sections about Mathinna and the history of the Tasmanian Aboriginal people.

I strove to be historically accurate as much as possible, but ultimately *The Exiles* is a work of fiction. For example, while Mathinna's family history is factual, her real-life counterpart was five years old, not eight, when the Franklins brought her to Hobart Town. The question of whether free settlers dropped handkerchiefs at the feet of the convict women is disputed; I chose to include it. The novel was fact-checked by Dr. Alexander, Dr. Lehman, and others; the few changes I made to the historical record were done consciously and in service to the story.

Today, about 20 percent of Australians—a total of nearly five million people—are descended from transported British convicts. But only recently have many Australians begun embracing their convict heritage and coming to terms with the legacy of colonization. I was lucky to research this book when I did; a number of historic sites and museum exhibits are new. Though descendants of convicts now make up three quarters of Tasmania's white population, when I first visited the island several years ago the convict museum at the Cascades Female Factory was only three years old. The permanent exhibitions showcasing Aboriginal history, art, and culture at the Tasmanian Museum & Art Gallery had opened two weeks earlier. In addition to these places, I visited Runnymede, a National Trust site preserved as an 1840s whaling captain's house, in New Town, Tasmania; the Hobart Convict Penitentiary; the Richmond Gaol Historic Site; the Maritime Museum of Tasmania; and convict sites and museums in Sydney and Melbourne.

I AM LUCKY to have an editor, Katherine Nintzel, who is willing to read and critique multiple drafts and engage every nuance, no matter how slight. With this novel she was like a personal trainer for my brain, motivating me to dig deeper and work harder than I ever have before; I can't overstate how grateful I am for her wisdom and patience. Thanks also to the rest of my team at William Morrow/HarperCollins for their unstinting support: Brian Murray, Liate Stehlik, Frank Albanese, Jennifer Hart, Brittani Hilles, Kelly Rudolph, Kaitlin Harri, Amelia

Wood, Molly Gendell, and Stephanie Vallejo. To Mumtaz Mustafa for the stunning cover. To Lisa Sharkey for sage advice. Eric Simonoff at WME, Geri Thoma at Writers House, and Julie Barer at The Book Group have been trusted advisors.

Bonnie Friedman read every page of the manuscript more than once and engaged with me so deeply that I felt I had a true ally, a reader who understood what I was trying to do as well as if not better than I did, and inspired me to get there. Amanda Eyre Ward dropped everything to read when I needed a pair of fresh eyes (and quickly saw that Mathinna's story should begin the book). Anne Burt, Alice Elliott Dark, and Matthew Thomas provided welcome insights. Carolyn Fagan was an invaluable support at every stage.

Writing a novel can be a lonely enterprise. I am grateful for the camaraderie of the Grove Street Gang, a writers' reading group that includes Bonnie, Anne, and Alice, as well as Marina Budhos and Alexandra Enders. Kristin Hannah, Paula McLain, Meg Wolitzer, Lisa Gornick, Jane Green, Jean Hanff Korelitz, Maureen Connolly, Pamela Redmond, Laurie Albanese, John Veague, and Nancy Star have been true writerly friends and allies. Thanks to my stalwart Montclair Writers' Group and the NYC-based novelists' group Word of Mouth (WOM), as well as MoMoLo and KauaiGals (you know who you are!).

My sisters—Cynthia Baker, Clara Baker, and Catherine Baker-Pitts—mean everything to me. They read early drafts, helped to hash out storylines, and are my fellow adventurers in life. I am grateful for moral support from my father, William

Baker, his partner, Jane Wright, and my mother-in-law, Carole Kline. My three sons, Hayden, Will, and Eli, bring me endless joy. And what is there left to say about my husband, David Kline, who has been with me at every step and makes my life richer in every way?

About the author

About the book

Insights,
Interviews
& More . . .

Read on

Meet Christina Baker Kline

Beowulf Sheehan

A #1 *New York Times* bestselling author of eight novels, including *Orphan Train* and *A Piece of the World*, CHRISTINA BAKER KLINE is published in forty countries. Her novels have been awarded the New England Society Book Award for Fiction, the Maine Literary Award, and a Barnes & Noble Discover Award, among other accolades, and have been chosen by hundreds of communities, universities, and schools as "One Book, One Read" selections. She has also written or edited five nonfiction books. Her essays, articles, and reviews have appeared in publications such as the *New York Times* and the *New York Times Book Review,* the *Boston Globe,* the *San Francisco Chronicle, Psychology Today, Poets & Writers,* and Salon. Born in England and raised in the American South and Maine, she lives in New York City and on Mount Desert Island in Maine. ᨀ

Behind the Book

In a *New Yorker* essay titled "Just the Facts, Ma'am," Jill Lepore writes, "Fiction can do what history doesn't but should. It can tell the story of ordinary people. It's the history of private life, the history of obscure men." Reading this, I understood something about my own work. In my three latest novels, in particular, I've written about people, real and imagined, who have historically been on the fringes of society, whose stories have been unnoticed or obscured. *Orphan Train* is about immigrants in destitute circumstances; *A Piece of the World* tells the story of an ordinary farm woman, Christina Olson, who became the subject of Andrew Wyeth's best-known painting; *The Exiles* is about poor women exiled from their homelands.

In the essay, Lepore goes on to ask: "Who are these obscure men?" And answers: "Well, a lot of them are women." The truth is, throughout history, women kept journals and wrote letters, but few had the time, means, or education to write books. Researching the story of Australia's convicts, for example, I found a trove of contemporaneous accounts written by men about their experiences, but few by women.

Three decades ago, when I traveled to Australia on a Rotary fellowship, I encountered a society that—much like America—was only beginning to come to terms with its complex history of racism and oppression. Even today, the plight of the nineteenth-century female prisoners sent from Britain and Ireland to populate a new land—and the Aboriginal people whose way of life was destroyed when colonists landed on their shores—is unknown by many.

As I considered how I might write about the predicament of the women sent on convict ships, I realized how crucial it was to show the arc of their stories from the beginning. Few of them ever returned to their places of origin. What was it like ▶

Behind the Book *(continued)*

to be sentenced to seven or fourteen years in prison to "the land beyond the seas," as Australia was known, given that it was, for almost all of them, a life sentence? How long did it take for cold, hard reality to sink in? I wanted readers to experience what happened at every step along the way. The four-month voyage was not just a transition from one place to another; it was transformative. It was when these women realized that they were no longer English or Scottish or Irish; they were on their way to becoming new citizens in a new world.

When I first conceived of *The Exiles*, I planned to write only about the British convict women. But the more I read about the period, the more convinced I became that it would be irresponsible not to address the history of the Aboriginal people who lived on the island of Tasmania for thousands of years before being exiled by the British. I read the real-life story of Mathinna, the orphaned daughter of a chieftain who was taken on a whim and later abandoned by the British governor and his wife, and felt that she needed to be part of this story.

I envisioned this novel as a passing of the baton from one convict woman to the next, to the next—with Mathinna's story providing crucial perspective on the British colonization of Australia. But writing about cultures other than your own is fraught and complicated. I felt a weight of responsibility in writing about Australia—and even more so in writing about its indigenous people. The convict women, sent by the British government to populate this fledgling colony, endured terrible hardship. But when they left Victorian England—one of the most stratified societies in history, where the slightest slip of your accent determined which social class you were in—those rules no longer applied. Once they became freed of their literal shackles, they could reinvent themselves. For the Aboriginal people whose land was usurped, it was a different story. Opportunity for some did not mean opportunity for all.

Today, about 20 percent of Australians—a total of nearly five million people—are descended from transported British convicts. But only recently have many Australians begun embracing their convict heritage and coming to terms with the legacy of colonization. I hope this novel will transport readers to a different time and place; I hope it illuminates a piece of previously unknown history. And I also hope it gives context, as historical fiction, at best, can do, to some of the issues we grapple with today.

A 1789 illustration of convicts arriving in Botany Bay. Transport to Australia began the year before and would continue for another eighty years.

There was no social safety net in England, and living conditions could quickly become grim for anyone fallen on hard times. This illustration by Sir Hubert von Herkomer depicts women in a lodging house in the London neighborhood of St. Giles. Most women sentenced to transport were convicted of crimes of poverty—ironically, if they could survive the journey and subsequent sentence, convict women had more opportunity to rise out of poverty than their nonconvict peers in England. ▶

Behind the Book *(continued)*

Newgate prison, approximately 1810. Conditions at Newgate were appalling, particularly for women and their children. Quaker social reformer Elizabeth Fry championed better conditions for prisoners, particularly women, both at Newgate and during transport to Australia.

The Thomas Bock portrait of Mathinna, painted in 1842, when the real-life Mathinna was approximately seven years old.

An interior photograph of the Cascades Female Factory, which operated for nearly thirty years, from 1828 to 1856. Today it is a UNESCO World Heritage Site and museum. ◠

Tell It Slant: An Interview with Christina Baker Kline

This interview by Jennifer Solheim was originally published in the Fiction Writers Review *in September 2020*

The story goes that when Émile Zola began research for *Germinal*, his masterpiece about the nineteenth-century French miners' revolution, he toured the working mines firsthand. He noticed a broad, muscled Percheron pulling a sled through a tunnel. The foreman explained that they brought the horses down as foals. Yet when Zola asked him how they got them in and out of the mines each day, the foreman responded that they didn't: "He hauls coal down here until he can't anymore, and then he dies down here, and his bones are buried down here." This was the seed for Zola. His descriptions of the mine horses in *Germinal* shed light on the harsh treatment of all workers, whether human or animal, and lend a concretized pathos to the majestic narrative rail against worker exploitation.

It's a similar case in Christina Baker Kline's new novel, *The Exiles* (HarperCollins), which might be understood as literary historical fiction with a feminist slant: within a depiction of the history of British convicts sent to Australia (marginalized people already), Baker Kline represents women's experience, and within women's experience those who left few traces: an indigenous girl, an orphaned young woman with neither financial means nor practical skills, and the fatherless teenage daughter of a drunken midwife. The three protagonists are of the margins within the margins—people whose stories were unrecorded, and so have gone untold.

Baker Kline's storytelling reads so effortlessly and true that it's easy to overlook the painstaking research that went into this novel, and the careful balance between vivid detail and larger questions about these women's human experience. But let's be clear: *The Exiles* is a masterful high-wire act. As both writer and reader, it's thrilling to read.

The Exiles is Christina's eighth novel. Her work has been published in over forty countries, and her novels have received the

New England Prize for Fiction, the Maine Literary Award, and a Barnes & Noble Discover Award, among other prizes, and have been chosen by hundreds of communities, universities, and schools as "One Book, One Read" selections. Her essays, articles, and reviews have appeared in publications such as the *New York Times* and the *NYT Book Review,* the *Boston Globe,* the *San Francisco Chronicle,* Lit Hub, *Psychology Today,* and Salon. She is a graduate of Yale, Cambridge, and the University of Virginia M.F.A. program, where she was a Hoyns Fellow in Fiction Writing. She is an Artist-Mentor for StudioDuke at Duke University and the BookEnds program at Stony Brook University, where, as a Fellow, I was so lucky to work with her.

Jennifer Solheim: In discussing the fictionalization of historical events in my novel, you quoted Emily Dickinson: "Tell all the truth but tell it slant." But as an edict, the Dickinson line isn't only about recuperation or new perspectives; it's also about character and the particularities of individual experience. So how did you work with the idea of telling truth at a slant in* The Exiles?

Christina Baker Kline: You're right; it's about both things. The next line of the Dickinson poem is "Success in circuit lies." I kept thinking about this as I wrote *The Exiles*: How could I approach the story in roundabout ways to make it more intimate, more engaging, less like a rote history lesson? There's a danger, when you write novels that involve large amounts of research, of sounding didactic, or worse, dry. In ways large and small, the task of a novelist who writes about the past is to make it come to life, to find singular details that make the story breathe.

In *The Exiles,* I use a secondary character, bawdy, irreverent Olive, to recount the British plan to transport poor women to Australia as breeders. Her wry humor is a useful delivery system for this kind of exposition.

In general, my version of 1840s Australia is a blend of then and now. While I worked hard to avoid blatantly anachronistic language in dialogue, I didn't try to approximate the speech of the time. I wanted the book to feel contemporary. I wanted readers to feel as if they were immersed in that world. ▸

Tell It Slant: An Interview with Christina Baker Kline *(continued)*

You traveled to England, Scotland, and Australia to research The Exiles. *How did research and character development work in this novel? Did one inspire the other?*

Some novelists don't travel for research; they believe that imagination is all you need, and maybe they're right. But I find standing on the soil where my novel takes place incredibly inspiring. If I hadn't gone to Tasmania I wouldn't have known about the fluorescent orange lichen on the rocks of Mount Wellington, for example, or that wallabies gather by the hundreds on the outskirts of the city of Hobart at dusk. I wouldn't have known what the four-mile trek from the harbor to the Cascades Female Factory was like, or what it felt like to be inside the walls of that prison. I was in Scotland for a week and Glasgow for only a few days, but several months later, as I was describing Hazel's miserable life there, I could easily envision her making her way along the wynds and pilfering a silver spoon from a shop; I knew what the cobbles felt like under my shoes. Her flinty character was forged during that visit.

Your three main characters meet by chance and fate, in some ways— but they also encounter one another as a result of the cruelty of systems and individuals to which they are subject. How did you develop these three characters and bring them together in the story?

The constantly changing relationships among these women are at the heart of this novel. Without them, the book would be little more than a treatise on the systematic oppression of women and Aboriginal people by the British government.

I think of Evangeline—the book-smart but naïve daughter of a village vicar who finds herself accused of murder and sent on a repurposed slaving ship to Australia—as a stand-in for the reader. She is catapulted from a comfortable middle-class existence into a world she'd never imagined; each experience is a fresh shock. Hazel and Olive, the convict women she befriends on the ship, are accustomed to this kind of life, more tolerant of its indignities and outrages. Mathinna, an Aboriginal girl, is torn from her home and family and must figure out how to navigate life in a household filled with uncaring British aristocrats. Hazel, working as a maid in the governor's house where Mathinna lives, is the only person who shows her genuine affection.

An Aboriginal girl dependent upon a British aristocrat's wife and amateur anthropologist, Mathinna is ultimately granted even fewer rights than the convicts. How did you approach writing Mathinna and her story? What inspired you to include her as part of the story of the convicts?

When I conceived of this novel, I planned to write about the British convict women exiled to Australia. But the more I read about the period, the more convinced I became that it would be irresponsible not to address the history of the Aboriginal people who lived on the island of Tasmania for thousands of years before being exiled by the British. I read the real-life story of Mathinna, the orphaned daughter of a chieftain who was taken on a whim and later abandoned by the British governor and his wife, and knew that she needed to be part of this story. It's complicated to write about real people whose lives ended long ago, their fates solidified. As I did in my previous novel, *A Piece of the World*, I chose to end Mathinna's story with a moment of connection, of recognition. Like Mathinna's, the final years of Christina Olson, the real-life person who inspired that novel, were bleak. I wanted to end the stories from Mathinna's and Christina's perspectives by highlighting their resilience as well as their vulnerability while they contended with forces beyond their control.

I've always admired the way your characters inhabit their bodies. I think of the bitter cold in the harrowing scene in Orphan Train *when preteen heroine Dorothy traverses four miles through a snowy winter night in Minnesota, or of Christina's pleasure in bathing before meeting her paramour in* A Piece of the World. *Now, in* The Exiles, *there are vivid descriptions throughout of the female body's survival against horrifying conditions—the convicts are granted only slightly better conditions than the enslaved Africans who crossed the ocean in the very same ship hold, before the abolition of slavery. How do you approach embodying your characters as you write?*

When I'm writing a book set in the past, I get completely obsessed with contemporaneous first-person narratives. While writing *Orphan Train*, I found a slim memoir at the Heartland Museum in Fargo, North Dakota, titled *Rachel Calof's Story:* ▶

Jewish Homesteader on the Northern Plains. It's filled with hard-to-believe details about what it was like to live through Midwestern winters in the 1900s. For *The Exiles*, I read ship surgeons' logs, letters from female convicts, and newspaper articles from the 1800s about conditions on the ships.

But I understand that your question is larger than that. I work hard to convey the physical details of my characters' lives, because I know that in order for a book to sing it needs to be fully felt in the body. Physical trials teach us what we can endure, what our limits are. We remember them vividly. Evangeline's journey to the (literal) underworld of Newgate Prison and the bowels of the ship is horrifying, yes, but it is filled with self-discovery.

Newgate no longer exists, but I visited the prison site in London and similar historic sites in England and Australia. I also drew on my own life experiences; years ago, I taught at a jail in Maine and a women's prison in New Jersey.

I'd like to conclude with a question for fiction writers about the research and writing of historical fiction that portray brutal realities, as you have done so movingly in **The Exiles**: *How do we stay true to the tales we tell while also giving them life beyond the margins?*

The lives of the convict women in the early-to-mid-eighteenth century were indeed brutal and unfair. It was even worse for the Aboriginal people. I didn't want to minimize the hardship, but I was determined to celebrate the women's victories, large and small. Though only one of the three main characters ultimately thrives, many of the minor characters—including Olive!—find ways to forge a life in this strange new land. They are the foremothers of the Australia we know today. ∿

Reading Group Guide

1. Were you familiar with this part of Australia's history before reading *The Exiles*? Was there anything new you learned that particularly surprised you?

2. Mathinna and Evangeline are both orphans, and Hazel is estranged from her mother and doesn't know her father. What impact does this have on their characters, and how do you think their stories would have been different if their families were present in their lives?

3. The Franklins treat Mathinna like an outsider in Van Diemen's Land, yet Mrs. Wilson tells Mathinna that they are the ones who don't belong. What does it mean to belong to a place? Who decides who does and does not belong?

4. Were you surprised by Evangeline's fate? Why do you think Kline made this decision?

5. What is the significance of Mathinna losing her language? Of all the ways she changes after leaving Flinders, why does this loss feel the most important to her, and mark such a clear divide from her old life?

6. Throughout the book, multiple characters reference and find comfort in Shakespeare's *The Tempest*. If you've read *The Tempest*, why do you think the author chose this play in particular? What connections and common themes does it share with *The Exiles*?

7. At one point, Mathinna thinks to herself "She was tired of feeling as if she lived between worlds. This was the world she lived in now." In what way does Van Diemen's Land act as a "between world" for the different characters? How do they each struggle with leaving behind their old lives and adapting to new ones? ▶

8. When Hazel is in solitary confinement at the Cascades, she is finally able to forgive her mother. How does Hazel's experience lead her to this moment? Would you have been able to grant forgiveness in Hazel's situation?

9. Ruby thinks about her "many mothers," and how each played a key role in taking care of her and making her the person she became. What role do found families, and found mothers in particular, play throughout the story?

10. Dr. Garrett reflects on the privileges granted the residents of Van Diemen's Land, saying, "It is my sense that, despite its hardships and limitations, living in a new world accords one certain freedoms. Social hierarchies are not as rigidly enforced." In what ways is this both true and not true for each of the characters in *The Exiles*? What are the limitations of these freedoms—which characters are allowed them, and why are others excluded?

11. What parallels do you see between the world of *The Exiles* and today? How does this history connect to issues of race, class, and culture that we grapple with today? ∾

More Books by Christina Baker Kline

A PIECE OF THE WORLD

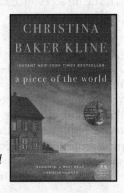

An instant *New York Times* bestseller

"Graceful, moving, and powerful." —Michael Chabon

"Later he told me he'd been afraid to show me the painting . . ."

To Christina Olson, the entire world is her family farm in the small coastal town of Cushing, Maine. The only daughter in a family of sons, Christina is tied to her home by health and circumstance, and seems destined for a small life. Instead, she becomes Andrew Wyeth's greatest inspiration, and the subject of one of the best-known paintings of the twentieth century, *Christina's World*.

As she did in her beloved bestseller *Orphan Train*, Christina Baker Kline interweaves fact and fiction to vividly reimagine a real moment in history. *A Piece of the World* is a powerful story of the flesh-and-blood woman behind the portrait, her complicated relationship to her family and inheritance, and how artist and muse can come together to forge a new and timeless legacy.

"Another winner from the author of *Orphan Train*. . . . [A] beautifully observed fictional memoir."
　　　　　　　　　　—*People* (Book of the Week)

"Like Wyeth's paintings, this is a vivid novel about hardscrabble lives and prairie grit and the seemingly small but significant beauties found there."
　　　　　　　　　　—*Minneapolis Star Tribune*

More Books by Christina Baker Kline *(continued)*

"Evokes the somber grace of [Wyeth's] paintings. . . . A story for those who want the mysterious made real."
—*New York Times Book Review*

ORPHAN TRAIN ....

The #1 *New York Times* Bestseller

"A lovely novel about the search for family that also happens to illuminate a fascinating and forgotten chapter of American history. Beautiful."
—Ann Packer

"I believe in ghosts. They're the ones who haunt us, the ones who have left us behind . . ."

Between 1854 and 1929, so-called orphan trains ran regularly from the cities of the East Coast to the farmlands of the Midwest, carrying thousands of abandoned children whose fates would be determined by chance and circumstance.

As a young Irish immigrant, Vivian Daly was one such child, sent by rail from New York City to an uncertain future a world away. Returning east later in life, Vivian leads a quiet, peaceful existence on the coast of Maine. But in her attic, hidden in trunks, are vestiges of a turbulent past.

Seventeen-year-old Molly Ayer knows that a community-service position helping an elderly widow clean out her attic is the only thing keeping her out of juvenile hall. But as Molly helps Vivian sort through her possessions, she discovers that she and Vivian aren't as different as they appear.

"A gem." —Huffington Post

"Poignant. . . . Affirms our hope that the present can redeem the past and that love has a genuine power to heal." —Mary Morris

"Powerful. . . . You'll be talking about it for years to come."
—*Naples Daily News* (FL)